D1526702

Rachel Jonas

A BADDIES BOOK BOX
EXCLUSIVE EDITION

BREAK
THE
GIRL

WARNING

This book is dark and twisted, but keep in mind that it's a work of fiction. Nothing between these pages reflects the authors' views, nor does it imply that they condone any of the situations or actions you'll read within the series.

Authors' Note/Trigger Warning: This book was written purely for your entertainment. Be advised, this series contains the following scenarios and themes that may not be suitable for all readers: *violence, drug use, dubious consent, mention of various forms of abuse, reference to off-page sexual assault, reference to off-page suicide, and kidnapping.*

This list is in no way exhaustive, so please read responsibly and at your own risk.

H ot June mornings are made for sleeping in late beneath the breeze of a ceiling fan or lazing beside a clear pool with no concept of time.

What hot June mornings are *not* made for is lugging a heavy tote filled with new-student paraphernalia across the expanse of Bradwyn University's campus. And yet, here I am.

My tour guide, Ellen—a wiry blonde with a rather eclectic sense of style—hasn't offered to carry a single thing. Instead, she continues to speed-walk from building to building, seeming to forget that the registrar's office loaded me up with school apparel and a ton of paperwork. But I suppose this is my punishment for deciding to transfer at the last minute. As if she's heard my thoughts and means to reassure me, Ellen passes a smile over her shoulder as she pushes her glasses up the bridge of her nose.

"You made a great choice coming to Bradwyn. We have tons of clubs you can get involved in. Think you'll join any?"

The question has me revisiting the *real* reason I'm here, and it's not to socialize. Despite the gorgeous campus and long list of amenities, I'm not here for that either.

"The plan is to focus on academics."

That's the safe answer, and Ellen buys it before rambling again.

"You've probably seen pics online, or maybe you've even

1

visited since you're local, but we've also got world-class botanical gardens. They're absolutely breathtaking this time of year. Also, the school's recently invested a ton into renovating the dorms. You'll be living on campus, right?" She finally takes a breath and waits for me to answer.

"Um, no, actually. But I did manage to secure space in a rental nearby. The house is occupied by students and, lucky for me, they had a spare room."

"Oh, nice! Those are hard to come by these days. Have you started moving in?"

I shake my head and tug the collar of my shirt a few times to get some air moving underneath it. Long, dark strands cling to my skin where my hair has fallen from my ponytail. But Ellen doesn't seem to notice I'm on the brink of a heat stroke and keeps pace toward the library.

"The girls I'll be living with all have crazy schedules, so I haven't even been able to *see* the house yet. I move in next week, though."

Ellen's eyes stretch wide. "Yikes! You're brave, aren't you?"

"How so?" I shoot her a look and, her eyes soften.

"Oh, it's just that a lot of ads for rooms around here are pretty liberal with their wording, so you don't often get what you bargain for is all. But I'm sure you'll be perfectly fine," she rushes to add.

The casual dismissal does nothing to settle my nerves now that she's made me question things.

Thanks, Ellen.

She focuses on our destination as we bypass the Athletic Building, then changes the subject.

"Mrs. Peterson mentioned something about you starting a support group on the grounds, didn't she?"

"It's not a support group, but you got the rest right," I say with a smile. "They're letting me use the auditorium for meetings, though, which is pretty cool. You know, assuming people show up."

"What's your objective?"

"Body positivity," I answer. "You know, just doing my small part to help others learn to be comfortable in their skin."

Ellen glances toward me again as we step onto the curb. "Cool!" she beams. "What makes you so passionate about your cause?"

There are two answers I could give. The main one being that I made someone a promise a while ago that I'd see this idea through, but I give Ellen the simpler response. The one that won't create more questions.

"Being plus-sized and having been taunted in the past, I know how damaging that can be. So, I thought I'd turn my experience into a bridge of sorts, one that will hopefully help people get through their *own* shit."

We ascend the steps of the library, and Ellen opens up a bit. "I was bullied all through high school. Pretty hardcore, actually," she adds, tugging the side of her plaid pants with a laugh. "As you can see, I have my own style and it's not always a hit with the crowd. Add in that I'm awkward as hell and would rather play D&D than party, and you have the perfect storm. I learned the hard way that people can be real assholes."

I smile but don't respond. I'd never minimize another person's experience, but my situation was a bit different. When the taunting comes from within your home, from someone you know should be a protector, it sort of pulls the rug out from under you. Because of it, I don't really know what it's like to have a safe space. One where I've felt unconditional love.

"Anyway, shall we go inside?" Ellen asks with a huge grin, which tells me this might be one of her favorite spots on campus. "We've got a great fiction selection. I'm a huge sci-fi fan, so I peruse that area pretty often."

My face hurts from the fake smile I put on to avoid hurting her feelings, but I honestly couldn't care less about any of this.

She reaches for the door but then comes to an abrupt stop. "Hey!"

She aims that word at the back of some guy's head as he makes his way down the sidewalk. He looks back, and Ellen points at the lidded coffee cup now lying on the pavement.

"You missed the trashcan. Don't you think you ought to pick that up?" she asks.

The accused doubles back, and it turns into a full-blown argument between them. Meanwhile, I'm actively trying to ignore the stares we're getting from those passing by.

Instead, I focus on the building adjacent to this one when the double doors fly open as someone exits toward the parking lot. From the brief glimpse I get of the inside, it looks like your standard fitness center—rows and rows of gym equipment like weight benches, treadmills, and a bunch of other shit that makes me tired just looking at it.

The entrance opens again, and a guy steps out, holding the door with his foot just long enough for two others to exit behind him. They rest against the brick wall, and they have my full attention. So much that I hardly notice when Ellen calls the stranger she's just picked a fight with an *'Earth-killing dickbag'*.

I zone out as sweat-drenched Bradwyn U t-shirts cling to two hard bodies. Their cutoff sleeves show off the ink that trails up their arms—one with colorful art all the way up to his neck. The third is completely shirtless with dark athletic shorts riding low on his waist, but no tatts. This trio are just magnificent enough that, if I weren't already perspiring like crazy, I would be now. They're tall, plus their shoulders and biceps look rock solid from here, leaving me to wonder what sport they're training for.

One with wild blond hair takes a small box from his pocket and it isn't until he pulls a white stick from inside it that I realize it's cigarettes. He has a lighter in his hand the next second, but before he can light up, the one with the neck tatts slaps the cigarette to the ground. There's a standoff between them, and for a moment, I wonder if I'm witnessing the makings of a fight. But when the blond one simply gives the other the finger and returns the lighter to his pocket, the dynamic between them confuses me a bit.

I was so focused on the exchange between *those* two, that I hadn't laid eyes on the shirtless one in a few seconds, but when I do, I gasp to myself, realizing he's watching me. I can't say for how long, but I feel frozen, like if I look away too abruptly it'll seem even more suspicious. So, I just stand there, blinking like an idiot.

My heart skips a beat when he lightly elbows the blond one,

never breaking eye contact with me. The others follow his gaze, and now they notice I'm standing here, too. There's enough distance between us that I can't make out what the shirtless one is mouthing to them. However, when all three smirk and the shirtless one nods this way, acknowledging that he knows I exist, I want to crawl in a hole and die.

Even more than I did when Ellen first started making a scene.

Only now am I able to break eye contact. Ellen's still on her rant when she flails her arms to prove some ridiculous point to the guy she's laying into and, of course, she hits my arm in the process. The stack of papers in my hand goes flying all over the sidewalk, and while I don't look around to confirm, I know all eyes are on us.

"Oh my gosh, Stevie, I'm sorry," she says, finally ending her lecture. Instead of helping with the mess, the guy she'd held hostage takes the opportunity to break free, and I don't blame him.

Ellen and I lower to the ground, gathering up what feels like endless sheets of paper that are now out of order. The only lucky thing is that there's zero wind today, so I guess I should be grateful for small favors.

Ellen glances up as she hands me a thin packet to place back inside my folder, and in my peripheral vision, I see her do a doubletake as she whispers one panicked word.

"Shit!"

I follow her gaze to the three near the Athletic Building. The same three who'd nearly given me a waking wet dream a moment ago. They're watching us, and that fact seems to have Ellen shaken. She quickly glances away, like eye contact with them will literally steal her soul.

"You know them or something?" I ask.

Still picking up stray pieces of paper, Ellen steals another look at the guys. Her face is redder now, which I'm pretty sure has nothing to do with the heat.

"They're on the hockey team. Actually, they're kind of the star players, which may as well make them local gods," she adds. "But to me, they're just glorified campus playboys—assholes who use girls up and never call afterward."

I smirk a bit. "Are you... speaking from experience?"

She peers up at me and seems a little embarrassed. "Me? Oh, God no! I'd never even be able to formulate a *sentence* around them, let alone... get physical," she adds with a whisper. "I've heard things around the dorms, though. Girls talk."

"They do," I say with a nod, standing now that we have everything cleaned up.

"Half the team are also frat members, so you can imagine how *that* goes," she says with an eye roll, but my interest suddenly piques with this new information.

"I thought universities frowned on being involved in sports *and* Greek life?"

Ellen nods. "Yeah, but not at Bradwyn. We're one of the few that actually encourage it, wanting students to get the most out of their experience without having to choose between the two."

I mean to listen, but her answer goes in one ear and out the other because I suddenly feel like a ship being lured in by a siren's call. The one with blond, shoulder-length hair just motioned with his head for me to come to them. He's quite bold, maybe even a little cocky to think I'd drop everything and prance over like some bitch in heat. I can't even imagine what he'd say or do if I were to obey, but we'll never know.

Now that Ellen's made it clear they're not only jocks, but also frat boys, there's no way in hell I'd let myself get anywhere near them. But then the doors to their building open and fate intervenes, ensuring that I don't answer their silent call. The three are suddenly lost in the crowd who join them beside the wall, deeming the moment officially over. And just like that, it feels like time is moving forward again.

"Which frat did you say they're in?" I ask.

Ellen shakes her head. "I *didn't* say, actually. Because I don't really know," she adds with a laugh. "Around here, everyone just calls them The Savages."

Her words linger with me a moment as I zone out on a thought. It isn't until she speaks again that I force my gaze her way.

"Ready to head in?" she asks.

"Yep," I smile. "Whenever you are."

She bounds into the library, and I try my best not to look back as we cross the threshold, but who am I kidding...

Somehow, with all those bodies swarming around them, I find those three sets of eyes locked on me like heat-seeking missiles.

I don't know them, don't know what they're about, but I do know of their brotherhood. And as fun as they are to look at and fantasize about, when all is said and done, it's entirely possible that my mission on this campus will burn their organization to the ground.

So, as I break this strange hold these boys have on me, I tear my eyes from theirs and face forward. Whoever they are, whatever role they play within their brotherhood, their involvement makes them enemies, casualties of war.

CHAPTER 2
STEVIE

THREE MONTHS LATER...

In a perfect world, the noise and chaos of the party will be an adequate distraction. Enough that I'll easily slip upstairs without being noticed, then slip out just as smoothly. After that, my night will hopefully be spent digging into evidence by way of the leather-bound book no one outside their brotherhood should even know exists.

However, thanks to my mother's husband-to-be having loose lips when he's a few drinks in, I know much more than I should.

I make my exit and the thick, steel door I've just eased closed acts as a barrier between me and the party raging inside. The music's now quiet enough to hear myself think, and to hear Maddox, too.

"All clear," I whisper.

He sighs in my ear. "Fucking finally. I'll help you navigate. You're still in the courtyard?"

My gaze shifts to the turquoise pool with bright lights glowing beneath the water. "Yep, heading across the breezeway as we speak. Double doors ahead."

"That should be the game room."

I smile as he gives a play-by-play. We studied the frat's website together, watched the video tour together, and memorized the old blueprint we dug up online together. Which means we both know I'm not some damsel in distress. Maddox can't help but be protective, though. It's always been that way. Since we were kids.

More than once tonight, he's complained about only being here in spirit, but I wouldn't have it any other way. If things go bad —which they very well could—this can't fall on anyone but me. He's got a scholarship and a clean rep to protect, while mine, on the other hand, is already shot to hell. So, much to Maddox's dismay, he's currently sitting in his dorm room on the campus of Elmcrest University one town away. And I'm here, alone in frat boy paradise—the aged manor situated at the end of Bradwyn U's Greek Row, a dwelling affectionately known as *The Den*.

"I don't like this. It's weird being *here* while you're behind enemy lines."

A laugh leaves me. "Behind enemy lines? Someone's got a flare for the dramatic tonight."

"Am I wrong, though?"

His question has me arching a brow, picturing the crowd I just left. Those not wearing t-shirts with the school logo and crossed hockey sticks underneath it, were sporting shirts and hoodies with the word "SAVAGE" printed across the chest. What was once simply the last name of the frat's founder, is now an adjective describing the brotherhood itself, and they certainly live up to the label.

These boys are wild, their parties are wilder, and sometimes... bad things happen.

"Ok, so maybe that's pretty spot on," I concede.

"Exactly, so I'm allowed to be a bit on edge."

I glance over my shoulder to make sure I'm still alone. No one followed, so a sigh of relief leaves me before sharing something with Maddox.

"I was thinking, even if I *do* get caught, which I'm not saying I will, but I could always just pretend I'm drunk and wandered off."

"Or how about you just run?" Maddox growls. "None of that hero bullshit, Stevie. I fucking mean it."

I mock him until he's done preaching to me, then silence creeps in. All because it weirds me out when he gets like this. All... boyfriend-y. There's no shortage of girls who'd *love* to be with him in that way. I'm just not one of them. All I've ever wanted from Maddox is friendship, even if others find it hard to believe we're strictly platonic.

I scan the length of the courtyard and take note of the lion statue that reps the school and hockey team—The Kings. Someone's even decided to be cheeky and slipped a burgundy and black hockey jersey over the lion's head. Next, my gaze shifts to the lawn furniture not too far away. It's mismatched, and the garden is overgrown. The grass, however, is cut and well-maintained. It's a bit of a shocker that they even give a shit, but maybe they're not all Neanderthals.

Maybe.

The door hinges squeak lightly when I let myself in and my heart races double-time. The actual house *should* be empty, thanks to the party raging in the gathering hall behind me, but I'm still on edge. The eerie quietness isn't helping.

"Ok, I'm in," I whisper, then sidestep the massive pool table in the middle of the room. As I do, a deep breath hisses in my ear.

"I can't believe I let you do this alone, knowing what they're capable of," Maddox groans. "I swear, if something—"

"No bad vibes!" I cut in. "Nothing will happen. I'll be in and out in no time."

My throat feels tight, a sign that I'm not actually sure it'll be so easy.

"Where are you looking first? The study?" Maddox asks.

"Don't you think that'd be too obvious? When Rob slipped up and mentioned the book, the look Tate shot him could've killed. Which means this thing is sacred to these guys. It won't be illuminated in a display case. I'm thinking I should start with bedrooms. Probably the upperclassmen."

Maddox is quiet, and a memory bleeds into my thoughts. It's of the night I found out the book even existed. I was seated at the dinner table with Mom and her fiancé, Rob. It was my second or third time meeting him, but the first I'd ever seen of his son, Tate—a graduate student at Bradwyn U, who my mom basically thinks of as a saint. I didn't realize it until later, but fate had brought him and I to the table that night.

Once I left for school, visits home became rare for me, so Mom and Rob seized the opportunity one weekend when I stopped in unannounced last spring. They thought it might be important that I finally put a face with Tate's name before the wedding. So, I put on a t-shirt and jeans instead of the dress Mom requested, then made her semi-happy for an evening by actually showing up to dinner with her *new* family.

As far as first impressions go, I can admit that one look at Tate had me imagining a world where we weren't technically about to be related. His merciless flirting right under our parents' noses didn't help either. More than once that night, he'd given me this look that made me feel undeniably... dirty. It also made me wonder if he even cared about that '*technically related*' part. And if I'm being honest, it may have also caused me to question whether *I* did.

Dimples melted me every time he smiled or laughed, and even beneath his crisp, white button-down, I could make out the detail of a meticulously toned physique. Rob had spent a fair amount of time bragging about what a star Tate was on the ice during his years at Bradwyn, so it was safe to assume hockey had accounted for the added layer of muscle.

The color of his shirt stands out in my memory. I recall how it contrasted his sun-kissed skin and the darkness of his hair and eyes.

His eyes...

They were intense and beautiful, their subtle upward arc being his one and only feature that isn't the spitting image of his father. Instead, they hint at his late mother's Southeast Asian roots. Within an hour of meeting him, the general consensus I reached was... yeah, I could easily learn to overlook our familial ties.

Stepbrother Dearest had started a fire. My vivid imagination fanned the flames.

Dinner was going well for the most part. Mom and Rob were entertaining to watch, at least. Both had a bit too much wine, so eventually they were behaving more like children while Tate and I were somehow roped into parenting them. What I thought would be a dull, stale night in, actually turned into a good time.

Right up until Rob rolled both sleeves to his elbows before clearing the table.

That's when I noticed it—the four-inch scar in the shape of an 'S' with a devil tail on the end that had been branded on his forearm. I hadn't been around him enough to spot it before, living on opposite sides of the country and all, but when I asked to get a better look, he proudly stepped closer. This was my first *in-person* look at the brand of the Savage Brotherhood, but I'd seen it before in a picture. A picture I don't think anyone knows exists but me.

No one *living*, that is.

The branding tradition has been ongoing among the Savages for years. Even before Rob attended Bradwyn and joined the frat decades ago. But if that gleam in his eye was any indication, he was still just as loyal to the affiliation *today* as he ever was.

Well, he was loyal until Mom started pumping him full of wine, anyway.

The moment Rob sensed my interest in the brotherhood, he started spilling intel. Among that intel was the revelation that the *Book of Secrets* was a thing. I felt the importance of that moment as soon as those words left his mouth, but I wasn't the only one. Tate did, too. He was quick to silence his father, but not before Rob disclosed the book's purpose.

He described it as *'a means for the brotherhood to purge their sins, a vessel to free themselves of their deepest, darkest secrets.'*

That got me to thinking. That sounded like the perfect piece of evidence to bring the brotherhood to its knees. The perfect place for a twisted frat boy to confess to a crime. One he got away with.

One that had a devastating ripple effect, of which he could never understand the magnitude.

It was a small glimmer of hope, but a glimmer nonetheless. Enough that I decided in that moment to quit school in California and enroll at Bradwyn U for the upcoming fall semester. It was the only way to get closer to the Savages.

The only way to find... *him.*

I was honestly content thinking I'd have to search for a needle in a haystack. Especially when Rob mentioned that the entire brotherhood—past and present—are marked with the same scar, just on various parts of their bodies. However, when he eagerly lifted his beloved son's sleeve to show that he'd followed in his old man's footsteps, my world stopped spinning.

Completely.

Tate had clearly also been a Savage. His brand was in the exact same location on his forearm as his father's, but that wasn't the detail that nearly had me crawling over the table to get a closer look. It was the unique beaded bracelet on Tate's wrist.

In an instant, everything changed, and no one in the room realized it but me.

It hadn't been some random stranger I was looking for. The one responsible for the pain that tore my family apart at the seams was seated right across the table, cringing as his father spilled copious amounts of information to us outsiders and eating food my mother prepared with love.

Fucking Tate...

Now, here I am, standing inside the residence of the Savage Brotherhood, on the hunt for a book that could possibly prove my stepbrother's guilt.

The memory fades, and I swear I feel Maddox's anxiety through the phone. Probably at the thought of me venturing into the guys' rooms. It might seem like a suicide mission, but that's partly why I'm glad to be doing this on my own.

He's been with me every step of the way, even though he's kind of blind to many of the details and the madness that drives me forward. He knows I hold the frat responsible for what happened, knows I believe there are clues in that book, but he has no idea about Tate and the horrible things I think he's done.

And I intend to keep it that way.

"Any chance I can still talk you out of this?" he asks. "You could walk out right now, Stevie. We could pretend none of this ever happened."

I hear his plea, know he's one hundred percent right about this being a terrible idea, but stopping before I have answers is simply out of the question.

"I have to do this," I answer, and I think he feels the finality in the response. There is no changing my mind.

He sighs at my stubbornness, maybe only now accepting defeat. Then, he gives his final word of advice before I continue.

"Fine, but do us both a favor and just... make it fast."

P assing through another set of doors, I enter the hallway. At either side, mounted glass cabinets showcase awards, trophies, and accolades signed by prominent politicians from local and larger sects of government.

I stop for a better look. These guys' social reps on campus are a shitshow, but their academic standing? Completely different story. Most are rough around the edges, underdogs from the wrong side of the tracks, but they're also notoriously intelligent.

Photos of those responsible for this wicked alliance's existence are hung between two cases. Like idols. False gods. Of course, Reginald Savage—their founder—is front and center.

"Something wrong?"

Maddox's voice has my eyes shifting from the portraits, and my feet move again. "No, just getting my bearings."

"When you get to the elevator, I vote you bypass it and take the stairs."

I hear his instructions, but they go in one ear and out the other.

"Yeah, well, I worked today, so my feet and I say your vote doesn't count, sir." I'm already pressing the button, calling the elevator to take me up.

Another hard sigh leaves him, and I know he's given up his argument. In fact, he's silent the entire ride up, until I speak again.

"Ok, all clear."

"What do you see? Where are you now?"

"Um... Second floor, hallway," I answer.

"*Which* hallway?"

The question has me racking my brain, remembering how different areas of the house were labeled.

"*Knight's corridor*," I answer, referencing the sleeping quarters for juniors, second-year members.

"Sweet, you should run into *Kings' Passage* on the left. See it?"

"Uhh... yep. Found it." With those words, I tug open the double-doors leading to the south wing designated for seniors to room. If anyone is to be trusted with that damn book, it's them.

"Hear anything?" Maddox whispers, like the volume of his voice on *his* end will be heard on *mine*.

"Nope, still silent. Pretty sure everyone's down at the party," I answer, pausing at the end of the hallway. "Right or left?"

"What?"

"Right or left?" I whisper louder.

"How the hell should *I* know? Right, I guess."

After hesitating for a moment, I go for it, opening the first door I come to. Cautiously, of course. It's dark inside and so quiet I can hear myself breathing. The thought of knowing I've just trespassed into someone's bedroom has me freaking, so a few seconds pass before I get up the nerve to turn on the light.

I have to make this quick, so the three questions Maddox rapid fires in my ear go unanswered. My eyes shift to the dresser where I take a quick note of what I spot there—a half-empty pack of gum, a guest nametag from the hospital, and a university ID printed with the same name as the hospital tag—*Ashton Blaine*.

Observing the pic, I arch a brow. My first thought is that dude is fucking hot, but then I take a closer look. Something about him seems familiar and it takes me a moment to pin down where I've seen him before. Then, it hits me. It was the day of my tour. He made up one third of the trio I locked eyes with as they stood outside the Athletic Building, and it's the generous amount of ink covering his skin that gives him away.

My gaze lingers on the pic. He gives off 'loose cannon' vibes if it's possible to tell that from an image. He also looks like he hasn't eaten a carb in his entire adult life. But even in all his tatted, chiseled perfection, my money's on him being a complete psycho. I can usually spot them from a mile away. The shelf lined with hockey trophies I lay eyes on next makes me certain of it. They mean he's likely excessively aggressive and violent on the ice, in a sport that's *already* notoriously ruthless.

The only thing worse than a hot jock is a hot jock with rage issues.

"What the hell's happening?" Maddox asks, and I realize I've been silent for a while.

"I'm just looking around," I say, keeping my eyes peeled for anything that stands out.

The next place I look is under the bed. It's hard to see, so I lean down and feel my way around. More random shit—a sock, a condom wrapper, and... oh, God! There's the condom!

Dry heaving, I sit straight and wipe my hand clean on the guy's blanket. I mean, I'd rather the gym rat have his *own* DNA as opposed to it being on my palm.

"What is it?" Maddox asks, hearing me heave again.

"Just... I don't wanna talk about it." My throat feels thick with saliva, but I talk myself down from vomiting and refocus.

"At least tell me what you see," he says.

I rear back on my shins. "Nothing yet. Just your average, disgusting guy's bedroom."

Maddox sighs on the other end. "I still say you should've checked the study."

"This is only the first place I've looked. It'll be fine."

I lean in again, reaching closer to the headboard this time. All I find are a couple of shoeboxes, which I think might be promising at first, but nope. Just two new pairs of sneakers inside.

Standing, I head to the closet. Full hamper, a stack of papers, more new sneakers, and a bag of clothes with the tags still on. Nothing of interest in the corners or on the top shelf.

"It's a bust. I'm moving on."

My heart's racing when I sigh. That ticking clock inside my head may be imagined, but that doesn't make it any less urgent.

I enter the next bedroom with reckless abandon, not bothering to be anywhere near as delicate as before. There's no hesitation to turn on the light, either. A soft rug cushions my knees when I drop down to search underneath the bed. This one's cleaner than the last, and it actually smells nice. Like there'd been a candle burning recently.

But alas, nothing.

Empty again.

Frustrated, I grip the edge of the bed when I stand, going straight to the closet since there's not a single book on the dresser or desk. The door squeals on its hinges when I open it and pull the string for the light. It's organized, nothing on the floor but a pair of shin guards sticking out of a Bradwyn U sports bag. All his clothes are hung on actual hangers, and dude loves his brand names. Every t-shirt, every hoodie, every pair of jeans, every belt...

The door is nearly shut when I remember the light, and as I reach for the string, I notice a tripod in the corner. Then, I notice the expensive-ass camera equipment on the shelf. It's weird how vastly different this space is from the last, which leaves me to wonder how the guys under this enormous roof can be so unique, and yet, still the same.

There's a weight on my shoulders as I come up empty. Again. I don't bother updating Maddox, instead heading right to the next bedroom. Flinging the door open, I do the same routine as with the last two, pushing worn hockey gear aside to do a thorough check underneath the bed, inside the closet. And like the last two times, there's nothing.

"Think, Stevie," I say, feeling myself get even more flustered as I turn to the desk against the far wall. Computer parts are strewn everywhere—sound cards, CPU fans, and a bunch of other techy shit I can't name. But that's when I see it.

A lockbox beneath an open laptop.

Breathing like a mad woman, I move the computer aside and almost shed a tear when the lid to the safe budges. All it takes is the press of a button on the side of the combination lock and...

"Shit!"

"What happened? What is it?" Maddox asks in a panic.

Before I can even answer, disappointment washes over me when I find absolutely nothing in the most promising space yet.

"I'm gonna need you to say something, Stevie, or I swear I'm coming over there," Maddox threatens.

"No, I'm fine, I just... I thought I had something."

"That's it. Time to bail. I have a bad feeling and you know my gut's never wrong about this shit," he says.

"I know. I just..."

Desperation becomes something else. Something tangible I can't quite put into words. Yes, it'd be easy to run because this is an *incredibly* stupid thing to be doing, but I need to know the truth. And if the one person who could've given me answers is gone... I'll do whatever it takes.

"Get out of there," Maddox warns again. "And put everything back the way you found it."

I'm a fucking failure. This was my one chance, and I blew it.

Brushing a tear from my eye, I close the lockbox and reach to place the laptop back on the lid. Tears blur my vision, but a bright red light beside the tiny camera lens above the screen has me blinking them away.

"Fuck!" My first thought is to cover my face, but I'm terrified it's already too late.

"Something happen?"

"The laptop," I say, dropping down to the floor to hide myself. I only sit there a moment before ultimately deciding that running for it is an even better idea.

Leaving this guy's shit exactly the way it is, I put as much distance between me and that room as possible. The hallway feels like it goes on for miles as I book it toward the staircase, glancing over my shoulder every few seconds out of paranoia. *My* scared ass didn't even turn off the light or close the door, because all I could think about was getting the hell out of there.

But if that red indicator light means what I think it means... I'm fucked anyway.

I take the stairs, flying down them faster than I think I've ever run before, replaying everything that just happened. If I'm lucky, the shadow of my hood hid my face well enough, but there's no way to be sure.

"Damn it!" More tears spill from my eyes as the weight of how royally screwed I am fully hits me.

"You're not saying anything, Stevie. I need to know you're good," Maddox says sternly. As if he's trying to hide that he's just as scared for me as I am. Judging by how he's breathing, I'm beginning to think he's rushing around his room, putting on clothes and shoes to head this way. Actually, I'm almost certain that's what he's doing. And, I don't know, maybe that's not such a bad idea.

"I think someone was watching me," I say just above a whisper, retracing my steps through the dark corridors.

"Someone saw you?"

"Yes! I mean... I don't know! I moved the laptop to open the safe it was sitting on, but when I went to put the laptop back, there was a red light beside the camera at the top."

"It wasn't on before?"

"No. At least I don't think it was," I answer, my voice quivering.

"Shit. You must've triggered it somehow. I shouldn't have let you do this."

"It wasn't your choice!" I nearly yell. I'm certain I would have if I hadn't remembered at the last possible second that I'm trespassing.

I slip out the front door and race down the hill toward the sidewalk, deciding I've spent about as much time in this house as I can stomach. There, hidden in the bushes, is my bike.

Freedom.

People are scattered across the lawn, but I don't care. They're not paying me any attention anyway. But even if they are, I don't really give a shit, seeing as how I may have already blown my cover.

"I only meant that we should've found another way. You can't afford to get in trouble again," he says in a much quieter tone, smoothing the rough edges that made me lash out before.

"I know, I just... I had to do it. I need to know. For her," I add, but I leave it at that when my voice breaks.

The water pooling in my eyes is the reason I don't see the rock at the edge of the sidewalk and stumble over it, landing on all fours on the ground. The skin on my knee stings when my jeans tear, and flesh meets cement.

"Fuck!" My frustration spills over completely now as tears flow. I don't even know how to control them at this point, so I don't bother trying. Instead, I lift myself from the ground and snatch my bike from the branches propping it up.

Maddox stays silent on the other end of the line, but he's still with me, listening as I breathe deep, struggling to cope with the botched mission. I know who these boys are, know all too well what their brotherhood is capable of, but I may have to just live with the fact that what's done is done.

A warm breeze whips over my face and through my hair as I ride, picking up speed, pedaling like my life depends on it. Because, shit... maybe it does.

It's entirely possible that tonight was an absolute bust, one that could land me right back in court, but a small part of me refuses to regret it. *Any* of it. Because if the shoe were on the other foot, the person I risked it all for, the one no longer here to speak for herself, would've done the same for me.

Because that's the true meaning of the word that binds us in life and in death...

Sister.

CHAPTER 4
ASHTON

W ithout fail, the defiant ones seem to end up being *my* problem. It's like I'm strapped to a beacon that draws out the smart-asses and shit-talkers from the group, the ones who glare at me when they think I'm not looking.

Like Enzo, here.

He wants to be one of us so bad he can taste it. Problem is, he thinks he can force his way in without submitting, without bending. That shit won't fly, though.

"On your knees!"

Enzo tightens both fists at the sound of my voice. I glance down, seeing his hands clenched at his sides. We lock eyes again.

"Tell me you're not that stupid," I growl, smirking at the thought of him swinging on me. "Do it. *Please.* I want you to."

He flinches with every syllable that leaves my mouth. Not out of fear, but because it's taking everything in him to fight the urge. There's darkness inside this one. All our pledges are a little rough around the edges, but this one's seen some shit. I can always spot them because *I've* seen some shit. He stares me down and I'm all out of patience.

"On your *fucking* knees!"

This time, he shudders when I yell and I don't hate it, witnessing the very moment this asshole falls in line.

My voice ricochets off the trees and can probably be heard for miles. Only, there's no one out here but us.

No one to help.

No one to hear them scream.

I'm nose-to-nose with this year's problem child, backing his punk-ass down while the other pledges watch from the circle they've formed around us. Enzo glares up at me, flexing his jaw, and then does as he's told. A smile curves my mouth the moment his knees touch dirt.

"Now, that wasn't so hard, was it?"

He's practically shaking with rage when he answers. "No."

I stoop down so we're at eye level. "No... what?"

Tension ticks in his jaw like before. "No, Big Brother Ashton."

Perfect. Looks like someone finally knows their place.

Nodding slowly, I hold his gaze and stand. Most who pledge Savage are turned away before they even get their foot in the door. In other words, my new friend Enzo should be thanking his lucky stars he's even here. A hundred other guys would kill to be in his spot right now, kneeling in the mud, moments from being buried chin-deep like the other pledges. They might resent the hell out of us right now, but soon, they'll get it. They'll see they're gaining a brotherhood for life.

For some, for *most,* this is the closest thing they'll ever have to family.

When I nod toward the hole dug beside Enzo, he climbs in. Micah smirks and hands me a shovel. I fill in the space around Enzo with damp soil and he fumes the entire time. Once his head is all that's visible, I pack the dirt tightly around him.

With a sigh, I rest my foot on the shovel head, then prop my elbow on the handle.

"Now that everyone's all tucked in for the night, Vince's gonna put in a call to the other pledges. What happens next is up to you," I warn them. "The others are about two miles away and we've armed them with flashlights, a compass, and the knowledge that you're buried somewhere in the general direction of north."

"I know what you're all thinking," Micah interjects, pausing to puff smoke from his mouth. "You're planning to yell, make as much noise as possible so they find you quicker, but I wouldn't if I were you. Not only is that a bitch move, it's also against the rules."

"How the hell are they supposed to know where we are if we're not allowed to make noise?" Enzo asks. "I was at every team workout this week just like you three were. I'm fucking exhausted."

Slowly, Micah turns. Having known him so long, I'm aware of how much he hates being challenged. In our brotherhood, *and* on the ice, respect from underclassmen isn't simply preferred, it's demanded.

"First, don't be such a fucking pussy," he growls. "Second, shouldn't you have a little more faith in your brothers?"

Enzo doesn't answer, just glares and breathes hard as it starts drizzling again.

"Well, just in case any of you get the bright idea to defy us, I've mounted a camera on this tree here," Micah explains, slapping the trunk of it as he speaks. "Everything that happens here tonight will be uploaded to the cloud. Audio and all."

"This is bullshit."

Pretty sure Enzo thought he mumbled that under his breath, but he wasn't quiet enough.

Micah's reaching his limit if he hasn't already. Taking unhurried steps, he stops with the toes of his dark boots inches from Enzo's face. Honestly, I half expect him to break the dickhead's nose. It's not like he doesn't deserve it. But my guess is that Micah's in a good mood tonight when he crouches down and takes a handful of Enzo's hair instead, using it to jerk our problem child's head back.

Micah studies him for a moment, taking a drag on his cigarette while he thinks.

"Don't you ever get tired of hearing yourself speak? Because I sure fucking do," he adds, blowing a ribbon of smoke into Enzo's eyes.

The dark-blond mess Micah calls hair falls toward his face a little, touching his chin. The strands are damp from the rain, and it makes him look psychotic. With his deep-set eyes and humorless expression, he's been likened to at least a hundred movie villains over the years. Tonight, I'd have to agree.

"All I'm saying is it could take them hours to find us if they don't know where to look," Enzo explains. "They could *literally* walk right past us a dozen times and not even know we're here."

Micah's hard glare is still fixed on him when he answers. "Sounds like a *you* problem," he concludes, shoving Enzo's head when he lets his hair go.

"Sleep tight," Vince adds, bidding the pledges farewell with a salute as he pushes off from a tree.

We all know tonight will thin the herd, but that's the point. Only the strong survive because Savages don't do soft. Don't do weak. Which is why, despite Enzo's fire annoying the shit out of me, I tolerate it. Because we all know he's a perfect fit.

Quiet conversation picks up behind us as we walk away. Vince pulls out his phone and dials.

"You're on," is all he says, then hangs up before shoving his cell back into his pocket.

Somewhere, miles away, that command just sent a dozen pledges scurrying across these very woods in search of the others. It's well after midnight and they have until sunup to complete the task if they intend to qualify for the next phase.

"Wait!" someone calls out. There's desperation in his voice but he hides it when he speaks again. "You're taking the shovels. How will they get us out?"

Vince turns and walks backwards instead of stopping his stride, smirking when he answers. "Guess they'll have to get their hands dirty. Otherwise, you motherfuckers might be here a while."

He faces forward and we're probably being called all kinds of '*assholes*' and '*dickheads*' behind our backs, but we don't give a shit. In fact, the moment we're back at my truck, my mind's already on other things. Like getting to the house in time to catch the last couple hours of the party. It's been a few weeks since I've defiled anyone's daughter. Tonight's as good a night as any.

The engine rumbles when I press the button on the keyring,

then climb in. Micah tosses the shovels into the bed, and I glance at Vince through the rearview mirror when he speaks.

"Think they'll make the deadline?" There's no real concern on his face as he stares at his phone, likely checking the live feed.

"Half will. Maybe not even that," I answer. "The rest are gonna dig their way out within the next couple hours because they're pussies."

I shift into drive once Micah's in his seat, but don't take my foot off the brake.

"Put that shit out before you close the door."

He cuts me a look when I nod toward his cigarette. We do this almost every day. It's fine that he refuses to quit or even cut back during the season, but he can light up somewhere other than my truck.

Mumbling under his breath, he tosses the stick out into the rain before slamming the door shut. Then, I'm not surprised his attention immediately goes to his phone. We're not new to any of this, which is why we know pledges cut corners when they think no one's watching. Which is why we're *always* watching. It'll be interesting, though, to see which ones play fair and which ones try to game the system, disqualifying themselves.

"What the fuck?" Micah growls, sitting straighter in his seat.

I lift my foot off the brake and pull forward with a smirk. "You good?"

He takes a while to answer but when I glance over, his face is in a full-blown scowl now. "Someone's in my *fucking* room!"

"My money's on Fletcher," Vince laughs. "Probably stealing condoms again."

Micah pushes a hand through his wild hair, frustration marking his expression. "Not Fletcher. Some bitch."

I pull the truck over and Vince leans in for a better look. "You sure?" His question has Micah's jaw ticking.

"Yes, Vince, I'm pretty fucking sure." When he turns the screen so we can all see it, I focus on the girl. My first observation is that she's got nice tits. More than a mouthful.

"Nope, definitely not Fletcher," I say under my breath.

Micah shoots me a look. It's one that usually intimidates

people to bend to his will, but it doesn't work on me and Vince. While most would cower, I give him the finger, then snatch his phone to get a better view of the video. The girl—whoever she is—is clearly on a mission. She's all over Micah's room, snooping through his shit like it's hers—under his bed, in his closet, then she finally rummages through the mess on his desk.

"Doesn't look like she took anything," I point out.

"Because she realized she triggered the camera," Micah grumbles. "This has Whitlock written all over it. No way him and his boys didn't put her up to this."

There's silence when I rewind the footage, watching as the girl gets down on all fours to reach under the bed, her perfectly round ass pointed skyward. Micah's probably right about her. Leo Whitlock—captain of our rival team—is among the few brave enough, and *stupid* enough, to pull some shit like this.

Vince stares for a moment, then leans back in his seat. "Is it just me or does this chick look familiar to anyone else?"

My gaze goes back to the footage and my brow tenses. Micah bounces a look between my face and his phone when I take it from him, zooming in on a still of the girl as she stands at his desk.

"No fucking way." The guys watch in silence when I toss the phone back to Micah, then reach into the backseat. After digging through shit in my bag, I find what I'm looking for—the smooth, glossed pages of a brochure I hadn't gotten around to throwing away yet. Pulling it free, I turn to the back page and... damn. There it is.

Or should I say, there *she* is.

Without speaking, I compare the image in my hand to the one on Micah's phone. Staring back with a big-ass grin on her face is the chick who thought it wise to cross into forbidden territory. If Whitlock *did* talk her into this, it'd mean our truce has been violated. Which would mean things are about to get *real* fucking interesting on the ice this season.

Focusing again, I study the back of the brochure. Her face is framed by a full head of dark hair. It's longer than I realized. In the video, her hoodie mostly covered it, but in the picture, I can see it touches her elbow. Next, I zero in on her lips—full, glossed.

The only thing that would make them look better is if they were wrapped around my dick.

Yep, she's definitely fuckable. Well, she *would* be... if she wasn't officially marked—a dead girl walking.

I study the brochure a bit longer, then Vince's words echo in my head. He asked if she looked familiar and I'll be damned if he isn't right. Only, I can't place when or where our paths crossed.

"What the fuck is this anyway?" Micah asks, nodding toward the brochure.

"Looks like she runs some body-positivity bullshit," I answer with a sigh. "A chick handed it to me in the quad a few days ago. A member of the group, I'm guessing."

Micah nods thoughtfully but doesn't speak.

"This is definitely her, though, right?" I ask.

"It is. And it looks like there's a meeting tomorrow night. Which means we have an official time we'll enter this girl's world and start fucking shit up." His eyes narrow, then his smile grows, proving once again that he might be more villain than hero. Just like people have said for years. "Her name on there?" he asks.

I study the caption under her picture, skimming past her backstory and the part about why she's passionate about her cause.

"Stevie," I answer. "Might be short for something. Might not."

"Last name?" Vince asks from the back.

I scan the page again. "Heron. Like the bird."

He's motionless when I glance at him through the rearview mirror, and his only response is a mumbled, "Hm."

Micah settles into his seat, finally relaxing now that our target has a name. It's like he's found peace knowing we've got this girl right where we want her. Trapped. Not knowing when or where we'll strike.

"Well, it sounds like we just found ourselves a new pet," Micah announces, and I like the thought of it. No one fucks with our brotherhood and just walks away. There are consequences.

Always consequences.

Not sure what she thought would happen, but Stevie Heron is about to come face-to-face with her worst nightmare—three motherfuckers who don't know the meaning of '*forgive and forget*'.

Her last name rings inside my head.

Heron...

We've set our share of traps over the years, and surprisingly enough, this is the first time we've managed to catch ourselves a bird.

And something tells me we're gonna enjoy taking this one out of her cage to play. But the part I'm looking forward to most? The part that brings me so much joy it makes my dick hard just thinking about it?

Clipping her fucking wings.

Tonight was heavy.

It's been a while since I've shared my own damage out loud. When I do, it always feels like reopening an old wound. My role within this group is that of a listening ear, and maybe an occasional advisor, but when a shy newcomer seemed to be struggling with her own issues, I stepped up.

She mentioned how I seem so confident, so together, and that she couldn't imagine ever being this comfortable in her own skin. So, I felt compelled to tell her a bit about my journey getting here.

I shared how I used to hate what I saw in the mirror.

Shared how, sometimes, that self-hating monster still rears its ugly head when I'm having an off day.

And I shared how my most memorable interactions with my father are of him belittling me because I was never as thin as he wanted me to be. His favorite point to harp on was how if I didn't *'get the weight off'*, boys would never take a second look at me. Like having some guys' approval of my figure was the be all and end all. Comments like that would stick inside *anyone's* head, but for me, hearing them as young as age eight, they shaped my entire world. As far as I was concerned, everyone saw me exactly as my father did. And those who said otherwise were merely trying to spare my feelings.

It's a dark, fucked up perspective, but I actively fight this particular demon daily. I've finally gotten to a place where, on most days, I come out the winner.

Now, as tonight's meeting draws to a close, I feel the aftermath of opening up, of letting the darkness in, but the sacrifice was for a worthy cause. Because I shared, one of our members now sees a light at the end of the tunnel.

"So... I think that's everything. Be safe and I'll see everyone soon." Smiling after having dismissed them from tonight's meeting, I watch the group start toward the double doors at the far side of the room.

It isn't until their quiet chatter picks up that I remember one incredibly important thing I forgot to announce.

"Don't forget to grab a packet off the back table if you're volunteering at the fundraiser. It'll be a great way to spread awareness and maybe help our numbers increase. Plus, you know, I could use the help," I add with a laugh.

The reminder has most who showed up tonight moving toward the table to grab paperwork.

"Be there with bells on," Claire adds, saluting me with two fingers as she pushes the silver bar and releases the door.

"Wouldn't miss it for the world," Misty chimes in with a wink. Then, she and her twin, Marley, follow Claire out to the parking lot.

Drew adjusts the brim of his hat when he speaks. "I'll be there early to help set up. I'm off work that day, so..."

"You're a godsend. Seriously," I say with a smile. "Oh! And great work on the pamphlets! I mean, I could've gone my whole life not seeing my face on the back of it, but still, it's the thought that counts."

"Are you kidding me? You're doing great work here. You deserve all the credit for starting this group. The campus needed something like this."

I take his words to heart, knowing what it would've meant to me having a safe space like this. At the height of my father's emotional and verbal abuse, I had no one to turn to.

Not even Mom. She was too busy trying to convince me he

didn't mean the things he said, convincing me I was just too sensitive for my own good.

I pull myself out of the thought and focus on Drew again.

"We've only had a few meetings so far, but I appreciate the compliment. Hopefully, things pick up a bit," I add, noting how we've seemingly stalled at a turnout of seven people each time we meet up.

"You know what they say. If you build it, they will come. So, moral of the story, just keep building," Drew winks.

He leans in for a hug, then once he's gone, I straighten the chairs back into a circle. His words linger with me, and I've taken his instructions to heart.

Just keep building...

I'm still lost in thought when the sound of the door unlatching has me smiling.

"Let me guess. You left your keys again?"

When I turn, I expect to see that Drew's stepped back inside, patting both pockets as he searches for his keyring, but it isn't Drew at all.

"Well, look who it is, boys."

A raspy voice echoes into the rafters of the auditorium and I'm frozen. The three taking slow steps toward me are strangers, yes, but not ones I don't recognize. Their faces are engraved in my memory, and their reputations are etched there, too. During the campus tour, Ellen described them as the ultimate fuckboy trifecta—hockey playing frat boys who get off on breaking girls' hearts.

One, I know by name. I'd seen his school ID on the dresser in one of the bedrooms last night—Ashton Blaine. I force my attention elsewhere to avoid his suspicious gaze. Their presence triggers something inside me. Something that screams for me to keep my distance. Here I was thinking I might've gotten away with trespassing in their house, thinking last night's misadventure might not blow up in my face, but I was wrong to assume that so quickly.

Very wrong, apparently.

When I first encountered them a few months back, I felt it in my gut—our paths would one day cross again. However, this isn't quite the reunion I had in mind.

I lift my eyes and the one in the middle gives *'leader of the pack'* vibes. No, he isn't bigger or taller than the others—they're all well over six feet and broad everywhere it counts. It's just his presence. Like he's deemed himself the protector, the one who'd enter a dark room first to make sure there's no danger awaiting the other two. But all that matters in this moment is that, from where I'm standing, this entire trio is scary as hell.

The one who thinks he's running shit hasn't taken his eyes off me since he and the others first began stalking in my direction. He pushes a hand through his hair in vain. It doesn't help tame it because it's still all over the place—loose, dirty-blond waves I'm guessing he hasn't washed or combed in a few days. His chiseled jaw, perfect nose, and sharp glare scream "pretty boy", but he's 90s grunge in the flesh. A nightmare personified for any father with a daughter whose innocence he hopes to protect.

Shit, Stevie. Deflect.

I force a smile. "Sorry, but you guys just missed the meeting. We're usually done by eight, so...."

My attempt at playing it cool goes from bad to worse when I try to slip past them, only to feel Ashton grip my arm. He has me tight, and my skin stings where his short nails bite into it.

"Told you she'd run," he grumbles to the others, his grip tightening.

My eyes cut to Ashton as he holds me in place. He's completely covered in tattoos. The grungy, psychotic one has them, too, but only on his arms and hands from what I can tell. But Ashton's got ink everywhere there's exposed skin, colorful pictures that run the length of both arms from beneath his short sleeves, down to his ring-clad knuckles. The color spreads upward to his neck, stopping just beneath his jaw.

Without the tatts and large gauges in both ears, he'd look like a perfectly chiseled mannequin. Hair the color of rich, dark chocolate hangs in his face, but the sides are cut short. An icy blue stare lingers on me, and I swear it's sharp enough to cut down to the bone when our gazes lock.

"You're hurting me!" There's no hiding the tremble in my voice when I try to snatch my arm from Ashton's grip, only to be yanked toward him so hard that I trip over my own feet. The rough motion has my shoulder slamming the center of his chest, but the force hardly moves him.

"Try that shit again and see what fucking happens," he warns, growling the words directly against my ear.

"I need to get home. My roommates are expecting me," I lie.

Maybe if they think the people I live with actually give a shit about what happens to me, they'll think twice about whatever they have planned.

"Then, I guess you'd better start talking," Ashton snaps.

"About what? I—I don't even know why you're..."

"She *wants* me to lose my shit," the psychotic one cuts in, speaking only to the others as a menacing smile curves his lips.

His gaze settles on me next, and I swallow loudly, unable to blink for fear of what might happen if my eyes leave him for even a second. He steps closer and does that thing again, where he moves his fingers through his hair only for it to still be a mess.

"We all know why we're here, and we all know what you fucking did," he says. "So, why don't you just save us a shitload of time and frustration and just... tell us what you were looking for last night and who sent you."

I struggle against Ashton, but his grip doesn't ease at all. "I already told you; I don't know what you're talking about."

Those words leave me, but I've got this sinking feeling I should've heeded the warning. All three smirk and my heart skips a beat as the walls close in.

The quiet one sighs and my eyes flit toward him just as his jaw ticks. Maybe it's impatience. Maybe it's frustration. He still says nothing, but he's also saying so much with that look he's giving. It's as though he wants it to be clear there's no way I get out of this without it costing me.

And damn it, I'm starting to believe that, too.

Ash's grip squeezes around my arm and I whimper when I'm forced down onto my knees. They hit the tile with a thud, causing the one I injured during last night's fall to throb and burn. Water pools in my eyes and then rolls down both cheeks. Because I'm certain these three are short on compassion, I don't speak up or bother trying to appeal to their humanity. However, when I sniffle involuntarily, I have Ash's full attention.

He leans down, heat from his lips teasing the rim of my ear. "Damn, are those tears for me?" he whispers. "Because that shit's like music to my ears."

He enjoys my pain.

Enjoys that he and his boys are the ones causing it.

My arm is finally released, and Ashton's hands shift to my shoulders instead. He lowers to the ground to kneel behind me, and I'm completely aware of being at their mercy.

The one with the untamed hair aims his gaze toward Ashton, then his eyes dart toward me again. In such a way that I sense his patience has worn even thinner.

"Shit, where are my manners?" he says. His voice is deep and melodic, a stark contrast from the malice in his eyes. "I know why you tried to run. It's because we haven't properly introduced ourselves, right?"

I don't move an inch or say a word when he continues.

"As you might've heard, this is my boy Ashton. You can call him *that* or Ash. He doesn't give a shit," he adds, dismissively pointing toward the one behind me.

I glance at Ashton from over my shoulder, only to find his eyes are already trained on me. Like a predator.

"And this is Vince," the guy says next, pointing toward the quiet one. "He's a man of few words, but trust me, if he has something on his mind, you'll know it."

Another quiet laugh filled with darkness leaves his mouth and it's only now that I realize I'm trembling. There's no way Ashton hasn't noticed, seeing as how he's completely locked my body against his.

"Lastly, allow me to introduce myself," he says, stepping closer as the smile leaves him. "You can call me, Micah."

My breath stills as he bends at his waist, lowering until his face is level with mine. So close I can smell the hint of tobacco lingering on his clothes.

"Now, this is the part where you tell us *your* name." His tone is beyond patronizing, but it doesn't matter. I have no intention of responding anyway.

Anger bleeds into his stare when I don't play along. He straightens and shoves both hands inside the pockets of his black, ripped jeans.

"Suit yourself, Stevie Heron," he says, letting me know he's fully aware of who I am even without my help. "So, now you know our names, which may or may not be important. But you know what definitely *is* important?" he asks, smirking. "That you remember we will fuck up your entire world if you don't start talking."

His voice echoes through the nearly empty room and I flinch. He didn't need to yell because the bass alone is enough to make it reverberate off the hard surfaces around us. There's no denying that I'm terrified, cowering in these assholes' shadows like some scared, timid bitch. Visions of my past seep in and it's like I'm that scared shell of a girl from years ago. The thought of it enrages me because I haven't been her in a very, very long time, and I refuse to go back.

"Now, let's try this again." Micah says, stepping closer, dragging a chair behind him. He stops directly in front of me and straddles the seat backwards, propping both his forearms across the top.

He locks eyes with Ashton behind me and then nods. I don't realize the gesture was meant as a signal, but an audible gasp leaves me as Ashton presses a knife firm against my throat. My pulse throbs against the blade, and when I swallow, the sharp edge bites into my skin, breaking it.

It's just enough to make it clear they're not above hurting me.

Just enough that more tears sting in the corners of my eyes when I realize shit just got incredibly fucking real.

Micah's gaze lowers to my neck and I flinch when he reaches out. Then, my skin warms to his touch when he gently swipes his finger across the cut. He's *so* gentle, in fact, the gesture feels out of place. Considering I'm being held against my will and could possibly be tortured before all is said and done. He pulls away and seems fascinated by the sight of my blood coating his fingertip. A fingertip he then swipes down the front of his white t-shirt. I focus on the red streak now marking him as he shifts in the seat. Then, my eyes find his.

"Now that we all seem to have an understanding... I mean, we *do* have an understanding, don't we, Stevie?" Micah asks.

Anger flares within me, but I'm in no position to lash out. Instead, I nod, not missing how he smiles at my compliance.

"Good," he croons. "Then, I'd like to know why you were in my room last night." When he finishes, he taps the tip of my nose once, being condescending as hell, like I'm a child.

My heart thunders behind my ribs and I know these guys won't settle for me playing dumb again. Not only has that ship sailed, it got swallowed up by a category 5 hurricane, never to be seen or heard from again.

Think, Stevie.

Micah's eyes bore a hole through me and it's uncomfortable. Like, he hears my thoughts. Like he's two steps ahead of me.

"Fine, it was me," I confess. "But you already knew that. I wasn't there to cause trouble, though. It's just that... a friend needed a favor. One of my housemates."

I feel Ashton's chest move with a short laugh. "You've gotta be fucking kidding me," he grumbles.

"That's the truth! She was at The Den with some guy from your frat, but she doesn't know who," I explain. "Apparently, knowing his name wasn't all that important the night it happened."

"The night *what* happened?"

I peer up when the quiet one, Vince, speaks. It's the first time he's said a single word. I get the feeling he knows the answer to his question, but wants to make me sweat as much as possible.

"She hooked up with one of you. Well, maybe not one of *you,* exactly, but an upperclassman." I hold eye contact with him, trying to make the story more believable. "I mean, she said the guy had dark hair, kind of low-cut like yours. So, I guess it *could've* been you."

Something I've said has Micah's eyes narrowing and Vince

levels an intense glare my way.

"Nah, try pinning that shit on someone else," he grumbles, insisting he wasn't the guy.

Little do they know, *no one* was the guy.

"Well, okay, but it was definitely someone from your brotherhood," I go on. "Anyway, she left an item behind and needed me to retrieve it. You know, before her boyfriend realizes something's up."

"What did she leave behind exactly?" Vince asks.

I blink a few times before an answer comes to me. "It was her phone. She told her guy she left it in a friend's car, so the lie will only hold for so long, which is why I was trying to help."

"Trying to help your cheating housemate deceive her boyfriend. Nice. And might I add, quite noble," Vince comments, holding my gaze with this judgmental-ass look on his face.

"I admit, it was a stupid thing to do and, believe me, I regret it."

"I'll bet," Micah says with a laugh as his eyes flit down toward the blade at my throat. Then, his gaze shifts toward Vince and Ashton. "Well, what do you two propose we do about our new friend, Stevie? Either of you believe this bullshit story?"

My breathing deepens and I'm starting to perspire.

"Nope," Ashton says behind me, which has Vince shaking his head in agreement.

"I swear that's the truth. She was too embarrassed to run into the guy again and didn't want her boyfriend to figure things out, so I offered to go. What's so hard to believe about that?"

"Know what I'm thinking?" Micah pipes up, addressing the guys while completely ignoring my explanation. "I think we should let the brotherhood decide. I'll call a special meeting and wash my hands of it."

"Not a bad idea," Ashton replies. "They'll have fun coming up with interesting ways to make her work off her debt."

My brow tenses.

What fucking debt?

"Or they'll put her out of her misery quickly and just hand her off to the dean, let him decide what to do. I'm sure he'd love to see the footage of her trespassing. Hell, maybe we should just turn her over to the cops," Vince concludes.

"No!" That word flies from my mouth before I consider the message it will send to the guys, but my offense *cannot* go any further than this room.

Micah's brow arches with intrigue. It's like he smells my desperation, knows all my secrets.

"Damn, you running from the law or something, Bird?" he teases, but I don't give an answer. "If you're gonna plead your case, speak now or forever hold your peace."

My nostrils flare hearing him call me that, but I don't react to it. "Just don't tell the others. Don't report me to Dean Emerson. And, please... no cops," I add.

With a smirk, Micah leans forward to rest his arms across the back of the chair again.

"Then, tell me," he says. "How do you think we should settle things between us? I mean, you *must've* known we couldn't just let you walk away from this. Sends a bad message if there's no cost."

"Then, we'll settle it. Just the four of us. Whatever you want."

Instantly, I regret saying these words, but it's my only option.

Vince and Micah study me for a moment, and I imagine Ashton's doing the same over my shoulder. Maybe wondering what I could possibly have to offer them that would make it worth their while to keep quiet.

Maybe wondering why I'm so adamant about this entire situation staying contained.

"Hm."

I blink up toward Vince when that sound leaves him.

Then, the next voice I hear is Ashton's, right in my ear. "Just how badly do you want your secret kept?"

"Bad. I'll do whatever it takes."

I feel Ashton's chin graze my hair when he shifts behind me. He's pressed against my ass, leaving no space between us.

"Then we *own* you," he begins. "Whatever we say, whenever we say it, until we say it's done."

My body shudders and I know he feels it.

"Okay," I answer. "But, please, I need to know this stays with the three of you. No one else will ever know. I need you to swear."

They meet one another's gazes, then it's Vince who nods, tucking both hands inside his pockets.

"You keep your end of the bargain, we'll keep ours. Scout's honor," he adds with a wicked smile, knowing nothing about him or the others screams *Boy Scout*.

I keep my eyes trained on him for a moment, then give a slight nod, still mindful of the blade against my skin.

"Then, that's that," I say, keenly aware of having just made a deal with three devils. A deal in which the full terms are a complete mystery to me. But it had to be done. For so many reasons.

Metal scrapes tile when Micah stands and moves the chair across the floor. At full height, he's even more intimidating than just a moment ago and I'm grateful this ordeal appears to be coming to a close.

"Unlock your phone and hand it over," he demands.

It takes half a moment for my body to catch up with my brain, then I do as I was told. Powerless, I'm still on my knees before him as he taps around on the screen. Finally, he dials his phone from mine and appears to lock my number in before handing it over again.

"Take it," he says. I blink into his dark stare and then accept my phone, having no idea what he's done to it. "We'll be in touch. Don't be hard to find," he adds.

The tension on my neck finally lets up, then I hear Ashton flip the blade closed behind me. He's still tucking it into his back pocket as he stands, and I'm still too shaken to move.

Without another word, the three of them trudge toward the door, laughing and chatting it up like they *didn't* just come into my world like a storm, blowing shit around like the disasters they are. Before they go, Micah grabs a volunteer packet off the back table just for shits and giggles, then leaves me with a smile and a nod.

These three are nightmares in the flesh, and unfortunately for me... I'm positive I haven't seen the last of them.

My bike falls into the bushes. It's a miracle I've made it home with how my hands shook the entire way. Twice, I nearly rolled right into busy intersections because my brain's currently stuck in '*WHAT THE FUCK?*' mode.

But seriously, what the actual fuck?

The faces of the three who barged into the auditorium today are emblazoned in my head. Every time I close my eyes, they're all I see. Devilishly attractive faces with so much darkness within them. I don't know when they'll be back, but they will be.

Beyond the shadow of a doubt.

Noise from inside the house bleeds out through an open window while I pace. My housemates have guests again. Like always. But I'm even less in the mood for their bullshit than usual, which means it's best to just hang out here. The fresh air might do me some good anyway.

Besides, the longer I avoid them, the longer I avoid an uncomfortable conversation about how close I am to getting them this month's rent.

And maybe *last* month's rent.

My phone sounds off. I'm half relieved and half worried when I see Maddox's name flash across the screen. He can't know how things went today. If he did, he'd want to get involved and that can't happen.

"What's up?"

"You home? I'm up the street and thought I'd stop by for a sec."

I pass a look toward the house again, hearing Dahlia—the chick who has the room right above my space in the basement—asking if anyone else heard a voice outside. How she heard me over all their loud-ass talking, I'll never know, but sure enough, her head pops through the ugly, floral curtains in the living room.

As soon as our gazes lock, she rolls her eyes, then retreats without even a simple greeting.

Back at you, dickhead.

The curtains fall closed, then I hear the words *'fat bitch'* leave Dahlia's mouth. Whenever she can't think of anything else rude or demeaning to call me, she resorts to pointing out that I'm not exactly thin, like I'd somehow forgotten.

Or like I give a shit.

"I'm here. Just hanging outside," I say, finally answering Maddox's question.

He laughs a bit. "Can't say I blame you for not wanting to go in. I'm guessing all the assholes are home, too."

"Looks like."

"Still don't know why you wouldn't just let me hunt down a studio apartment we could've shared. I'm honestly over dorm life anyway," he adds.

I imagine what it would be like to share a place with him—stepping over his messes, having the TV on ESPN twenty-four-seven. It'd be a recipe for disaster and our friendship would never survive it.

No thanks.

"Maybe next semester," I lie.

When he's silent on the other end, I imagine he didn't buy a single word that just left my mouth, but God bless him for not pushing. He pulls up to the curb and I end the call without saying goodbye. A few seconds later, he's taking long strides up the walkway wearing dark sweats and a t-shirt repping his university. It reminds me of when we were kids, watching as he'd cross the street from his house to mine. Back then, things were much simpler, but there's something to be said about a friend who sticks with you through all the rough shit.

Maddox drops down onto the step where I've taken a seat and he reads me. Without me even speaking a word.

"What happened?"

I'm still on edge but know I can't tell him everything. The plan is to only share enough to get him off my case. A simple *'everything's fine'* response would never fly with him, so...

"Some of the Savages paid me a visit tonight," I admit, and the look on Maddox's face confirms why he can only know so much.

"What the fuck? Did you get names?" he asks with a sudden flare of anger in his tone. He stands to his feet again and I reach for his wrist, pulling him back down beside me.

"It wasn't a big deal," I lie, remembering to adjust my hoodie to cover the cut on the side of my neck.

"What did they want?"

"Well, I was right about them having me on camera, so, naturally, they wanted to know why I was there."

"What'd you tell them?"

"Obviously, not the truth," I scoff. "As far as they know, I was there on behalf of a friend who'd screwed around with someone in the brotherhood and left her phone."

Maddox eyes me, scanning me with a scrutinizing look. "And they bought it?"

I shrug. "More or less. But the important thing is they said they won't report me to the university or, you know... the police."

He's silent when I add that part, likely reliving the same incident in his head that I'm reliving in mine.

"If they show up again, or if you even *think* they're gonna be a problem, call me. I fucking mean it, Stevie. Day, night, whenever."

I nod and stand with him when he gets to his feet again. "Yes, sir."

He shakes his head like he always does when I call him out for being bossy.

"I'm glad you stopped by."

He nods and glances toward the house. "You sure you're okay going in there?"

I shoot an incredulous look at the brick university housing unit I share with four co-eds and sometimes two of their boyfriends. "If you think I'm gonna let Dahlia ruin my night, you don't know me very well."

He smiles again. "She's such a bitch."

"*Such*... a bitch," I echo, tilting my head back to the sky.

Maddox's smile turns into a laugh. "I'll check in tomorrow," he says, bringing me into a bear hug, but before I'm released, the sound of an engine rumbling up the street catches my attention. There's a black pickup slow-rolling past the house, but the windows are too darkly tinted to see who's inside. They definitely slowed down to get a better look at either me or Maddox, though.

He lets go without noticing a thing, and I'm feeling a little sick when a thought hits me.

What if that was them?

What if they know where I live now?

"The fundraiser for your group at the rink is coming up soon, isn't it?" Maddox asks, jarring me from my thoughts.

I offer an aimless nod before answering. "Um... yeah. Everything's pretty much all set."

He scans me with a look, maybe noticing that I'm shaken. "Sure you're okay?"

I quickly fix my expression and shove him toward his truck. "I'm fine. Go home. We'll talk tomorrow."

He lingers for a bit but finally takes off. Then, I'm alone, stalking back toward the house. Before opening the front door, I take a deep breath. Yes, in part because I'm undoubtedly walking into a cloud of cigarette smoke, but also because I just really don't feel like dealing with the girls' shit tonight.

The door is barely open when...

"Well, if it isn't our non-rent-paying—"

"Save it, Dahlia. I'm not in the fucking mood. And like I said a million times already, you'll get paid when I get the bedroom I was promised. A corner of the basement with three walls doesn't count."

I keep my feet moving in the direction of the basement door, but the pillow Dahlia held in her lap falls to the floor when she hops off the couch. Heavy steps charge toward me as she stomps over like the brat she is.

Her hand grips my arm and I immediately pull free. At my sides, my fists are tight and I want nothing more than to lay into her, but I can't. No matter how badly I want to... I can't.

Dahlia has this snotty-ass look on her face, reminding me that she's been thinking she's hot shit since being invited to pledge. Doesn't help that the invitation came from the number-one sorority on her list.

"Don't ever touch me like that," I growl, stepping closer, backing her down.

A collective, 'Oooohhh!' becomes our soundtrack as the others observe, treating this moment like their nightly entertainment.

I keep my eyes trained on Dahlia and she does the same, blinking at me from behind thick, dark bangs. It'd be so satisfying to punch her right out of the pink baby-tee she's wearing, but despite how she grates my nerves, I see through the act. See that she's nothing but an insecure girl who can't stand that she doesn't intimidate me. It burns her up that I—a curvy size-sixteen—don't cower in shame in the presence of her size-two frame.

Disgusted by this whole situation, I roll my eyes and walk away.

"And for the last time, the fucking rent's due on the first!" Dahlia screams down the basement steps before slamming the door shut.

Rage fills me and I want to hit this bitch so badly I can fucking taste it. I go as far as climbing several steps with exactly that end in mind before reminding myself why that's a terrible idea. There's too much at stake if I lose control and let myself go there.

So, I stand on the stairs a moment to gather myself, then choose instead to bask in the fact that I'm alone and in my own space.

Safe.

Even if it is a musty old basement with webs I have to clear out every couple days. Even with the inconveniences and less-than-pleasing aesthetic, it sure as hell beats having to constantly deal with the girls upstairs. Down here, I can shut out everyone and everything until I'm good and damn ready to deal with them.

The mattress swallows me up when I fall into it. Had it not been for a very specific notification bell, I might've laid there all night. But instead, I roll over onto my side and stare at the phone screen.

He's online.

The one and only guy I'd ever put off sleep for. And to think, he's all mine for the very low price of $12.99 a month.

I smile at the thought then fall back again, holding the phone above my face as I watch an empty seat become occupied by an exquisite body. A shirtless torso and dark jean-clad thighs are all I see so far, but damn if that isn't enough. You'd think my day had been a breeze with how the sight of him calms me. It doesn't matter that he's careful to keep his face hidden by a shadow, or that I only know him by his username.

It's enough.

He doesn't speak, ever, but it's just as well. Knowing he's a real person with the same mess of emotions and problems as the rest of us would only ruin the illusion anyway. So, instead, I enjoy the silence just like the other eighty-seven sets of eyes currently on him. That's according to the counter in the top left corner, and as I stare at that figure, it climbs by another twenty.

Without a doubt, there will eventually be several hundred of us here, all tuning in to watch whatever show he's in the mood to put on. But it always feels like it's just me and him. Like he does this for me. Like he *touches himself* for me.

Without even thinking about how to respond when his hand moves to his waistband, mine follows, lowering into my jeans once I unzip them. For now, my fingertips tease the elastic of my panties, but I'm already wet for him. He strokes himself beneath the fabric and I gawk at the size of his cock. It hangs against his thigh, several inches of mouthwatering thickness.

A small scar on his right side is his only telling feature. No body hair. No tattoos. No visible piercings. My lip aches from biting it when he lifts his hips from his seat to lower his jeans a bit. Just enough to free his cock from his boxers. I draw in a breath

46

watching his hand slip slowly down every single inch, and I trace the slit of my pussy through the fabric of my underwear. He pauses to reach out of frame for a moment, then returns with a bottle. He tilts it slowly and a thin drizzle of oil falls from the opening and drenches the tip of his cock, running down the length of him.

I don't even blink while I watch him pour with reckless abandon, giving zero fucks about the mess. His fingers wrap around his dick again, and he begins to pump slowly as the head swells, glistens. It's at this point that I stop torturing myself and allow my imagination to run wild, pretending my touch is his when I slide two fingers between my lower lips. A whimper leaves me when I tease my clit, churning small, gentle circles as I get wetter for him.

This stranger who has no idea who the fuck I even am.

His head falls back against his chair and against his black background, all I see is him. His dick—magnificent and solid— points skyward. The comments are starting to scroll on the side of the feed, and I have no clue how anyone's hands are free right now.

Anonymous: (*$10 tip pledged*) *"No way he's a virgin IRL. At least ten girls—or guys—have defiled this man. TODAY ALONE!"*

Anonymous: (*$25 tip pledged*) *"If it's true that he's keeping all that dick to himself, what a fucking waste."*

Anonymous: (*$25 tip pledged*) *"If I lick it, does that mean it's mine?"*

The chat is always incredibly colorful, but with a smile, I promptly disable the feed. No distractions. Not from him.

His hand slicks up and down the solid length faster and I imagine how his flesh is throbbing against the heat of his own palm. His stomach contracts when pleasure gets the best of him, and his chest moves quickly as his breathing picks up. He's close and so am I. He massages himself with a few more strokes and then...

"Shit..."

That word spills from my lips as cum spills from his dick. First, a powerful burst, then a glistening flow of white liquid that runs down his knuckles. Starting at my clit, a surge of pleasure spreads upward, to my stomach, then my chest, filling my entire body. The addictive pulsation in my pussy has me wishing like hell I could be wherever he is right now, touching him while he touches me. My thighs clamp tight around my hand when the last few aftershocks leave me quaking on the mattress.

My lids feel heavy when the orgasm ends, but I don't close my eyes. I want to see it all, every second he gives us, his captivated audience. He reaches off frame for a dark towel and cleans himself, ridding his fingers of the white stickiness I believe any one of us viewers would've volunteered to lick clean.

He stands and we're left watching an empty chair, which is how he ends every livestream, so I know it's safe to resume the comments.

Anonymous: ($15 tip pledged) 'Newbie here and, I kid you not, I've never come so hard in my fucking life. Take my money, sir. You just gained yourself a lifer.'

Anonymous: ($100 tip pledged) "A pleasure as always."

Anonymous: ($5 tip pledged) "I vote we beg our star to lose his V-card on livestream. I'd personally tip $500 to see that. Not even kidding."

I scroll for a bit more, then close out of the app, even more tired than I was before. Forcing myself off the bed to head to the shower, all the shit that happened today comes flooding back, but I have a new outlook. Maybe, just maybe, my visitors just wanted to put the fear of God in me, which they certainly did. Maybe that was the last I'll see of them, and I can go on about my life without having to look over my shoulder.

As the shower cuts on and I hold my hand beneath the water, reality hits. An image of that dark pickup passing comes back to me, and while I couldn't see who was inside, my gut confirms.

Beyond the shadow of a doubt, it was them.

And if I'm honest with myself, I know this nightmare is far from over.

1 o A.M.

Feels like I slept *maybe* an hour. With one eye open, I kiss two fingers and press them to my phone as a pic of my sister brightens the dark space.

"Morning, Mellie Bean," I say quietly, and then read the texts that came through while I slept.

Maddox: Just checking in. You didn't seem okay last night.

He worries too much, so I hit him with a casual '*All good, bro,*' and then scroll down and find Mom's left a voice memo. It's sure to be about the wedding, because that's *all* she thinks about these days. So, I roll over onto my side and press play.

'*Morning, Sweetheart. Thought you might be up by now, but it's okay. You probably had a late night. I'm still knee-deep in planning if you were wondering. It'd be nice to have your help sometimes. I know you have class starting soon and you work, but... it'd be nice is all. Rob and Tate have really stepped up lately to help with things. Speaking of Tate, he's asked about you. My hope is that you two can bond a bit before Rob and I exchange vows. You know, since you'll be family soon. Brother and sister, really. Plus, I think it's nice that you're at his school now that you transferred. It actually gives me peace of mind knowing he's on staff, looking out for you. I know he's no replacement for Melanie, and that's not what I'm trying to say. I just... I want you to be okay, Stevie. That's all I've ever wanted. I know you're busy and probably won't call back, but I'm just letting you know I'm officially jealous that Rob gets to see his kid more than I get to see mine, and they live the exact same distance apart that we do. Anyway, the three of us are getting together tonight for dinner at the house. Hope you can make it. Love you.'*

A sigh leaves me. The woman is a master guilt tripper. One who sometimes seems completely aloof to the strain that wears on our relationship. To her, I'm hardly around because I'm too caught up in my own life to pay her the attention she believes she deserves. But in truth, I'm not around because I find it difficult to cater to her needs when she chose to turn a blind eye to mine for so many years.

I give her request some thought, but then remember how much I really don't want to sit at a table with not only her, but her husband-to-be, and his fucking son. Already, she's put him on a pedestal, and I can't help but wonder how she'd feel if she knew what I know about him. Would she feel all warm and fuzzy about him looking after me on campus then?

I roll out of bed with a groan, wishing I didn't have to move at all today, but I need food and work starts in about an hour. There's a bottle of juice and a muffin upstairs with my name on them—literally—so my destination is set for the kitchen. Halfway up the steps, my phone buzzes in the pocket of my shorts and I pause to look at it. There's a number I don't recognize, but the message clears up any questions I might've had.

Unknown: Morning, Bird. You'll want to lock this number in. Trust me. It's best if you answer when I call. Be at Henley Park in thirty. Life will be a lot less complicated if you know the rules up front—Micah

My face warms when I frown, and my fingers move quickly across the screen, tapping out a response.

Stevie: Rules?

Tossing my phone back to my bed, I continue up the steps, headed toward the kitchen. Half-empty condiment bottles rattle on the fridge door when I pull it open, and of course, some asshole drank my juice. There's nothing left but *maybe* a quarter cup in the bottom.

"Son of a bitch! Who did it?"

The fridge door slams shut and seated behind me at the table, the not-so-innocent faces of my housemates all stare back at me. Some with faint smiles, others with snarls.

"Who... the fuck... drank my shit?" I ask again, but this time I lock eyes with Dahlia. She makes it a point to get under my skin whenever she can, so my money's on her.

"My bad. Was that yours?" she asks. "I just got so thirsty in the middle of the night. You know, when you woke everyone up screaming?"

I hold her gaze, only now realizing I'd even been loud enough for someone to hear. It was a nightmare. The same one that's haunted me off and on for the past year, but I don't go into detail explaining that to Dahlia.

"So, let me get this straight. You're complaining about me keeping you awake *one* night, meanwhile, no one has shit to say about Kelsey riding her boyfriend into the sunset nearly *every* night?" My gaze shifts to Kelsey and Logan, the stallion in question. "And by the way, it shouldn't take one human being that long to get off, Kelsey. My guess? He's fucking someone else, and whoever she is, she drains him dry before he comes over and you get whatever the fuck is left."

I've already turned away when Logan starts choking on his toast. Meeting Dahlia's gaze, she's wide-eyed like *I'm* the asshole here.

"Why are you such a damn bitch?" she snipes. "Could it be because no one's trying to fuck *your* fat ass?"

Her arms cross over her chest and the taste of blood lets me know just how deeply I've bitten into my cheek. It's all that kept me from lighting into this cunt.

I step closer, until we're nearly nose-to-nose. She flinches, her brow tenses with concern, and I love that she knows I could destroy her.

"One of these days," I whisper, "I'm gonna forget that I'm

technically not allowed to beat your ass, Dahlia. And when that happens, the reward will *totally* be worth the punishment."

Her breathing quickens and I know she can tell this is a warning, and that I mean every damn word. Slowly backing away, I trudge toward the basement. I've already had it up to here, and it's not even noon. It feels great to tell Dahlia exactly how I feel. Now, if only I could find a loophole and act on it.

Dropping down to sit on the edge of my bed, I let out a sigh and reach for my phone. I intend to do a bit of mindless scrolling to clear my head, but there's a response to my text.

Micah: No questions. Just be there. Henley Park. Twenty-five minutes.

I fall against my bed with a sigh, wishing I could have a normal existence just once. For maybe like a month, at least so I can catch my breath. However, every time I ask, the universe just gives me a big, fat nope.

MICAH

"She's late. Which means *we'll* be late, and I'm expected to lead the workout this morning."

"Quit grumbling. It's only a few minutes past," Ash answers. "She'll show."

"If she knows what's good for her," Vince adds under his breath.

The truck shifts slightly when I lean against the passenger side door, keeping my eyes trained down the street, anticipating the arrival of our new pet. My thoughts go back to the fear I saw in her eyes last night and I believe Ash is right. She *will* show.

Because she knows shit will get ugly if she doesn't.

Just when I think I'll have to send a text as her one-minute warning, guess who bounds around the corner. The seat of a vintage, teal bicycle disappears between her thighs as she pedals toward us, wind moving the length of her brown hair in a spiral behind her. Vince sees her approaching and leans away from the truck to get a better look, gnawing the toothpick between his teeth twice as hard now. In my peripheral, I spot Ash eyeing her, too, maybe wondering what the hell she's wearing.

Old-school tube socks with two blue stripes at the top are pulled all the way up to her knees, drawing my eye to the one marked with a nasty bruise and band-aid in the center. A white tank top reads 'Go-Go's Galactic Skate Rink'. When I factor in the pink, glittery skates draped over her shoulders by the laces, and the corded whistle squeezed between her tits, I assume the logo on the shirt must be where she works.

A pair of purple, spandex shorts barely cover her, and I'm finding it hard to ignore her figure while she rides. But honestly, I noticed last night. As a self-professed ass-man, I didn't miss how her jeans melted over her curves. Didn't miss how they fit over her hips like a glove. Didn't miss how the seam pushed between the lips of her pussy just enough to make out the outline. She's a far cry from the size zero, blonde Barbie-types Ash usually goes for, but judging by how he hasn't blinked since she started coming this way, I'm guessing he likes what he sees.

Too bad she's a walking target.

Our walking target.

She stops right in front of us on the sidewalk and she's a feisty one. I can sense that about her already, but when we lock eyes, there's just enough self-control in her gaze that I'm certain she knows her place.

Good girl. Don't make this harder than it has to be.

"Nice seeing you again, Bird. Glad you could join us." There's no hiding my smile when she winces at her new nickname.

"Can we just get this over with," she huffs, scraping the rubber ridges of her handlebar with her thumbnail. A sign of annoyance, I imagine.

Ignoring her request, I nod toward her bike. "Car in the shop?"

She doesn't take well to being teased and rolls her eyes. "These are my wheels. My *only* wheels," she adds with a sigh.

"Hm." That's about all the response I can muster as I get distracted, staring at her bike seat again.

That lucky fucking bike seat.

"Like I said, I've got someplace to be," she huffs. "So..."

Ash steps up and I'm intrigued to see how Bird will respond when he reaches for her, lightly plucking the whistle from her cleavage with his finger. When he drops it back down to her chest, she doesn't even flinch.

Looks like we caught ourselves a tough one.

"Go-Go's," Ash says. "Worked there long?"

"Long enough," she hisses. "Now, can you *please* tell me what this is about? You mentioned rules or something."

I nod once. "We figured things would be simpler—*cleaner*—if we break this down to a formula. A template you can easily follow."

She cocks her head, crosses her arms, confirming what I already knew—she's gutsy. Or, you know, she could just be a bitch.

"Just tell me what I have to do to make this go away. Like I said, I have shit to do."

I laugh. Have to. She really thinks this'll be a one and done situation.

"One hundred points," Vince speaks up, causing Bird's eyes to cut to him.

Her fists tighten around the handlebars. "What's that even mean?"

"Earn a hundred points and it'll be like none of this ever happened," he answers. "No one else will ever know what you did, and we'll consider your debt paid. That means no Savages giving you shit, your family won't have to see you get expelled, and more importantly, no cops," he adds. "That is what's most important to you, isn't it?"

I glance toward Bird when Vince taunts her, but she's stone-faced. Keeping her secrets to herself.

For now.

"And in the meantime, we own you," Ash adds. "Whatever possibilities are swirling around inside your head right now, whatever questions you have about what that might mean, the answer is 'yes'. We own you in every way imaginable."

Bird's throat moves when she swallows. It's the only sign Ash has her shaken because you'd never guess it from that mean-ass look on her face.

"This is bullshit," she mumbles.

"You're right. It *is* bullshit. It's bullshit that you broke into my room. It's bullshit that you didn't think you'd have to pay for that." The words leave my mouth through gritted teeth because she still doesn't seem to grasp that this is all on her. Not us.

"Whatever, just tell me what I need to know," she hisses.

Ash smirks, shamelessly staring at Bird's tits before meeting her gaze. "You earn your hundred points by doing whatever the hell we say, whenever we say it. The quicker you break and realize that your most important role right now is being our bitch, the easier this will be."

"So, basically, I'm being hazed," she says flatly.

Ash grins. "Call it what you want, but as long as you don't give *us* trouble, we won't give *you* trouble. Simple."

If looks could kill, we'd be burying Ash next week, because it's painfully obvious we struck one of Bird's nerves.

"How can I not give you trouble if you're not being clear," she snaps. "I mean, okay, you think you own me, but what the fuck does that even mean? What do I have to do to keep you assholes from getting cranky and ruining my life just for the hell of it?"

"It means exactly what the fuck it sounds like, and let's be clear on one thing," Ash growls. "We don't *think* we own you. That shit may as well be written in blood."

With those words, he reaches for her again, slowly moving his finger across the little reminder his blade left on her neck. Bird snatches away and it's her first act of defiance.

Shit... this is gonna be even more fun than I thought.

The way Ash's mouth curves into a smile, one filled with darkness and malice, means he's likely having the same thought.

"Let us make this simple for you," Vince says, moving in on our prey. "We'll start small with your tasks, let you get acclimated, but we won't tolerate bullshit. No second chances. You fuck up, we fuck you over. Also, the guy you were with last night? End it."

Vince finishes and the look on Bird's face is priceless. Like she's just had an epiphany of some sort.

"That *was* you. The truck that drove past my house." Her eyes shift to Ash's pick-up, maybe just now having a clear enough head to notice it's the same one she'd seen.

"Seemed wise to check in on our property before heading home," Vince teases, but his face goes blank the next second. "Now, like I said, shut that shit down. Immediately. Last thing we need is some roid-raged dick bag giving us shit about our little arrangement. So, to summarize, the only motherfuckers with dicks you're allowed to have in your life for the foreseeable future... is us. Right up until those points are earned," he adds.

Bird's brow twitches as the seriousness of Vince's statement seems to sink in.

"I don't have a boyfriend, so... there's no issue," she answers.

I study her expression, looking for signs of deceit. When she blinks her large, brown eyes at me, they give a false sense of innocence I'm not falling for, but I won't push for now.

My gaze lowers and I tap the butterfly clipped to the lace of her skate. Her eyes follow as I back up, heading toward the truck.

"See you soon, Bird," I call out. "And be a good girl. You never know where we might show up next."

This was lesson number one, so she doesn't quite get it yet. But she will.

Her full lips curve into a scowl as I climb into the truck. Hopefully, now she realizes she's no longer in control of her life. Because *we* are.

Nodding once in her direction, I get the feeling we're off to a pretty solid start.

Not bad for day one.

"This shit can't keep happening. Unauthorized social events while under probation is a surefire way to get that status escalated to a total suspension of the fraternity. Is that what you fucking want?"

I stare out the window as Eros paces the length of the study. The moment we got back from the gym, he pulled up to the house, waiting to hand us our asses. I'm aware of the fact that he's one of the few people—if not the only person—who speaks to us like this and walks away without blood loss. Comes with the territory of the brotherhood, though. Doesn't matter a whole lot that he graduated and left the house. Once a big brother, *always* a big brother.

"Do any of you give a damn how this could affect your eligibility to play once the season starts?" he asks. "At least tell me you three had no clue they were planning it." The statement has me glancing at Vince from the corner of my eye, then Micah. "You've gotta be shitting me," Eros sighs.

"In our defense, we told them to keep it small," Micah reasons, letting his shoulder fall against the mantle.

Eros laughs one of those laughs that lets you know there isn't a damn thing funny.

"And then what?" he asks. "You left and did your own thing while no one stuck around to supervise? Real fucking smart."

"Actually, we were in the woods, dealing with pledges," Vince interjects. "But what's done is done. We just need to know what steps to take from here."

Eros meets Vince's gaze. "Well, the first step sure as shit better be punishment. If they were given directions to keep things small, that's how it should've been. Teach these guys that they can't just defy you and get away with it. Yes, they're your brothers, and some of them are even your teammates, but there's still an order to things. If their respect for you isn't enough to keep them in line, then maybe having them fear you will get the job done."

Silence fills the room, then Eros sighs.

"Listen, I know this isn't all on you guys, but in a way, it is. You're the overseers here now and that's not a role to be taken lightly," he explains. "If the interfraternity Council catches wind of this, or if whoever the fuck keeps making these reports decides to make up some more shit, they're shutting us down."

Eros falls silent and it isn't lost on any of us how important our brotherhood is. Unlike most of the frats, none of us were born with silver spoons in our mouths. In fact, several of us didn't have food to even put *on* a spoon growing up. Which makes the Savage Brotherhood a lot of these guys' only option, their only ticket to a better life.

There are sixty members in-house and a hundred thirty-six on campus. That's a lot of futures at stake.

Which is why we protect what we have here at all costs.

Which is also why even those who finish usually continue their work. Like Eros, who's part of the graduate chapter and still participates in the frat's philanthropic endeavors. Just proves that you're a Savage for life.

"Let's just hope this stays under wraps," he concludes with a hard sigh. "The less the guys know the better. The last thing we need is for support to decrease. If they find out there won't be any parties, pledges will start dropping off like flies, then dues will dry up. Eventually, that would be the death of the frat."

Listening, I'm starting to question things. None of us bought Bird's story about her playing Captain Save-A-Hoe for some bitch who left her phone at the house. So, the likelihood of her being a puppet for Whitlock just shot through the roof. The reports against us haven't come out of thin air. They're an act of sabotage and we all know it.

Our rivals, the Jaguars, are a bunch of rich dickheads from across town at Elmcrest University. They hate that us *regular* dickheads kick their asses every time we step out on the ice. Things only went from bad to worse last year when they swore we cheated them out of a win at regionals, killing their chance of making it to the Frozen Four.

They just can't seem to accept the truth.

That we're better than them.

Period.

"Any luck filling the gap in the volunteer schedule?" Eros asks. "It needs to be a worthy cause, something that'll impress the IFC, something to help the Council see that we're about our business, an asset to the community."

On request, I reach for the packet beside me on the table and walk it over. He takes it but looks confused.

"What's this?" he asks.

"It's a body positivity group here on campus. We attended a meeting last night and thought it might be a good fit."

My explanation conveniently leaves off the part about holding Bird at knifepoint before snagging the info off a card table near the door.

Eros pulls some of the paperwork from the large envelope and scans it dismissively. "This is a start, I guess, but there needs to be more."

"We'll keep looking," Vince answers.

"Good," Eros says, checking his watch. "How long until the season officially starts?"

"We already work out a few times a week getting ready, but practice doesn't start until the first week of October. Then, the first game's scheduled just before Halloween."

Eros takes in Vince's response, seeming to calculate where we are on time, and then he nods.

"Question... with all the shit that's been happening, especially the probation, should we cancel The Hunt?" Micah asks.

Eros' gaze shifts to the dark rug beneath his feet. I'm actually surprised he's giving Micah's question so much thought because I assumed it'd be an immediate no, but...

"For now, we'll keep plans as they are. And I'll be there to make sure things don't get out of hand."

With the morale of the brotherhood being as important a factor as anything else, I get why he's not shutting it down despite the risk. But before I get the chance to respond, my phone vibrates with a text.

Louis: "Where the fuck are you? You don't call or text back. I've left you at least fifteen messages. The nurse said you stopped by, but that was over a week ago. My mother—your grandmother, your flesh and blood—is asking for you and I don't have shit to tell her. Why? Because you're in the fucking wind again. Shit... sometimes, I don't even know why she bothers with you. That woman's been nothing but good to your ungrateful ass, so the least you could do is be available when she wants to see you."

I zone out, processing the barrage of insults and accusations. As far as uncles go, Louis is about as shit as they come. With only eleven years between us, we grew up in the same household, but he bailed and went to the military when I was maybe seven. Hence the reason he has it in his head that my childhood was as simple and easy as his.

Well, it fucking wasn't.

My gaze lowers to my arm, where my fingertips trace the pale edges of raised scars. The many that can't be seen beneath my ink. I feel them, though—a collection of pain and hatred I'll wear forever. Tattoos helped hide them from the world, but I'll always remember.

Always.

Tonight, they remind me why I don't feel guilt over Louis' bullshit text. He doesn't get to give me shit for not being there *now*, because he wasn't there *then*. No one was.

Just me.

"That a hookup?" Micah teases as he nods toward my screen.

I force a laugh then tuck my phone away. "Nope. Family shit."

Hearing my answer, he rolls his eyes. "Must be something in

the fucking air. My dad's been blowing my phone up all week, asking if I'm coming home anytime soon."

"You going?" I ask.

When he shoots back an emphatic, "*Fuck* no," that clears up any confusion.

I glance at Eros just as he's checking his watch again and have to ask. "We keeping you from something?"

"No," he answers, then closes his eyes for a few seconds. "Actually, I do have to take off. I've got some family shit of my own."

"Fuck. You, too?" Micah laughs.

"Unfortunately." Eros pauses to answer a text then meets my gaze. "You three getting into any trouble tonight?"

Vince shrugs. "Nothing special. We'll probably shower, then maybe work on training our new pet."

Eros arches a brow. "Do I even want to know?"

"Probably not," Vince smirks.

"Didn't think so. I'll catch you guys later."

Eros' footsteps fade as he leaves the study then exits the house, leaving the three of us to decide how to protect our household. On one hand, we have to keep our noses clean, stay off the IFC's radar. But on the other, we have a brotherhood *and* a bird to keep in check.

Running shit isn't always an easy job, but someone has to do it.

"Go over the floor one more time with the dust mop, then you can take off for the night," Kip calls out over the music. "You've got your keys to lock up, don't you?"

Instead of yelling back, I smile, giving him a thumbs up and he does the same. He heads toward the back office, the gray man-bun at the base of his neck bobbing with his quick stride. My skates glide over the rink's glistening slats. I push the duster to gather anything I may have missed the first two times, then the show begins. The tall handle acts as my makeshift microphone while I multitask—cleaning and putting on a concert for my audience of one—me.

I belt out the lyrics, enjoying that I don't have to be mindful of running over anyone's brats. My whistle is officially retired for the night and so am I. Well, I will be in about fifteen minutes at least.

This place is magical after close, like a party for one. Kip leaves the colored lights swirling above just for me. He knows I like to vibe out while I do the last of my tasks. And I'm doing exactly that, right up until the music stops.

I'm mid-note, which is a little embarrassing, but the feeling is quickly replaced with confusion when I spot my mom offering Kip a polite wave. He heads back to the office and it's just me and Mom, making our way toward one another in silence. Me on wheels, her in gym shoes.

"Hey," she says with a hesitant smile.

"Hey."

Things have been weird between us for a while, and it's always more noticeable in person.

"Missed you tonight at dinner."

"Well, Kip had me on the schedule to close, so..."

She gives that same barely-there smile and I hate it. It always makes me feel guilty, then I get mad at myself for *feeling* guilty. The strain between us isn't my fault. It's on her. Completely.

"You came all the way down here to tell me you missed me?" I ask, hoping the air of skepticism isn't apparent on my face.

"No," she says. "Or, I don't know, maybe I did. I guess I'm never sure you'll answer my calls these days, so maybe I just needed to see your face. Needed to know for myself that you're okay."

My eyes widen and I shrug. "As you can see, all is well."

Her brow creases, and she shifts her weight to one foot. "But... are you really?"

Here we fucking go. I look everywhere but at her, needing an out. "I'm still on the clock, so I can't do this right now."

"When Kip let me in, he said to take as long as I needed. No one's rushing me out of here but you," she counters.

"Well, Kip doesn't have a fifteen-minute bike ride home in the dark, so that's not really his call."

"I'm sorry my being here is such an inconvenience to you, but maybe if you'd responded to my dinner invite, I wouldn't have had to show up unannounced."

Pushing a hand through my hair, I take a breath.

"What do you need from me, Mom? You have my full attention."

"Fuck," she says with a shrug, laughing a bit to dispel frustration. "I just want you to *talk* to me, Stevie! Or maybe come by the house every now and then. Something!"

"I can't be there."

She steps closer and her eyes narrow. "You think it's easy for me?" she snaps. "I wake up and fall asleep in the house where one of my little girls... where she..."

Her voice trails off and I'm grateful she didn't say it. Grateful she didn't finish that sentence. Instead, she wipes her tears and backs off.

"You're missed is all. Not just tonight at dinner. Always."

I push one of my skates back and forth across the floor and try to empty my thoughts of the images and memories she just sent rushing back.

"Tate was there," she adds. "He thought you might come, so he was just as bummed as Rob and me when you didn't show. He mentioned that you two should grab coffee or something sometime since you're on his campus."

"It's not *his* campus," I say, correcting her, hating that she makes that monster sound like some kind of fucking saint. If only she knew...

"I didn't mean it that way. It's just that he's a TA there, too, so... I only meant—"

"What's your angle?"

Her eyes flicker when the question leaves me.

"I... Well, I only want you two to be more than strangers. Maybe friends," she adds. "You'll be family soon and—"

"I need you to just... *stop!*"

"Stop what?"

"Stop pushing him on me!" I snap. "I had a sibling, now she's gone, so stop trying to replace Mel with your fiancé's asshole son! I get it, you need to rebuild the family you lost, have a perfect kid for once, but... please... just leave me out of it."

I'm breathless when I finish, seeing the hurt that instantly fills my mother's expression. But as badly as I know I should've held that in, something wouldn't let me.

Completely at a loss and probably thinking what a bitch she raised, she turns to leave, and I come to my senses.

"Mom, wait. Please."

She doesn't stop until I have her wrist, doing my best to hold her back despite being on wheels. She faces me and can't hide the hurt behind her eyes. Pain I caused, sadness I'm responsible for this time.

"I didn't mean that."

"I think you did, actually," she counters.

I don't respond right away, still searching for the right words when she speaks again.

"I know you feel I didn't protect you from your father, from his *words*," she says. "And I know that, in your eyes, that makes me just as guilty as him, but there has to be a way to move past this. It's not enough that I tell you I don't give a shit about your size, or even if you had an extra foot growing out the side of your head, Stevie, but... I love you. With everything in me," she adds.

Her words stick with me, and I try to make them make sense, but it's nearly impossible to convince myself she's being honest. Do I believe she loves me? I do, but I also believe that her silence said a ton.

It said that she didn't stand up to my father for taunting me because he was only saying what *she* didn't have the balls to say. Like, when he'd make pig noises at me from across the dinner table when he felt I was eating too fast. Or when he'd purposely buy my school clothes two sizes too small, encouraging me to starve myself until I could fit into them. By standing in silence and letting it all pile up, my mother may as well have done all that shit herself.

I let out a breath and remember the boatload of emotional work I've done to leave this dark place. A place filled with wrath and unforgiveness. Eventually, I'm able to let some of the anger fade, partly because the bits and pieces I've heard about Mom's past may be the reason she never stepped up. She was raised in a family with an overbearing patriarchal presence that I can imagine made her feel powerless, like she couldn't speak up. So, I guess she has her damage, too. Because of this, I choose to move forward, let the past be the past.

"Full disclosure, I meant some of what I said," I admit, "but I didn't mean to hurt you."

Mom lowers her head. "I get it."

"I've just got so much going on," I add, not even tempted to share about the trouble I've gotten myself into lately. "Sometimes, life feels so much harder than it has to be and... I just—"

"You miss her."

I hold Mom's gaze, seeing my little sister in her features, and I nod with tears welling in my eyes. She squeezes my hand in hers and I know we're nowhere near perfect, but what family is?

"When's the next dinner?" I ask. "Just name the time and place and I'll be there."

Please, don't say it's at the house. Please.

She studies my face and seems to read my vibe. "I'll see if Rob minds hosting next time."

A weak smile curves my lips and it's all I can muster up for her.

"Okay. Good."

I nod, and then her arms are around my neck, squeezing like she hasn't seen me in years.

"We'll aim for midweek," she says, "but shoot me a text with your availability since classes are starting up."

"Sure. As soon as I get home," I promise.

Now that she's gotten what she wanted, she's gone and it's just me and the echo of my skates wheeling across the floor. My phone buzzes in my pocket and a growl leaves me—a group chat with the guys. How lovely.

Micah: You around for a snack run?

Micah: Here's a hint... this is where you say yes.

I hold the phone and imagine him smiling that wicked smile that makes my skin crawl.

Stevie: Still at work.

Vince: Funny. I don't recall anyone asking. Snack list incoming.

Stevie: You do remember I don't have a car, right? It'd take me until midnight to get to the store and then to your place.

Vince: Sounds like you'd better pedal like the wind, Bird. Standby for the list...

One by one they flood my phone with notifications, requesting all kinds of chips, soda, and candy. Items that will apparently all be at my expense.

As if to punctuate just how fucked up things are for me right now, the rink goes completely dark, which means Kip's apparently forgotten I'm still here.

Great.
Fuck-ing great.

H ow many sketchy humans does a girl pass while riding her bike down a dark road in the middle of the night?

Answer: a shit-ton.

I stand at the front door of the Savage's Den in one piece, but as luck would have it, rain started falling about halfway here. Now, I'm soaked and exhausted, so the sooner I can get this over with, the better.

Someone's coming and I readjust the heavy bags in my hand, praying the person opens up before I lose feeling in my fingers.

The door pulls back and it's Vince. His stare always gives me chills. Maybe because he's so quiet, so hard to read. The house is somewhat lively behind him, filled with ambient chatter and laughter flowing out of nearly all the rooms.

"Your things," I say, lifting the bags to hand them off.

Only, he doesn't take them. Instead, he widens the gap in the door, and I realize my work here isn't done. Apparently, I'm expected to bring their snacks in myself.

Rolling my eyes, I step in and glance around while he closes the door behind me. The place is just as I remember it. Except, I'm not running through its dark corridors tonight, sweating bullets as I fear for my life.

"Should I set them here?" I ask.

Vince shakes his head and gestures toward the back of the manor. "The kitchen," he says with an annoyed groan.

Sighing, my focus is on keeping my cool as I follow him through the foyer, around the corner through the rec room, and then into the kitchen. It's a surprisingly well-lit space that's not in shambles like I would've expected. It's also not empty. Micah and Ashton are there, and I try to hide how the sight of them startles me. No sooner than I get the bags onto the tiled countertop, my phone rings, breaking the silence.

Without looking, I'm certain it's Maddox. We have a long-standing routine where I call him when I get in late from work, then we game until one of us can't keep our eyes open any longer. He knows I've been off for more than an hour and I don't have to wonder if he's freaking out.

He definitely is.

"Need to get that?" Micah asks, suspicion in his eyes.

I play it cool, though, thinking up a quick lie. "Nope. Just my mom checking in."

He studies me for a moment, then lets it go. At least he seems to. Mostly because his focus has shifted to my tits.

The white tank top of my uniform got drenched on the way over, making my purple bra show through the fabric. He stares shamelessly at my nipples, and it's not until I cross both arms over my chest that he remembers I have eyes. He meets my gaze and there's not even an ounce of embarrassment on his face knowing he's been caught.

"Classes start this week, so we'll need a copy of your schedule. A picture of it is fine," he adds, maybe thinking that makes his request more reasonable.

I don't answer right away, and he arches a brow.

"Understood?" His tone is scolding. Again, making me feel like a child in their presence.

"Understood," I nod.

"Good." A smile crosses his lips as he pushes a hand through those wild, blond waves.

The layer of thick muscle padding his chest flexes with the movement, and so does his bicep. On the inside of his left one, I

69

spot the brand many members of the brotherhood have marked themselves with. It makes me curious where Vince is hiding his. I wouldn't even know where to start looking for Ash's. His body is a canvas, and no space was wasted.

Ash glances at the large clock on the far wall, then back at me. "Cut it close, didn't you?"

I fight the urge to mouth off, knowing it'll only make things worse.

"I'm tired, it's raining, and it's dark. I did the best I could."

His head tilts when I finish speaking. He does a better job of maintaining eye contact than Micah did, but not by much.

"Can I go now?"

He stares when I ask, and I get the feeling he thinks I've spoken out of turn. Beneath the hair that's fallen into his face, his eyes narrow.

What wicked thing is he thinking up now?

A breath hitches in my throat when he stands, very clearly towering over my five-foot-five frame with his height of maybe six-three or six-four. I do my best not to let him see I'm intimidated, but it's hard not to be. Especially with the memory of him holding a blade to my throat being so fresh.

"You can leave."

He's hardly gotten those words out when I take a step toward the exit, but he catches my wrist before I get too far. My breathing's erratic now and the rapid up and down movement of my chest has his attention, drawing his eyes *there* instead of my face when I speak.

"What?" I hiss. "You just said I could go."

His eyes—burning with frustration—slowly lift to meet mine. "And you can... as soon as you turn down our beds and leave *these* on our nightstands."

He lets go to grab three bottles of water off the counter, then shoves them into my arms.

"Don't linger, and don't touch anything," he warns.

My heart skips and I start toward the exit again. This time, with my destination being the upperclassman hallway. I take one step away, but Ashton's glare halts me.

70

"Back hallway, first three rooms on the right," he says. "But I'm guessing you already knew that."

There's no detectible malice in his tone, but I'm frozen anyway. "Got it. Is that all? I can go after that?"

His deep gaze has me locked in. And when he takes my chin in his hand—firm but not overly aggressive—I feel things a girl shouldn't feel for a guy like him. Not under these circumstances, anyway. He stares down on me like he'd easily eat me alive, making me feel small and vulnerable, and... lust swells within me.

"That's all," he answers, his voice low and raspy, still lightly squeezing my jaw. "Unless... you'd like to earn a little extra credit tonight."

The others chuckle in the background, but not Ashton.

Not me.

Shit. He's dangerous. In more ways than one.

Somehow, I break the spell and back away.

"I'll... go do the beds and be out of your hair," I say softly.

I'm not sure how he reads that, my docile tone, but that makes two of us because I'm confused as hell, too. I should be repulsed, enraged by the pass he just made at me, but instead... I'm turned on.

A revelation that leaves me feeling sick and twisted.

The rims of my nostrils flare like an animal in heat when he wets his lips. His eyes lower to my breasts again and I'm greedily wishing I could be inside his head, hearing his thoughts. And it's the realization that he's actually piqued my interest that cues me to leave.

Ashton holds my gaze until I lose sight of him and fade into the darkness of the rec room where he can't track me. I make quick work of heading up to their rooms, dodging the curious stares of their other brothers along the way. One, in particular, seems to notice something's up and stops speaking mid-conversation as I pass through. But I'm gone before my expression can give away anything more.

I quickly do what I was asked—turn down all three beds and place a bottle of water beside each one. After that, I rush toward the exit because my stupid brain can't help but imagine what

71

would happen if I didn't. For instance, I'm tempted to walk back into the kitchen, step up to Ashton, and settle my curiosity. But if I'm being honest, the only thing stopping me tonight is one lonely fact.

That giving in, being weak in the moment... would make him my first.

Ever.

I slam the door to The Den closed behind me and hop onto my bike, hardly aware of the rain as I scold myself for even considering it.

Their goal is to break me, but my dad already did the bulk of the work. The fact that I gave Ash's suggestion any kind of thought at all means, I don't know... maybe I'm already in pieces.

"So, what's the verdict? Did she behave herself this time?"

I glance over my shoulder when Vince speaks. I hadn't even noticed he came into the room. My attention was... elsewhere.

"Looks like it," I answer with a nod, observing our bird onscreen as she leans across my bed to smooth the comforter. Those tight *'work shorts'* barely cover her ass, which I'm sure earns her plenty of male attention on the job. The thought crosses my mind that this sort of attention could tempt her to break the rules—a factor that might need to be addressed later.

The footage I've scanned three times now is from twenty minutes ago, when we sent her up alone. To my surprise, she didn't touch anything she wasn't given permission to touch, which means she's learning her place. Learning to only do as she's told.

"Did she send her schedule? Didn't see it in the group chat."

I shake my head. "Not yet, but I have a feeling she'll cooperate. She has so far."

When I glance back, Vince nods with a yawn. "Probably right. Anyway, see you in the morning."

"Going to bed already? It's not even one." The statement has him stopping in my doorway.

"I've got some work to do before bed," he smirks.

I nod, thinking he'll elaborate, but he doesn't. "Cool. Night."

"Night," he says.

I pause the playback on a shot of Bird exiting my room. My head tilts, taking her in from a new angle, and it isn't until I hear Ashton snickering behind me that I realize *he's* watching me now.

"Damn. Caught in the act."

"Shut the fuck up," I shoot back with a smile, but I'm not embarrassed. "Been thinking. Maybe we could make better use of this arrangement," I say distractedly.

"How so?"

I shrug and lean back in my seat, my attention never leaving the screen. Bird is stacked as hell. Any asshole with eyes can see that.

"I think we might be wasting her talents, having her do menial shit like making late-night food runs. She might be useful in *other* ways."

"What are you thinking?"

I shrug and weigh my words before saying them. "I'm thinking we invite her on The Hunt."

I turn and face Ash now to get a read on his expression. Doesn't surprise me that he seems intrigued. If the look on Bird's face earlier was any indication, she damn-near soaked her panties when Ash made a pass at her. Now, he and I are *both* quiet, and I'm willing to bet money we're thinking the same thing.

That our focus shouldn't just be on *working* Bird...

It should be on *fucking* her.

"Just keep me in the loop," Ash says, so casually I smile a little.

"Will do."

"Anyway, I'm heading down to the basement. I think a second workout might do me some good."

On his way out, he winces, working his shoulder. It isn't lost on me that he sometimes hits the weights to push through the pain. I try not to think too hard on why it bugs him from time-to-time, but part of being brothers is knowing the stories behind one another's pain. Knowing the stories behind the scars.

"Think fast."

I launch a bottle of painkillers through the air, and it rattles in his hand when he catches it. He eyes the label, then nods to say

74

thanks. A look passes between us and it's a silent acknowledgement of me having his back like he's always had mine.

Always.

Through everything.

I'm alone again and take one last look at our prey, remembering how she practically melted at Ash's feet tonight.

I see you, Little Bird. I see you and I know what you want.

Even if you're not ready to admit it yet.

STEVIE

My soaked clothes lie in a pile on the floor. I didn't bother with pajamas, instead cranking up my heater and climbing into bed naked. Turns out I'm not the only one who had a sucky night. Upstairs, Dahlia's crying on the couch while the other girls crowd around to console her. From what I gather, pledging is taking a toll on her, but this is what she wanted. So, she'll just have to suck it up, I guess. Also, I don't exactly give a shit about her drama, and I'm finally in bed after a long, grueling day. This is all I need right now.

At least, that's true until my phone dings with my favorite notification.

He's online again. Another livestream. Looks like it's viewer's choice tonight, which means somebody's about to earn himself a shit-ton of money. And someone else—meaning me—is about to enjoy watching.

I nestle deeper beneath the comforter, suddenly more aware of being naked than I was before. All because *he's* on the screen now. Reaching blindly toward my nightstand, I open the drawer and grab my vibrator—fully charged, ready to go.

He sits silently as always, but he decided to cut to the chase and came to his adoring fans completely nude. Beside him, there's a table stocked with goodies I can't even focus on because all I see is tan skin and corded muscle that wraps around his biceps, pecs, abs, and thighs. The only visible blemish being the tiny scar on the right side of his torso. He's a chiseled work of art, but his face is hidden. Not beneath a mask this time, but beneath the shadow of a dark baseball cap. He's completely still, awaiting instructions.

Anonymous: ($10 tip pledged) "Touch your balls. Rub them. Not too fast."

The words scroll up the side of the screen and my teeth sink into my lip, never blinking my eyes as he does what he's told. Slowly, making a show of it, he caresses the solid mass of his inner thigh, eventually reaching his sac. He's smooth, clean shaven everywhere, so there's nothing to obstruct the view. The tips of his fingers tease the delicate skin first, then he gently squeezes, massaging himself as his dick slowly begins to awaken. I'm hypnotized, watching it rise, once flaccid against his leg, now fully erect and standing at attention. His veins are more visible now, winding mesmerizing trails up the shaft, all the way to the swollen tip.

A work of fucking art.

Anonymous: ($20 tip pledged) "I see a marker on the table. Write the word 'taken' on your chest for me. Let the world know you're mine."

His chest moves once and I believe he just laughed, but without seeing his face there's no way to tell. He grabs the marker and writes in large, bold letters... TAKEN.

Anonymous: ($50 tip pledged) "You never speak and I'm dying to hear your voice. I just DM'd you. Please read it aloud and put us all out of our misery."

I'm intrigued as hell to see whether he'll actually take the bait, but when he begins clicking around on the screen, I'm hopeful. So hopeful that my head lifts off the pillow and not a single ounce of air leaves me while I wait.

"I'm sooo *fucking* hard for you," he reads with a growl, and the sound of his low, gravelly voice does it for me. My toy buzzes to life and I shudder when the smooth tip of it nudges my clit.

Anonymous: ($15 tip pledged) "Since you're speaking tonight, tell us... are you really a virgin like it says in your bio?"

His hand gently squeezes his sac again while he decides how

to answer. But then he nods once—his only response to the member's question.

Anonymous: ($40 *tip pledged*) *"Fuck the Q&A. I'm a mom with twin four-year-olds and this is my one and only guilty pleasure. Anyone else just here to watch this man's beautiful cock explode? Stroke while you talk, sir. Please."*

Sensing the woman's frustration through the screen, I smirk a bit, and I *think* he does, too. Again, the covered face makes it hard to be sure.

Anonymous: ($35 *tip pledged*) *"I'm with you, sister, but I have a request for our star. No lube or oil... spit on it."*

I draw in a deep surge of air, forcing myself to blink when my dry eyes remind me that I haven't. The object of our obsession obliges as usual, tightening his abs as he arches forward, then spits a stream of saliva that lands right on the slit at the tip of his cock, and slides down the shaft. My lip aches from biting into it so hard, but I can't fucking help it. He rubs the moisture into his skin and breathes a relaxed sigh as his hand begins to work.

Anonymous: ($65 *tip pledged*) *"Shit... pledging just to say that I've never wanted to sit on a man's cock more than I want to sit on yours. Thank you for existing."*

The sound of my wet pussy responding to the show accompanies a breathy sigh coming through my phone's speaker. He's getting into it. So much that I sometimes wonder if he forgets we're here, forgets we're watching. I like to think that's the case, that his pleasure is authentic instead of just a part of some performance.

As if responding to my thoughts, a whispered, "Oh, shit..." falls from his lips and he's definitely more turned on than usual. It makes me wonder what transpired during his day that left him aching for this moment, aching to come.

I think back on my own incident with Ash earlier. It's undoubtedly the reason my clit's already throbbing and on the verge of sending shockwaves through my entire body. So, now I'm curious. Who did he cross paths with today that he let get away? Who did he want to fuck so badly he can hardly hold it in now?

A quiet moan leaves my lips and the need to touch him is

overwhelming. He teases the head of his dick with his thumb and his breathing's erratic. I want to come but not until *he* does. It adds to the illusion, makes it feel more real.

His stomach and thighs tense with restraint, but I wish he'd just let go already. It would free *me* if he did. But then it's like he's heard me again, making it feel as though I'm there in the flesh when his body lurches forward, and then cum erupts from his dick like a damn fountain.

"Fuck. Yes." I'm a bit louder than intended, but who gives a shit?

My clit pulses against the vibrator and I can't keep my eyes open as I'm rocked with pleasure, imagining his cum covering me, filling me. By the time I'm able to pry my eyelids open again, he pumps the last surge into his fist, then just breathes. His heart beats so fast the hollow of his throat throbs.

Anonymous: ($50 tip pledged) "Rub cum on your chest for us. Right over the word you wrote. Feels like the perfect end to a perfect performance."

Sated and spent, he lifts his hand to the word 'TAKEN' printed on his skin, and wipes sticky, white liquid over the letters, smearing ink as he drags his palm over it.

Anonymous: ($30 tip pledged) "I always leave these livestreams wet, relaxed, and recharging my toy. Much appreciated. See you next time."

Anonymous: ($100 tip pledged) "Show your face."

Host: -$100 (Pledge Reversed)

Anonymous: ($100 tip pledged) "Well, shit. Can't blame me for trying. Keep the money anyway. Add it to the pile of cash we all throw at you with hopes that you'll one day let us witness some lucky girl—or guy—defiling you for the first time. Love and peace, Your Highness."

The screen goes dark when the stream ends, and I tuck my toy away inside my drawer with plans to clean it later. My heart still hasn't slowed, and I can't admit what just happened. Yes, I got off watching the livestream, but once or twice... *he* wasn't the only one I thought of. Three faces flashed interchangeably in my head as I came. It seems that they don't only rule my life, they rule my fantasies, too.

The thought reminds me of something I need to do. So, I forward the screenshot of my schedule to the group chat per Micah's request.

As badly as I want to distance myself from these three—for *so* many reasons—there's nothing I can say or do to make that happen. Because it turns out, once the devils know your name... they're not likely to forget it.

CHAPTER 12
STEVIE

At the top corner of my page, what started as a random, blue spiral of ink has morphed into a tiny universe, complete with moon and stars. This work of art is all that's kept me from dozing off this morning. I'd stake my life on this being my most boring class this semester and it's only day one.

Professor Lange has lulled three students to sleep with his monotone delivery and I'm fighting not to be the fourth. He pauses, returns to his desk, then takes a seat—the most exciting thing that's happened so far. Meanwhile, I reach to sip from my water bottle, wishing I'd thought to fill it with coffee.

Or Vodka.

"Now, if you'll turn to page two of your syllabus, my TA will take over from here to explain the attendance policy for this course, as well as the grading rubric. His is a voice you'll be hearing a lot around here," Professor Lange says, prompting me to nearly thank God out loud. "As someone I've personally mentored over the years, I've had the opportunity to watch him develop into an exceptional, trustworthy young man, and I'm certain you'll find there's a lot to glean from him over the next several months. So, without further ado, allow me to introduce you to my protégé, Mr. Ford."

My ears perk up a bit hearing that last name. Then, Professor

Lange gestures to the front row of the lecture hall and that's when I spot him—the last person I wanted to see today. Well, *one* of the last people I wanted to see today.

The first thing I notice is his hair. It's thick, dark, and has a bit of length to it. Then, his tall frame rises from the seat. He turns and faces the room, and that's when my heart sinks.

Holy fucking shit.

Professor Lange's assistant, Mr. Ford... is Tate.

Two girls in the row behind me whisper, and while I can't hear exactly what's being said, I can bet they're swooning over him. Most girls would. He's got that *'Tall, dark, and God's gift to women'* thing going on, but I'm not moved.

A gray dress shirt is tucked into the waistband of dark slacks. I can't see it because it's hidden beneath his sleeve, but I envision that fucking brand on his forearm. My gaze shifts to the black, beaded bracelet he wears, and I'm triggered, remembering the moment I linked that bracelet and his scar to one of the worst moments of my life. Those two pieces of evidence are how I knew the universe had led me to the right guy. How I knew I'd found my smoking gun. My proof.

He paces in front of Professor Lange's desk like he's *'King Dick'* or some shit, hands tucked in his pockets all casual. His confidence annoys the hell out of me. Maybe because... how dare he pretend he's just some regular guy, leading a regular life?

Like there isn't a world of darkness inside him.

His eyes find mine and he stops in the middle of formally introducing himself to the class. First, his eyes narrow as he questions whether he's mistaken, then they widen once he's certain it's me. A faint smile curves this fucker's lips, prompting me to look down at my paper instead of him.

The audacity.

"As I was saying," he continues, "this semester will be a breeze as long as you don't slack on your reading and you're mindful of your attendance. Professor Lange had a saying when I was his student. It was *'showing up for class is showing up for yourself.'* What I took from that was that we should all treat being here, right here in this room, like it's more than a means to an end. It's an investment, a sign that you see the importance of adding to your arsenal of knowledge, properly arming yourself for the world that awaits you."

He finishes and I can't help the hard eye roll I give him.

Shut the fuck up, dick.

"I'll go over the grading rubric next, then we'll do a fun little icebreaker to help us all get better acquainted. Most of your faces are new for me, but... I recognize a few."

I don't know why I glance up at him, but I do. And sure enough, he's staring right at me. Those damn dimples don't work on me, though. I'm immune to them *and* his bullshit.

I've gone back to doodling on my paper when my purse begins to buzz on top of my desk. I quickly find my phone and silence the call, but when I check to see who I missed...

"Shit..."

The whispered word hisses from my lips and the guy in front of me glances at me over his shoulder.

"Sorry."

He responds to the apology with a short nod, and then faces forward again.

Stevie: Can't pick up. In class.

Vince: Looks like you're in the Hillbury Building. Come to the main entrance. 2 minutes.

Stevie: I'm in Hillbury because I'm IN CLASS...

Vince: 1 minute

These assholes know exactly how to get under my skin. So thoroughly, you'd think they've known me for years, know all my triggers. Turns out they're just incredibly annoying and that covers all the bases, I guess.

Stevie: Can I at least know why I'm being summoned?

Ashton: Simple. We forgot to take care of something this morning. Thought we'd stop by and correct that.

Fucking hell...

My knee bounces with frustration and it doesn't help hearing Tate's voice over the mounted speakers. I swear, he shoots a look my way between what feels like every sentence he completes. And if I'm not mistaken, my perpetual annoyance with his existence is some kind of a sick thrill to him.

Snatching my bag and hoodie off the edge of my seat, I snarl at him one last time as I stand and rush toward the exit, hoping to be as little a distraction as possible. It doesn't work. All eyes are on me because I'm clearly pissed and moving quickly to avoid angering my new rulers.

Having given up on a discreet exit, I burst through the doors of the lecture hall and into the hallway. Vaulted ceilings and stained-glass age the university. The shadows of vines that have slowly inched their way up the brick exterior block out a small bit of light, a mix of craftsmanship and nature, beauty and divinity. My steps echo when I reach the broad staircase that spills down into the atrium, and there they are, impatiently waiting.

My steps slow and when I realize I'm holding my breath, I consciously draw in air with hopes of appearing less rattled when I'm standing at their feet. Speaking of feet, my slouchy socks and slides seem out of place as I look the guys over. Each one with his own style, but they all look... expensive. Where the money comes from, I have no clue, but I feel out of place. T-shirt, yoga pants, and a hoodie seemed fine for a first-day outfit. Until now, that is.

Struggling to keep a hold on my confidence, I square my shoulders. "I need to get back to class, so..."

Vince smirks and I'm convinced he gets off on making me uncomfortable. His intensity and tendency to keep silent are unnerving, to say the least. But today, he speaks.

"This should be quick. Follow us."

He nods toward a narrow corridor off to the left and they start walking that way. I hesitate, but then my steps trail behind them. There's no staff or students around because all classes in this building are already in session, but I find myself wishing for at least one eyewitness. Someone who could say they've seen me, someone who could say they've seen who I'm *with*.

The hinges of a door squeal when Ashton pushes it open, then gestures for me to enter first. It's a dark, windowless room, and once I'm inside, I realize it's a supply closet. Steps shuffle inside behind me just before the door closes and the four of us are in what feels like a small, pitch-black abyss. Seconds later, there's a click. We're bathed in soft, yellow light, and Micah's hand falls from the string attached to the bulb above.

Vince slips a backpack off his shoulder and sets it on the floor. I stare without blinking as he stoops down to unzip it, then pulls out a hideous, fur monstrosity that looks like a... *rug* maybe? Next, he tosses old sneakers at my feet. A pair that looks like they've been worn to cut grass, tar a roof, and take a shortcut through hell. The final piece? An actual potato sack.

When I meet the guys' gazes, they're smirking, and I'm starting to see where this is going.

"Can't have our little girl attending her first day of school without her new school clothes, now can we?" Micah teases.

I glance down at the pile of '*clothes*' and shake my head. "Fuck you. *All* of you. I'm not wearing this shit, so..."

I take one step when Micah's solid arm loops around my waist from one direction, and Vince's from another. Then I feel fingers against my scalp just before the stinging starts. It's Ashton who's grabbed a handful of my hair and yanks me back, slamming me into his hard, wall-like chest. He tugs my head to the side, stretching the tendon where his mouth now grazes my skin just near the cut he made.

"Don't... run from us," he breathes. His voice is deep and quiet, almost soothing. Meanwhile, my scalp is on fire and he's not loosening his grip.

"You see what nice things we brought for you?" he croons. "Only an ungrateful bitch would make us ask her twice to change. However, the choice is yours."

That's funny, seeing as how I'm *literally* being held against my will. My breathing's wild and I bounce a look back and forth between Vince and Micah.

"How many points?" I ask.

Micah's brow arches when he smirks. "Mm... let's say three. With the grocery run the other day, that'd bring you to six points total."

My eyes stretch wide. "Are you kidding me? The grocery run was only three points? I rode my bike in the fucking rain to—"

"Okay, now it's worth *one* point. How's that?" His jaw ticks, waiting to see if I've got anything else to say.

My entire body vibrates with rage. Fiery words burn my throat when he knocks my score down, but speaking them out loud would only make things worse. If his goal was to show me what happens when I defy them, when I fight back, message received.

After a long stare down between us, Micah's gaze softens. The hand he's left settled against my waist, squeezes me a little, and then he lets go.

"Where should we start?"

He's asking Vince and Ash, not me.

"Well, we can't put *new* clothes on her without removing the old ones, so..."

Ashton's answer has my heart going wild, thinking and feeling so many things, but the stupidest of them all?

I don't want them to see me naked.

I envision my body, like I'm standing before a mirror, seeing myself as *they* will. My stomach is soft and a little puffy, even when I suck it in. My thighs touch when I walk or, hell, even when I'm just standing still. My hips—blighted by a few stretchmarks that showed up during puberty—aren't exactly slim and trim either. I hate that this is the narrative running through my head, but it is, and I can't seem to filter out the negative thoughts.

Can't seem to filter out my father's voice.

I hear him, hear his insults and berating. I hear his disapproval, his disappointment.

He religiously filled my mind with his bullshit as a kid, leaving me just as messed up in the head as he hoped I'd be. Now, in the presence of these three, I don't stand a chance of remaining confident. They're almost ethereal where looks are concerned. It isn't lost on me that, typically, guys like this are extremely superficial and cruel.

They're oblivious to how I'm struggling inwardly as Ashton's grip on my hair finally eases up.

"Should *you* do it, or should *we*?" Micah asks, arching a brow. It takes a moment, but I realize he's asking if I'll be removing my own clothes, or if they should do it *for* me.

"You can't be fucking serious," I say, laughing a bit, but their stoic faces mean they're not joking about making me undress.

"Wrong answer. Arms up." The order comes from behind me, from Ashton.

"W—what?" I say shakily.

"You had your chance, now the decision's been made *for* you," he says. "You think you're the only one with places to be?"

"No, but I—"

"Arms. Up," he repeats, and my head burns again when his fist twists in my hair.

Trembling, my hands stretch toward the ceiling.

Ash's deep timbre edges on amused when it ripples through me, whispering two words into my ear.

"Good girl."

Vince grips the hem of my tee and my skin cools as he lifts the fabric above the strawberry-print bra I'm wearing. Knowing he's just exposed me to the others, my eyes fall closed as I become painfully aware of what parts of me they can see. The shirt slips over my head, then I hear it fall to the floor.

I'm trying to will myself to have an out of body experience when the humiliation gets to be too much, but it doesn't work.

I flinch when heat from Ashton's hand presses to my stomach. He still has me from behind, but there's less tension on my hair now. Slowly, my eyes open and I see Micah stooping down to remove my slides and socks. He stands and nods at Ashton, then that hand radiating heat through my torso slips down into my yoga pants.

"What're you doing?" I ask in a sudden flare of panic.

"Relax," Ash answers, pushing the spandex fabric down off my hips.

His fingertips graze my ass, cupping it a little to get my waistband down to my thighs. His offer from the other night is with me again, taunting me. Not because I'm tempted, but because my pride is wounded. I imagine what his thoughts must be now that he's seen so much of me, probably wishing he could take back those words.

Micah takes over, pulling the pants off the rest of the way. I step out of them and only what's hidden beneath my bra and panties is still sacred. When Micah smirks, I die a little on the inside, imagining a hundred snide remarks he could be thinking right now.

"A little old for printed underwear, aren't you?" His eyes are on my panties, and I hate having his attention.

"Cute," Vince teases, wearing a smile himself.

Micah steps closer and I feel stuck, trapped between *his* formidable body and Ashton's. His eyes darken when they meet mine and I'm panting, subconsciously leaning into Ashton, only to find there's no escaping either one of them.

"New rule," Micah growls. "From now on, you either wear silk or nothing."

To drive his point home, he slips a finger beneath the center of my bra, then lets it snap against my skin.

"W—why?" I force out. "You'll never see them anyway."

I'm not being a bitch when I say that, although I'd be well within my rights. I'm just stating a fact. But when Micah flashes a white smile, I'm confused.

"Silk... or nothing. Am I understood?"

That same finger he used to tug my bra is now beneath my chin, lifting it, forcing my eyes to meet his. When I nod, he's visibly pleased. I expect him to back off, but instead, he lingers in my space, silent. Until a bold claim falls from his lips.

"The other night, you were into Ashton's suggestion, weren't you?" he blurts out. "I saw it in your eyes."

I swallow deeply, and my first instinct is to lie, deny the accusation.

"I don't know what you're talking about," I practically whisper.

Micah's eyes narrow and when I glance toward Vince, he's

giving the same look. "You've gotta do better than that, Bird," Micah accuses again.

We fall into another of those silent standoffs and my *second* instinct is to weaken Micah's statement with a laugh. Only, I mean for it to sound casual, but instead it sounds nervous and thin.

"No!" I snap, being mindful of not shouting in case someone walks past, but I'm desperate for them to believe me.

Desperate for *me* to believe me.

"Then fucking prove it," he growls. "Prove you don't want us, prove you weren't tempted, and it'll never come up again."

I laugh to deflect just like before. "Fine. Tell me how to prove that and I'll do it. Gladly."

I'm still holding Micah's stern gaze, awaiting instructions when his hand lifts to that string again, and with one pull, we're surrounded by darkness.

The only sound is my breathing. I have questions, *so* many questions, but only ask one.

"What do you want from me?"

I can't see anyone's faces, but I imagine their smiles broadening when Micah gives his answer.

"Finger yourself."

I manage to choke out one word. "What?"

His steps can be heard, bringing him just a little closer to speak directly in front of me.

"I want you to finger your pussy while we touch you," he explains, rendering me silent. "And if you don't come, you'll prove your point."

I scoff, feeling disoriented and a little like I'm stuck in a fever dream. "You're insane."

"Maybe," he laughs. "Or maybe I'm dead-on and you're terrified that we know the truth about you."

Blinking, I breathe him in and ask a question that can barely be heard. "And what truth is that?"

His fingertip starts at my chin like before, but then it trails down my throat as I swallow beneath his touch.

"On one hand, you wish you'd never met us," he says in that

growly tone of his, causing a breath to still in my chest. "But now that we're here... you want us to fuck you. Hard. Wild. All the time."

I'm speechless. The only sign of life is my heart, which is sprinting right now. I hate myself for what I feel, for letting them get to me.

Hate that, on every level... he's one hundred percent right.

My head reels, trying to connect my expectations with reality.

Just a moment ago, I was filled with thoughts and concerns about how these three would judge me, but now I'm not sure *what* to think. Nothing they've said or done has quite fit how I saw it playing out in my head. Mostly because a girl knows when a guy is turned off, and from what I gathered, they are *not* turned off.

I feel the rise and fall of Ashton's chest behind me as I'm held, braced against him. I'm breathing like I'm short on air and I can't make heads or tails of what's happening. I'm angry, *livid* even, but... I'm also wet. I'd think it strange to be turned on in this moment, but I'm not the only one.

I shift my weight from one foot to the other and brush against the front of Ashton's jeans in the process, only to feel solid steel persisting beneath the rough fabric. His response isn't to back away or hide the secret I've just discovered. Instead, he settles against the rack behind him for leverage, then he pulls me closer to rest against him as he slowly presses his hips forward. The hard rod of his dick fits right between my ass cheeks and he's giving off major *'look what you fucking do to me'* vibes.

And at this moment, something becomes clear... I'm into that shit.

I'm twisted and know I shouldn't play along, but I push my

hips back, wanting to feel him. *All* of him. The reaction I get is unexpected, but not unpleasant. His grip on my hair tightens again, drawing my head back to his shoulder. Once he realizes I'm no longer fighting, he releases my hair. Now, the hand once used to control me, moves to my neck. The metal of his rings is cool against my skin when he grips my throat, stroking his thumb just beneath my ear.

I'm not convinced I'm awake when the straps of my bra are pushed down both shoulders. Then, I'm even *more* dazed when warm, damp lips meet my nipple with a gentle kiss. I confirm it's Micah when I place my hand on his head, feeling his wavy strands between my fingers. He settles one hand against my waist and uses the other to lift my breast to his mouth. More wetness pools between my legs as he flicks his tongue over my nipple until it's so hard it hurts, and then draws it into his mouth.

Reaching for something to brace myself when my knees weaken, my fingers land on Vince's chest. With how distant and cold he's been, I'm inclined to pull away, but before I'm able to, his palm flattens over the back of my hand, holding it in place. His heart's beating so fast it seems dangerous, and that's when I realize he's the only one not touching me, not taking advantage of this moment.

He's always so hard to read, so hard to pin down, but right now, I feel him. He wants in on this, wants to touch and be touched, but doesn't seem like the kind of guy who goes after what he wants or makes the first move.

With his hand still on mine, I lower it down his stomach to his waist, moving slowly because I sense that's his preferred pace. But the second I touch his zipper, he stops me, curling his fingers between mine as he brings my hand to the back of his neck instead. Soft, buzzed hair meets my fingertips and he sighs a little at my touch. I squeeze his nape as I feel him coming closer. Then, as I hold in a breath, his tongue separates my lips, and all rational thought is gone.

They're all over me, large bodies maneuvering around one another to ensure each one has a piece to himself, and I'm a lost cause. Even before Ashton whispers another command.

91

"Touch yourself," he beckons.

With one hand snaked around Vince's neck, the other is free, resting on my quivering stomach. It's the only part of my body that has yet to submit to these three. That is, until Ashton takes charge, positioning me like his doll, sliding my fingers into my panties, then letting my own desperation do the rest.

"Fuck," I cry out, letting Vince swallow the moan that leaves me right after.

My pussy is so slick the sound of the wetness coating my fingers fills the small space.

"That's it, Bird. Come for us," Ash croons.

Micah's mouth on my tits has me dazed as I slide two fingers over my swollen clit. Ashton grips one hip, slowly grinding his dick against my ass while his once gentle hold on my throat begins to tighten. My pussy clenches around my fingers when I sink them inside and I'm grateful for Vince's kiss. I whimper into it while he sucks my tongue into his mouth, muffling the sound of my pleasure as my body coils toward Micah.

"Damn, do you always sound this fucking hot when you come?"

Ashton rasps that question into my hair as my fingers work me through the last of one intensely pleasurable orgasm. So pleasurable, I'm already longing for another. The darkness surrounding me adds to the surrealness that has my head spinning. Or maybe... that feeling is just being near *them*.

Vince lingers in my space for a moment, and I'm surprised by the feel of soft kisses to my lips and cheek before he backs away. Part of me feels like he and I are meeting for the first time today, right now.

Micah's mouth audibly breaks suction from my nipple, then immediately finds my lips. I'm like a dead fish against him at first, wondering if he missed that I just finished kissing his friend a matter of seconds ago, but then it hits me.

He doesn't actually seem to care.

He freely explores my mouth with his tongue, and I'm only half aware of my hand being pulled free from my panties by one of the others. But then the fingers that were just inside me are

92

drawn into the warmth of Ashton's mouth. A gasp hitches in my throat but kissing Micah drowns it out. Ash's tongue is like wet silk as he sucks softly, making sure all traces of me that were left behind are his now.

"Shit, you're so fucking sweet," he whispers, speaking the words around my fingers.

Hearing Ashton's declaration, Micah smiles against my mouth and then pecks my lips once before putting space between us. The unexpected passion these three brought to this moment tempts me to pull Micah close again just so it's not lost.

"Well, shit. *That* went a bit left," he admits with a quiet laugh, and I couldn't agree more. When he pulls the switch again, my eyes squint while adjusting to the light.

It was as if I'd lost all sense of time and space for a while, only now remembering I ducked out of class for this. Well, not for *this* exactly. The guys adjust their clothing, mostly the fronts of their jeans, and I bend toward the bag to gather my things, too.

"What do you think you're doing?"

Micah has my wrist, stopping me a few inches from grabbing my pants.

"I'm... getting dressed."

That answer seems pretty standard to me, but he seems confused. "We already told you, we *brought* what you're wearing for the rest of the day. That didn't change."

My mouth falls open and I don't even know why I would've thought anything different. They touch me, kiss me, make me give myself an orgasm for their fucking entertainment, but I'm still being forced to dress like a maniac. Again, strictly for their entertainment.

Vince holds out the potato sac with a hole for my head and arms cut out, and I glare at him while I snatch it over my head. He smirks when he holds out a rope.

"To use as a belt," he explains.

I slap it out of his hand, and they all laugh when it hits the floor.

If I didn't already, I'd certainly feel like a fool *now*. What girl in her right mind lets guys who treat her like this touch her in *any* way?

I have that answer.

Only me.

I'm silent while slipping on the shoes I'm pretty sure they fished out of a dumpster, then top it all off with an ugly fur vest that smells like vinegar. I step toward the door, but Micah stands in front of it, halting me. He waits until I meet his gaze, then makes it abundantly clear what my place is.

"Don't you get it yet, Bird? You even *come* when we tell you to," he smirks. "Let that sink in."

Tears sting my eyes and I'm furious. Mostly with myself, but definitely at these three assholes.

"Move," I growl, attempting to shove Micah aside, but with a mass of solid muscle that shields him like armor, he doesn't even budge.

"Hang on. One more thing," he says, halting me. "We've had something hanging around the house and didn't think we'd get anymore use out of it. Which is a shame, because it was custom made for last year's recruits." He motions for Vince to toss him something, and that something is a stamp. He removes the cover, then presses it to my forehead before stepping aside. "There. Now you're ready."

I snatch the door open so fast, I nearly rip it off its hinges, armed with only my purse because those fuckers kept all my clothes. Even my hoodie, which means I can't cover up.

Fucking great.

They exit the supply closet behind me, but I don't look their way. They're dead to me.

I make it to the end of the hallway before finding a bathroom. Rushing toward the mirror, I'm finally able to see what the stamp says, and I'm not sure which of their antics has me more pissed. The outfit or... this—the words *'Certified Dick Tease'* marking my forehead.

And to top off my shitty morning, a text just dropped into the group chat.

94

Micah: Congrats, Bird. You earned yourself some extra credit today... 1 point.

One. Damn. Point.

Fuck him.

And fuck whatever she-devil birthed his sorry ass into this world.

CHAPTER 14
STEVIE

E ven with my return to class being marked by whispers and laughter, I'm still more pissed than humiliated.

But I'm definitely feeling pretty fucking humiliated, too.

Tate stumbles over his words as I ease into a seat. Without meeting his gaze, I'm positive I'm the distraction. There's no sense in trying to pretend I don't look like a huge jackass, so I settle in and just accept that this is my life. Yep, I'm the loser who just debased herself for three cocky assholes, and then still had to put on this ridiculous outfit.

One thing is clearer than ever... the Savages are completely and undeniably heartless—a fact I should've accepted before it came to this.

Professor Lange clears his throat, standing from his seat despite Tate technically still having the floor. "Excuse me, miss, what is your name?"

I meet his gaze, hoping he's talking to someone else, but of course he isn't.

"Stevie," I answer, observing as both Professor Lange and Tate struggle to hold their composure.

"Right. Ms. Heron," he continues. "We noticed you took a bit of a hiatus a moment ago and, considering the circumstances, it'd be remiss of me not to ask, but... is everything alright?"

The class *and* Tate chuckle and I feel my face heating up.

likely turning redder by the second. But I'm stronger than that. This isn't the first time I've been the butt of someone's joke in a classroom. Only this time, the taunting has nothing to do with being the chubby girl in class.

"I'm fine. Just had to take a bit of a break and... freshen up." I flash a smile after answering, then it quickly fades.

The class laughs louder and I'm starting to care a little less.

"I pledged in college, so I get it," Professor Lange says, tucking one hand in his pocket. "I just hope disrupting class won't be a regular occurrence."

He smiles a bit and, surprisingly, he's not being a dick about it. Which I appreciate.

"No, sir. I promise."

The professor nods once and takes his seat again. Then, my gaze shifts to Tate as he pushes off from the desk where he'd been leaning. He gives a few final words and luckily, we're dismissed.

I'm slow to gather my things because I'm still a little distraught from my latest run-in with the guys, but I eventually make it to the door as the last few students exit. I try to avoid Tate's gaze, so I'm not obligated to speak, but he doesn't seem to catch the hint.

He steps into my path, mere feet before I make my clean getaway, and he has on that good guy smile I hate. Because he is *not* a good guy.

Shit, here we go...

Dark eyes are digging into me when I peer up. I always get that sense with him. That he's desperate to get inside my head.

"You, uh... decided to pledge?" he says, sounding almost nervous to address me. That could be because our interactions are never quite friendly on my part.

"Yep. Now, if you'll excuse me..."

I step left to get around him and he moves with me, one hand gently gripping my elbow. He lets go right away, so it doesn't trigger me or anything, but still.

"Listen, I mentioned to Val that it'd be nice if you and I could grab coffee sometime," he says, this hopeful twinge in his voice. Honestly, it makes me want to gouge out his eyes. "So, if you don't have a class to rush off to, I've got a couple free hours. If you're interested, that is. I'm buying," he adds with a smile.

When I glance down at my outfit, he laughs a little.

"And if you want to stop by your place and change first, that'd be fine, too. *If* you're allowed to change," he adds. "I know sometimes that's against the rules, but honestly, I'd take you however you want me to."

My brow lifts, and he lowers his head, seeming to have just realized how that came out. He laughs at himself, but I hold mine in.

"I... that didn't come out right. I just mean that... never mind."

I study him for a moment—his posture, his tone. Is he... losing his shit because he's talking to me? I mean, the rambling, backtracking, that look in his eyes that screams *'please say yes'*. It's all so hard to believe because, with that face and that physique, he could probably have any girl on this campus on her back before I can even make it out to the atrium. But here he is, feeling awkward talking to *me*.

Something doesn't add up.

"So, you're trying to tell me that you'd actually sit somewhere with me, in public, dressed like... *this?*" I'm unable to hold in a laugh, holding out the sides of the fur vest that might just be from a badger, because that is complete bullshit.

Tate shrugs, then scans me from head to toe. "I mean, I know what you really look like, so yeah, I would. In a heartbeat," he adds, but it's more so the way he says it. With this deep, heartfelt tone as he holds my gaze.

How fucking naïve does he think I am?

My lips part and I'm just about to tell him to go to hell, but a text interrupts, and Tate falls silent.

"One sec," I say, just beginning to scan what the boys sent to the chat.

Ashton: The Den. Tonight at nine. Just wired cash to your bank account to buy yourself some lingerie. Something slutty in black.

As soon as the message comes through, so does an alert from my bank, letting me know $200 was just deposited. I think back to

Micah taking my phone and I'm starting to see the scope of what he's done to it.

Stevie: I have class. When am I supposed to shop? And you can't possibly expect me to walk into the mall or anyplace *dressed like this.*

Ashton: How and when you get the shit isn't our concern. Just make sure you're where we told you to be, wearing what we told you to wear.

Great.

I glance up at Tate. My plan was always to turn him down, but now I have a legitimate excuse for why I have to decline.

"Looks like something's just come up. You know, sorority shit," I lie, seeing as how he already believes I'm pledging.

The disappointment on his face is almost believable.

"No, it's cool. I completely understand," he says, finally stepping out of the way. "Maybe some other time."

"Yeah, maybe."

"See you in class Thursday," he calls out.

I pass him without a word, then shoot him a peace sign over my shoulder.

My life's got enough dick-bags in it without adding *him* to the mix. Besides, once I finally get the info I need, his ass won't be around anyway.

Fingers crossed.

CHAPTER 15
STEVIE

A new face greets me at the door, and from the looks of things, he's already a little tipsy, but not quite drunk yet.

He eyes the black sweats and matching hoodie I threw on before riding over.

"A little overdressed, aren't you?" he says with a smirk.

On cue, a half-dressed redhead passes behind him, balancing a tray of beer bottles.

I fake a smile. "Sure. If you say so. Can I come in?"

He steps aside then closes the door behind me. "I'm Fletcher," he says, introducing himself. "You're here to serve with the other girls, right?"

Until now, I had no idea this was the guys' plan, but here I am, I guess.

"I'm honestly not sure what's going on, so would you mind getting Vince for me?"

Fletcher seems a bit confused, but takes me over to the study and closes me in. I'm guessing to grab Vince like I asked. He's the least toxic of the three, but still a world-class asshole.

I pace in front of the French doors, listening to what sounds like a lowkey party somewhere within the huge manor. My heart races at the thought of stripping down to what I bought today, at the thought of wearing so little in a room full of strangers.

100

I'm mid-thought when the doors swing open. I lose my breath as the three wicked ones catch me off guard.

"I—only asked for Vince."

Ashton's grin turns devious. "Then, it must be your lucky day because you got all three of us."

Swallowing hard, I try to forget how my encounter went with them earlier, but there's no use. A girl doesn't easily forget a thing like that.

Micah's expression is the first to turn cold, then the others follow. "What the fuck are you wearing?" he says with such a chill I almost stutter my answer.

But instead, I unzip my hoodie, revealing a black, steel-boned corset underneath. It's covered in lace and my tits are nearly touching my chin with all the lift, but surprisingly enough, I don't hate the way I look in it. Or the way I feel in it.

I slide the sweats down my hips and reveal the rest—matching, silk panties with a garter belt strapped to sheer, thigh-high stockings.

At first, the guys' silence is a little unnerving, so I focus on shoving the clothes I just shed into the backpack I wore over.

"Well, *fuck*."

The emphatic reaction fell from Vince's lips, surprisingly. He's typically somewhat reserved compared to the others, but apparently, I hit a nerve tonight.

Perhaps, one below the belt.

Makes it feel kind of worth it that I shaved *everything* to make this look work. It's not like my ego couldn't use the boost. Especially after only earning one extra credit point for my performance this afternoon.

Dickheads.

"Vince is right. You clean up well, Bird." Ashton's smirk accompanies the slow scan he does of my outfit from head to toe. But when he gets to my feet, his brow arches. "No heels?"

I look down at my purple sneakers and shrug. "Nope. These will do."

Micah also nods toward my footwear, but he has a question.

"What's with the butterfly clip on your laces? You had one on your skates, too."

I take a deep breath and actively block them from digging too deep. They can't. Not on *this* subject anyway.

"It's nothing. It *means* nothing," I add, forcing a tight smile right after.

Lucky for me, he lets it go at that, but I feel like prey the next moment as the three circle me. Like sharks in the water. A figure in the doorway grabs my attention, though, and I do a double-take when I recognize the face staring back at me—Dahlia. Yes, there's hatred in her eyes, but also curiosity.

Judging by the bright red body suit she's wearing, and the tray balanced against her shoulder, I'm guessing she's here for the same reason I am. To wait on the Savage's hand and foot.

Seeing her quickly sobers me up, and then she's gone.

"These are for you."

I stare at what Vince has just handed me—a pair of black cat ears attached to a headband. I'd seen some of the other girls bounce by wearing random animal ears but thought they brought them on their own. I make my way over to the antique, floor-to-ceiling mirror propped in the corner. The guys stand in silence behind me, shamelessly observing as I readjust my corset, then the straps of the garter belt.

"So, what is this anyway? A boy scout meeting or something?" I ask with a disinterested sigh.

In the mirror's reflection, I spot Ashton as he props his elbow on top of the bar, then casually leans against it. "It's an event meeting."

I nod. "You mean frat boys do shit other than feast on the tormented souls of unsuspecting women?"

I hadn't meant for the joke to be so on the nose, but there's no taking it back.

"On occasion," Micah chuckles and I roll my eyes at him in annoyance. "But if you must know, we were mostly organizing The Hunt."

His explanation only confuses me more. "What the hell is that?"

"Something you'll find out about soon enough. Because, lucky for you, we've decided we're taking you with us."

It's like a record screeches to a halt in my head. "You never said that was part of the deal. I never agreed to go *anywhere* with you."

It's also on the tip of my tongue to tell them to go fuck themselves.

"You look worried," Vince says, approaching me from behind, stepping unnervingly close as he strokes my hair. "Relax. It'll be fun. Besides, you'll get to meet Big Brother Eros."

My face morphs into a scowl. "Big Brother who?"

Ashton lets out a soft laugh. "It's not his real name, obviously. Eros is the Greek god of sex, and during *our* Eros' time here among the Savages, dude got more ass than a toilet seat."

The others laugh, but I'm disgusted.

"Hm... how delightful," I chime in. "Anyway, a little info about this *hunt* thing would be nice, seeing as how there's no way I can get out of it," I add under my breath.

Micah grabs a pack of cigarettes from his pocket, which has Ashton shooting him an annoyed glance. He lights up and puffs smoke before even attempting to respond to me.

"Don't worry your pretty little head about it. You'll know all you need to know in due time," he says. "But what I *will* share, is that tonight was also about bringing the others up to speed on our volunteer schedule."

"One guess which cause is at the top of our list," Ashton adds.

"No clue," I answer, running a hand through my hair before facing the guys head-on again.

Ashton tilts his head and smirks just enough to make me uneasy. "You sure about that? You can't think of a *single* cause we might've recently gained interest in lately?"

It takes a moment, but I'm finally putting the pieces together. Specifically, I recall Micah grabbing a volunteer packet off the table the night we met. Inside, they would've found all the details laid out about the fundraiser at the skate rink.

"You fucking wouldn't."

"Oh, yes, we fucking would," Ash shoots back, flashing a smile at me. "What's yours is ours, Bird. *Everything* that's yours... is ours."

I'm seeing red but try to calm down. If I explode, they won't hear me and... I need them to hear me.

"You don't understand," I snap. "A lot of our members have body image issues for various reasons, and the club is their safe space. It's *my* safe space. Most of them avoid guys like you. At all costs," I add. "You'll make them uncomfortable, and you'll make them lose trust in me, because they'll think I'm the one who set this up."

Three blank stares are aimed right at me.

"Avoid guys like us why?"

I nearly scream in Micah's face when he asks because he should already know the fucking answer. But instead, I pace, working to suppress my anger.

"Seriously?" I scoff. "Do you not know what your kind are like? If a girl isn't a Barbie Doll with an impossibly small waist, huge tits, and an ass so tight you can play beer pong on it, guys like you aren't always the nicest to encounter. But you *obviously* don't understand shit like that, hence the reason you asked *my* size sixteen ass to show up wearing... *this* tonight. On display for every asshole here to point at and judge."

I'm fuming, amazed by the lack of awareness.

"Is that what you think this was about? Embarrassing you?"

I don't meet Micah's gaze when he asks. Partly, because I'm starting to tear up and don't want him to have the satisfaction of knowing this is getting to me.

"Whether that was your goal or not, you had to have known I'd be uncomfortable."

Micah slips a hand to the back of his neck and leaves it there while he thinks. "We never meant to embarrass you or—"

"Bullshit," I interject. "Your intention may not have been to make this about my weight, but you *absolutely* wanted to humiliate me, to show me how much of a puppet I've become for you assholes. You're a lot of things, Micah, but a saint sure as hell isn't one of them."

He stares back and I note that he doesn't deny a single thing

I've just said. His silence goes on too long and the others don't seem to have anything else to say either, so I'm done with this.

"Just... tell me what I'm here to do, so I can do it and go home." I don't have it in me to look them in their eyes.

"You're serving drinks, waiting on the guys hand and foot just like the other girls."

I hear Micah, but don't feel the need for a verbal response, but when I move to walk away, he grips my arm. We're close and I hate that I can't escape him.

"You can be pissed all you want, but don't forget how this arrangement works," he warns through gritted teeth. "You haven't been dismissed, therefore your ass stays exactly where you're standing. Am I clear on that?"

Lava rushes through my veins and I want to explode, want to burn them all alive with my rage.

"I understand, now let my fucking arm go," I hiss, realizing the only power I wield when it comes to them is verbal.

A few seconds lapse, then finally, Micah eases his grip and I snatch away. The hatred I hold for them is tangible, and it couldn't possibly run any deeper. They get off on making me feel weak and broken, but I'm only hardwired to take so much. Just like anyone else.

Something tells me they won't stop until they draw the darkness out of me. And if that happens.... I'm not so sure I can lure her back inside her cage.

CHAPTER 16
STEVIE

I don't want to think right now. All I want to do is figure out what the hell I'm supposed to be doing. The sooner that happens, the sooner I can get the fuck out of here.

The other girls are rushing in and out of the kitchen, so I head that way, too, which means passing through the game room. It's packed wall-to-wall with members of the brotherhood. As discreetly as possible, I breathe deep, feeling their judgmental stares crawling all over me. I stand out here. I haven't had a fucking thigh gap since maybe kindergarten, and I probably couldn't even fit my arm through some of the shit these girls are wearing. So, yeah... I'm not exactly blending in right now.

Especially when my attempt at keeping my eyes trained straight ahead goes left. *Way* left. Clumsy and never missing an opportunity to call unwanted attention to myself, the toe of my sneaker catches the corner of the pool table as I'm passing by. And in a desperate attempt to steady myself, I grab the felt-covered ledge just as a guy's taking his shot.

Of fucking course.

The cue ball bounces off my fingertips, which means I'm now in pain *and* embarrassed.

"Shit!" I clasp the sore hand, waiting for the stinging to stop.

Heat spreads across my cheeks as I observe the faces of the ones whose game I just ruined. Staring, I hold my breath, waiting for one or all to explode in a rage, telling me what a clumsy bitch I am, but that never happens. A few smile, others don't even seem aware of what just took place. In other words, no one's making a big deal of things but me.

I lock eyes with the one who made the shot. Still clutching his pool stick, he points at my hand. "You okay?"

The pain's already starting to subside when I nod. "All good. Just can't seem to walk in a straight line tonight."

He moves toward me while someone else positions himself to take a shot, like nothing ever happened.

"Enzo," he says, introducing himself. His hand lingers in the air. My palm touches his and I realize I've seen him before. He was here during my grocery run—the only one who seemed to notice I wasn't just making a friendly house call.

"Stevie." My palm warms against his and he flashes a smile. "I —I'm sorry about ruining your shot. I was—"

"Don't worry about it," he cuts in. "If anything, you made the game more interesting."

His green eyes stay trained on me, and I realize he still has my hand. He seems to become aware of it at the same time and pulls away.

"I think I've seen you around here before," he says. "A few nights ago. You brought groceries by or something."

My face feels warm again as it sinks in that I hadn't imagined his awareness of me.

"Yeah, I drop in sometimes," is all I say, hoping the look on my face isn't giving away more.

"Then, hopefully we'll be seeing a lot more of each other." His eyes flash down toward my breasts before he meets my gaze again. "Unless... you give me your number, so we're not leaving things to chance."

Enzo barely finishes his sentence when a large hand lands on his shoulder. I follow the length of that tan arm to Vince's cold gaze. It's focused right on me, and I hate how he and the others think they can chastise me with that same, scathing look. Apparently, I'm not allowed to disturb their bros because I'm a peasant or some shit.

Whatever.

My weight shifts to one foot and I can't fight the eye roll that follows as I wait for Vince to speak up.

"Enzo, you heard the rules when you walked in tonight, didn't you?" he asks, still with his eyes locked on mine.

"Yeah, but—"

"You heard the part about pledges not being allowed to even *look* at the girls?"

"I did, but—"

"Then why the *fuck* did I just see your eyes on this one's tits a few seconds ago?" he snaps. "Get back to your game, Enzo. And if I were you... I'd keep my eyes on that fucking pool table and no place else. Got it?"

When Vince finishes, his gaze lifts over my shoulder, and he stares behind me. My head turns, following his line of sight. Ashton and Micah's wicked glares are aimed this way, and there's no missing that they're deadlocked on Enzo.

Without so much as a slight rebuttal, Enzo does as he's told and walks away. He leans over the edge of the pool table to make his shot, only glancing up in my direction once.

I shoot Vince a look. "Well, *that* was incredibly fucked up."

"Watch it, Bird," he says low and calm, clenching his jaw. "If you make a scene, you can guarantee that *we'll* make a scene. Is that really what you want?"

My heart races when he asks that. I think it may be that we both know I can't even begin to imagine what these three '*making a scene*' would look like. But still, I have a hard time walking away from a fight. Including ones I know I can't win.

"Just curious. Do you guys make it a priority to castrate *all* your newcomers or is it only the hot ones?"

"You're trying to fuck my pledges?"

I gasp at the sound of Micah's voice behind me, just as deep as Vince's, but ten times more menacing. More... *threatening.*

I meet Micah's stare and he's still smiling after his question's been asked. Beside him, Ashton's clearly amused as well. He crosses his thick biceps over his chest, and I'm caged in, surrounded by all three. I'm curious who's watching, what they're making of this, but instead my gaze shifts from one set of my tormentors' eyes to the others. From Ashton's ice-blues, to Vince's otherworldly green, to the wells I swear reflect the darkness of Micah's soul.

"Answer the question, Bird," Micah taunts. "Are you trying to fuck Enzo? Because if I'm being honest, I'm not sure how we'd have to punish you for that kind of disobedience."

He steps closer, invading my personal space without a second thought, then reaches for my hair, twirling the length of it in his fingers. Heat creeps up my torso to my neck, and then my face. When he leans in, I stop breathing altogether, but maybe that's the point. He wants to be sure I'm listening, hearing very clearly.

"Don't make me show you my dark side, Bird. Neither of us wants that. Trust me."

He backs away then, and all three put distance between us, eventually turning their backs to walk away. I watch as they blend in with the others, two dropping down into armchairs, one leaning against the wall. Within seconds, they fall into casual conversation with their brothers. Like the things they do and say to me are nothing. I'm appalled, but also... a little curious.

What sort of fucked up things have happened to them that *this* is normal?

Torture. Cruelty. Pain.

My shoulder flies forward when someone bumps into me. "What the hell are *you* doing here?"

When my head whirls around, Dahlia's staring down her nose at me. She looks over my outfit, how it fits my body, and it's no surprise when she frowns with disgust.

"Seriously? You *had* to know this was a poor choice," she scoffs.

I don't give a response. Bitch doesn't deserve one. So, deciding to be the mature one this time, I step around her, only to have her grab my arm. Having been manhandled enough this week, I snatch free and shoot her a look that screams my thoughts loud and clear.

Don't. Fucking. Touch me.

She sighs, rolling her eyes, but doesn't try it again. "What the fuck are you doing here, Stevie? It's pledges only," she points out.

"Yeah, so, maybe I'm pledging." I'm on the move, making my way toward the kitchen, but she's following me now.

I catch her shooting me this snooty-ass look from the corner of my eye. It has me wanting to rip her extensions right out of her scalp.

"Bullshit. And why were you in the study with those three?" she asks next.

I step in line behind the other girls waiting to grab a tray of drinks when a laugh slips out. "Why do you care?"

"Because they haven't made eye contact with a single pledge tonight. Until *your* ass walked through the door."

What Dahlia *isn't* saying is that, from the outside looking in, it seems like the guys are interested in me. Only, in Dahlia's twisted little world, that's one-hundred-percent impossible. Which explains that suspicious look that hasn't left her face since she first walked up.

The girl in line in front of me gets her things and moves on. I grab a tray of drinks and do the same, moving through the room like some disgruntled bar wench. Meanwhile, I feel Dahlia's eyes on me as I walk away without giving an explanation she can digest. Sure, she'd never guess the *true* reason the guys haven't let me out of their sight since I got here, but I'm content to know the suspense is killing her.

Now, if only she'd *actually* die.

The only twist that'd make it even better is if she'd take the three whispering across the room with her.

"Damn, they're really going through this shit, aren't they? I might have to send someone to make a beer run if they don't slow down," Grace says.

We introduced ourselves about an hour ago. She's been filling trays all night, keeping things running smoothly. From what I've gathered, she's the only girl who's already a seasoned member of her sorority rather than an inexperienced pledge like the others. Most of the guys appear to know her and she doesn't seem nearly as nervous as the rest of us.

"I'd go grab some, but I'm on my bike."

"Oh! Well, that's good for the environment, I guess," she says with a quick laugh, wiping her brow with the back of her lacy gloved hand. They even have *her* dressed in this shit.

I decide I've been working hard enough to earn myself a break, so my hip settles against the counter as Grace nods toward the game room. Our view is limited through the kitchen doorway, but we've got a clear line of sight to the pool table.

"Looks like you have an admirer," she points out, bringing my gaze to Enzo where he's perched on a stool near the window. His brow arches when our eyes lock, and the rebel even dares to smile at me, defying the guys' warning.

"He's just being nice."

Grace chuffs another short laugh. "Girl, look at those devious eyes. Nothing *about* him says 'nice'. Granted, he's a sophomore and I don't know much about him, but I think we can both agree he's a hot one."

I don't respond, but definitely don't disagree. I'm unsure of his ethnicity, but his skin is deeply tanned. Naturally so. His hair is dark and a little curly, and twice he's done that thing Micah does. The thing where he runs a hand through it, only for it to be even *more* of a mess as it settles in this annoyingly hot way. He's tall like the guys, earrings in both ears, clean shaven. He's dressed like a fuck-boy in jeans and a well-fitting t-shirt, but yeah, Grace isn't wrong about him being fun to look at.

"So, you gonna go chat him up?" she asks.

I laugh and tear my gaze away from Enzo. "Nah, I'm good. Probably best I don't ruin the illusion, right?"

She shrugs, gulping water from a bottle she's kept beside her tonight. "Suit yourself, but if I were you, I'd already be in the coat room fucking him."

A laugh slips and I push off from the wall, adjusting my corset where it digs into my side a little. Grace is about to set more bottles on my tray when a random from the frat calls out from the doorway.

"Game time," he announces, prompting the girls to sigh with relief as they set down their trays and head toward the game room. Some even pause to slide out of their heels because they weren't smart enough to wear sneakers like me.

Grace walks beside me and we find a wall to prop ourselves against while the other girls seat themselves in spaces within the loose circle the guys formed in the center of the room. Directly in the middle, an empty bottle.

"Shit," Grace sighs. "This night might get interesting after all."

I laugh but there's the slightest discomfort knowing so many eyes are likely on me right now. The guys, Enzo, Dahlia. I ignore them all and watch the last spaces of the circle fill. However, my stomach sinks when another member of the house motions toward Grace and I to join, too.

My eyes flit to the guys before I can stop myself, and I know why. Because I'm on their turf, under their supervision, and I'm expected to obey their rules. Realizing how they've trained me to seek their approval, I get pissed off, like this is day one. Like I don't already know how things work around here.

Vince's brow arches and I know it's a warning, his way of saying what he's too chill to say out loud. Still, I hear him in my head all the same.

'Don't fucking do it, Bird.'

But contrary to popular belief, they don't own me. So, whether it's pride or defiance, I find it impossible to ignore how my gut is twisting and turning, screaming at me to break this hold they have on me. And that's when I do it.

I join the circle.

I can't even look at the guys when I drop down into a tight space between Grace and another girl. There's a huge lump in my throat, but I willfully ignore it. They wanted me here tonight, wanted me to behave like the other girls, so that's what I'll do.

The game begins and that knot slowly begins to ease. I still don't have it in me to look at the guys, but I feel them. Standing across the room like three big bad wolves in a row, waiting for me to fuck up so they can pounce. Grace is up, so she gets to the center of the circle and twirls the bottle with her fingers. It lands on one of her sorority sisters. I gather as much when they squeal and call each other 'bestie' when they get paired to smooch. They plant one on each other, but it's not quite the show the male population in the room hoped for. In other words, there was no tongue action.

Grace's friend gives the bottle a spin and it lands on a dude who's clearly had more than a few beers. I saw him stumbling into the yard to pee in a bush earlier, and as he sits with glazed eyes and his cheeks bright red, I know he's still just as wasted. The girl reluctantly tiptoes over to him and pauses to greet him with a look of disgust. She plays it smart and grabs his jaw in both hands and plants one on his forehead.

"What the hell was that?" one guy says.

"It was a kiss," the girl shoots back, adding a snide, "Deal with it," as she drops back down in her seat.

Drunk dude takes his turn with the bottle, and wouldn't you know it, it lands right on me. My stomach twists at the thought of having to put my lips on his, taste the stale beer on his breath.

He eyes me and a faint grin on his face has me regretting thinking this was a feasible way to get under the guys' skin. If anything, *I'll* be the one upset at the end of the night.

My eyes flash toward them, seeing exactly what I expect— three angry glares boring a hole through me. Micah's jaw ticks and there's the purest form of rage in his eyes I think I've ever seen. I look away, focusing on the drunk one again.

"Make it fucking good this time," someone calls out.

I hold my hand out when the prick comes in hot and fast, thinking he's about to give me everything he's got, but instead, I take a page from the last girl's book. He seems confused when I hold him by the shoulders and place a kiss on his cheek.

The guys in the crowd protest heavily as I make my way back to my seat.

"New rule. No more of this kindergarten shit. No more forehead kisses like we're freaking kissing our grandmothers. Lips and tongue," a guy declares. Of course, nearly all the others back him up because that's what horny frat boys do.

"It's your turn," Grace nudges me, reminding me I have to spin next.

Reaching toward the middle, I twist the cool glass and watch it spin, slowly coming to a stop directly across from me.

On Enzo.

My eyelashes flutter up when I meet his gaze. He's nearly expressionless, but there's a slight smirk on his lips.

"Fate," Grace whispers.

My heart races and I hate that it has nothing to do with the fact that my target is a super-hot guy who I'm pretty sure is into me. No. It's because the three standing directly behind me are so focused that their glares are tangible. I can literally feel them, their energy warning me to find a way out of this or feel their wrath.

But I *want* them angry, seeing red. Because they leave me feeling those things and so much more. Every single day. So, maybe it'll do them some good to feel it too. Sure, there will be a cost for disobeying, but in this moment?

Completely fucking worth it.

My knees press into the rug as I crawl on all fours. Enzo's teeth sink into his lip as he stands and walks to meet me in the middle, crouching down on one knee so we're at eye-level with one another. That knot is in my throat again, doubling in size when heat from his fingers warms the back of my neck. I feel dizzy from breathing so heavily, filled with equal parts fear and excitement.

Moist heat from his mouth meets my lips and he inhales as my eyes fall closed. He grips the back of my neck tighter, and... this is happening. His tongue nudges my bottom lip, but he doesn't force it into my mouth, which honestly makes me *want* him to. And just like that, I'm starting to forget there are other people in the room.

Suddenly, the words, "Fuck this," have Enzo abruptly pulling away.

I peer up just as a massive shadow darkens the space, and I find Ash looming over us. Before I can protest, his hands slide under my arms and he lifts me off the ground with ease. It isn't until he tosses me over his shoulder like a toddler that I'm past the shock and able to speak.

"What the hell do you think you're doing?"

The question slips out before I can stop myself, but Vince's glare reminds me that I'm not to cause a scene. Well, no more of a scene than I already have. I'm livid, but there's also a sense of satisfaction I can't ignore. I take this outburst to mean I've thoroughly gotten under their skin, which was always my best-case scenario.

One of Ash's hands spreads flat against my ass as he carries me. I can only guess what everyone's thinking seeing him and Vince escort me from the game room. I flip my head up from Ash's back just in time to see Micah take Enzo by the front of his t-shirt and slam him against the wall. After that, Ash turns the corner and I'm no longer able to see what unfolds next.

But I can definitely hear it...

Micah telling Enzo what an insubordinate, ungrateful piece of shit he is.

Enzo matching Micah's anger as he tells him that he may be pledging, but he's not anyone's bitch.

There's another loud thud and I assume that's Enzo's back being slammed against the wall again. Then, there's a wild commotion that sounds like furniture being rearranged. A fight.

Because of me.

"Put me down," I growl, pummeling Ash's back with my fists when kicking against him doesn't work. He's solid, like a wall. Nothing I do seems to faze him, which is why he gets me upstairs and into a bedroom with ease. As if I weren't even trying to stop him.

I'm dropped on top of a bed, and now that I'm right-side-up, I recognize the room.

"Micah said they're in the bottom drawer. I'll grab them," Ash says to Vince, but then his eyes dart toward me. "Don't fucking move."

I'm breathing wildly, but other than my chest heaving when I draw in air, I do as I'm told.

"Hold her hands."

Vince grips both my wrists and I'm shocked by the feel of cool steel on my ankles when Ash cuffs me to the bars of Micah's footboard, then slips my sneakers off before tossing them across the room.

"You've gotta be shitting me," I say under my breath, letting a frustrated laugh slip.

Ash tosses two pairs of cuffs up the bed to Vince and, within seconds, I'm completely helpless, even more at their mercy than I already was.

"No fucking way this is happening right now," I groan to myself, staring at the ceiling, wondering how the hell I got here.

"Wrong, Bird. This *is* happening. And it's happening because *your* disobedient ass thought it'd be fun to play with fire tonight," Vince says. "I'm interested to hear how you think that went for you."

I sigh in exasperation. "Whatever. So, what now? Am I gonna

be forced to lie here and listen to a lecture? Are you going to keep me here until morning, then make me fix you assholes breakfast? Or do you have some *other* chauvinistic bullshit in mind?"

I expect some sort of a smart-ass comeback from one of them, but when my eyes flash toward Vince, there isn't much of an expression on his face. Instead, he looks away and silently drops down into the chair at Micah's desk, slowly spinning while he stares at the ceiling. He eventually responds, but the vagueness only sets my nerves on edge, all while being just cryptic enough to also spur fear.

"Guess you'll just have to wait and see what prize you've earned yourself this time, Bird."

His eyes drift closed as a faint smile touches his lips.

Whatever they have in mind, it'll be wicked as usual.

I can feel it.

F irst, there are footsteps coming from somewhere down the long, dark hallway. Then, water rushes from a faucet. Neither Vince nor Ash say a word while I lie there, dying a slow death brought on by suspense and fear.

The footsteps are coming this way again and I feel exposed. Even more than I did before. Micah's massive frame darkens the doorway and I'm shaken by the sight of him. His chest, face, and hair are damp. A small cut on his top lip means Enzo went down with a fight, but when I take note of the bloody shirt Micah's just tossed into the hamper, a clearer picture begins to unfold.

As if he realizes I've just made the connection, he flashes a brief look toward me while emptying the pockets of his jeans at his dresser. Then, I lose his attention again when he turns to close his bedroom door. I'm filled with panic a moment later when he locks it, sealing me inside with the three of them.

If I could take back what I did downstairs, I would. In a heartbeat. Not only because of my current predicament, but because someone else paid the price for me not listening.

"He didn't deserve it."

The sound of my voice stops Micah mid-stride. He'd made it halfway to the bed, but now he's just staring.

"It was a fucking game and he didn't know about our...

118

arrangement," I say, feeling hatred flowing freely as I utter that word.

Micah's head cocks to one side and his eyes move down the length of my body when he speaks.

"Thing is, you don't get to pick and choose how this all plays out. When you fuck up, you don't get to define the blast radius. Whatever or whoever is in our way... all becomes collateral damage."

My eyes sting but not with tears this time. With rage.

"So that's it?" I ask. "Enzo's your pledge, someone who had potential to be a future member of your brotherhood, and now you're just done with him because of some bullshit game?"

Micah's gaze narrows. "Done with him?"

I study his expression, try to read him. "I... heard you two fighting down there. I assumed he'd be disqualified after that."

Before another word leaves his mouth, Micah shoots Vince and Ash a look. It's filled with annoyance, like he'd rather not be having this conversation, but then his eyes land on me again.

"The blood isn't Enzo's," he reveals.

"It's yours?"

Micah shakes his head. "No. Apparently, you aren't the only one with a soft spot for Enzo."

The look he shoots me cuts like a dagger, and I can't help but squirm when he finally takes his focus off me.

"Enzo and I were in the middle of sorting things out when some *other* asshole thought it wise to intervene. He sucker-punched me, then I shut that shit down. Which brings me to my next point," he says, meeting Vince's gaze. "We're officially one pledge short."

I'm confused but the others don't seem to be. Enzo is the one who crossed him, but he kept him around instead of the other guy? I won't pretend to understand the dynamic around here, but their sense of loyalty and brotherhood is beyond my comprehension.

But as long as Enzo didn't miss out on his opportunity to be a Savage because of me, I'm good with that.

I'm suddenly the center of attention again and I can't take my

119

eyes off Micah. He's a little too close. And that look in his eyes is a little too wild.

"Hit the light," he says.

Ash reaches toward the lamp on the nightstand. The next second, darkness. The bed dips beneath Micah's weight when he sits to my right, but I don't see or feel him.

My heart races.

A girl with monsters like these three, menacing souls who haunt every dark corner of her life, should always keep eyes on them.

Always.

The bed dips again when Ash drops down to my left. A shadow and movement near the headboard has to be Vince. They have me surrounded again.

"Vince? Ash? I'm curious to hear what you two thought about tonight."

They both mull over Micah's question for a bit, then it's Ash who speaks first. "No doubt about it. Our rules were blatantly ignored. Like none of the shit we said even registered in this pretty little head of hers."

His light caress grazes my cheek, then moves into my hair where it spreads over the pillow.

"Seeing as how I issued an additional warning," Vince says, "Yeah, I gotta admit. I'm feeling a bit disrespected."

I roll my eyes at the dramatic spiels, which means I'm grateful they can't see my expression at the moment.

"Well, you heard it for yourself, Bird. We feel disrespected. So, now I have to ask... Was it worth it?"

I sigh in exasperation. "Was *what* worth it? I'm a little disoriented right now. Being handcuffed to a bed against my will tends to have that effect on me."

I hear Micah laugh to himself and it's always such a dreadful sound.

"I'm asking if putting your fucking mouth on Enzo—someone we expressly told you not to wag your ass in front of—was worth the punishment," he clarifies. "Because we both know there's always a punishment."

Air rushes into my nostrils and the blinds above my head splash just enough moonlight across my chest that I'm sure the guys see the rapid movement.

My eyes flash toward Vince when he speaks. "Would you have fucked him tonight? If we hadn't been there to stop you?"

He has no idea what he's asking, seeing as how I've never fucked *anyone*. Let alone some stranger I just met tonight. I've done other things, yeah, but not... that.

"What? No!" I protest. "I've already told you it was just a game. I wasn't even looking at him in that way."

The sight of my breasts heaving when I finish answering makes my response hard to believe, I'm sure.

"Hmm..."

The disapproving sound came from Micah, and I scramble to tighten up my story.

"He was just being nice," I reason.

"Bullshit." I peer up at Vince as he stares down on me from his post near the headboard.

"Then why ask questions if you're not going to believe a single word I say anyway?"

"Because we all saw the way he looked at you," Micah reasons, leaning up to my ear to add, "And we sure as *shit* saw the way you looked at *him*."

The vibration of my pulse is unnerving, making it feel as though there's electricity racing through my body.

"Know what I think?" he asks. "That kiss got to you. It made your pussy so wet you've got a fucking river between your legs right now."

"You're wrong. It was all just friendly." A quivering breath leaves me, and my eyes are wide. I can only make out his silhouette, but he's definitely staring right into me while I speak. "Besides, those weren't the rules."

I make out the outline of Micah's damp curls when his head tilts curiously to one side. He doesn't speak, so I jump right into explaining.

"The rules weren't about my feelings or how my body responds to someone. No one can control that. Not even you," I

121

point out. "The rules said I couldn't date, couldn't get involved with anyone. Not that I couldn't have natural human responses."

"So, are you confessing to having a *'natural human response'* when Enzo kissed you?"

I have every intention of giving him a suitable answer, but instead, I lie there. Completely silent.

"And the truth comes out," Vince croons, the deep rumble of his voice causing goosebumps to prickle my skin.

"And so it does," Micah adds. "But now, I'm honestly a little curious. Just how big an impression did our friend Enzo make on our little bird tonight?"

His shoulders move with labored breaths while darkness flows through his thoughts. I'm pretty sure those are the only kinds of thoughts he has. I watch him like a hawk when he lifts his hand, still and silent as he smooths his fingertip across the waistband of my panties. My stomach quivers and I'm frozen, staring down my body when he slides that same finger down the seam connecting two very thin pieces of silk between my thighs.

My pussy responds to his touch by sending a current of carnal energy pulsing through my entire body. The ripple of pleasure makes me quake all over and I wish like hell I could control it. It's not a reaction he deserves.

He smooths his way down the silk again, this time being bold enough to lightly press harder, teasing my clit through the delicate fabric.

A moan leaves my mouth and, immediately, I wish I could take it back. Again, they don't deserve to draw even an ounce of pleasure from me, but my body has this way of betraying me when it comes to them. Making me do, think, and feel things I shouldn't.

Like now, as Micah pulls the silk away from my skin, I don't protest, knowing I should. His hand slips into the side of my panties and he smooths his palm over my bare skin, then gently squeezes the lips of my pussy, familiarizing himself with my body. Breathing hard and fast, he appears to be of two minds, at war with himself. He takes his time and it's enough that I have a chance to start thinking clearly again. So, I open my mouth to tell him this ends here, to tell him he's not allowed to touch me, but before the words leave my mouth, the length of two warm fingers slowly slip inside me.

His breathing deepens as the sound of my sticky wetness fills the room.

"Tsk tsk, Little Bird. Looks like you told a lie." His voice low and raspy as his fingers move in and out. "And one kiss from him did this to you?" he asks.

This question is somehow the least hostile he's asked tonight. If I'm not mistaken, he sounds more curious than anything.

"I—it wasn't like that. I—"

I fall silent, deciding I'd rather not speak while unable to form coherent sentences. Plus, being silent means getting to keep my secrets.

"Tell us why you're so wet, Bird," he croons.

My eyes are locked on him, watching like a woman obsessed as he angles his palm toward the ceiling and plunges his middle and forefinger deeper inside me. Now that my vision has adjusted to the darkness, I can see the detail of his tatted forearm, the roadmap of thick veins beneath his skin, the slight twitches of muscles and tendons that flex with every motion. His wrist twists and his fingers move in a slow circle within my core.

Another quiet moan leaves me, and I hear soft laughter from Micah as the others watch.

"Damn, you like that shit?" he rasps. "Say it. Tell me you like when we touch you."

The request has a spark of defiance igniting within me. The answer is annoyingly obvious, but I can't bring myself to say it.

"Do you wish it was him?" Micah asks next.

Before I can even think, my head shakes and the word, "No," falls from my lips.

"Mmm...," is his thoughtful reply. "Then why... are you so... fucking wet for him?"

"I'm—"

I breathe through the swell of pleasure that has me trying to clamp my legs together, but the restraints on my ankles prevent it.

"What are you trying to tell us?"

Vince's lips are at my ear, his warm breath moving over my

123

skin as the sound of him invites a memory to swim into my head. A memory of how much I enjoyed being touched by all three at the same time just this morning. Now, every inch of me wants that again.

Desperately.

Micah's fingers stir inside me more and my eyes roll back. "Say it. Tell us why you're so fucking wet."

I squirm on his comforter and toss my head to the side, catching his scent on his pillow. It has me panting like I'll die if I can't have what I want tonight.

All three of them.

"Because... I like when you watch me," I admit. "I liked knowing I had your undivided attention while he kissed me."

Micah's hand falls still, but he doesn't pull away. No one speaks and the pause in action gives me just enough time to think too deeply and begin shutting down. Maybe from shame, or embarrassment, or... hell if I know, but I'm slipping out of the moment. The room goes completely dark again when I squeeze my eyes shut.

"I know how that makes me sound. Like some crazy bitch who likes being finger-fucked and felt up by the same assholes trying to ruin her, but... shit. I guess that's where I am. Completely twisted and fucked up."

Words fail me and I feel pathetic. And then, when Micah pulls away, that feeling only worsens. An echo of my father's insults creep in just to make me feel even *more* like shit, and it works like a charm. He's in my head, clear as day, telling me how boys think girls like me are easy, desperate. I can't help but wonder if that's how *these three* see me. As some overweight slut who'll take what she can get from whoever will give it to her.

A tear trails down my cheek and into my hair and the night's ruined.

God, listen to me. I'm in a room with a trio of sick fucks who chained me to the bed, and yet, some corrupt part of my brain only *now* felt the night had been ruined.

"There is so much wrong with me."

The sound of my voice is startling because I only meant to *think* those words, but they somehow escaped for the guys to hear.

"Please, just… let me go."

I sound small and weak, which seems fitting.

"You're not going anywhere," Ash asserts, and I feel rage seeping into my veins.

Frustrated, I pull against the cuffs, making them scrape the metal post of the headboard as I flail wildly.

"Why the hell are you doing this to me?" When my limbs go limp, I've clearly lost what little fight I still had in me.

Maybe this is what they wanted. Their goal has been to leave me a shell of the person I was before they found me that night, so maybe I've reached that point.

Rock bottom.

I give up completely and decide to just lie here until they see fit to let me go. With the first floor still full and lively, it's not like anyone would hear me call out for help. As if the brotherhood would cross these three anyway.

Basically, they've won.

I give.

This thought has barely had time to sink in when a firm hand grips my chin, then a set of hot, damp lips press to mine. Vince is a man of few words, but his kiss tells me so much. That he's deep and complex beyond what anyone can see. That he knows there's an art to making someone feel who you are through touch. That he has a gift for knowing what I need. Like now, when he slowly opens his mouth, drags his tongue over mine, like my taste is all he's ever wanted or needed.

Something dawns on me, an explanation for how the lines between us are so harsh at times, then blurred the next second. Whatever's broken in me is addicted to whatever is broken in them, making me feel just a little more whole when I'm drunk on lust.

Ashton undoes the cuffs on my hands, but leaves my feet bound to the footboard. A soft touch to my inner thigh startles me, but Micah's fingers sinking deep into my core relaxes me quickly. My arm snakes around Vince's neck, pulling him closer. He kneels into the mattress, bracing himself against the headboard with one hand while a rough squeeze to my breast tells me where his other has gone.

The chill of Ashton's rings on my thigh enlivens my skin when he lifts it, placing his forearm beneath me. He positions me in just the right way that I'm open for Micah, whose pace quickens as he drills his fingers in deeper.

"Fuck, yes," I whisper against Vince's soft lips as Ashton's hand slinks across my corset. It only lingers there for a few seconds before he pushes his way into my panties, too, joining Micah. While one fills me with the heat of his long, hot fingers, the other rubs my slippery, swollen clit, and I moan into Vince's mouth.

My hands are unnervingly idle and I need to feel something. Skin. Muscle. Heat.

I reach for Ashton and realize he removed his shirt without me noticing. I'm elated at the feel of my palm being met with warm flesh instead of fabric. I envision his ink, the colorful pictures that add to him being a work of art, but... there's something else. Something I wouldn't have known just looking at him. Irregular patches of skin raise questions in my head. Some sections are pitted and rough, only to move a few inches to find a smooth plane bordered by puffy ridges. My first thought is that he's been injured during hockey over the years, but not like this. There are too many tiny wounds.

Too many scars with stories attached that I'll likely never hear.

Ashton's fingers go still and it's then that I realize he knows what I'm doing—studying him, wondering things I shouldn't be wondering. So, I push my fingers into his hair instead, gripping it lightly to distract him. Only then does he touch me like he'd done before, making my pussy weep with need.

Reaching to my right, my hand lands on Vince's waist and he's solid, covered in smooth, taught skin that begs to be touched. I manage to undo his belt, button, and zipper with one hand, and he doesn't object when I push inside his jeans. Hot steel fills my hand when I explore the length of his cock down his thigh, gripping him through his boxer briefs. He moans in response to my touch, sending one hell of a chill racing down my spine, and my back arches toward the ceiling.

Ashton squeezes my thigh, bracing it against his torso. If I didn't know any better, I'd say there's something other than hatred emanating from their touches. Something else in those long caresses that soothes pain no one sees. Something that dispels the darkness.

Even if only for a little while.

"Damn. You're so fucking close, Bird," Micah says, and this is the first time their nickname for me feels less like an insult and more like a term of endearment.

I must be high, though, because there's no chance they'd ever mean it any other way.

Still, he isn't wrong. I *am* so fucking close.

Vince's hand pushes upward, leaving my nipple hard enough to cut glass when his hand settles around my throat instead. Soft and easy at first, but his grip slowly tightens around my airway. I'm fully aware of this being a great time to be scared shitless, but I don't feel fear. Only turned on and craving more.

"Tighter," I whisper against his lips.

I'm relieved when he doesn't hesitate even a little, but instead meets my request, gripping harder.

"Like that?" he whispers into my mouth.

I nod and his tongue plunges between my lips. I squeeze him inside his jeans and his dick swells in my hand. It seems that, as much as I like to receive a little pain with my pleasure, he likes *giving* a little pain.

Ash's fingertips dig into my thigh when I tense, feeling that addictively sweet throb pulse in my clit.

"Don't stop. Right there," I plead as the sensation spreads all over me. Vince somehow senses that I want him to squeeze harder, then the next second, I'm a screaming, quaking mess on Micah's mattress. The three, collectively, make me come so hard the bed is completely soaked beneath me.

Ashton traces small circles on my inner thigh while I relax, and it feels... intimate. Almost as intimate as Vince's kiss lingering with me until I've fully settled down, and Micah's hand casually resting on top of my foot.

Damn, I swear if these three weren't psychos, I'm woman enough to admit I'd be addicted to everything about them.

My pulse slows and I feel like I could drift off, which has me dreading the long bike ride home.

The guys stand and I can't tear my eyes away from them. When my gaze leaves one, it settles on the other, admiring what I can make out of their features with the light off. My hands are free and uncuffed, so I sit up and rest on the heels of my palms. Beside me, Vince zips his pants and I note that he's still hard as a brick, showing through his jeans. Under different circumstances, I wouldn't expect them to leave without a release, but our situation isn't exactly typical.

Actually, it's anything but that.

Ashton slips on his t-shirt and the room lights up a bit when he checks his phone.

"What time is it?" I ask.

"Almost midnight."

I have class in the morning, then work after that. I wiggle my ankles and the cuffs rattle. "Does someone mind undoing these? I should probably get going."

The guys stop what they're doing and share a look. "You're staying until the party ends."

There's tension in my brow when confusion sets in. "What do you mean? I thought—"

"You thought we'd make you come, then send you home with a smile on your face," Ash teases. "That it?"

I don't speak, feeling the familiar sting of betrayal. Just like when I allowed them to push the boundaries in the supply closet on campus.

I fight in vain when the cuffs are placed on my wrists again.

"What the fuck?"

They watch me writhe and thrash around on the bed, getting absolutely nowhere.

"Everyone should be leaving within the next couple hours. When that happens, we'll release you."

"Two hours? What the hell am I supposed to do until then?"

Vince shoves both hands in his pockets, then shrugs. "I'm sure you could probably use a nap after coming so hard. Get some sleep."

Not only did I get carried out of the game room like a toddler, now I'm being put to bed like one.

"Fuck you. *All* of you," I growl, but they only laugh at my rage.

"In due time, Bird. In due time."

I'm too pissed to even wonder which of them has just spoken, but I'm determined to kill whatever this physical hold is they have over me.

They don't get to run my life *and* have full access to my body, too.

No fucking way.

Not even a shower could make me feel clean. Every time I close my eyes, I see or feel them.

Everywhere.

This twisted journey began with me content, sitting on my high horse, feeling all righteous and shit. In my head, *they* were the sick ones. Only, the passage of time seems to prove me wrong. Yes, the guys are the definition of depraved, but... maybe I'm no better.

Just the thought of them makes me more aware of my nakedness beneath the towel. I tried rinsing my sins down the drain, but they linger, wicked images of my body being used in ways I should never allow. And now, I'm wet all over again just thinking about it.

I reach beside me on the bed when a text comes through. Seeing Ash's name has me both frustrated and anxious.

Ash: I still have you on my fingers, and your scent might just be my new obsession. It's... fucking addictive.

My stupid heart races as I envision him, lying in the dark, inhaling traces of me left behind on his skin. But before I get too carried away with *that* thought, another rushes in. It's of how once he and the others had their way with me, I was left tied to Micah's bed for hours. All of a sudden, his flattery feels a bit less substantial.

Stevie: Go fuck yourself.

Ash: Is this how you respond to compliments?

Stevie: No, this is how I respond to assholes.

I picture him again. This time he's smiling, knowing I'm annoyed.

Ash: You know, I think I'm starting to learn what makes you tick.

I see his text but make him wait. The basement always has a slight chill, so I slip out of my towel and into the plaid flannels and t-shirt draped over my footboard. Once I'm done, I sprawl out on the mattress again.

Stevie: How have I lived these twenty years without having the great Ashton Blaine mansplain the innerworkings of my mind. So, please, by all means, tell me what you think makes me tick.

He takes no time at all responding.

Ash: ...Us. WE make you fucking tick.

I stare at my phone for what feels like an eternity, amazed by the sheer audacity, but it fades. It fades because... he isn't wrong. A fact I will *never* admit to out loud.

Stevie: I'm convinced the only thing you're obsessed with is yourself.

Ash: Trust me, there's only one thing on my mind right now.

I breathe deeply, wondering if he means what I *think* he means. Drawing both feet beneath the blanket to warm them, I type out a response, but hesitate to send it.

Stevie: Like what?

Again, he doesn't hold back. Not even a little.

Ash: Fucking you.

I smirk because this sickness of theirs is contagious. It's clearly taken a hold of me and I'm a lost cause.

Stevie: I'm confused. You three have made my life a living hell, so which is it? Do you want to bring me pain or pleasure? It can't be both.

Ash: You sure about that?

I close my eyes but don't open them right away, remembering the feel of his hands around my throat, the burn of his fingernails digging into my arm, being handled roughly when he tossed me over his shoulder tonight.

Each time, there was pain, but the end result was me getting wet for them.

Stevie: It's late. I should go.

Ash: Just admit that you're turned on and don't know how to process that shit.

Again, I hear his dark, quiet laughter in my head.

Stevie: Actually, I have class in the morning, so I should've been in bed hours ago. Besides, I'm sure there's some other girl who'd love to have her phone blown up by you tonight.

Ash: None as interesting as you.

Heat flashes to my face and I'm positive I'm red now.

Stevie: As flattering as that is, I have to go.

Ash: Fine, but only if you admit something first.

I sigh and let my back fall against the headboard.

Stevie: I'm listening.

Ash: Tell me you enjoyed tonight, enjoyed what we did to you.

A breath hitches in my throat and it's like I'm back there, back in Micah's bed while his fingers plunge into my pussy, while Ashton teases my clit, while Vince kisses me with the heat of a million suns.

I consider lying, but I wouldn't be fooling either of us.

Stevie: Yes.

At first, I think he's just taking his precious time responding, then I realize that's just the end of the conversation. I answered his question, now he's done. Typical of him to get what he wants and then bail.

I set my phone aside, and no sooner than I do, it sounds off again. It's not a text this time, but my favorite livestream coming through in the clutch. I'm definitely spent from my encounter with the guys, but I'll still tune in.

Only to be supportive, of course.

Flipping open my laptop, I log in and see nothing but an empty chair, which means the show hasn't started. I grab my vibrator from the nightstand just in case I change my mind, then hop up to brush my teeth. There's no rush because he always gives his subscribers time to get settled. So, I take my time, cleaning a glob of toothpaste out of the sink, and then hit the lights.

I step back into my room, but at the realization that I'm no longer alone, I nearly jump out of my skin. At first, I'm unsure which emotion I'm feeling more strongly, anger or embarrassment. Standing beside my bed, staring at the screen of my laptop with disbelief in her eyes, and a huge grin on her face, is the bitch I frequently fantasize about killing—Dahlia.

Time moves in slow motion as I take it all in, her seeing my setup—vibrator and all. I've unwittingly just given her even more ammunition to use in the undeclared war between us.

"Are you fucking kidding me? Is this the kind of pathetic shit you sit down here doing all day?" She belts a wicked laugh and I'm fuming.

"What the fuck are you doing down here?" I rush toward the laptop, but by the time I slam it shut, she's already seen enough.

A stranger seated in a dark room, undoing the drawstring of his sweats. Any idiot can draw a conclusion on what happens next. Even *this* idiot, I guess.

"And did I read that correctly? You're a paid subscriber?" she asks, still pointing at the laptop. "I mean, I know you're not exactly anyone's fantasy, but there's gotta be *someone* out there who'd get you off for free. I mean... right?"

As she cackles, I realize she had time to read the welcome message that scrolls across the screen for contributors. There's still a smirk on her face as she stares at me, thinking thoughts I wish weren't so transparent. Only, I've heard it all before, in my father's voice no less.

Like him, she's thinking I'm desperate.

"So, let me get this straight. You can pay to watch some guy jerk off—a guy who'd *never* actually have anything to do with you in real life—but you haven't paid rent?" she asks with a scoff. "Real fucking classy."

My blood runs hot, turning my body into a furnace. "Get the hell out of my room!"

I'm tempted to shove her toward the steps but the last time I let someone push my buttons and I lost my temper, things didn't end well.

"Relax," she says, rolling her eyes like *I'm* the problematic one. "I only popped in to chat about earlier. First, there was the thing with those three guys cornering you in the study, then they went batshit crazy during spin the bottle. Honestly, believe it or not, I'm just making sure everything's cool," she says, pretending to care.

"Are you fucking kidding me?" I scoff, having a hard time believing my ears. "You've been up my ass since I moved in, and *now* you're concerned about me. Please. Save your B.S. for someone else."

"Our beef doesn't trump girl code," she argues. "We have to look out for each other. Which is why I'm wondering how you know them. Are you maybe related in some way?"

Un-fucking-believable.

I'm not even sure where to *begin* unpacking her bullshit. Not only is she borderline obsessed with whatever my connection is to the guys, but now I'm understanding that *this* is how she's rationalized it. Because, God forbid, there be any sort of attraction on their part toward me.

I recall how my tour guide, Ellen, reacted when we spotted them near the Athletic Building this summer. It was my first encounter with Bradwyn U's golden boys of hockey, but Ellen was beyond shaken. In fact, she could hardly even look their way for fear of turning into a pillar of salt or some shit. If that's the case, if *all* the girls on campus are like that in their presence, I'm starting to understand Dahlia's obsession. She wants to sink her claws into one of them.

Or maybe *all* of them.

My stomach turns at the thought of it, and it jars me out of my rage. All because what I'm feeling more powerfully now is... jealousy.

My fists clench and it's on the tip of my tongue to tell Dahlia about how my night *really* went. How their hands and mouths were all over me, but then I remember this isn't something to brag about. Being perceived as someone's toy, their *property*, is more humiliating than anything.

Still, I'm tempted. Just to wipe that smug look off her face.

"Get the fuck out, Dahlia! Before I lose my shit," I hiss through gritted teeth. It's all I can do to keep from waking the entire house.

When I snap, she falls silent, but she's clearly frustrated, wanting answers. But what the fuck did she expect? Coming down here uninvited, invading my space. All because it's *killing* her not knowing what my business is with Ash, Vince, and Micah.

With a sigh and another eye roll, she finally starts toward the stairs, but when she reaches the top, she turns to speak again.

"A little word of advice—the next time you're planning to practice self-love, lock the fucking door like the rest of us."

She barely finishes her statement and I race up the staircase and slam the door shut, clicking the deadbolt right after. Had I done so in the first place, had I not still been thinking about the guys... my night might not have gone from bad to worse.

CHAPTER 20
VINCE

We've been through some shit, we've seen some shit, and we've done some shit, so we can usually shake things off pretty quickly.

But not this.

Not her.

It's been four days of no contact, four days of not so much as saying Bird's name, and she's still stuck in our heads. The others haven't admitted it out loud, but one of the curses of knowing Ash and Micah like we're blood means there's no hiding from each other.

Not even in our own thoughts.

Sweat pours down my face and I lower the weights to the mat and glance up at my reflection in the mirror, still feeling like I'm someone else. The demons from my past are familiar and I've learned to live with them, because they're all I've ever known. But I'm not a fan of change. What happened the other night was different. Me *allowing* it was different.

And now my head's fucked up because of it.

My eyes flit toward Micah when I spot him in the mirror, moving across the weight room with his stare locked on a target. Following his gaze, I realize what that target is. Or rather *who* that target is.

Enzo.

As if our radar is dialed in to the same frequency, Ash follows through with his last chin-up, then his feet drop down to the mat. His brow arches as he observes Micah, then I'm not surprised when his feet start in that direction just as I stand. We move toward Micah in sync, both still a little winded from our workouts, but I'm guessing we sense the same thing.

Trouble.

Loud music blasts from the speakers minimizing the sound of metal on metal as the rest of the team put in their time on the equipment. There don't seem to be eyes on us as Ash and I meet up with Micah in the aisleway, all moving in the same direction now. No clue what Micah's endgame is, but I *do* know he's still not over the run-in with Enzo the other night. The blatant disregard for the expressed rules and having him go rogue again didn't go unnoticed.

And no one is more pissed about that than Micah.

Fletcher spots us coming toward him, and then locks eyes with Micah. One nod toward the other side of the room has Fletcher abandoning his post where he stood spotting Enzo, leaving him with the barbell suspended in midair.

"Dude, where the hell are you going?"

Fletcher doesn't even look back when Enzo calls out as he watches his safety net casually walk off. He's breathing wildly, puffing his cheeks as he guides the barbell back toward the rack, but Micah redirects him, slowly lowering the bar down to Enzo's chest. Then, a flash of panic fills his eyes as he realizes who his new spotter is.

Outwardly, I don't react to seeing Micah lean over Enzo, adding his own weight to the bar currently crushing our pledge's chest. But on the inside, I'm always alert and ready to intervene if my brother goes too far. He doesn't always seem to have access to his off-switch, so Ashton and I sometimes have to *become* his off-switch.

Maybe this is one of those times.

"Good to see you again, Enzo," Micah says calmly. Meanwhile, Enzo's pulse thunders at the base of his throat—

currently the only visible sign that he's worried how this might turn out. Even his expression has gone blank.

"What the fuck do you want?"

"That doesn't sound like much of a greeting," Micah teases. "It's almost like... *you're* the one in charge and *I'm* the one who disrespected *you*."

Enzo rolls his eyes, trying to readjust himself on the bench, but the more he moves, the more Micah leans in, adding to the three-hundred pounds already on the barbell.

"What the fuck do you want me to say?" Enzo yells out. "That I'm sorry I made a move on a girl I didn't realize you'd get in your fucking feelings about? Then you have it, my sincerest apology."

A laugh leaves Micah and he glances up at Ash and me. "Damn! This guy talks a lot of shit for someone who's life I could end right now, doesn't he?"

Neither Ash nor I respond or change expressions, because it's starting to feel like one of those moments where we need to intervene and save Micah from himself. There were times in the past—one in particular—that I wish I'd had the balls to step in sooner. Now, because I know how quickly things can go bad, I no longer hesitate. He's got mere seconds to pull his shit together.

Micah shifts his gaze back toward Enzo.

"Is that what you think? That this is about some bitch?" he asks. "No, this is about you needing constant reminders that you aren't shit around here. I don't know what it was like wherever you transferred in from, but on *this* campus, you're a fucking cockroach. And I promise, if you keep stepping out of line, not only will you find your ass on the outside of this brotherhood looking in, but we will fucking destroy you."

The sound of Enzo wheezing as his hands tighten around the bar has me uncrossing my arms to lift it from his chest, but before I can even touch it, Micah lets up. His stare lingers on Enzo as he struggles to tip the weight of the bar to one side. It slams the ground with a thud and a handful of guys who'd been watching nearby rush over to help. Micah rubs his nose as pure, undiluted rage flows through his veins. He storms toward the locker room, slams the double doors open with both hands, and we're right behind him. The sound echoes on the other side, ricocheting off the tiled walls and floors, the metal lockers. Breathing wildly, he drops down onto the first bench he comes to, and I see it all over him.

The frustration of having Enzo call it like he saw it.

Having Enzo call it *right*.

Bird *is* getting in our heads. Like no other girl has done before. Now, it's starting to affect our business within the brotherhood. If we'd kept our cool when Bird broke the rules, if we'd dealt with it later instead of carrying her off to discipline her like cavemen, none of this would've happened.

But... fuck. Some discipline that was—kissing her, finger-fucking her until she came.

None of this was what we had planned, but here we are. Angry and avoiding the source of our frustration. The girl we started out only wanting to break, who's now breaking *us*.

"Enough of this shit."

Ash and I watch as Micah goes to his locker and works the combination. The first thing he reaches for when he gets it open is his phone. He drops back down to the bench and dials. It isn't until he puts the call on speaker and lowers it to the bench that we're able to see who he's called.

Leo Whitlock—the guy with the most solid motive for crossing us. The guy who'd most likely convince a girl to trespass in our house.

There's lots of chatter in the background when he picks up, which means he'll be especially dickish since he has an audience.

"Always good to hear from you, Locke. How can I be of service?"

Micah's nostrils flare when Whitlock addresses him like they're old friends. When, in actuality, they've hated each other since battling on the ice in high school.

"Cut the shit, Leo. Tell me what your deal is with Stevie. What info do you want reported back, and what's it costing you in return?"

There's anger in Micah's tone, of course, but there's something else. He's grasping at straws, thinking Stevie and Leo are in on something together. Initially, it was the only thing that made sense, but there's been no proof. Which makes it feel like Micah's desperate, looking for a way to deepen his hate for her. Possibly to mask that she gets to him. No, it's not love, or even *like* for that matter, but she does have this way of making us deviate from our plan. Even if the deviations are only ever slight.

Leo laughs and Micah's face reddens a little more. "Who the fuck is Stevie and why would I know something about him?"

My brow tenses hearing that, hearing Leo refer to Stevie as *him*. It's entirely possible he's just fucking with us, but the response was too abrupt, too quick for him to have had time to think on it. Which has me reconsidering again. Maybe we *have* been wrong about Stevie's connection to Whitlock all this time.

Micah goes quiet and I'm guessing he's had the same thought. Then, Ash shoots me a look before we both refocus on the call.

"You're barking up the wrong tree, Locke. And judging by your silence, I'm guessing you just realized that," Leo sighs.

"Let me find out you're behind this shit, and I swear to you—"

"Damn!" Leo cuts in. "What'd this guy do to get under your skin? Here I was thinking I'm the only one who can piss you off this thoroughly, but it sounds like I should be taking notes."

"Fuck you," Micah growls, ending the call.

While it should maybe give us at least a mild sense of relief to know Stevie isn't Leo's puppet, it only raises more questions. Like, why the fuck was she going through our shit that night? And what's so damn important that she risked getting caught, considering she seems to have some sort of legal shit hanging over her head?

I don't like unpredictable situations. And if there's one thing I can say for sure about this girl, it's that she's proving to be one hell of a wildcard.

CHAPTER 21
STEVIE

So, this is happening, I guess. Here I was, enjoying a little peace and quiet since I haven't heard from the guys in a few days, then Mom called. I promised I'd make it to the next dinner and, of course, she's holding me to that.

Standing outside Rob's door, I'm having some pretty major second-thoughts. It would've been easy to say no, easy to pretend I had too much studying to do, but the moment's passed and I'm locked in now.

"Uh oh! You've got a hair that's gone rogue," Mom says, reaching to brush a strand from my cheek. I let her, but I'm definitely annoyed. Just during the car ride over she told me my lipstick's too red and asked if I was behind on laundry because I chose to wear a tank top tonight.

Rob's steps approach from the other side of the threshold. I let out a sigh at the thought of there still being hours of this left to endure. Mom made me promise to be on my best behavior, so I'm going to give it a shot. However, I can only be in Tate's presence for so long before feeling like I'll lose my shit.

Guess we'll see what happens.

The door of Rob's newly updated craftsman swings open, and I force a smile when he greets me and Mom with hugs.

"Come in, come in!" he beckons, stepping aside so we can enter.

I look around while Mom talks his ear off about God knows what. It's my first time visiting, so I'm taking it all in. The smell of varnish and fresh paint are present but faint enough that it's not bothersome. I slip my sneakers off and feel the smoothness of the shiny wood floors beneath my socks.

Mom's spent a lot of time here lately, helping Rob renovate. She plans to move in after the wedding, so it makes sense that she'd want to make it feel like it's her space, too. But if I'm honest, the idea of her selling our old place bugs me a bit. I mean, it's hard for me to even step foot inside the *foyer*, but it isn't lost on me that our memories are there. Memories that will all be left behind soon.

The good.

The bad.

Rob's light touch to my shoulder has the thoughts fading when I fake another smile.

"So, what do you think of the place?" he asks, gesturing around the large foyer where nearly the entire first floor is visible.

"Looks great!"

He smiles and nods in agreement. "I wish you'd seen what it looked like before, but your mom's warmed it up quite a bit in here. I swear, I've never owned so many rugs and throw pillows in my life. And now, thanks to her, I know what a duvet is."

Rob squeezes Mom with a side hug and I fight the feeling that bubbles inside me. I have nothing against seeing her happy, seeing her move on, but I always have this sense of her joy being unfair or imbalanced.

She allowed so much to slide, allowed so many things to happen that she could've stopped. Sometimes the thought crosses my mind that... maybe she *doesn't* deserve to move on so easily.

"Well, the pizza's almost done in the oven, and the movie's ready to go in the living room. Tate should be pulling up any minute," Rob adds, and I suppress an eye roll.

"Fun."

Neither he nor mom seem to catch the sarcasm, and I'm left to find my way to the living room as they disappear in the kitchen.

Dropping down onto a large sectional, I prop my heels on the coffee table for about two seconds before remembering this isn't my house. I lower my feet to the floor again as I scan the room, looking at the many photos that line the walls. Most are of Tate, from hockey events over the years, dating back to his childhood. There are pics from formal dances he's gone to as well. All with model-types on his arm.

Back then, he seemed innocent enough, but I'm well aware of who and what he turned out to be. He's living proof that outward appearances can be very deceiving.

"Looks like you can use some company," a deep voice says, startling me a bit.

I glance left and meet Tate's gaze, only now realizing I'm no longer alone. He's dressed down tonight, wearing a pair of light, distressed jeans, and a gray tee. I realize my tank and denim shorts match his look, as if we planned to coordinate tonight.

Not awkward at all.

"I'm guessing our parents are in the kitchen finishing up dinner?"

Taking a deep breath first, I nod, but don't return his smile. Which he should be used to by now.

He leans forward to place his cell on the coffee table, then drops down onto the couch, leaving one cushion between us. He always makes me feel so exposed, which is why I cross both arms over my chest even though he's not staring there. He's looking at my face, which I can see in my peripheral vision.

Since our run-in outside the door of Professor Lange's lecture hall, I've now managed to duck out after every class, before Tate has time to speak. Because of that fact, this is the most he's said to me since offering to buy me coffee.

"So... are you always this standoffish, or is it just with me?"

I meet his gaze, and *now* I smile. "It's just you."

When I face forward again, staring at the movie paused on the opening credits, Tate laughs.

"That's funny, because I don't recall you always being like this. The first time we met, I don't know, I thought we might've connected. Unless I imagined that."

"You did. There was never any kind of 'connection' or... whatever you're implying."

A quiet laugh leaves him. "I didn't mean it like that. I just... it seemed like you were more *open* then."

I slide him a slow look, not bothering to hide my annoyance. "Open to what, exactly?"

Tate shrugs and he's thoughtful for a moment. "Maybe just to the idea of getting to know me before deciding to hate me."

My stare lingers on him as his mood deflates a bit. His head slowly settles against the headrest. Unlike me, this *was* once his home, so when his foot lands on the table, he leaves it there.

Our parents' laughter drifts in from the kitchen, contrasting the tension here in the living room. At this rate, the night will be ruined because the energy between us is off. And if that happens, Mom will never let me hear the end of it.

"Fine," I sigh, tearing my eyes off him when I sink deeper into my corner of the sofa. "Tell me about yourself."

First, his head shifts, and he shoots me a suspicious glare. "Where would you like me to start?" he asks, his tone hinting that he's at least mildly frustrated.

"Start at the beginning, I guess."

From the corner of my eye, I see his chest rise when he breathes deep.

"Okay, the beginning," he says seemingly to himself as he gathers his thoughts. "Well, my parents met one summer my dad spent in the Philippines. Neither expected it to be more than a fling, but then their fun resulted in... *me,*" he adds with a quiet laugh. "That changed things a bit. My dad came home to the States, and Mom stayed on the island with her family. Then, about a month before she had me, my dad convinced her to come here to try and make things work."

"How'd *that* turn out?" I ask dryly.

Tate shrugs. "About as well as you'd expect. They lasted just over five years, divorced, and my mom did most of the heavy lifting where raising me was concerned. Right up until... she died."

My gaze shifts to him when he finishes. I was set to just nod and fire off another question, but hearing about his mom made me pause.

"I heard that you lost her. I didn't mean—."

"It's been years, so... you're good," he says.

He ends his statement there, but when his expression becomes solemn, I sense there's still considerable pain that accompanies conversations like these.

"But anyway, that's pretty much my life in a nutshell. After she passed, I went to kind of a dark place, got in a ton of trouble, but my dad got me involved in some of the brotherhood's programs for youths. Honestly, it helped. And maybe even saved my life."

It isn't until I feel my expression softening that I realize just how cunning he is. I nearly fell for his good guy, innocent act, but I jolt myself back to reality, remembering who I'm dealing with.

"What about you?" he asks, drawing my eyes to him.

"My parents divorced a few years ago, I've spoken to my dad less than a handful of times since then, and I'm currently just kind of winging it."

He smirks at my answer, which was significantly less detailed than his.

His head falls back against the couch again. "Sometimes I think I might've been more grounded after everything if my parents had a second kid, someone for me to look after, to be accountable for. But maybe that's wrong. I might've just dragged them down the same path I traveled."

I get lost in my thoughts for a bit and don't answer right away.

"What about you? Ever wish you weren't an only child?"

The question hits my heart before my brain, but once it finally registers, my eyes are fixed on him. His expression shifts from curious to confused.

"Did I... say something wrong?"

It takes me several seconds to gather my thoughts, and once I do, I don't even process them before they convert into words.

"I'm *not* an only child," I hiss.

Tate's posture shifts toward me. "I—I didn't realize. My dad hasn't said anything, and your mom never mentioned—"

"Of *course,* she fucking didn't."

When I stand and grab my phone from the armrest, he seems to realize I'm done here.

"What did I say?" he asks, and when my gaze falls on him, I realize he could never possibly understand why *he,* of all people, doesn't want to ask me that question.

It's bad enough that he's the root cause of me having to do life without my sister, but he doesn't even fucking know she existed. The thoughts are twisted in my head and not making perfect sense because, of course he doesn't realize that the girl he hurt was a member of this family. But it just adds insult to injury hearing her mentioned like some fucking afterthought. Starting with my mother who conveniently kept those details under wraps, treating my sister's death like some dirty little secret.

"Please, tell me what I said wrong," Tate pleads, and I meet his gaze with tears blurring my vision.

"I had a younger sister," I hiss. "And some asshole..."

My voice trails off there, and I hate that I'm not strong enough to say the rest. That some asshole raped her, and it fucked with her head.

That I know *he's* the one to blame.

"Don't fucking follow me," I warn, glaring with hellfire in my eyes. He stands and I shoulder-check him on my way toward the exit, swiping Mom's keys from the table near the door. I hear her and Rob rushing toward the foyer, likely to see what all the commotion is about, but I'm out before they can ask.

Speeding and crying, I pull into the driveway of my childhood home in under ten minutes. My first thought is to grab my bike and go, but something won't let me leave. I'm raw and hurting in ways I haven't let myself hurt in months. It's a deep, sinking sensation, one that makes me fear I could fall forever if I let myself.

Fall until I find my sister in death.

I slam the door shut behind me when I climb out, and I find the key on Mom's ring, letting myself into the house. It's rare that I come here because of the pain, but tonight I need this. Need to feel close to my sister in the last place I heard her laugh, smelled her hair, felt her arms around my neck.

A life full of potential and unfulfilled dreams is now just this. A memory.

I take the stairs slowly, not bothering with lights. As much as I hate it here now, it's still home and I could find my way through blind if I had to. I know which floorboards creak, know which doorknobs are tricky, because this place is a part of me. As much as the family that once inhabited it.

I stand at Mel's closed door several seconds before getting up the nerve to turn the knob. My breaths are wild and dizzying as I build up the nerve, reliving the nightmare that awaited me on the other side a year ago.

The door slams against the stopper when I push it wide. I step inside and it still feels like her in here. I don't know what becomes of a soul once it leaves the body, but my hope for her is that she's free. From all that hurt her in this life. From all that made her feel like staying here with us was no longer an option.

My fingertips trail the edge of her bed cover and I remember nights spent in here, laughing for hours at absolutely nothing, braiding her hair, listening to her plans for life. Now, those thoughts only add to the holes she left in mine.

It looks like Mom left things mostly as they were the last time I was here. I'd gone through Mel's room, nearly ransacking it for details or clues as to who hurt her, but something I learned about my sister is that she was good at hiding things. Good at keeping secrets. Which meant anything she didn't want found, wouldn't be found.

I managed to get her laptop and cell phone shortly after the incident. I've kept both but having her phone has been the most therapeutic. It holds all her pictures, the little moments that made her who she was. It's like a time capsule, frozen in place from the day she left.

But it's also where I found the picture that ignited my obsession with uncovering the whole truth. The one of Tate's arm around her shoulders at a Savage party hosted at The Den the night she was assaulted.

Her closet's dark and still filled with her clothes, shoes, and her clarinet case rests on the top shelf. My heart wrenches inside my chest and I take it as a sign that I've reached my limit. I turn to leave and if I weren't so in tune with every nuance about this house, I might've missed it.

A floorboard that squeaks differently than the others.

Kneeling, I pull back the rug and begin stepping over the boards again, in search of the one that sounded a bit off. After a few seconds, I find it and I'm back on my knees, plucking at the edges of the slat until it finally budges. I hold my breath as I pull it free and set it aside, finding a tin canister underneath.

Yellow with blue butterflies printed all over.

Of course, she'd choose something with butterflies. They were always her favorite.

My fingers grip the edge of the tin, but I can't do this here. I'm guessing Mom and Rob—and maybe even Tate—are on their way after how I stormed off. So, I put everything back as I found it instead, then lock up the house. All while my heart races and my hands tremble.

I said before that my sister was a master at hiding things, keeping secrets, and that nothing she wanted to stay hidden would ever be found. So, maybe she led me here tonight. Led me to that exact spot to make this discovery.

I'm both terrified and anxious to find out what was so important that she went to such great lengths to hide it, but I have hope.

Maybe, if luck is on my side tonight, I'll have the one thing I've wanted since the moment of her death.

Irrefutable proof, pointing directly at the one who hurt her.

A flash of lightning.

The steady lull of falling rain.

It all seems fitting as I stare at the canister I found hidden beneath Mel's floorboards. To think, had I not gone inside today, whatever this is could've been lost forever once Mom sells the house.

The basement lights flicker when a deep clap of thunder shakes the entire foundation, and I've finally gotten up the nerve to remove the lid. It feels like my heart's in my throat, though. Breathing deep, I peer inside. Mostly, it just seems like a random collection of things, but for some reason, I can't bring myself to touch them.

Maybe out of sentiment, knowing Mel was the last to place them here.

Maybe for fear of what I might find once I start digging.

Another deep breath and I reach inside to pull out a napkin. It's from a diner I've never heard of or been to, so I set it aside. Next, I pick up a small slip of paper. Turning it over, I find the words 'So many secrets, so little truth,' scribbled on one side. The ink is heavy, Mel's penmanship intense. So much that I imagine the pen's tip must have carved into whatever surface she wrote on. My gaze lingers on her chaotic writing, and I swear I can see her scrawling this message clear as day. Toward the end, she seemed to always be in a rush. Who or what she was racing against, I may never know.

I scan the rest—a blue wristband from go-kart racing. A movie ticket dated about six weeks before she passed. A receipt from mini golf for two players.

I'm still not able to make complete sense of it all, because everything that comes to mind is purely speculation, but a picture is beginning to form. One that suggests my sister was seeing someone. Someone she decided not to tell me about, which leaves me to wonder why she hid it. The first possibility that comes to mind is that this guy was older, had no business being in a relationship with a minor.

A guy like Tate, for instance.

Anger has my hands shaking as I rifle through the remaining items with less caution. Beneath a receipt from an ice cream shop downtown, there's a keychain that reads '*I love you to the moon and back,*' and I can imagine it came from the same guy who took her to all these different places.

A moment of selfishness creeps in and anger spikes. It's like she had this whole other life no one knew about, but maybe that's not true. Maybe it's just a life that *I* didn't know about. I used to consider myself a good sister, one Mel could tell anything, depend on for anything, but I've questioned the truth in that statement for the past year. And now, as I accept that she had so much more going on than I ever could've realized, I'm certain I was completely wrong. It doesn't matter that *I* believed I was a good sister. Mel didn't.

Thunder booms outside, matching my frustration as I slam her items back inside the box—that stupid keychain, the receipts, all the other bullshit mementos, and then the napkin.

I've already closed the tin when it dawns on me that I missed something. Setting the lid aside again, I stare at the napkin. Or rather, the name and phone number I hadn't noticed were written on it the first time.

Some girl—Scarlett R.

I turn to the front again and read the name of the restaurant out loud.

"Dusty's Diner."

I rack my brain, wondering if maybe I've been there and just don't remember, but a quick search on my phone confirms that I haven't. The place is more than an hour away, in a city called Cypress Pointe. I haven't been there but know of it. Still, I don't get why this phone number is so important. Why Mel wouldn't just save it in her phone and toss the napkin.

Without thinking, I start to dial, but only get so far before something stops me. Instinct maybe. It's just that there's no telling what this girl might know or how sensitive the information she holds might be, so I don't want to chance it. I need to handle this in a controlled situation, which means I need a new plan, and I at least know what the first step has to be.

I'll be taking a ride out to Cypress Pointe and paying Dusty's Diner a visit. With any luck, someone there will know who Scarlett R. is and tell me a little bit about her. After that, if I'm lucky, I might be able to convince her to meet with me.

'So many secrets, so little truth.'

Mel's words ring inside my head and I'm starting to see she wasn't just speaking about the world around her. My sister had her share of secrets, too, and now that she's gone, I'm determined to unravel them all myself.

As far as closure goes, sorting out the other side of her life is about as close as I'll get.

A quick check of the app shows that Bird finally made it home. With limited contact this week, I'm not sure where she's been tonight, but I had a feeling she'd at least get her ass home before the storm hit. As I think it, lightning brightens my room for a few seconds, then a loud roll of thunder follows.

Checking Bird's whereabouts wasn't the only reason I reached for my phone, but it helped me stall before returning my dad's call. When he hit me up a few hours ago, I wasn't sure I'd call back. Not until just now. The thought crosses my mind that maybe I should just text. That way, if shit goes sideways, I can easily ghost him and pretend he doesn't exist.

"Fuck it."

I dial and fall back on my pillow, staring at the ceiling.

"Micah?" he answers in a rush. More than once, I've purposely hung up after two rings to avoid him. Looks like he's getting quicker on the draw.

"Yeah, it's me."

"Shit, I didn't think I'd hear back from you. How are you?"

It takes a sec to answer because I hate small talk. "Fine. Busy."

"I figured with classes starting, plus practice. Has the season kicked off yet?"

"Nope, still a month out. But the team meets up for workouts and pick-up matches to stay active."

"That's good," he says. "If you stay ready, you don't have to *get* ready, right?"

"Pretty much."

"Maybe you can send me your schedule and I can come see you play. I've always loved watching you out on the ice."

My fist clenches against my chest, recalling maybe a dozen matches he's attended since I got into hockey eight years ago.

"Sure," I answer with a sigh. "It's posted online, so I'll shoot you the link when we hang up."

"Good. Thanks."

We reach that point where we start running out of things to say, so I switch to a topic I couldn't care less about.

"How's Mom?"

He blows out a long breath. "Still a bitch. Still married to the same asshole. Still squatting in my fucking house while I slowly go insane."

I don't jump to defend my mother because, well, he's right. She *is* a bitch, and her husband's definitely an asshole.

"So, what's your plan to get them out?"

"It's pretty simple, really. I moved into the pool house," he says. "Now, I'm too close to ignore and I can bug the shit out of them and possibly get them to stop dragging their feet."

"Damn. Sounds like a Nate Locke move if I ever heard one. It also sounds just fucked up enough to work," I add with a smirk.

"Here's hoping."

A long pause has me thinking about hanging up. Then, I decide to do exactly that while things are still going okay.

"Listen, I should—"

"I miss you, Micah," he blurts. "It's been months since I've heard from you or since you've returned one of my texts or calls. I'm not sure if you've checked in with your mom at all since then, but... I miss you," he says again, and a pang of guilt hits me out of nowhere.

My eyes slam shut, and I shake it off.

"Yeah, well, nothing's changed. I'm still the same fuck-up I've always been, so you're not missing anything."

"Don't say that." There's a sternness to his tone that isn't lost on me. "You're doing well for yourself out there. I should know, I saw your final grades from last semester online. You finished the year out with nothing lower than a ninety-seven percent. That doesn't sound like the work of a fuck-up to me."

I'm honestly surprised he still checks.

"And I'm willing to bet that if you commit to applying for an internship from that list I emailed, you'd be *every* company's number-one pick," he adds. "I'm telling you, Mic, the second they see how good you are with all that techy stuff, it'll be love at first sight," he adds with a laugh.

I know the list of internships he's referring to, and also recall conveniently forgetting having seen it. "Yeah, well..."

His silence indicates that the tone of the conversation is getting ready to shift, which has me even more convinced I don't want to do this.

"Look, I think we both wish things were different between us, and I take full ownership of that, but... I'd like to think it won't always be like this. Tense, strained, like I'm talking to someone who doesn't know me."

I scoff at that last part. "I *don't* know you. That's kind of what happens when someone chooses not to be in the picture."

"Micah, it's not like I was just out barhopping. I worked my ass off, held down *two* jobs to provide for you kids. Trust me, if I could go back in time and do things differently, I would."

"Even the part where you sent me away?"

My question leaves him speechless. At least, that's what I gather from the silence on the other end.

"I mean, you've gotta admit, that part was kind of fucked up, right?" I add with a somber laugh. "I was in mourning and my own parents couldn't see that. Cam's death was..."

I lose my words and anger flares inside me, thinking about how it could've all been avoided. Thinking about how she'd still be here if it weren't for my parents' bullshit.

"You got rid of me because I was being eaten alive by grief and didn't know how to deal with that shit. Fuck that I was in pain. Fuck that I was just a thirteen-year-old kid. You just did what you had to do, right?"

"Damn it, Micah! We did what we thought was best for *you*, not us. Are you planning to hold this shit over my head for the rest of my life? Mistakes were made. I'm man enough to admit that, but you're twenty-one. Are you man enough to accept my apology? I mean, I'm fucking begging you at this point."

I let out a breath when I realize I should've stuck with my plan and left his ass unanswered.

"Speaking of mistakes, this was a big one."

"No, this is how we fix our shit—two adults who both know nothing's ever perfect," he corrects. "This isn't your problem, but I was a sixteen-year-old kid when I found out you were on your way into my world. There was never a chance in hell I was going to get everything right. But, shit, I'm trying to make it better. I'm trying to *be* better," he adds. "I get it, I was never around, but I can't undo that. My only option is to be here *now*. But I can only do that if you'll let me."

My chest tightens and I feel sick hearing him pare down my entire fucked up childhood to one singular issue. That he worked too much. No mention of how their bullshit before they finally divorced fucked us up. No mention of how we were treated like pawns during their entire marriage, a means of one parent hurting the other. No mention of how the incessant arguing is the reason he and Mom weren't paying attention to Loren that day, and then...

"Well, I'm alive and I'm guessing that's all you needed to know. So—"

"Micah, it's time to stop running," he cuts in. "How can you still feel like I don't have your back? What I did for you... what I *covered up* for you... I could've lost everything. But I risked it. I risked it because you're my kid, I love you, and that's what dad's do."

His words have an image forcing its way into my head—flashing red and blue lights, my dad hiding Vince, Ash, and I in the woods behind a house as it went up in flames.

"I can't do this."

"Micah, wait!"

I hang up, feeling myself lose it. My heart feels like it's about to claw its way up my throat right as I launch my phone across the room.

"Son of a bitch!"

The throbbing in my head means Loren is stuck inside it for the night. Not that she ever leaves, but I can usually block her out. But tonight, after that call, I'm certain the pain isn't going to die down anytime soon.

Serves me right because I should've known better than to make that call. It's fine, though. Lesson learned. Won't happen again.

Ever.

W hen I dozed, I was pulling out from a bus station near the university. So, it's a bit disorienting when the next time I open my eyes, I'm in a big city—glittering lights, bodies packed on the street.

Passengers exit the bus while I gather my things. And my nerve. I know nothing about Cypress Pointe, which means I'm literally going into this situation blind, armed with nothing but a napkin with a stranger's name and phone number written on it. It's somewhere to start, though, I guess.

Maddox: You haven't answered my calls or texts in days. Where the fuck are you? I only know you're alive because I called the rink and Kip said I just missed you. Just... call me.

I tuck my phone away and leave the text unanswered. I'm not in the mood to explain something I'm not even sure *how* to explain yet. So, I step off the bus and head toward the front of the station. Quickly spotting the car I requested on the app, I climb in and try not to overthink things. We're only a ten-minute drive from my destination—Dusty's Diner. Hopefully, someone there can tell me if this Scarlett person is a regular. If not, I guess I'll be giving her a call.

It dawns on me that I should've gone with my first thought and called *before* making this trip, but I'm admittedly not thinking all that clearly these days. So, I choose not to consider the one million other ways I could've handled this and just try to clear my head during the ride.

"Looks like we're here," the driver announces. I stare up at the sign from the backseat, having second thoughts. But I didn't come all this way to let my nerves get the best of me, so I'm doing this. Just like Mel did.

"Thanks."

"No problem. Have a good night."

The driver pulls off and I'm on my own, standing in the small parking lot with my heart in my throat. The walk to the entrance feels like it takes hours, and you'd think the glass door in my hand weighs a thousand pounds with how slowly I open it.

A tiny bell above the door chimes and I take a look around. I've got no clue what I'm hoping to spot, but it's driving me insane to know Mel was in this exact place and I have no idea why.

"Seat yourself. I'll be over to your table with some water in a sec," one of the waitresses calls out over her shoulder. She flashes a quick smile before whipping a blonde ponytail with purple tips as she turns back toward her customer.

I scan the place and find a booth in the corner. It's got a good view of everything, so I take it. Chatter fills the small space and there seems to be a steady flow of patrons. With only a handful of empty seats in the place, I imagine they stay pretty busy.

Behind the counter, a cook mans the grill with speed and efficiency. In the few minutes I've been observing him, he's plated four meals and has barely broken a sweat. Three waitresses take turns circulating behind the counter with pitchers of water and coffee, wearing powder blue uniforms that make even the young one who first spoke look like she's straight out of the eighties. As I think of her, she bounds my way, wearing a smile despite how busy she seems to be.

"Sorry about that," she says, delivering the cold water she promised. My glass is filled to the brim, and she makes eye contact with me again. "Take a look at your menu and I'll circle back to take your order. Name's Scar, by the way."

I'd just smiled back when she said that. Her name. And hearing it, the grin fades almost instantly. My eyes lower to her nametag to confirm and, sure enough, Scar's definitely short for Scarlett.

Air rushes into my lungs and I'm certain I look like I'm having some sort of episode, but I didn't see this coming. Here she is, the girl I drove all this way to see, standing right in front of me.

Ignoring my weirdness, she walks off and grabs another meal and then drops it off a few booths away. I'm in shock, scrambling for where I plan to go from here, because I definitely thought there'd be more legwork involved. But I was wrong. Mel led me right to her.

"Sorry again," she says breathily. "We're unusually busy, even for a Saturday night."

"No worries. I'm in no rush."

She smiles again, reaching for the notepad in her apron. "Have you had time to look over the menu?"

"I—uh, yes. A grilled cheese with tomato soup, please."

"Got it. And to drink?"

"I'm good with the water actually."

She finishes jotting down my order and then meets my gaze again. "Should be up quickly. Just wave me down if you need anything else."

She's gone again and I'm reeling, wanting to ask this girl all the things, but also not wanting to reveal all my cards. So, to keep my nerves from fraying while I wait, I respond to Maddox, hoping to settle him down before he sends out a search party.

Stevie: I'm alive. Stop worrying.

Maddox: Where the hell are you?"

I type out a message, and then delete it, deciding to lie. He'd have too many questions if I told him I drove two hours to Cypress Pointe.

Stevie: Just hanging out. I'm around.

He takes a bit to answer, and I can guess he didn't like my response. I wouldn't have if he'd given it to *me*.

Maddox: Everything cool between you and your mom? I called looking for you and I got the sense that things might be tense between you two right now.

I roll my eyes, wishing he hadn't done that.

159

Stevie: All good.

I set my phone on the table when I spot Scarlett coming back this way. "Here you go."

"Wow, that was fast."

She shrugs and sets the bowl of soup down last. "The cook's been at this a while, so he rarely keeps people waiting."

I glance toward the cook when she mentions him, and then back at her. I'm completely aware of seeming like some creep who's maybe trying to decide how to make a move on her or something, but I'm literally at a loss right now. I need to get her talking in the least conspicuous way possible.

"Well, anyway, enjoy," she adds, turning to leave.

"I... I'm not from around here," I stammer. "Anything fun to do while I'm in town for the weekend?"

She meets my gaze and looks a little less weirded out than a moment ago. "You staying on the Northside or Southside?"

I assume the bewildered look on my face lets her know I have no idea what she's talking about.

"Sorry. You're on the Southside now. The Northside is a bit more... posh. Downtown is Northside."

I nod like I'm not making this up as I go. "Ah, gotcha. Yep, I'm staying downtown."

She smiles again. "Well, there's a club I know of. It's owned by a friend of the family, but I'm not quite old enough to get in yet. So, I guess I can only tell you what I've heard," she says with a laugh.

"How old are you?" Lucky for me, she doesn't seem to mind that I've asked.

"Seventeen. I'll be eighteen in a few months. You?"

"Twenty."

"Shit, you aren't legal yet either," she grins. "Sounds like you'll have to get creative like the rest of us. There are a couple movie theaters, a few bowling alleys. You could take a walk along the boardwalk. If you'd been a couple weeks earlier, you could've caught the fair downtown. They close an entire city block down for all the rides and vendors. It's huge."

"I'm sorry I missed it. Movie it is, I guess."

She gives a polite grin and props the tray against her hip. "What's your name?"

"St—ephanie. Stephanie," I lie.

Her brow arches. "Nice to meet you. We don't get a lot of tourists on this side of town, so it's nice having you here."

"Thanks."

She gets away from me this time and I want to kick myself for not thinking of more to say. This is a once in a lifetime opportunity and I'm fucking blowing it. But then the universe throws me a bone. Scarlett unties her apron and after chatting with one of the waitresses for a moment, it looks like she's going on break. She glances this way for the fraction of a second, and I manage to flag her down. She walks over and that's about all the time I have to think of what I'll say.

"Need something?"

"Not really but it looks like you're about to break, so I thought you could keep me company?"

There's a look of skepticism that leaves her just as quickly as it comes, then after glancing toward the door for a moment, she decides to sit.

Thank you, God, for small favors.

"Did you have something else to do? I'm sorry. I should've asked that first."

She waves me off. "No, you're fine. I was just going to sit in my car and rest my feet. But nothing's stopping me from doing that here, right?"

I take a sip of my soup and try to chill on the intense eye contact. Poor girl's gonna think I'm a serial killer.

"What kind of car do you drive?"

"A blue Cutlass. It used to be my sister's."

"She upgraded?"

Scarlett nods with a laugh. "You could say that. Not just her car, though. Her entire life."

She laughs and so do I. "That sounds interesting."

Scarlett adds. "She tried to buy me something new, but I didn't want it. The Cutlass is basically a part of the family, ya know? It used to be my uncle's before he gave it to her."

When Scarlett nods toward the cook behind the grill, I make the connection. "He's your uncle?"

"Yep," she nods. "And he's also the man behind the diner's name."

He locks eyes with his niece and winks at her when he smiles. She returns a smile of her own and I get the sense that they're close.

"So, it's just you and your sister?"

"Nope, we have a brother, too. He's the oldest and he's been in the wind ever since he got home," she answers.

"Got home from... the military? College?"

"Prison," she shares. "He was mostly innocent, though, if that matters." Her laugh makes it clear she's not uptight talking about it. I am curious about her brother now, though. Maybe *he's* got something to do with my sister visiting this city?

"Sorry, I shouldn't have—"

She waves me off again before I finish.

"You're fine," she says. "Just don't tell my sister I'm talking so much. She'd kill me."

I force another smile while thinking. I need to know more, but also don't want to pry. But... shit, what if this is important?

"If I'm not being too nosey, how long was your brother away?"

"A few years," she answers. "And he made it home this summer. Just in time for my sister's wedding."

The timeline is off. He was gone too long for him to have ever known Mel, which makes him a dead end. I smile and eat a bit more of my soup while I think.

"What about you? Got any siblings?"

Scarlett's question has me hesitating with the spoon hovering over my bowl. Guess I walked right into that one.

"I... no. It's just me."

"Sometimes I think that'd be kind of cool—no one to fight with. No one to take your shit, use it, then never put it back. Having your parents' all to yourself."

"Yeah, unless your parents aren't the kind you *want* all to yourself."

When she arches a brow, that knowing look on her face leads me to believe she might know a thing or two about that.

"If it hadn't been for my sister and my uncle, I would've practically raised myself, so... I can definitely relate," she admits.

I'm midchew when she waves her uncle down, calling him over to the table. The big, burly guy I spotted when I walked in puts up a finger to buy himself a moment, then slips his apron off over his head. Out from behind that cutout in the wall, he seems bigger and broader. He gives off lumberjack vibes. Especially with the thick, gold-toned beard hiding half his face. He's solid and looks like he'd give a truck a run for its money if it collided into him, but according to Scar, he's nowhere near as intimidating as he looks.

"Uncle Dusty, this is Stephanie. She's visiting from out of town."

Dusty's eyes flash toward mine and I don't expect the warmth in his expression. "It's not often we get a face in here I don't recognize, but it's always a welcomed surprise. I'm glad you popped in to check us out."

"And I'm glad I found you guys," I say back.

"How's the food?"

I glance down at my nearly empty plate and bowl as I laugh. "Well, I think you can guess it was good."

His hand lands on my shoulder when he grins. "Happy you enjoyed it. And tell you what, first meal's on me. Just make sure you stop back in if you're ever visiting again."

"I—really? Thanks so much."

He nods in this polite way that makes him seem like a gentle giant. "Pleasure's all ours."

With that, he's gone and back on the grill to fill orders.

"You're welcome," Scar says with a wink.

"That was your plan?"

When she shrugs with this less than innocent face, I know I'm right. "He calls it the traveler's discount, and that's just code for free. So, when we get new people in that I actually like, I make sure he knows they're not from around here and hooks them up."

"Well, I appreciate it."

She nods again and then checks the time. "Shit, break's over."

Those words make my heart skip a beat and I realize that my attempt at breaking the ice took longer than planned.

Scar begins scooting out of the booth and I'm scrambling.

"Wait..."

Her eyes lock with mine.

I don't know what to say to make her stay. Don't know what to say to help me get down to the bottom of what this place meant to my sister. So, it's time to just come out with it.

At least some of it.

"I... have a bit of a confession."

Scarlett's brow arches. "Ooo-kay."

Curious, she settles into the seat again, but her eyes never leave me.

"Me showing up here wasn't random," I admit. "I was looking for this place. I was looking for *you*."

Now she's super confused. "Why?"

I reach for my bag and feel her eyes on me while I dig. Then, when I place the napkin with her name and phone number on top of the table, she's clearly lost.

"I gave this to you?"

Shaking my head, I fold both hands in my lap, wringing them together when I feel myself starting to stress.

"No, not me. My sister," I reveal. "Her name is Mel."

"But... you just said you were an only child." A look flashes up at me and I sense her distrust.

"I know. I panicked and... I guess I didn't really know how much I should say."

Scarlett's thoughtful for a moment and I imagine she's trying to make sense of it all, so I help her out a bit. Her eyes shift to my phone when I unlock it and show her the pic of Mel I keep on my screen.

"This is her. The most I can gather is that she came in one day and you two had a conversation. About what, I have no idea, but it was important enough that she kept this napkin in a very special, very *secret* place. So, I'm hoping you can tell me why."

My chest is heaving wildly while I await an answer. Hopefully, something that can make this all seem worthwhile.

"I remember her."

It feels like the floor just fell out from under my feet. "Y—you do?"

Scarlett nods. "She came in late one night, acting a little weird. All she ordered was a milkshake. Said she wasn't hungry. So, she just sat in her seat, mostly staring at my uncle."

My brow tenses. "Why?"

Scarlett shrugs. "First, she asked if his name was Dusty, and when I said yes, she got really quiet. Then, her eyes started watering. I'm not sure what upset her, but it was definitely something," Scarlett explains. "She got up and I knew she was going to run, so I grabbed her hand and got her to stop. She thought it was because she owed me for the milkshake, but that wasn't it. I wanted to give her this."

Scarlett taps the napkin.

My head's swimming. She's said so much, but not enough. Things still don't make sense.

"Did she say anything else? Do anything else?"

"No. I was surprised she even accepted my number. After that, she just ran off."

"Did you ever hear from her?"

Scarlett shakes her head. "No, and I didn't expect to. But I had to at least make sure she had a way to contact me if she needed help. She... *seemed* like she needed help."

Those words hit me hard. Suddenly, my heart feels heavy and I'm beginning to spiral.

"What's going on? Is she okay?"

My throat seizes up and I zone out, staring toward the kitchen. Staring at *Dusty*.

"No," I answer. "She's not okay. She took her own life."

There's silence at the table and it feels like I'm having an out of body experience. In this moment, everything feels so black and white, a series of truths and fallacies with no gray areas in between. And I realize I was going about this the wrong way all along.

"I need to speak to your uncle," I blurt, standing from my seat. "Mel seemed to be here for him, so maybe he's who I should be talking to."

"I can see if he has a sec," Scar offers, then she's on her feet, too, headed toward the grill. I focus on them as she gives her uncle a quick rundown, and when he gestures for me to come back to the kitchen, I'm relieved they're both being so cooperative.

I push through the door into the kitchen and Dusty waves for me to follow him out the back.

"Keep an eye on those burgers, then once they come off, plate 'em and make sure you serve them hot," he instructs Scarlett.

"On it," she nods, and then I'm following this wall of a man into an alley.

Not the smartest thing I've done, but I'm desperate. And I feel like I'm so close.

The solid metal door slams behind us and we stand beneath a streetlamp that bathes us in orange-colored light.

"My niece told me the gist of what's going on, but I don't know if I can be much help. She didn't tell me about your sister until after we closed that night, so I didn't even get a good look at her."

"I understand, but... is there *anything?*" I plead, hearing my own desperation.

He feels sorry for me. I see it in his eyes. I'm not one to seek the pity of others, but in this case, I'm praying it helps in some way. Whatever it takes.

"I'm sorry, sweetheart. I can see this is important to you, and if I'm being honest, it's haunted me since that night."

I feel winded and lean forward, resting my hands on my knees as tears come.

"Shit."

Dusty steps closer. "I wish there was more I could say or do to help, but I'm afraid this might be a dead end for now."

"I can't take anymore dead ends. That's all she's left me with are dead fucking ends!"

The feel of his broad hand on my shoulder is a surprise, but

166

I'm not inclined to shrug it off. He and his niece have only been kind to me tonight. Helpful, even.

"I'm gonna give you my cell number. Promise me you'll use it. If you find out *anything,* give me a call," he pleads. "I know this is something personal for you, but I need to know what your sister came here to sort out that night."

I nod aimlessly, and I'm only half aware of what's happening when he takes a notepad from his pocket and scribbles his information down for me. He takes my hand and folds my fingers around the piece of paper.

"Call me. Please," he says again, and then leaves me to catch my breath in peace.

It's not until I'm alone that the tears fall in sheets. I'm tired beyond belief. Emotionally, mentally.

And now this.

Another empty lead.

Another false hope.

CHAPTER 25
MICAH

You know you're in a shitty mood when not even porn can fix it.

A full twenty-four hours after hearing from my father, my head's still a clusterfuck, but that's on me. I shouldn't have called back.

The chick onscreen is over-the-top with the screaming as she rides some guy's dick. I hit mute, but the vibe's already dead. With a pick-up match scheduled for tomorrow morning, I have to get my shit together before then. Heading out on the ice in this state would fuck things up for the whole team. So, for a second, I consider venturing downstairs to see who's still up, maybe to shoot pool for a bit, but then I'm hit with a better idea.

It's been a week since we've seen or talked to Bird. The distance felt necessary for a number of reasons, but her break from us ends tonight. She's got points to earn, and she won't earn them sitting on her ass, pretending she doesn't owe us. So, as of this exact moment, she's officially back on duty, back to being at our beck and call.

Before dialing, I check the app for the first time today. She's not far away. Looks like she's heading toward campus, but much faster than if she were on her bike, which means she's in someone's car.

If she's smart, it's not a *guy's* car.

The line trills and I switch to speakerphone.

"Hello?"

She's whispering. *Why* is she whispering?

"Where are you?"

"On a bus," she says, and she doesn't sound like herself. Usually, there's some bite to her words, but not tonight.

"On a bus coming from where?"

She yawns before answering, "Cypress Pointe."

My brow tenses, thinking of the route from here to there. It's not around the corner.

"Ever been there?" she asks.

I don't respond right away because this feels a lot like normal conversation. And we don't *have* normal conversation.

"Cypress Pointe University has a hockey team. We play them sometimes. But why were *you* there?"

There's a deep breath but no words yet. Bird's quieter than usual and I know I wasn't wrong to assume something's up with her tonight.

"It's nothing really. Turned out to be a waste of time, so I'm just ready to get home. I'm beat," she adds.

Maybe that's the reason she seems so soft today. She's tired.

"I need you to drop by."

"Please, Micah," she sighs. "It's been a long day and—"

"An Uber will meet you at the bus station," I cut in, reminding her how this arrangement goes. It's not based on her feelings or preferences. When she's given an order, her only option is to obey.

"Can you at least tell me what this is about?"

Slowly, I rub my cock through my shorts. "Just need your help with something."

She's quiet and I check the app again. "Looks like you're about twenty minutes out. I'll leave the door unlocked downstairs. Let yourself in and don't talk to anyone on your way up."

She hesitates, then agrees. "Fine. Okay."

I'm good with that answer, but I'm sure she doesn't understand the request. Bottomline is that Enzo's eager ass is downstairs with some of the guys, and I can bet on him thinking she's fair game because I'm not around to remind him otherwise.

169

So, this is my failsafe. If I can't trust *him* yet, I'll control the situation by controlling Bird.

Unlike him, she listens, knows her place.

"Twenty minutes to the bus station. Ten to get here. No extra stops. I'm waiting."

STEVIE

Of *course*, Micah would call tonight. After the fucked up day I've had, while I'm feeling spent in every way imaginable. The only good thing is, I'm numb. Completely.

Details from my encounter at Dusty's have been swimming through my head the entire bus ride home. He and Scar seemed like nice enough people, but what if I'm wrong? What if it was an act and they know more than they're letting on? It all has to mean something, but Mel didn't leave me a single clue. Now, I may as well be wandering through the dark without a flashlight.

I climb out of the car and stand on the sidewalk, phone in hand as the driver pulls off. I've been on the fence about texting my mother all night, but I'm desperate. What if *she* has answers? What if she knows something I don't that could help me sort through the pieces? I've made it a point to avoid her this past week, but maybe it's time to put an end to the silence.

For Mel.

Before I lose the nerve, I shoot her a message.

Stevie: Hey. I need to ask a question and please be honest.

I add the last part because, since losing Mel, Mom tiptoes around my feelings sometimes. But if she knows something, even if she thinks I can't handle it, I need her to tell me.

Mom: Of course, but where have you been? I've been calling since you stormed off at Rob's.

Stevie: I need to know why Mel might've taken a trip out to Cypress Pointe?

Here's hoping she answers despite me ignoring *her* question. Right now, our issues are secondary. The focus should be on Mel.

While I wait for a reply that might not even come, I stare up the side of the manor, noting that most of the windows are dark. All except the lower level. I dread going inside, dread the noise and whatever task Micah has awaiting me, but there's no avoiding it or him.

My phone sounds off and my eyes flash down toward the screen.

Mom: What? When?

Stevie: Not sure exactly, but I need to know why she might've gone. Do you have any idea what she could've been looking for?

Mom: No, she never mentioned it. What's happening? Where'd you hear about this? You need to talk to me, Stevie.

I sigh and accept that I've just run headfirst into yet another brick wall. Like always. Frustrated, I shove the phone back in my pocket without responding. Doesn't seem to be a point anyway.

I ascend the front steps of The Den and turn the knob. It's unlocked like Micah said it would be, so I let myself in. It seems like no matter the time of day or night, this place is always lively, buzzing with laughter and masculine energy.

On cue, loud cheering erupts from the game room as I move through the hallway undetected. Walking past the game room, I spot Enzo among the crowd, sipping a beer. He laughs at something that's said just out of earshot, but then his eyes catch mine. Almost right away, the expression slides from his face and I decide against waving. My hesitation isn't brought on by the sound of Micah's grave warning echoing in my thoughts. Instead, I stop myself because Enzo's looked away. So quickly I'm not certain he isn't angry with me for the trouble I caused him the other night.

The night I met him, he was sweet and a little flirtatious. Ok, maybe more than a *little* flirtatious. But now things have changed. My best guess is that the guys have issued some sort of warning, drawn a line in the sand he's mindful not to cross for fear of feeling their wrath. Whatever's been done or said was enough to convince him that I'm completely off limits. So much that he knows not to even make eye contact anymore.

The possessiveness of those three is astounding, and I'm just

171

some random girl. No one special. I can't imagine being someone they love or even just care about. Whoever they end up with down the road better have the patience of a saint.

Patience and one hell of a right hook.

She'll need it keeping one of them in line.

I don't hit any other snags moving through the first floor virtually undetected. It's best that way. The fewer witnesses there are to my humiliation the better.

Pressing the button to call the elevator, I cross both arms over my chest, sighing as I try to imagine what on Earth Micah could want from me. Am I picking up a late-night snack order? Turning down his bed because he didn't feel like it? Or maybe I'll be rubbing his feet.

I never know with these assholes.

The elevator bell rings, and the doors slide open. I step in and press '2', following the now familiar path to Micah's door. I stand there, gathering myself for a moment, then finally, I knock.

A relaxed, "Come in," prompts me to turn the knob, unsure of what to expect.

I lay eyes on him, a pair of navy-blue basketball shorts riding low on his waist. He's shirtless, sprawled out on his bed with one leg hanging off the side, and the other propped up on the footboard. The tip of his cigarette glows as it burns between two fingers, but the heavy aroma of weed leads me to believe he'd been smoking something else before I got here. Without making eye contact, a slow plume of smoke billows from his lips and floats toward the ceiling.

"Lock the door," he rasps.

I do it, but I'm starting to think this isn't going to be a snack run.

"I thought athletes were supposed to be careful about what they put into their bodies." I nod toward the cigarette as I speak.

He lifts his head and it's the first time he's looked at me since I walked in. "Now you sound like Ash."

Another puff of smoke clouds from his lips and his stare deepens. "Why'd you say you were in Cypress Pointe again?"

"I was checking out a place I heard about, but it wasn't what I expected. It was actually kind of a letdown if I'm being honest."

He doesn't blink. "You were alone?"

It's obvious he's trying to catch me in a lie, or maybe see if I'll slip up and admit to breaking his rules. A breath hitches in my throat. "I was."

More staring and silence while he studies me.

"But anyway," I sigh. "You said you needed something, so I'm here. What is it?"

That look lingers on me a few more seconds before he brings the cigarette to his lips again. "The last few days were shit. I could use some help clearing my head."

I'm confused, not understanding what that has to do with me. "Sounds like a job for your therapist."

He smirks at that. "Maybe. But you're here, and you're free, so..."

We lock eyes again and it's confirmed—he's more than a little high.

His laptop is muted on his nightstand with two girls going down on the same guy. Gesturing toward the screen, my lips curve into a nervous smirk.

"Your night seems like it's been pretty interesting already, so I should probably just go and—"

"On the bed."

His voice sounds low and menacing, matching the ferocity in his eyes. My heart races as I take slow steps toward him. And by the time I reach his bed, I'm holding my breath, having a pretty clear understanding of what he wants as I sit.

My leg settles beside him, and he reaches for me, slipping the length of his fingers between my thighs, gripping the inside to pull me closer. The hold he has on me is tight, but not so rough that it's painful. He places his cigarette on the edge of the ashtray without his eyes leaving mine. I'm focused on the ribbon of smoke that rises from the tip when Micah's lips make their way to my skin. The end of his tongue traces a small target on the side of my neck, then I feel the gentle throb as he sucks the hollow of my throat.

My eyes fall closed as the drama that filled my day starts to become an afterthought. Micah's hand moves higher, until he's nudging the seam of my jeans between my legs.

"What is it exactly that you need my help with?" I ask, expecting him to pull away and *speak* his answer. But instead, he shows me, placing my hand on his cock, gently squeezing to form my fingers around the solid rod resting on his thigh.

"This," he whispers over my skin. "*This...* is why I need you. Make me fucking come."

CHAPTER 26
STEVIE

I swallow deeply as Micah's request drives all my senses through the roof. In particular, my sense of touch as he kisses my neck again.

"You called me over for sex?" I scoff, thinking the joke will be on him when I tell him one of *many* reasons that isn't happening.

He laughs and the soft rumble of it vibrates my throat. "Baby steps," he teases with a rasp. "Tonight, I'll settle for your mouth."

A breath hitches in my throat and I'm completely dumbstruck, finding it impossible to believe the words leaving his mouth.

"You can't be serious."

"Ten points," he shoots back, and then leans away until we lock eyes. Which is when I realize this isn't a bluff.

"No. Fuck you and fuck the points." I shift on his bed, preparing to stand, when he grips my wrist. I expect him to rub it in my face that, technically, per our agreement, I'm not at liberty to deny him or the others *anything* they ask of me, but he doesn't do that. Instead, he's silent. For so long that I turn to face him, observing while he studies me with this dark look in his eyes.

I'd love to break free, but he has this unnerving effect on me. His gaze narrows and something shifts. I can't put my finger on it, but it's as if he suddenly recognizes that I'm not quite stable right now. And what's even weirder, it almost feels like that actually matters.

"What happened tonight?" he asks, his tone losing its brash edge. Still, I try to snatch out of his grasp, but it doesn't work. His grip is too tight.

"Nothing happened," I hiss. "Pardon me for not wanting to suck your dick on command. You know, our arrangement wasn't even supposed to be... *that* type of arrangement."

"Funny, you weren't saying that shit while Ash and I finger fucked you last week. Seemed like that type of arrangement *then*," he adds coldly.

"Fuck. You. I'm not your whore, Micah. You can't dangle points in my face and—"

"Fine, no points," he cuts in, tilting his head as he studies my reaction. "You don't want this to be about our pact, then fuck it. It's not about that. In fact, we can make this a *mutual* encounter."

It doesn't take long to catch his meaning. Nor does it take long for me to get wet imagining it. I fight the urge to give in, though. He's transparent. A fuck boy in the wild.

"We'll keep things simple," he continues. "I'm horny as hell and you're—"

"I'm what? Here? Available? Your pet?" I scoff, shaking my head when I can't look at him any longer, but his fingers warm my chin when he turns my face.

"You're all those things," he says with an infuriating smirk. "But more importantly... you're exactly *who* and *what* I want right now."

His tone is raw and the sound of it has my nipples hardening against my bra. I'm livid, seething with anger, but not only because he'd have the audacity to proposition me. It's mostly because he and his brothers have given me so many reasons to hate them, so many reasons to resist. Yet, there's still something that draws me in, something powerful enough to melt some of this anger down into lust.

He's close again. His lips grazing my skin. His chin nudging my throat.

"Just admit that you need this, Bird. I heard it in your voice when I called—the tension, the sadness. Let me fix it," he says with a breathy groan. "Think about how good we can make each other feel. My dick between your lips. Your pussy... dripping while I tongue the absolute *fuck* out of it."

A chill races down my spine and I shiver against him, wishing for the freedom to finally give in. Wishing for the freedom to want him uninhibited, without all the negative shit that comes with it—pain, frustration, guilt. But the toxicity between us makes that impossible. When it comes to wanting Micah and the others, there will *always* be darkness.

Because that's who we are.

"Get naked," he breathes into my ear, "then bring your ass back to this bed."

He kisses my neck as his fingers twist into my hair, and his words twist my insides. I stare over his shoulder at his laptop, seeing the pleasure and relief on the stars' faces. I'm envious. Enough that it weakens my will, ignites my imagination.

The plan was to head home, crawl into bed and pray for sleep with hopes of leaving this shitty day behind, but... I'm not so sure I ever really *want* to be alone. Maybe I thought that's all there was. Maybe I need comfort tonight.

Maybe I need... *this*.

The bed creaks when I stand, unable to tear my eyes from Micah's. His stare is intense, clocking me as I slip out of my jeans and underwear. Thick muscle shields his chest like armor, moving more rapidly now. It occurs to me that he could've called any number of girls tonight—girls that wouldn't have put up a fight, I'm sure—but he didn't call them.

He called me.

I hesitate to think what that means. I wasted a lot of time and energy feeling ashamed of my body, a lot of time hiding from the world in oversized clothes or not bothering to go out at all. But as Micah's eyes wander up my thighs, I feel something I don't always feel.

Sexy.

I press my palms into the mattress, ready to climb into the bed when Micah shakes his head.

"Your shirt," he says, staring at my breasts through my tee.

"But I—"

"Everything comes off." His tone is deeper this time, darker.

I need to stall. "Fine, but you first."

Smirking, he arches a brow when I flip the script, making a demand of my own. "Fair enough."

He stands, and without breaking eye contact, tucks his thumbs into his waistband. He bends, lowering the dark shorts to his ankles, then stands tall as he steps out of them. Confidence doesn't quite cover it. He's downright cocky as he stands before me naked, sheathed in muscle and tattoos down both arms. My eyes lower to his ripped stomach, then, when I can't help myself, his dick. He's huge, as big as I expected, as big as I saw through his shorts, but I can't stop staring.

Blond waves touch his shoulders and I compare him to a Viking. God knows he's brutal enough to fit the bill. He rips the comforter off his bed and tosses it out of the way before dropping back down onto the mattress. He smirks again, then nods at me.

"There. Now you."

There's visible trembling in my hands when I pull off my shirt. It crosses my thoughts to leave my bra on, but he'd never have it. I unhook the clasp and my breasts fall—heavy, dense, far from perky. Nothing like the girls on his laptop.

The comparison has me in my head again, thinking that's what he'd prefer, but when I join him in bed, his kiss says otherwise. It says he's different tonight, bleeding emotion like an open wound. If there wasn't an ocean of hatred ebbing and flowing between us, I might call this feeling passion. Only, I know that's the wrong word. It can't be that.

Not when it comes to us.

Micha's lips travel up my jaw. Then, I melt against him when he whispers into my ear. "My dick should already be in your mouth, Bird. Don't make me wait."

There's a smart-ass remark on the tip of my tongue, but I don't get the chance to unleash it. Micah cups my breast, craning his neck until he reaches my nipple, drawing it into the moist heat of his mouth.

My fingers splay across the ripples of his abdomen and the muscle quivers at my touch. So, I slide my palm lower, to the smooth plane at the base of his stomach, just above his dick.

"Grab it," he breathes over my skin. I do as I'm told, shocked by the heat that fills my hand.

Heat and an erection so solid that it makes his need crystal clear.

I move my hand up and down his length, brushing the tip with my thumb, teasing him. This is the most power I've had over him... *ever.*

He groans, turning to stare down his torso to where I'm gripping him. "You're killing me, Bird. I need your mouth," he rasps.

Rising to my knees, I lean in, hovering over his waist, eyeing his remarkably large dick. My hair cascades onto his stomach when I bend closer, and he gathers it gently. He holds it in his fist, out of the way so his view is unobstructed.

"Holy shit," he growls, tensing his hips the second there's contact, the second I draw him into my mouth.

The hand not holding my hair lands on my ass, squeezing it tight.

"I swear on everything, you're fucking perfect. Your tits, this beautiful ass of yours... every inch of you," he breathes, sounding almost delirious. In fact, he must be, because these aren't the compliments of an enemy.

Hearing him about to lose his shit, I suck harder, pulling him deeper into my mouth as my lips slip up and down his cock. It grows firmer against my tongue and the feel of soft veins beneath his skin makes my pulse race. My cheeks hollow when I suck the tip, drawing another groan from him like I hoped I would.

"Feels so damn good," he whispers. "Don't you dare fucking stop."

I glance toward him just to steal a peek, just in time to see his eyes drift close, his head slowly fall to the pillow. His bliss has me impatient for him to make good on his promise, impatient for him to return the favor.

I zone out on a fantasy, imagining his mouth on me, but the

feel of Micah's hand on the back of my head pulls me right out of it. He presses gently, pushing me down on his cock. Before I can even process his actions, I react, slapping his hand away.

"Don't."

We lock eyes, staring one another down, and I think I might actually lose my shit when he smirks. Yes, this cheeky asshole has the nerve to laugh while I'm clearly not amused.

"Damn, Bird, lighten up," he chuckles, pulling me toward him by my hip. "Bring me your pussy. The quicker I can get you off, the sooner you'll stop being such a bitch."

He pulls me to him again, but I plant my knees firmly in the mattress. "No, not like that."

When I glance at him, he's confused. "Not like what?"

My stomach twists, knowing I'll have to explain because I don't think he's ever been with a girl my size.

"Not with me... *on* you," I practically whisper. "It's uncomfortable."

He chuckles again. "What the fuck are you talking about? How the hell is having your pussy eaten uncomfortable?"

Damn him. Damn him for not getting it.

My lips part to explain, but I can't. I don't want him even thinking about it, so I turn away with hopes that once I start sucking him off again he'll stop asking, but the light tug to my arm tells me that's not happening.

"Talk to me."

The depth of his voice always makes everything he says sound scolding, but this time, maybe that's intentional.

I meet his gaze, but not before rolling my eyes in frustration. "It's a weight thing," I sigh.

He's quiet for an incredibly awkward stretch of time before finally speaking.

"Are you fucking insane?"

That wasn't quite the reaction I expected, but he has my attention.

"Have you seen yourself in the mirror?" he asks next. "Have you completely missed how my brothers and I can't be in the same fucking room with you for more than five minutes without breaking our *own* damn rules?"

My heart races and I'm not even sure why. Maybe because... I believe him?

"I hear you, but in case you missed the memo, I'm not exactly a small girl, Micah."

"And in case *you* missed it, I'm a big guy," he points out.

Those words have me sizing him up, following the length of his calves to his powerful thighs. He's still hard as a brick and is definitely big in *that* respect. Then, I study his chiseled abdomen, his wide chest and shoulders where his hair rests over them, topping off his six-foot-something frame. By the time I'm done admiring his body and reach his face, there's a smirk curving his lips.

"I'm *more* than capable of handling you," he says, grabbing my hip toward him again as he closes the subject.

I don't fight this time. He brings my thigh over his face and both my knees settle into the pillow at either side of his head.

"Spread them," he growls, guiding me down. "More."

Heat from his breath warms my pussy. I open my legs further, and the reward for my obedience is the feel of his silken tongue entering me. I squirm and he reacts quickly, before I can get away. With one solid arm, he catches my waist, locks me in. His abdomen flexes beneath me, every time he lifts his head, craning his neck to work his tongue into my center. I finally get my bearings enough to lower my lips to his cock, taking slow draws on his length, savoring the smoothness of the head against the roof of my mouth.

Still holding me in his grip, Micah's lips latch around my clit, sucking with slow, hypnotic pulses that flood my core, pushing me to my limit. Sounds seep up through the floorboards—laughter and loud conversation—and it's the only sign we're not the only two people on the planet. I've allowed myself to slip deeper than planned into his world, and I'm having one hell of a time finding a reason to regret it at the moment.

I gasp when the length of his fingers enters me, stretching me as he probes only a few times before taking them away. My pussy longs for the feeling again as soon as it leaves, craving the heat and friction. He finds a new use for his hands, though, gripping both my ass cheeks, spreading them as he gives my clit a long, slow lick, collecting my wetness on his tongue.

"Ash was right," he says. "You taste so good. So. Fucking. Good."

His words go straight to my head when he buries his face into me again. The moan that leaves me as I come is muffled by his dick, stretching my jaw when I take him deep. His palms knead my ass, rough, as his entire body tenses. Then, a stream of hot liquid bursts to the back of my throat, and his chest vibrates beneath my stomach. He's loud, moaning against my pussy as his cum spills onto my tongue and I swallow him down. He doesn't fall from my mouth until he's empty and soft.

Completely spent and sated.

Just like me.

"Fucking hell," Micah groans. I lift my thigh over his head and rest beside him on the bed.

Flashes of the day I've had burst into my thoughts—the diner, Scarlett, Dusty, me crying in the alley when I came up short.

Again.

Blinking my eyes tightly only quiets the recent memories, but they linger. Micah's also silent, and it dawns on me that I've maybe gotten a little too comfortable in his bed. So, I sit up and swing both legs off the edge, spotting my clothes near the window. Seems like the best idea, before Bruce Banner flips the script on me and turns into The Hulk. That's usually how things go with these three. They get what they want, then revert to their baseline asshole status. Which is why I'm not expecting anything different tonight.

My feet hover over the floor, but before they touch the carpet, a firm grip to my arm pulls me back. My shoulder falls against Micah's chest and as I lock in on his gaze, the softness of his lips presses to mine. There's a lightheartedness to the gesture, something I hadn't expected. He seems carefree and... normal.

The playfulness infects me, too, and I smile against his lips before shoving my tongue into his mouth, forcing him to taste remnants of his own pleasure. He knows exactly what I'm doing and smiles into our kiss.

"You're fucking disgusting," he laughs. "Lucky for you, I'm into kinky shit like that."

He kisses me deeper, letting me know I haven't rattled him, then pecks my lips one last time. I get the sense that he doesn't mind me not rushing off, so I lie back and stare at the ceiling, just existing with him, naked and warm. It dawns on me that he managed to do the one thing no one else has accomplished.

He made me feel comfortable.

As if he knows my guard is down, his hand lands gently on my stomach. He leaves it there, smoothing his fingertips over my skin. For once, I don't cringe at the thought of someone feeling the softness of this particular area, the imperfections.

"I've got a pickup game in the morning, so I need to crash, but... that doesn't mean you have to go."

I can hardly believe my ears but try to hide my shock. Lying there, with the warmth of his solid thigh against mine, I consider it, the idea of turning over in the middle of the night and finding him there, or waking up to him. But a large part of me knows not to trust him. Knows not to trust *this*.

Far too often, they've changed up on me. So quickly that it makes my head spin. What makes tonight any different?

"I should go."

He turns and I feel his eyes on me, but I don't have the courage to meet his gaze. In the past, he's been far too unpredictable, and for that reason, I'd rather sleep in the comfort of my own space.

Even if that space *is* just a basement all the way on the other side of town.

"Fine," he finally says. "But I'm taking you. Get dressed."

"I'm fine to take the—"

"Bus? No," he scoffs. "At this time of night, it's full of seedy assholes who think any girl riding this late is an easy target."

When I finally do look into his eyes again, there's a firmness in his expression that I take to mean he won't bend on this.

Instead of wasting my breath protesting, I grab my jeans and t-shirt while he pulls on his shorts. He moves to the dresser and slips a tee over his head, then waits while I tie my sneakers. As he passes through the doorframe, I note how close his head is to the top, how close his shoulders are to the sides, and I understand why he wasn't worried about 'handling me'. And with the others matching his size, I don't imagine that'd be a concern of theirs either.

I trail him, and when I catch a glimpse of his face in the light of the hallway, he's still flushed and red. His hair is more mussed than usual, too. Not only is he still hot as sin, I might find him hotter than ever in this moment, with thoughts of our wicked deed still fresh in my head.

He's none the wiser that he has my undivided attention when he taps Ash's door twice with his middle knuckle before letting himself in. Seated at his desk with a lamp beaming light onto a textbook, we find Ash. Right away, his curious blue eyes peek around Micah and then narrow when they land on me. He smirks and I adjust my shirt when his deep stare makes me feel naked.

"Well, *this* is a pleasant surprise," he says, leaning back in his seat.

From the looks of things, he was obviously studying before we wandered in. His hair's tousled, and he's shirtless with his extensive tattoo work exposed. A pair of black-framed glasses I've never seen him in offset his bad boy persona. He's got this whole 'hot nerd' thing going on, and I've gotta admit, that shit's working quite well for him.

"I need the truck," Micah speaks up. "It's late, so I'm gonna drive her."

Without a second thought, Ash's keys fly through the air and land in Micah's palm. "Thanks."

"Hang on a sec," Ash calls out, halting Micah's steps just as we turned to leave. "You two been partying without me?"

His eyes are fixed specifically on me. My cheeks feel warm and I'm certain that's because they're red as hell right now.

"Next time, you'll get an invite," Micah smirks, and I find their dynamic so fascinating.

Ash nods slowly, still with his eyes trained on me.

"Be back in a sec," Micah says, grabbing the doorknob.

I catch Ash's eyes again as the door closes, and as fun as my time was with Micah, I can't help but to think how much more it could've been if the others had been invited to join.

Micah's words ring in my thoughts.

'*Next time.*'

He's planning for there to be a next time...

WE MOSTLY RIDE TO MY PLACE IN SILENCE, WHICH IS perfect. I keep replaying my conversation with Scarlett, trying to connect the dots with half of them missing. And now, Mom's on high alert, texting back-to-back, trying to pry answers from me that I don't have. As my phone goes off for the tenth time since climbing into Ash's truck, I feel Micah's eyes on me.

"Did I keep you from something tonight?"

The chill tone he'd spoken to me with at the house is long gone, giving way to a harsher, colder sound. Something closer to his usual voice.

When I glance over, meeting his gaze, I see hints of something unexpected. Jealousy. Or maybe that's the wrong word. It's... possessiveness. Like, he can't stand the thought of something—or *someone*—he's deemed "his" being out of his control.

I'm keenly aware of the bright red flag waving right in front of my face.

"It's just my mom," I explain, although he's not owed an explanation.

His eyes shift back to the road, though, so I can only guess my answer appeased him. It's silent again, but not comfortably like before.

"Did you mention something about having a match tomorrow?" I ask, trying to fill the dead air.

"Yeah, sometimes we meet with local teams before the season kicks off. Keeps us in shape, quick on our feet."

My eyes shift in his direction when he mentions keeping in shape. I focus on his arm stretched to the steering wheel, the highly defined muscle, prominent veins running beneath his ink.

Through his t-shirt, his pecs protrude, and I don't hate how the fabric hugs his ridged abdomen and biceps.

He's perfect.

As long as you're only looking skin deep, anyway.

"You should come."

I stop ogling his physique just as his head turns my way. We lock eyes. "Come where?"

He laughs a bit at my airheaded moment. "To the match. Starts at eleven. We'll pick you up."

"You asking me or telling me?" I say with a smirk, facing out the window when we turn onto my street.

"Asking."

The response seems like a missed opportunity to kick dirt in my eyes, so I'm a little surprised.

"I would, but I've got a ton of shit to settle before tomorrow night," I answer, already thinking of the long list of things that have gone undone due to recent distractions.

"Right. The fundraiser. What's left to finish?"

The question draws a laugh from me. "Oh, I don't know, selling tickets? I hardly even put a dent in the number I intended to unload, but it is what it is at this point, I guess."

He's quiet. Thoughtful, even.

"Do you have the tickets on you?"

I do a double-take when he asks. "They're in my bag. Why?"

"Give them to me. I'll see what I can do."

After staring at him in disbelief—and also with a smidge of distrust—I dig into my bag and hand over a stack of purple tickets bound by a rubber band. He reaches over me to toss them into the glove box, then shuts it.

"What time's this thing start again?"

I suppress a deep sigh, controlling myself because, all-in-all, he's been less toxic tonight. Far be it for me to poke the bear.

"Since you're still planning to show up against my wishes... it starts at eight."

A nod is his only response as we pull up to my house. To my horror, all my housemates are seated out on the porch steps, laughing and talking like it's not nearly midnight. They glance this

187

way but I'm positive they can't see us through the tinted glass. Not sure if it's the sigh of dread that leaves me or my now sullen expression that gives me away, but Micah notices the shift in my mood.

"Shit, I know that look," he says with a laugh. "Which one of them do you hate?"

It's on the tip of my tongue to say all of them, but that'd ruin the mirage. My entire excuse for being inside The Den that night is hinged on some supposed allegiance to one of my housemates, so I'm forced to lie.

"The brunette with the bangs," I answer, pointing Dahlia out from the crowd.

Micah studies her for a moment. "Yeah, I've seen her around. I think she was at the house when—"

"She was," I cut in, feeling frustrated as I recall being hounded for answers from her that night.

"What'd she do? Or is she just a general bitch?" His wording makes me smile.

"She's definitely a general bitch, but... there's other shit, too."

"Like what?"

After the question leaves his mouth, he puts the truck in park, and I'm surprised. I expected to just get dumped out of the passenger seat when we got here, especially seeing as how he has an early morning.

"Like, a bunch of little things that add up," I share.

His brow arches when he repeats himself, sounding stern this time. "Like... what?"

I breathe deep and look at the dashboard instead of him. "For starters, she lied about the room I'd be renting at the house. A *cozy bedroom with a private bath* turned out to be a small corner of the basement."

Micah's quiet for so long that I turn to gauge his expression. I expected to see pity there, actually, but instead, I find anger.

"Your bedroom is in the fucking basement?"

I'm not sure how to respond, because I'm not sure what he's thinking, so I just nod and look away again.

"That started it," I continue, "but we just sort of naturally clash."

When I laugh, I feel Micah's stare on me again.

"The night of the meeting at The Den, when me and the other girls had to serve, her brain damn near short circuited trying to figure out what my connection was to you three. Believe it or not, my weight is a bigger issue for *her* than it is for me," I add. "So, she was on this insanely persistent mission to figure out what the connection was. Finally, she settled on thinking I *must* be related to one of you. What other way for her to rationalize how someone like *you* would be with someone like *me*?"

Emotion creeps in with those last words. Because some variation of them has been drilled into my head all my life, from one asshole or another wanting me to feel like I'm less than. It just so happens that, this time, that asshole was Dahlia.

"I'm coming around. Don't touch the door," Micah says through gritted teeth, and before I can sort out what's happening, he climbs out of the truck, slamming the door behind him.

I follow him around the hood of the truck, and when he stops at my window, I note that my housemates are staring, too. Staring *and* whispering.

I focus on Micah again when he unlatches my handle. He's intense. *Very* intense, actually. That's the only word that describes his rigid body language, his stern expression. He's not quite pissed, but on his way there.

He offers his hand, and after half a second, I realize he intends for me to take it, so I do, stepping out into the grass. Now, not only can I *see* my housemates' whispers, I can hear them too. Not actual conversation, but the hissing of venomous words leaving their lips.

I can only follow Micah's lead as he walks me to the end of the driveway, and then, before I can even process his actions, his arm loops around my waist and he kisses me. In front of everyone. With as much heat and passion as there'd just been in his bedroom.

My body eventually catches up to my brain and I turn into him, locking my fingers at the base of his neck, beneath the warmth of his hair. His tongue slowly dips into my mouth, and I breathe him in, experiencing a swell of excitement and vindication like I've never felt before.

Knowing there's at least some measure of a connection between us.

Knowing he kissed me because he wanted to.

Knowing those bitches on the porch are eating their fucking hearts out right now.

If I'm being honest, that's the best part.

He presses one last kiss to my mouth, and I swear I could die right here on the sidewalk. His gaze lowers to my lips like he wants more, but he leans toward my ear instead.

"They think you're one of us now," he whispers. "Don't ever let that bitch think she's got something over you again. Understood? We don't do weak."

His words run deep, and they have their intended effect on me. I hear *and* feel them. He can assume as much when he pulls away and I nod.

"Understood."

He smiles and it's like the rest of the world suddenly just came back into existence. As I'm walking away, he palms my ass, and I spot the other girls from the corner of my eye, watching in disbelief. I trudge toward the house, moving quickly so they don't see me grinning from ear to ear, because... it's definitely coming.

I turn when Micah's deep voice booms through the night air. My heart sinks, wondering what's up now, seeing as how this entire act is unscripted.

"Bird."

"Yeah?"

He arches a brow and gives me this insanely sexy, chill-inducing look that has me locked in. "Next time you stay this late, the guys and I already discussed it... you're ours for the entire night. It won't be up for debate."

That smile comes out now. "Understood."

He walks to his truck with a slick grin on his lips, knowing he just sold that shit. He starts the engine, revs it a few times, then he takes off down the street headed back to The Den. And just like that, my night is officially made.

What started out as a terribly emotional and gut-wrenching day has taken quite the drastic turn. Who knows? I might even sleep well. But the best part—the part that will have me grinning until dawn—is that Micah just helped me say my three favorite words without even having to open my mouth...

Fuck you, Dahlia.

Things are definitely off.

It's not always easy to pinpoint where a friendship has gone wrong, but there's no doubt about it. This is completely on me.

Maddox walks beside me in silence, clutching a stack of purple tickets, aiding in my last-ditch attempt at drumming up sales for the fundraiser tonight. We've spoken all of ten words to each other in the last hour. There's so much I *can't* say, I'm not really sure what *to* say anymore. If I'm not keeping my own secrets, I'm keeping Mel's, protecting her even in death.

In all the years Maddox and I have been close, there's never been a time when I've avoided him, never a time when I've avoided his phone calls, but that's been the case the last few weeks. He feels the strain, the disconnect. I'm certain of it. Which is why we've mostly walked in silence, pretending this is normal for us, while that couldn't be further from the truth.

He agreed to help me with this weeks ago, so it works out that the guys have a pickup match this morning. It means I can walk the streets with my best friend, without fear of being spotted and reprimanded for breaking their twisted rules. But honestly, I thought Maddox was going to bail on me. It's not like I haven't given him reason to, ghosting him so often lately. I should've known better, though. If there's one thing he's never done, it's disappear on me.

Even after my dad left.

Even when things got tough after Mel passed and I went dark for a while.

He was there.

Just like he is now, walking in the heat, as if he has nothing better to do.

My place is close enough that we could've walked downtown, but he insisted on driving us closer. I didn't argue. I did, however, toss my bike into the back of his SUV. He has to cut the morning of canvasing short to head to the airport to meet his grandmother, but I can't afford to end early. Attendance for the event is low. *Way* low.

We've spent the morning targeting local spots we know other students hang out on weekends—cafes, bookshops, laundromats. And despite all these places being packed, between the two of us, we've sold a whopping eleven tickets. Add that to what other members have reported back, the turnout will be embarrassingly small. Like, fifty attendees small. But if nothing else comes from Me and Maddox's early-morning sales efforts, it's at least an opportunity to patch things up with my best friend.

At least, I hope it is.

"Thanks for coming with me. Definitely beats doing this alone."

He's stone-faced at first, but then cracks a smile. "Hell, I'm just shocked we actually get to hang out."

"Fair enough," I say back. Sure, he just took a shot at me, but I kind of deserve it.

We cross the street when the light turns, then we cut through the alley behind a deli.

"I have questions," he says, keeping his eyes trained on the pavement beneath our feet.

"And I might have answers. Emphasis on the word *might*," I answer with a dim smile. One he doesn't reciprocate. Instead, he's got this serious look on his face, and it only adds to the awkwardness.

"I'm positive you won't answer both, so I'll let you choose between the two. So, first, where have you been hiding?" he asks. "Or, option two... *what* have you been hiding?"

His tone is light and unassuming, but the question is heavy. I weigh my options and one is clearly less intimidating to answer than the other.

"I haven't been hiding, per se. I've been busy."

"Bullshit."

The abrupt response has me snapping a look toward Maddox.

"We've been busy before, Stevie, and we've still managed to find time to catch up. But lately, you've been like a fucking ghost. I can't track you down anywhere."

"Between school, the group, work, and just surviving, I've been—"

"If you're not gonna be honest, I'd rather you just not answer at all."

The depth of his voice takes on a sternness I'm not used to hearing from him. It's a sign that he's not buying any of this, and if I want to salvage what's left of our friendship, I'll have to tell the truth.

Well, some of it, at least.

"I've still been trying to sort things out for Mel," I admit, and when he casts a look my way, it's softer, more understanding. "I made a run to Cypress Pointe."

His brow quirks as we round the corner and step back onto the sidewalk.

"That's a bit of a hike, isn't it? What's way out there?"

"A place called Dusty's Diner," I share. "Mel visited there before she..."

My voice trails off when I can't bring myself to finish the sentence.

"Does she know someone who works there?" he asks.

I shrug, wrestling with the wording. "Not exactly. She went in, asked about the man who owns the place, then left in tears, but not before one of the waitresses wrote her number on a napkin and gave it to her. That's how I knew the place existed."

"And the napkin was just... laying around?"

I envision the tin, covered in butterflies. Then, I envision the mementos it held inside. My sister's secrets.

"Yeah, I guess you could say that," I lie, deciding against sharing all the details. It's one thing for *me* to unearth the skeletons in my sister's closet, and another for the rest of the world to know they exist.

"So, nothing came of it? Still don't know why she went?"

I shake my head. "No clue."

"Have you mentioned it to your mom?"

"I did, but she didn't know anything either."

He's quiet and I know his wheels are turning. "Well, were the people at the diner suspicious or anything? Did it seem like they knew something?"

I shake my head again. "Nope. In fact, they were super helpful. In the sense that they were willing to answer all the questions they could, anyway. Problem is, no one seems to actually *have* answers."

A sigh of frustration leaves me when I finish speaking.

"Do you plan to go back? Dig deeper? Ask more questions?"

"Not unless I have reason to. They said they didn't know anything, and I believe them."

I replay that day in my head, talking to Dusty and Scarlett. They were only kind to me, and I didn't get the impression that was a front. So, I've had to think outside the box a bit, question other reasons my sister might have been there. It's possible Dusty wasn't Mel's direct target, but instead, maybe someone Dusty may have known. I didn't get around to asking Scar if maybe her uncle had a son. Perhaps a son Mel's age who she may have known. Hell, *he* might've been the guy she was seeing, but who the fuck even knows?

I have a million questions, a million scenarios floating around inside my head, and zero resolutions.

Maddox gets out one syllable of his response before shutting his mouth.

"What is it?" I ask. "If you have an idea, trust me, I'm all ears."

He hesitates again, but then just comes out with it.

"Have you considered the possibility of just... leaving this alone?" he asks, being gentle with his words. "I mean, Mel kept this shit to herself for a reason. And maybe that reason was that she wanted to protect you and your mom from whatever she was dealing with."

I hear him. In fact, these are thoughts I've had for a while now, but if I'm honest with myself, it would be impossible for me to go to bed at night knowing I stopped trying to avenge my sister.

"You're not wrong," I admit. "But the truth of the matter is, if I were at all capable of letting this go, I would've done it months ago. For my own sanity. It's just that... she's not here anymore. She'll never go to college, she'll never get to accomplish her dreams, she'll never get to win at life, or fuck up at life, or *any* of that shit and... I just need to know why."

When my eyes blur, I fight against my tears, refusing to let them fall. I'm sick of crying, but more than that, I'm sick of living my life in limbo.

"I hear you, and even if I don't fully agree with what you're doing, you know I support you."

He squeezes me with one arm in a half-hug as we walk and I appreciate him—for this, for being here despite feeling distant from me, for everything.

"Just promise me that if it gets to be too much, you'll stop."

I nod. "I can't promise, but I'll keep that in mind."

"Good enough." He kisses the top of my hair. "I have to go. The last time I was late picking up Grandma from the airport, she got into an argument with security and ended up getting detained."

I smile, remembering that incident very clearly.

"Tell her hello for me. I'll see you tonight, though, right?"

He shrugs and looks very unsure about that. "Probably not. Mom's doing a big family dinner since my grandmother's here."

It sucks, but I get it. Plus, I wasn't exactly looking forward to him crossing paths with the guys. "I know you'd be there if you could. We'll hang out soon."

He nods, agreeing.

"Yep. Soon."

"Thought you said ticket sales were shit," Kip whispers with a smile, nudging me as he walks past, carrying a few pairs of rental skates to the counter.

His question comes just as I observe the crowd forming at the door, all clutching purple tickets in their hands. I hadn't lied—sales *were* shit. Only, looking at the line with no end in sight, you'd never guess it.

"I think we're gonna need more t-shirts," Claire beams.

"Tell me about it."

I glance toward the pile of a hundred I honestly thought would mostly go to waste, but now I'm having second thoughts.

My eyes are fixed on the entrance, trying to count heads, when three who tower above most of the crowd walk up.

"You've got to be kidding me. No way *they* showed," Claire says to me as she, too, spots the guys.

It shouldn't surprise me that she already knows of them. Being hockey players means *most* people know them. The crowd parts as they walk into the lobby and I forget to breathe. No one protests when they jump the line and hand over their tickets to Liza behind the counter. She stamps their hands, damn-near needing to wipe drool from her lip, and then they enter—my smoking ho tormentors.

Beside me, Claire clears her throat and I'm aware of he

straightening her clothes, but then a tiny gasp leaves her as she realizes they're coming this way.

"Shit! Do you know them?" she asks, but there's no time to answer because they're here. Vince walks up first—a navy blue baseball cap shadowing his eyes, a fitted tee and gray sweats that leave *very* little to the imagination below his waist. Ash stops beside him—dark jeans with holes in both knees, with black sneakers and t-shirt. The turquoise gauges in his ears bring out the same vibrant hue in some of his tattoos, providing the only pop of color. Micah steps up last. The damp curls resting on his shoulders means he climbed out the shower, tossed on the jeans and snug-fitting gray tee right before arriving.

All eyes are on them and I'm trying not to gawk, but damn...

"Hey," I say casually, pretending not to be in awe of them along with everyone else. It's easy when I force myself to think of all the shit they've put me through, but it gets tougher when glimpses of the pleasure they've brought me creeps in, too.

"I believe this belongs to you," Ash speaks up, right before handing over an envelope of cash. "We sold what we could before and after the pickup game today. Sometimes we get a good crowd even though the season hasn't started. Today was one of those days."

I eye the money, imagining how many tickets they must have sold to earn so much.

"Thank you. *All* of you. This will mean so much to the group."

Ash nods and Claire clears her throat again, prompting me to remember she's even present.

"Oh! This is Claire." I gesture toward her with the introduction. "She was the first member of the group, actually. Well, besides me, I guess."

She snorts a laugh, then promptly covers her mouth with one hand, and waves at the guys with the other.

"Hi," she barely gets out. "I'm Claire. But... I guess you already know that."

My heart sinks when she stumbles. Mostly, because I feel her anxiety spike.

"Pleasure meeting you," Vince says, laying on the charm. He's not intentionally flirting, but that doesn't stop Claire from blushing.

My number-one concern with them being here was my crew being uncomfortable. But so far, we're off to a decent start.

"So, I should um... get the shirts organized by size and set up the table," she says, grinning as she excuses herself.

It's just me and the guys now and the mood shifts.

The kind expressions they'd donned to meet my friend have been replaced with deep, hooded stares that can be hard to read sometimes. With these three, it can either mean they're contemplating something wicked, or thinking of what filthy thing they'd like to do to me next.

Being honest, I don't hate that last idea.

Not like I used to.

A flash of my night with Micah creeps in, and when I glance up, he's already staring. Possibly having the same thought as me. I can practically feel his solid thighs in my hands, the ridges of his chiseled abdomen beneath me as I rested on him.

More people flood in through the entrance and it jars me back to the present.

"How was the match?" I ask. "Did you guys win?"

Vince chuffs this cocky laugh that's sexy as sin. "Of *course*, we won."

My heart does this quick throbby thing that has me scrambling for words.

"Well, I... Thanks again for your help. You didn't have to do this."

"Don't sweat it," Ash says with a casual nod. "Besides, we committed to doing this as part of the frat's volunteer obligation, so our asses are kind of on the line, too."

And just like that, the sweet gesture loses some of its magic. Of course, this wasn't just for me. They did it because they had to.

Drawing in a breath, I pull my gaze from the three and glance around the rink. For just one second, my head was in the clouds, but they always seem to pull me back down to earth.

"Well, I should go help Claire," I say, then attempt to dismiss myself. I'm feeling a bit embarrassed for forgetting who I'm dealing with, forgetting that I'm not special.

I take one step toward the table lined with purple t-shirts when a large hand encircles my wrist. I turn and stare Vince in his eyes. He's the one who's taken a hold of me this time.

"It wasn't just about the frat," he says.

I blink into his green stare, feeling confused.

"I saw your face a second ago, when Ash explained why we stepped up," he adds. "And... I thought you should know it wasn't about that."

I'm holding my breath, thinking I might understand what he's trying to say, but I keep my thoughts to myself for now. Then, when Vince realizes I'm still a little lost, he sighs. His discomfort is damn-near palpable. Over the past few weeks, one thing I've gathered is that he's not great at expressing himself, which explains that pained look on his face.

"Micah mentioned you were having a tough time moving tickets," he says. "Yeah, a good turnout reflects better on the frat, but... that was an afterthought."

I'm quiet, gauging whether or not he's got some other angle, some hidden agenda I don't quite see yet. Because if he doesn't, what he's just admitted might be perceived as... *sweet*.

Still, I'm not quite sure whether they're to be trusted.

"This group means something to you, and we know you were worried that our presence here would do more harm than good. So, I guess we also wanted to prove you wrong. We... wanted to help."

Despite the drab tone to Vince's speech, there's a hint of softness in his eyes. It's enough that I believe him. I mean, he nearly choked on every syllable, but he managed to get it all out without bursting into flames, so that's something.

When I nod, I feel some of my recent coldness disappear. "I appreciate that. Thank you."

Vince nods, then I'm distracted by a voice. "Stevie, get out here!" Marley—one of my very first members—yells from the rink. She and her twin are beckoning me to join them out on the floor.

I face the guys again. "Any of you skating?"

Ash scoffs. "Not unless it's on ice."

It feels strange leaving them standing there, but I also get the sense I should've already walked away.

"Well, I, um... I should get out there. Guess I'll see you around."

The guys nod, and I step away. All three sets of eyes linger on me just as a group of their brothers approach, but I'm certain I have their attention long after I turn.

This turnout still blows my mind. Yes, because I anticipated that this event would crash and burn, but also because of *them*.

I glance over my shoulder at Vince, Ash, and Micah standing there, and there's a feeling in my gut I never thought it possible to feel toward them.

I'm... grateful.

VINCE

"All right. Here's the deal. You bought your own tickets, we're here supporting a worthy cause, so have fun tonight," I announce, speaking up so the guys hear me over the music. "However, if *any* of us three hears one complaint, if we see anyone pulling some shit they know they shouldn't be pulling, there will be consequences."

I look at the pledges in particular when saying that part. If anyone's going to fuck up, it'll be them.

"So, to be clear, don't *do* dumb shit, and don't *say* dumb shit. If you do, we *will* find out about it. Understood?"

Everyone nods in agreement, keeping their eyes trained on me, Ash, and Micah.

"Good. Be on your best behavior tonight, fellas. Make the Savages look good. Dismissed."

The crowd disperses now that I've given permission, but Ash grabs Enzo by his shoulder before he can get too far.

"And *you'd* better be *particularly* careful," Ash warns. "Not much gets past us. Then again... you already know that, don't you?"

Smiling, Ash shoves Enzo off toward the others, and when Ash leans against the rail and shakes his head, I have a flashback of our brother, Eros, having to be especially tough on the three of us. We were a lot like Enzo—defiant, the definition of a challenge—but Eros didn't give up on us. Granted, he had to put his foot to our asses more times than we can count, but he stuck around.

He *still* sticks around.

As more bodies file into the building, the DJ turns up the volume a few notches. Mostly, we pretend to just be keeping an eye on things, making sure our boys don't get out of line, but it's painfully obvious where our attention truly lies. Case in point, each of our gazes slowly shifts toward the rink when Bird swings past.

The t-shirt with the name of her group over a huge, blue monarch butterfly only falls to her hips. Black stretch pants hug her round ass and it's out there for everyone to see. Including us, and we haven't been shy about looking.

She's admitted to being self-conscious about her body, but you'd never know with how she flaunts it. She speeds past again, smiling with her friends, never making eye contact with us, but she knows we're watching.

"Think she has any idea how fucking hot she looks?" Ash asks. He's been standing with his arms folded the last few minutes, staring only at Bird.

Micah smirks. "Sad thing is, no. I don't."

I couldn't agree more. Especially when I glance toward our guys and a good handful of them have their eyes glued to Bird's ass when she executes a skilled turn and starts skating backwards.

"It's like she's *trying* to make us fuck her," Ash says, gnawing the side of his lip with the words.

A laugh leaves Micah and he finally tears his eyes away, looking toward the entrance instead. It's then that an intense, "Oh, shit," leaves his mouth and has me turning to see what's up.

"There a problem?"

He answers my question with a nod toward the door. "Maybe."

Ash and I are both looking now, staring down the sorority

chicks all rocking red t-shirts with their letters in white across their chests.

"You been dodging one of these bitches or something?" Ash asks with a laugh, but Micah is stone-faced.

"No, it's just that Stevie's got a… thing with one of them. Which means they probably shouldn't be here."

"Shit, that's on me," Ash admits. "A few of the girls were at the match this morning and I thought it'd be an easy way to unload some tickets. You just told us to sell as many as we could, so…"

"It's cool. It's done now. We'll just have to keep an eye on things, make sure they don't start any shit."

Micah finishes speaking and his attention is still on the door. He doesn't look away until Ash laughs. "So, is this what we're doing now?" he asks. "A few weeks ago, we were all about burning Bird's world to the ground. Now, we're her personal bodyguards?"

There's no malice in his tone, or even any hint of protest, just amusement.

"Don't be an ass," Micah grumbles. "Nothing's changed."

Ash arches a brow. "Just saying… maybe this sudden change of heart has something to do with, I don't know, you and Bird hanging out last night? Alone," he adds.

"Shit! What the fuck? Why am I just now hearing about this?"

Ash laughs and Micah's jaw ticks as he stands between us as we talk over him. He knows we see that he's not as abrasive toward Bird as he was in the beginning. But he should be used to Ash giving him shit. For starters, we've *all* felt things shifting when it comes to Bird. Hence the reason we've deemed frequent breaks from her a necessity. It's all strategic, giving us time to regroup and regain some perspective when she gets inside our heads.

Only, sometimes I wonder if she ever really *leaves* our heads.

"While I could definitely give you shit about this, I won't," I say with a laugh. "So, just fill us in. What's the plan?"

He hesitates, then lets out a breath before giving me the rundown.

"I dropped her off at her place last night. We pulled up and her roommates were hanging out on the porch. Turns out, the brunette between those two blondes over there? She's one of them. Name's Dahlia," he says, nodding toward the girl he's talking about. "I asked Bird a few questions, found out this chick's been giving her shit about us."

My brow tenses. "About us?"

Micah shrugs. "Basically, she kept asking why she saw us all together so much, insinuating that we're out of Bird's league or some shit. So, long story short, I may or may not have made it seem like Bird's with us. And I mean... *all* of us."

He finishes and Ash and I are still staring in his direction, not saying a word. When he smirks and pushes a hand through his hair, we let him speak again.

"I know what this fucking looks like," he says. "And I know what our mission's been, but you two didn't see how that bitch affects her. I had to do something."

Because he cares.

He'd never say as much, but we know each other better than anyone. He opens his mouth to explain again, but I stop him.

"Fuck it. I'm in. I'll play along."

"Me, too," Ash chimes in, sealing the agreement with one last statement. "No one fucks with Bird but us."

STEVIE

"Thanks for your support."

I smile, handing over two shirts as I total in my head how many we've sold so far. Forty-seven in the couple hours since the event kicked off, which is forty-seven more than anticipated.

Beside me, Claire completes a sale of her own, and I step away to take a peek at my phone.

Maddox: Dinner ran long. Sorry. I know you needed me there.

Stevie: No worries. Things are running smoothly. Just have fun. We'll talk later.

I drop my phone into my bag and join Claire behind the table again.

"Who designed the shirts? They came out super cute!"

I'd let my eyes and attention wander toward the guys seated in a booth, dragging my gaze back to Claire when her voice snaps me out of the daze.

"Um... Marley and Misty know a guy. I just shot them the design in an email, and they took care of the rest. He donated them, actually."

"Nice! The butterfly really pops," she adds. "Any reason you made that the group logo? I notice it on a lot of our flyers and things. I also noticed the tattoo under your hair once when you had it in a ponytail."

Her words have my hand wandering there, aimlessly rubbing the raised edges of the art on the back of my neck.

"Uh, yeah. There's a reason, but... I'd rather not talk about it." I offer a weak smile, hoping my vague response hasn't hurt her feelings, but when she smiles again, I know it didn't.

"Oh! Of course! Well, whatever the inspiration, it fits. Not sure if this was your goal or not, but it makes me think of a caterpillar's transformation. It's poetic," she adds with a quiet laugh.

I nod and a memory flashes in my thoughts...

Mel and I are maybe six and eight. We're both smiling as we stare in awe at what she's caught. We stole an old Mason jar from Dad's shed. What once held the collection of nails we now left piled in the windowsill by the table saw, had become the temporary home to the most vibrantly colorful butterfly I'd ever seen in my life. I was in awe, but from that point on, my sister was obsessed. Everything she could buy with a butterfly printed on it, was hers. She drew them, sang about them, dreamed about them. And now, while not *my* obsession, I tend to keep them nearby as a reminder.

Claire handles the next customer that walks up and I reach for a fresh stack of shirts to place on the table. I set them down and casually glance toward the booth where the guys have been hanging out. Ash and Vince have wandered over to the concession stand, leaving Micah seated alone. Only, he's not exactly alone anymore.

A brunette in a tight, red t-shirt stands with her jean-clad hip resting against the edge of the table and it only takes half a second for my brain to catch up with what my eyes have already realized. That the girl smiling and pushing her tits out to get Micah's attention is Dahlia. On cue, she flips her hair and I feel my face growing hot.

Just last night, she'd seen me with Micah. There's no doubt that she got the message he sent when he kissed me in front of the house. And yet... she's still shooting her shot.

Fucking bitch.

I'm angry at myself for not noticing she was here. For God

206

knows how long. I've been so busy, running around like a chicken with her head cut off to make sure the night goes off without a hitch. Meanwhile, she's been right under my nose maybe this whole time.

It isn't until I realize my fists are clenched at both sides that a thought hits me.

If I'd known she was here, what would have changed? Would I have hovered over the guys, cockblocking? They're not mine. Hell, they're not even my friends, so why should I give a shit about who they give their attention to?

Even if that person happens to be Dahlia.

I try to settle my nerves, but who the hell am I kidding? Whether it's rational or not, I'm upset. No, I'm fucking *pissed,* actually. And I'm not sure if it's directed more at Dahlia for completely disregarding the boundary my display with Micah should've set. Or... if it's all on Micah.

He knows the drama between Dahlia and me. No, not every menial detail, but he knows enough. He knows she's on a mission to tear me down, on a mission to make me feel like the nothing *she* sees me as. And now, as she licks her lips and stares down on Micah as he sits there like the fuckboy he is, eating that shit up, he's feeding into her bullshit logic.

Feeding into her belief that because I don't fit her ideal, she's better than me.

"Stevie! Where are you going?"

I hear Claire calling after me as I walk away, but I don't stop, knowing it's best if I remove myself from all of this. She calls out again, and I walk faster because my eyes are already filling with tears. I fucking hate that I'm letting this shit get to me, but... it is.

Fuck Micah.

Fuck them *all*.

But most of all... fuck me for giving a shit.

MICAH

207

I turn in my seat, scanning the building for Bird's whereabouts. A moment ago, she was at the table with her friend, selling t-shirts. Now, it's like she vanished.

Dahlia's still talking when I stand, a strange feeling spreading across my chest as I do another sweep. I wouldn't even think twice about Bird going missing if it weren't for how I'm sure this probably looks from a distance—a girl she hates smiling in my face.

It's in the back of my mind that I've never been the kind of guy who cares about this kind of shit—or the kind who'd even be *aware* of this kind of shit—but I guess that's different now. There was a gnawing in my gut that made me turn to look for Bird. A small part of me hoped she wouldn't see me talking to Dahlia and jump to the wrong conclusion, but with her gone, I'm willing to bet that's exactly what happened.

I wave the guys in my direction, then I start toward where I'd last seen Stevie, leaving Dahlia in the middle of her sentence. Ash and Vince are right behind me when I get to Claire.

"Hey, where'd Stevie run off to?"

She collects money from a customer and meets my gaze with a mousy smile. "Not sure. I couldn't chase her down because I've had people coming over back to back, but she looked upset."

Fuck.

"Which way did she go?"

Claire points me toward a closed door. "I think she's in there."

The song changes and 'Love Shack' pours from the overhead speakers as I take long strides in that direction. Ash and Vince are right with me, and I don't bother knocking on the door when I get there. Instead, we enter what looks like a stock room with reckless abandon and close ourselves in, muffling the music on the other side of the threshold. We walk a few feet and turn a corner, and that's when we lay eyes on her.

Red rimmed eyes, crumpled tissue in her hand, her cheeks still wet with tears.

"Get the fuck out," she yells, pointing toward the door.

"We're not going anywhere."

She glares when those words leave my mouth, but because

she's perpetually defiant, I know what her next move will be even before she makes it.

"Fine, then *I'll* leave."

The three of us create a wall blocking her path. She makes her best attempt at pushing through, but Vince catches her waist and hoists her an entire foot off the ground as she shoves against his shoulder. He hardly notices her struggling when he places her down into a chair. A frustrated eye roll marks Bird's silent protest. She knows she won't get past us, but if she thought she stood a chance at bulldozing through, she'd try again.

"Tell me why you're upset."

I finish speaking and I swear the sound of my voice just made her face twice as red.

"Why do you even care?" she asks, throwing her hands into the air. "This is all one big fucking game to you, isn't it?"

I'm holding my tongue, clenching my fists. All that keeps me from putting everything out on the table is my pride.

"If you tell me why you're pissed, we can have a conversation," I offer, and it happens again. That thing where she looks more and more like an angry tomato about the face.

"Fuck you, Micah. The fact that you even know there needs to *be* a conversation means you know exactly what you fucking did."

Her words are venomous, and I'm not the only one who feels it. I guess as much when Ash nudges me.

"Dude, what the fuck did you do?" he asks quietly, never taking his eyes off Bird.

I let out a deep sigh, knowing she's right. I also know she wants me to be the one to start the discussion because, in her eyes, I'm at fault.

Silently, we stare one another down as I struggle to shove my ego aside. I've never explained myself to a chick in my entire life. Because I'm not the type to let someone feel they're entitled to such a thing. But... I see through her anger.

To the hurt.

I don't know all her secrets, but the bits and pieces she's allowed us to grasp have painted a pretty bleak picture. One that left her emotionally scarred and struggling to love herself.

Shit.

I'm gonna have to do this, aren't I?

Fuck me.

"That wasn't what it looked like."

Bird's expression doesn't change. It still looks like she wants to kill me with her bare hands.

"Dahlia approached me, but I shot her down."

Bird's eyes roll back again when she scoffs. "Sure, you did."

My eyes narrow at her. This already goes against everything I believe, and she isn't buying it, so what's the fucking point?

I breathe deep again, reminding myself that she's been through some shit. It's the only thing that settles me, helps me keep my composure.

"She approached me," I repeat, keeping my tone even. "She didn't miss what I hinted at last night. The part about you being with not only me, but... *us*."

Bird's anger has her winded, but she's at least listening.

"First, she asked if she misheard. Then, once I told her she hadn't, she weighed in with her opinion, saying the three of us can have any girl we want, adding that she doesn't understand why we'd *'agree to some shitty arrangement to share you'*. After that, she promised to keep things discrete if I ever wanted to hang out."

"What was your response?"

I scoff at Bird's question. "I'd be able to tell you if I hadn't cut her off in the middle of her sentence to find out where the fuck you went."

There's a lingering look in her eyes that I don't miss. Actually, I recognize it. It's distrust. I know because I wear that look often. Only, the longer she studies me, the more it fades.

"I've got no reason to lie to you, Bird."

That feeling hits me in my chest again and I'm not a fan of it.

"For what it's worth, I've known Micah for half my life and I know when he's bullshitting. This isn't one of those times," Vince adds.

Bird's gaze shifts to him, and she could easily call Vince out for covering for me, but she doesn't. Instead, I see the same burgeoning trust toward him.

Finally, she nods and her eyes soften. She wipes a tear from her cheek, and I think we're all surprised when a quiet laugh puffs from her lips.

"Have I mentioned that I hate that bitch?" she sniffles.

"It's pretty fucking clear," I tease, relaxing against the wall now that the fire inside her has gone out.

My chest is heaving after admitting so much. Most of what brews between us four is unspoken. No, my brothers and I never had a conversation about Bird being the hub between us, but that hasn't made this fact any less true. Any less real. I don't know what to call it, but those invisible spokes connecting us to her exist, growing stronger over time despite our best efforts to fuck this up.

But, whether any of us would ever say as much out loud, there's something there. Far from love, not even quite affection, but attachment maybe? Complicated by the tendency for the three of us to be obsessive and possessive to the point of it bordering on toxic—*those being the words of some fed up group counselor to us years ago.*

Ash goes to Bird and takes her hand, using it to pull her up from her seat. She lets him, but she seems confused. At least, she does until he grips her chin and claims her lips. This is what she does to us. Makes us crazier than we already are.

It's unhealthy and problematic as fuck, but this is our reality.

This is what we *want*.

Ash slowly backs her toward the wall, and she takes his tongue. Watching her deep-throat it reminds me how she took my dick last night, drained me, swallowed me down that pretty throat of hers. She rests against the exposed brick and her tits bounce when she makes contact. Her eyes open to tiny slits. Just enough to find Vince before closing them, luring him over with one bend of her finger. There's zero hesitation in Vince's steps as he approaches, accommodating for the difference between her height and his by leaning in, then craning his neck to bring his lips to the side of her throat.

Shit from the past has made him hate touch since I've known

him. However, that shit seems to go right out the window every time he's near her—our fucking kryptonite.

Bird's hands lower and she rubs the front of Ash's jeans, Vince's sweats. I see those slits in her eyes again and they land on me. I know she wants me closer, but I had my fun with her last night. So, for now, I'm content where I've posted against the opposite wall, watching.

Vince breathes deep against Bird's neck. She responds with a gentle squeeze to his cock, and he grips her tit, pushing his thumb over her pebbling nipple. I can't help but wonder if she knows his secrets. Wonder if she can sense them.

Ash, impatient and impulsive, undoes his belt and snatches his zipper down. Bird gets the hint and works her hand into his boxers. A long breath leaves my nostrils and it's like I feel the softness of her palm against *me*. Ash draws Bird's bottom lip between his. Hers are swollen and blushing from the kiss and I swear I can taste her. It's taking everything in me not to join, but observing has its perks, too. For instance, when Ash slips a tattooed hand into Bird's panties, I can make out every motion through her thin pants.

His fingers pushing between her thighs, separating her lips, and finally entering her pussy with a quick thrust that has her gasping into his mouth.

She's drenched. The sound of it fills the air and my dick throbs against my zipper. My brothers are thoroughly enjoying her. As they should.

Bird's mouth leaves Ash's when a soft moan passes from her lips. Her fingers slink around to the back of his neck and she squeezes until his forehead slowly presses to hers. They're breathing one another's air and my lip aches when my teeth sink into it, knowing she's a breath away from coming on his fingers.

And she would've...

If the door didn't swing open just as Ash's name rolls off the tip of her tongue.

The asshole who just crashed the party isn't a stranger. I've seen him before. He's the one Bird had in her arms the night we met her. The night we rolled by to scope out her place.

212

The one she assured us didn't mean shit to her.

The next few seconds play out in slow motion, and I don't miss a thing—the rage that fills this guys eyes, the panic that fills Bird's when she realizes I'm not the only one watching, and I sure as shit don't miss how she retreats from Ash and Vince.

At first, they're confused, but then their gazes follow Bird's when she speaks.

"Maddox. Wait. I can explain."

This Maddox guy takes one look around, like he's memorizing the scene, our faces, then explodes from the room just as quickly as he'd burst in. I don't move, though, instead staying perched against the wall to watch it all unfold.

To watch how Bird will handle this.

"Shit. Shit. Shit," she chants, adjusting her clothes and hair before charging toward the door. Then and only then do I intervene, taking her arm when she means to pass.

"Where the fuck do you think you're going?"

"Let go, Micah."

She sounds anxious. Like she stands to lose something if she just lets him leave.

"You said out of your own damn mouth that there wasn't anything between you," I growl. "Was that a fucking lie?"

She huffs, clearly agitated by my question. "There's nothing between us, but he *is* my best friend and I need to talk to him," she insists.

I've never seen her like this. The version of her *we* get is hard, defiant. And yet, she's tripping over herself to chase after *this* motherfucker.

Not sure if she knows this, but I'm taking notes.

Lots and lots of notes.

"Then, correct me if I'm wrong, but if he's only a friend, you haven't crossed a line, right? I mean, technically, there shouldn't be anything to smooth over. That is, if he's only a friend." I finish speaking and study her expression very, very carefully.

She snatches her arm free but doesn't try to leave.

"Yes, actually, there *is* something to smooth over," she insists.

"It's not so much *what* he walked in on, but who I'm *with* that's the problem."

I cock my head, waiting for an explanation.

"Fuck." She sighs and her frustration's brimming over. "He doesn't even attend our school and he *still* knows about you guys. Your frat. Not sure if you know this or not, but your reputation definitely precedes you," she says. "So, why *wouldn't* he be upset?"

I hold her gaze and don't blink when I ask a question.

"Are you fucking him?"

"Are you—" Her eyes flit to the ceiling when she scoffs. "I'm not having this conversation. If you don't believe me, that's on you. I've told you the truth and now, if you'll excuse me, I need to go talk to my *friend*," she says snidely, emphasizing that final word.

She turns the knob and it'd be remiss of me not to give one final warning. Negligent even.

"I sure as hell hope you know what you're doing."

She pauses as my words sink in, but the next second, she's gone, hunting down Maddox. God only knows where he's run off to lick his wounds, but the one thing I *do* know is that Bird made her choice.

And unfortunately for her, it was the *wrong* fucking choice.

T he parking lot is full, packed to capacity, but it's the only
place I can imagine Maddox being.

Because I know he wants to get as far away from me as
possible right now.

I replay the scenario in my head and... oh, God... what he
must have seen. What he must think of me.

I push both hands through my hair and do another slow scan,
and this time, I spot his truck and rush between parked cars and
groups of students who've begun to congregate because it's gotten
so crowded inside.

"Excuse me. Move!"

I push past a couple making out against the side of a van and
probably look like a crazy person when I jump in front of
Maddox's headlights just as he takes his foot off the brake.

"What the hell are you doing?" he yells out the window.

Breathless, I stand at the hood of his truck, hands in the air.

"I'm not moving until you talk to me."

"There's nothing to fucking talk *about*, Stevie! You've clearly
gone off the deep end and, I'm sorry, but I won't be a part of that
shit."

I feel defeated already, but refuse to let it end here.

"Maddox, please."

There's a stalemate between us and I'm positive that if he had clearance behind him, he'd back out of his space without a second thought, but he's trapped.

Cursing to himself, he shifts into '*park*', then kills the engine. I release a long breath of relief when he finally steps out and slams his door closed.

"Talk," he sighs, looking everywhere but at me. Maybe he *can't* look at me. Maybe I disgust him now.

"Look, I know that must've looked bad, but—"

"But what?" he scoffs. "What could you possibly say that would make what I just witnessed okay? If no one else knows why those guys are bad news, *you* should."

He's livid, doing his best to keep his voice down, but he's losing that battle quickly.

"What about what they did to Mel?" he forces out. "How can you even—"

He starts pacing as a frustrated growl leaves him.

"You know what? I'm just gonna say it. I think losing her really fucked you up. As your friend, you need to seek serious help."

My heart lurches in my chest and his words cut deep, the bluntness of them. Typically, he speaks about my sister with care, knowing it's a sore spot for me, but not today. That compassion is nowhere to be found.

"And you... you're fucking them, Stevie?" he snaps, getting redder by the second. "You've waited all this time, saved yourself, and now you gave in to *these* assholes of all people?"

I've let him throw his daggers, but I'm starting to lose my cool.

"What'd you think, Maddox? That I was saving myself for you?"

As soon as the words leave my mouth, I know I shouldn't have said them. His not-so-secret feelings for me are sort of our elephant in the room, that obvious thing that we don't speak about. *Ever.* But I'm raw and hurt and... so many things.

My head lowers and I stare at the pavement, realizing I've made an ass of myself *again* tonight. "I didn't mean that. I wasn't trying to—"

"No, fuck you, Stevie. I've only ever looked out for you, but

I'm starting to think you might be beyond my help any-fucking-way."

He turns and gets back in the truck and, this time, I move aside, letting him pass when he revs the engine. His tires burn rubber as he exits, and all eyes are on me as onlookers probably try to sort out what just happened.

But no one's more confused about that than me.

So much is going through my head. I couldn't explain to the guys that on top of Maddox being my best friend, I've also known that he's been in love with me almost our whole lives. Except, that love has only ever been one-sided.

Does it make things awkward when it comes to me and guys? Absolutely. But I'm usually really careful to keep that side of my life secret. Until tonight, that is.

When I shoved it right in his fucking face.

"Shit."

I'm pacing in Maddox's now empty parking space when a set of tires screech behind me. I don't even have to turn to see who it is. Not only do I recognize the rhythmic hum of Ash's truck, but I know I started a blaze leaving *them* to go after Maddox.

"Get in," Micah commands, the hollowness of his deep voice setting my nerves on edge. He doesn't sound like himself. Or, maybe that's the thing. He sounds *just* like himself. The version I came to know and hate when we first met.

I could delay the inevitable, could cause a scene and put them off for a few days, but what's the point?

In their eyes, I've broken their trust, undid the small amount of progress we've made. Tonight is sure to be one I won't soon forget despite this setback being steeped in miscommunication.

Without a word, I approach the back door as Micah pushes it open and then slides across the seat so I can get in. Wherever this is headed, whatever punishment awaits me... I'm certain they've convinced themselves I deserve it.

T hey're silent.
 Completely.
Even as we turn into the long driveway of The Den, then *pass*
the manor to head deeper into the property. Ash's truck finally
comes to a stop, and in his headlights, the large wooden doors of a
two-story stable. The slats are deteriorating and missing more than
half the green paint that once coated them.

My heart has been on overdrive since we left the rink, but
seeing that *this* is our destination has me feeling like I might
literally have a heart attack.

"Why are we here?"

My question goes unanswered as Micah climbs out and leaves
me in the backseat alone while he walks to the back of the truck. I
turn on the bench to watch, breathing wildly as he grabs a black
duffle bag from the bed, right beside where they apparently tossed
my bike. When he lowers the bag to the ground and stoops out of
my line of sight, I panic.

"What's he doing? What's in the bag?"

Again, no one answers, but this time Vince and Ash hop out of
the truck, too. My eyes dart to the tree line and I'm calculating
how far I could get before they catch me if I run for it, because
they *will* catch me, but I can't just sit here. Can't just let whatever
is happening happen.

Within seconds, I break out into a cold sweat and the truck suddenly feels smaller than it once had. My fingers grip the handle and I pull, thinking if I can just get to the road someone might see me and *help* me, but before I can even fully open the door, I'm yanked backwards by my waist, then forced down onto the seat.

"No! Let me go!" My cries may as well have gone into the ether, because no one responds.

Strong hands hold my wrists, and as I kick my feet against the door, it flies open, and a second set of hands grabs my ankles. They're freakishly strong and no matter how hard I fight against them, I can't make their grips budge. At the feel of rough rope cinching around my ankles, panic turns into sheer terror and I begin to imagine a number of terrible things that could come of this. And that level of terror rises when more rope is tightened around my wrists, and I'm dragged from the backseat by my hands. I squeeze my eyes shut and brace myself for the hard fall to the gravel below, but arms catch me before that happens. And with one easy motion, I'm tossed over Ash's shoulder, bobbing against his back while he carries me, and Vince unlatches the heavy chain secured to the double doors.

Micah stands behind us, and I lift my head to see his face. Much to my horror, he's smiling, getting off on my fear. Like always.

"Why are you doing this?" I ask, expecting to only get silence in return again, but he indulges me this time.

"Why are we doing this," he repeats with a sigh. "Well, the short answer is that we agreed it's time to restore the balance of things. Based on that shit you just pulled back there, it's clear you've forgotten how this is all supposed to work."

He reaches out to stroke my cheek and I snatch away.

"See what I mean?" he says, his grin widening. "Somewhere along the way, you forgot just who the fuck we are, but we thought of a way to make it so you *never* forget. And the best part is, you're about to earn yourself a whopping twenty points!"

Rage surges through me when he rustles my hair with the words, like I'm some wayward, family dog. I struggle to no avail against Ashton. All it does is infuriate me more to grasp just how powerless I truly am.

Micah holds my gaze and, finally, the smile slips a little. "In case you haven't figured it out yet, you fucked up," he says gravely. "Chasing after your boyfriend, defying me... it's gonna cost you."

"He's *not* my boyfriend!"

Micah shrugs and I get the feeling that nothing I say matters much. "Maybe not, but you're sure as shit fucking him. And, not sure if you remember or not, but that's against the rules, Bird."

I buck against Ashton again as the large chains Vince has been working on finally clatter to the ground. There's an eerily hollow sound that echoes back from inside the stable when he opens the doors.

"I'm not fucking Maddox, because I'm not fucking *anyone!*" I snap. "I'm a virgin, you asshole."

Whatever Vince was doing to the door stops. I know because the *sound* stops. Even Ash goes still beneath me. I imagine my claim has just given them all pause. Even Micah. His eyes narrow as he steps closer, tilting his head, looking like a true psychopath as he takes my chin rough. His stare deepens and I can't move.

"Shit," he says softly. "You might actually be telling the truth."

For the first time since leaving the rink, I feel a sense of relief and I half-believe this might not end badly. But that feeling is short lived, being snatched away when Micah speaks again.

"However... I'm not changing my mind on this. That defiance in your eyes right now? The defiance I saw when you ran off? It ends tonight."

Micah

My eyes leave Bird and shift to Vince. "Go to the loft. I'll toss the rope up."

Unfortunately for Bird, we keep a bag of goodies in the truck at all times. The original plan was to use it for something we had in mind for the pledges, but this works, too.

"No, no! Please!" she pleads, but it's too late for remorse. The fact that it took this to bring her ass into submission means we were too soft on her, means we allowed her to forget this shit isn't a game. But reminding her will be easy.

For *us* anyway.

I'm in my fucking head, replaying how this is mostly my fault. It started last night, with me taking points off the table and making what went down in my room less about our arrangement and more about... us. And tonight was a total shitshow tonight. We ran after her, concerned about her delicate fucking feelings, begging her to believe I had no interest in Dahlia.

And what does Bird's ass do?

Chases after some weak, punk-ass bitch who damn-near cried when he laid eyes on her with us. Shit's ironic as fuck.

If I weren't me, I'd kick my own ass.

There's no point in denying what I've now accepted as true. She's got some kind of wicked hold on us, but I'll be damned if I let her know that shit.

I peer up when Vince's steps creak above, and I toss the rope bundled in my hands toward the rafters. He catches it on the first try, then Ash lets Bird slip off his shoulder. She's only on her feet for half a second before Vince tightens the slack, then knots it when I raise my hand to signal him. Bird's toes are barely touching the ground, so she's balanced, but can't get any traction as the tips of her sneakers slip over the loose hay and dirt beneath her.

She's always so hard, so tough, but not tonight. Tonight, she's sweating and sobbing because she knows she's about to be punished for what she did.

Lighting a cigarette, I step around her until we're face-to-face. Gripping her mascara-streaked cheeks, I note that she's never been so alert, so focused on me. It's refreshing and, if I'm being honest, it's making my dick hard.

"You get it now, don't you?" I whisper, blowing a ribbon of smoke against her cheek.

She doesn't speak, but the way she's trembling in those ropes... it's like a fucking drug to me.

Addictive.

I can't help myself. I lean in and taste her mouth, the saltiness of her tears making it hard to pull away, but I manage it. Because there's work to be done.

Only now does Bird seem to realize that Ashton's lit the woodburning stove, and her eyes widen. Then, when he places the branding iron into the flames, her panicked stare shifts to me again.

She *does* get it...

"Micah, don't do this. It was a misunderstanding," she explains, sounding so sweet and docile. If only she'd had this disposition earlier, we wouldn't be wasting our evening here.

"A misunderstanding. Hmm. That's interesting, because I distinctly remember trying to *get* an understanding earlier. But you pulled away, ran after Maddox instead," I remind her. "Does that sound familiar?"

Her head falls to her shoulder, then she bites down on her lip as more tears rush from her eyes. I step close again, brush wetness from her cheek with the back of my hand.

"Do you remember what I told you last night?"

She shakes her head when I ask. "I'm not sure."

I nod. "When we put on that show for Dahlia, when I came through for you... I told you that you're one of us now. Didn't I?"

This time, she nods, and it seems to be coming back to her.

"That was me taking you from the outside. That was me letting you in. And not even a full twenty-four hours later, you shit all over it," I growl, leaning in until I'm right at her ear to ask, "Was it worth it?"

She doesn't answer, and I don't expect her to. So, when I step away and Ash walks up, Bird's eyes stretch with fear, staring at the orange glow at the end of the iron.

"If this doesn't help you remember whose you are... nothing fucking will." I hold her gaze a bit, then nod toward her hip. "Put it on the left one."

"No! Please! I'll do anything, just please don't do this! Please!" she begs, but it's like her words don't even register.

Vince approaches her from behind and tugs her pants down

her thighs. She squirms but the ropes only allow for so much movement.

Ash holds her gaze and she's pleading with her eyes. "On the count of three," he says, but as soon as the word, "One," leaves his mouth, the sound of searing flesh and Bird's bloodcurdling scream surround us in stereo.

We've done this dozens of times, but this is the first time I can say with a clear conscience that I've thoroughly enjoyed this shit. Whether it's the way pain sounds leaving those beautiful lips of hers, or the fact that this mark means that no matter where she goes, no matter what happens, we're now carved into her forever.

Deep.

Burned into her skin like she's burned into ours.

She'll never fucking forget.

Ten seconds pass and Ash lowers the iron. I walk up to Bird, making sure she hears me loud and clear. Even over the sound of her own wailing.

"Breathe a word of this to anyone, *show* anyone, and I promise... you will fucking regret that shit for the rest of your life."

Her voice softens to a quiet whimper as she pants, gasping for breath, likely experiencing the worst pain she's ever felt.

"Now, you'll always be ours," I say before my hand slips between her thighs, cupping her pussy through silk panties. "And since we know you've saved yourself, rest assured, soon, this will be ours, too."

Her lids grow heavy, and I recognize that look. She's passing out. But before she drifts, three words leave her lips...

"I hate you."

Hearing that, I smirk as my arm goes around her waist. I pull a knife from my back pocket and work it against the rope to cut her down.

"Can you keep a secret?" I whisper, feeling the weight of truth in these words as they leave my mouth. "I hate me, too."

The rope snaps, she goes limp in my arms, and just like that... our bird has completed another important lesson.

P ale light blinds me and I'm no longer waking subtly, but jolting into what *would* have been an upright position, but I'm stuck, tied down in someone's bed.

Micah's bed.

I swallow deeply and try to get my bearings, but searing pain in my left hip brings it all rushing back—the stable, the rope, the glowing tip of the branding iron. My attention shifts there, expecting to lay eyes on a mass of melted flesh, but instead, a pristine white bandage is taped in place, covering my marred skin.

The last thing I remember is staring into Micah's dark eyes after being mutilated by the sadistic fucks I would *love* to kill this morning.

A chair creaks across the room and I lift my head just as Ash turns. He's got a textbook in hand, black-framed glasses perched on his nose, and his feet are casually kicked up on Micah's desk.

Like they *didn't* hogtie and brand me last night.

"Morning, Sunshine," he grins, and I want to claw his eyes out.

"Don't you dare fucking speak to me," I hiss, trying and failing to stand, which only frustrates me further. "And why the fuck do you keep tying me up! Shit!"

When I growl and finally give up, the sound of Ashton's laugh nearly has me spitting fire.

"Calm down. You'll aggravate the wound," he warns calmly, as if he's *not* the one who caused said wound. He nods to the side of the bed. "I put pain killers, ointment, and bandages in your bag. Keep it clean and it'll heal up in a few weeks."

I hear him, but only one part of what he said even registered.

"You went through my bag?"

He stares. "First of all, you're welcome. We grabbed it on our way out of the rink last night. Second, I didn't go *through* it, I put something *in* it."

"Don't touch my things."

He laughs again, loud and deep. "Are you shitting me? Of all the places you've trusted me to put my hands, your bag is where you draw the line? Interesting."

"Keep mocking me and I swear to God—"

"Swear to God you'll what?" He tilts his head when asking, looking genuinely curious, and genuinely infuriating.

Another growl leaves me, and I kick against Micah's bed like a child, because that's how they fucking treat me. Telling me what to do, where to go, and punishing me when I disobey.

"I want to go home."

"Relax. We'll take you after you eat. Vince is fixing you something so you're not taking pills on an empty stomach."

On cue, as if waiting for those exact words before entering, the door opens and in walks Vince, tray in hand. On it, he's toasted a bagel and smeared cream cheese on both sides. A bottle of apple juice rests beside it with a banana.

"Eat," Vince instructs. "I won't ask twice."

"What will you do? Force it down my throat?"

He smirks and I get the feeling he imagines doing exactly that. "If I have to."

He sets the tray beside me, then loosens the cap on the juice before placing it on the nightstand. When he lifts the bagel like he might actually shove it into my mouth, I hold out my hand. Grinning, he sets it in my palm, then unties that wrist.

"Eat," he says again, then retreats to the other side of the room. He playfully shoves Ash's feet off the desk, then sits beside Micah's laptop.

I take a bite, but my throat feels tight. There's nothing *physical* causing it to restrict. Only frustration, rage. I swallow the bite I've taken just as Micah joins us, and seeing *his* smug ass sets me off.

It's like I'm having an out-of-body experience. Something comes over me, and before I can stop myself, I throw my half-eaten bagel in his direction. Unfortunately, he ducks just in time, and proceeds to gawk at the door where it sticks, the cream cheese acting as an adhesive. For several seconds, he stares there, but when he finally turns, his wicked glare lands right on me.

"Good morning to you, too," he teases with a smirk.

I've got one free hand and make the most I can of it, quickly reaching to the other side with hopes that I can untie it quickly. But my effort is in vain.

"We talked about this. Eat, take your pills, then we'll take you home," Ash says calmly, holding me still while Micah binds my wrist again.

"What is... *wrong* with you assholes? How fucked up do you have to be to think you can *burn* someone, then pretend you give a shit about my fucking health the next morning? We are *not* normalizing this shit! This isn't okay!"

I'm panting and writhing on the mattress, but the three surrounding me are silent, staring as I thrash around, until I eventually tire myself. But I've only given up in body, my mind is still racing, still fueling my anger.

"I shudder to think what kind of fucked up childhoods you fuckers must've had if the shit you do to me feels okay."

My head lifts from the pillow and I glare at Ashton, feeling particularly venomous today.

"You. You're covered in scars from head to toe. So, now, because someone did one hell of a job making sure *you're* numb to pain, you think everyone else should be, too? And you," I say next, laying eyes on Vince. "You think I haven't noticed how you get whenever I touch you? How you tense up and fight the urge to pull away? I've already pieced your whole story together because you're so fucking transparent. And I know what got you off last night was the fact that you *finally* got to be the one in control. Finally got to be the one with the power."

226

My heart races as he stares blankly, not giving anything away with his eyes, but I see him. See his trauma, see what he faced in the past, see how it's fucked him up. But that isn't an excuse. We *all* have shit! That doesn't mean we get to sharpen our hurt and turn it into weapons like they've done to me.

I narrow my eyes at Micah next.

"And you lost someone important. Someone who kept you balanced," I add. "And now, you're just... a fucking sadistic mess. Addicted to power and violence. Broken."

He doesn't flinch when I finish. In fact, it doesn't look like I've affected him at all. None of them do.

"You got my analysis wrong," Ash speaks up, casually pushing his pencil into Micah's electric sharpener. "Well, you got *part* of it wrong at least. Although, if it matters, you nailed Micah's and Vince's right on the nose."

I can hardly catch my breath as I focus so intently on him, it's like he's the only person in the room for a moment.

"You mentioned someone wanting me to be numb to pain," he says, blowing shavings off the pencil tip. "That's the part you missed. I assure you, that bastard wanted me to feel every second of what was done to me. Day in. Day out," he adds, seeming to zone out on a memory. "Thing is, I learned to flip that shit on its head. Not only do I feel pain... I'm fucking addicted to it."

My eyes flit to his tattoos and for the first time, I realize they serve a dual purpose—covering the scars *and* feeding his obsession. His gaze shifts to me, and several things sink in. His words. Mine. The fact that he all but confessed that I was spot-on about both Micah's and Vince's damage, too. I'd accurately summed up their history, all their pain in a few brief sentences, the collection of experiences that made them who they are today.

Monsters.

My head turns. Rage and the cocktail of heavy emotions has my eyes blurring with tears.

"People always point out how blood is thicker than water, but the part they leave off is that the one thing that's thicker than blood... is pain. That shit will bind people tighter than you'd ever fucking believe." I don't turn but recognize the sound of Micah's voice. "It's why the three of us are closer than brothers. And, like it or not, it's the reason we can't seem to keep our hands off you, when all we wanted was to ruin your fucking life."

I point to the burning wound on my hip. "I'd say you're doing a pretty good job of that life ruining part."

He scoffs, shaking his head. "Why is it so hard for you to see it?"

Rolling my eyes, I still don't look at him. "What the fuck are you talking about?"

"That we're not just drawn to each *other*... we're drawn to *you*, Bird."

Only now do I meet his gaze, seeing the gravity in his stare as he continues.

"We're drawn to the darkness you try to hide, drawn to those broken shards of rage that turned your heart into scar tissue. Other guys, they see that shit and run. But us? We want it all."

My heart races, but I'm fighting it. Fighting the way his words get to me, infecting me like poison. They bleed into what little light is left inside me, turning it dark as night, matching the voids in their chests where hearts used to be.

"And if you're honest with yourself," Micah rasps, "you love knowing that you drove us into such a blind rage that we had to *literally* mark you. Mark our territory, so it's clear to the entire fucking world that you're no longer free game," he says with a deepening tone. "Because you're ours."

Slowly, I turn toward the window and stare out, feeling like I'm living in a fever dream. An alternate reality where I actually believe they think their actions are romantic, grand gestures.

"I don't want to be here. Please, just... take me home."

That's all I can say. That's all that matters. I want to leave.

"Eat, take the pills, then we'll take you home," Ash repeats. "It'll hurt like a bitch to change the bandage later, but you have to keep it clean. Otherwise, you'll be in no shape to travel next weekend."

I sigh and look in his direction. "What are you talking about?"

He smirks and arches a brow. "We need you ready for The Hunt."

I hit the corner and double-back so quickly my sneakers squeak on the tile. Still, I wasn't fast enough to get away.

"We can't keep doing this."

I roll my eyes at the sound of Tate's voice, fighting the urge to growl when he steps in front of me, blocking my path to the steps. There are still students pouring out of the classroom, which means he jogged up the steps of the lecture hall to catch me. It's been so long since he's chased me down like this, I honestly thought he was done playing the good guy role, pretending to care.

"What do you want?"

"A conversation."

"I don't owe you anything," I hiss. "Now, if you'll excuse me."

My attempt to step past him falls flat when he moves with me. A hard sigh leaves me because I'm *so* not in the mood.

"Please, my weekend was shit and I just really want to get through today without any drama, and—"

"I've given you space," he cuts in. "I let you breathe and process our last conversation, but it's been weeks, Stevie. Weeks since you stormed out of my dad's house like I was the fucking bad guy and..." he pauses when he realizes we're drawing unwanted attention. "Your mom said to let you cool off, so I've done that. But we're both adults. That means we should be able to sit down and have a discussion without things going bad, right?" he asks.

229

I don't answer and he tosses his head back in frustration. When his dark eyes settle on me again, he's composed himself.

"It's been hell keeping my distance when I think about how our last conversation went, when I consider that something I said upset you so much. All I'm asking is for a chance to clear the air," he says. "That's it."

I clench the strap of my bag tightly, glancing around the broad hallway that's beginning to clear out as the building empties.

"I work tonight."

"Then, I'll come to you," he offers.

I consider that, but don't exactly want him knowing where my job's located, but also knowing the guys monitor my whereabouts. God knows *that's* a bag of shit I don't want to open today.

I take Tate's hand and grab a pen from the side pocket of my bag. He stares as I write the name of a shopping plaza on his palm, then the cross streets.

"My job's near here. I'll meet you at nine."

He studies the location, then nods. "I'll be there."

I sidestep him and head down the steps, deciding not to give him another second of my time. He wants to talk, so we'll talk.

But chances are, he won't like hearing what I have to say.

It's 8:59, and the second the clock hits 9:01, I'm out. He doesn't get a grace period because I didn't want to meet him in the first place. I check my phone again and it's exactly nine, so the countdown has officially begun. But as luck would have it, thirty seconds in, a silver sports car speeds into the lot and I recognize it as Tate's.

I let out a breath as I push off from the streetlamp I'd been leaning against for the past few minutes and walk over, wanting to get this over with as quickly as possible. I open the passenger side door and don't bother with eye contact as I climb in. The interior smells like him. Or rather, like his cologne. It has undertones of pine and clean linen, but it's muted after a long day assisting

Professor Lange. I feel his stare. My work uniform doesn't cover much, so he's getting an eyeful, but I don't really give a shit about all that. Right now, I just want to go home, change my bandage, and take as many painkillers as I'm allowed because this fucking wound hurts like a bitch.

"Talk," I huff, staring out the windshield as a semi passes the lot.

Beside me, Tate takes a breath and I can assume he didn't expect me to be so direct, but it's been a long day.

"Well, it feels appropriate to start with an apology. I didn't realize it at the time, but I said something that offended you or hurt you that night, and for that I'm truly sorry."

My eyes flit toward the roof of his car and I don't speak.

"Your mom filled me in on what happened," he says, and I finally snap a look his way. "She didn't give me details, only shared that you had a sister and you lost her. And honestly, that was enough. I don't need to know how or why. The fact that you lost her is explanation enough."

Here we go again. Tate, the smooth talker. He has no idea I see right through him and have had about all I can stand honestly.

"My sister's name was Mel, and she was raped," I say flatly. "The whole thing fucked with her head, so much that, shortly thereafter, she decided to just... end it, set herself free," I add, holding his gaze.

I need to see his eyes. Need to see the effect my words have when I tell him more than my mother would ever be able to stomach. But, as expected, there's no reaction. He's a great actor. The best I've ever seen.

"Shit. I'm so sorry, Stevie."

The car is dead silent for half a minute, and I consider ending it here, ending this conversation before it ever really starts.

"My... mother was a victim of sexual assault," he reveals, and I glance toward him again. His eyes are fixed on the steering wheel. "It was when she was young and still living in the Philippines. I get what you mean, though. The part about your sister not being able to move past it. My mom didn't take her life, but she did say it changed her forever."

I study him, wondering what his angle is, wondering if I can even believe his story.

"She talked about it?"

He nods. "Not often. But I think she figured it was important that I knew, thought it was important that I saw the long-term effects an act of violence like that has on a woman," he shares. "It made me sensitive to a woman's feelings, to making sure she feels heard and safe."

He looks my way before I can turn, and I'm caught in his stare. Only, a few seconds later, *he* breaks our gaze, slipping into a thought. A deeper one, it seems.

"I told you I lost her, but I didn't tell you how," he says. "She'd taken a second job to make ends meet because Christmas was coming up. She was really big on holidays," he adds with a distant smile. "Nothing bothered her more than the thought of the tree not being full, even though it was just the two of us. So, she'd work her day job, come home to fix dinner, made sure I got my homework done, then she'd drive a few miles to this convenience store not too far from the house. She didn't hate the job, but hated the hours. That didn't stop her from sticking with it, though. But this one particular night, she got held up at the register, and... the guy shot her."

I don't respond. His pain is tangible, and I wasn't prepared.

"$207.41," he says. "That's how much was in the register. That's the amount my mother's life was worth to him. $207.41."

Muffled traffic outside the car is the only sound as we sit in silence, dwelling in our own pain. He seems to remember he isn't alone and breathes deep.

"I didn't mean to bring the mood down," he says with a dim smile. "It's just that you shared and I wanted to make sure you knew I understood. I know what it feels like to lose someone who means the world to you, and then to have to go on and pretend like things are okay when... they're just fucking not."

He smiles again and it's even more faint than the last.

"After talking with your mom, I understood," he says. "She didn't keep your sister's death from me because she didn't think it was worth mentioning. She kept it to herself because if I didn't

232

know, she could pretend it wasn't real, could pretend she wasn't the mom of a girl who *isn't* anymore."

My stomach twists with his words and my eyes fall closed, thinking of my sister in that way. A girl who isn't anymore.

I didn't realize a tear slipped down my cheek until Tate lightly cups my chin and swipes it with his thumb. When my eyes open, his are trained on me, and this is when I realize it's still there. The strange spark that flared between us when we first met. Before I knew we were already connected by tragedy. And it's enough that I pull away.

He brings his hand to the arm rest and leaves it there. Even without meeting his gaze, I sense his defeat. His disappointment at the lack of progress between us.

"I need to go. It's dark and I can only go so fast on my bike."

"Let me take you. I—"

"No," I snap, already unlatching the door. "And now that we've talked, please don't come after me again. We'll deal with each other during Professor Lange's class because we have to, but outside of that... I'd appreciate you giving me space."

I've got one foot in his car and the other on the pavement, and that's where my eyes are focused, on the ground as I wait for his response. With any luck, he'll comply, and we won't have to keep doing this.

"Fine. If that's how you want it, I'll respect that. But I'm not happy with it," he adds. "Our parents will be married in a matter of months and we're worse off than strangers. And the worst part is, I honestly don't even know what the fuck I did to make you hate me so much."

I swallow and tighten the hold I have on the door handle, feeling so many emotions all at once it's overwhelming. I push up from the seat and place my hand on the hood of the car before turning to meet Tate's gaze.

"I have my reasons."

With that, I slam his door shut and hope and pray this counts as whatever version of closure he needed. Because as far as I'm concerned, I've already given him more than he deserves.

CHAPTER 35
ASH

I can't remember a time I've looked forward to The Hunt more than I do right now.

Forty-eight hours of who-gives-a-fuck activity, on a lake so far out there's no one around to hear the screams. It's all anyone in the house is talking about.

Vince and Micah's bags have been packed since yesterday, but I'm just now getting my shit together, despite our plan to leave later this afternoon. I've been in my head, though. Texts from my uncle early in the week have had me fucked up. More than I've admitted.

I toss a shirt to the hamper and catch a glimpse of Micah's phone as he rocks back in the chair. He's on the app. The one where he can track Bird's whereabouts. Or at least that's what he'd say if I asked what he's doing. But sometimes I think he checks it just to fill the void when we distance ourselves from her. Which has been the case again this week. Aside from the text we sent a few hours ago, letting her know we'd be by to get her later, contact has been minimal.

Things got out of hand this past weekend. They were... intense to say the least. Emotions ran incredibly fucking high, and shit went sideways. So much that none of us have talked about it since. Usually, it's only *one* of us raging and the others are thinking clearly enough to pull back. But this time, when it came to Bird, we *all* saw red. All felt the rage. All felt the sting of her walking out on *us* to chase after some asshole she says is only a friend. At the time, that seemed like total bullshit. But now that our heads are clear, who the fuck knows?

"Where is she?"

My question has Micah peering over his shoulder before focusing on his screen again. "Home. Packing, I think. She went to class, came right back, hasn't left since. It's been like that all week except the few times she went to work."

I'd expect a stronger reaction from him than this, seeing Bird follow the rules, but he doesn't have much of a reaction at all. I take it to mean his feelings are more complex where Bird's concerned, less black and white, more gray areas than any of us ever saw coming.

He's thoughtful for a few seconds and Vince and I lock eyes from where he's posted in the beanbag chair across the room.

"Talk to me." I study him again, waiting for a response.

He hears me, but takes his time. "Not sure what you mean."

"Bullshit. And if you can't talk to *us* about what you're thinking, things are worse than I thought."

He smirks and closes the app before tossing his phone to the desk. "My head's just... fucked up," he admits.

"That's sort of your default setting, though, isn't it?"

He lets out a dark laugh. "Yeah, but this feels different. There's something about this one girl that just... fuck. I don't even have the words," he admits. "It's like when you get a new toy and you're really into it, but you play with it too rough, then... ruin it."

There's another heavy exhale before he continues, locking his fingers behind his head. He's no better at expressing his feelings than me or Vince, so I try to help.

"Do you have regrets?"

He stares at the wall for a bit. "I think the point is... I don't really know what we're doing anymore. It was clear, then one day, it wasn't. At first, we did bad shit to her because that was the plan. We agreed that was what she deserved. But now, it's starting to feel like we do it because..."

His voice trails off and I finish the sentence in my head. He's wondering if *now* we do the bad shit out of rage.

Or worse...

Jealousy.

Bird came out of nowhere, caught us off guard in more ways than one. But the part that gets to me the most is that we've only scratched the surface when it comes to her. Right now, it's all sexual tension and curiosity. God forbid that we actually dig deeper, accidentally let this girl sink her hooks into us.

At first, it feels like I'm questioning everything, but that isn't true. I already know what the result would be. Something dark and toxic none of us could outrun. So, if we think we're fucked now...

Shit... I don't even want to imagine what that would look like.

"Do you think we went too far?" Vince's tone suggests that this isn't the first time the thoughts crossed *his* mind. But that's the thing about us. We move like one beast. What one does, what one builds, what one destroys, we *all* move in the same direction.

"Fuck no," Micah answers. "Bird's still guilty, this is still her fault, and I still want answers."

"She isn't budging on that," Vince says. "All we know is she's not working with Whitlock. But whatever she *is* hiding, she's not giving it up."

Micah nods in agreement.

"So... what now?" I ask. "What if we were right about her? What if this was all a setup and we just don't see it yet?" Another thought hits me. "Or what if that story we all thought was bullshit was actually legit?"

Surprisingly enough, Micah doesn't speak right away. Instead, he seems thoughtful, and maybe even a little troubled as he eyes me.

"Then, I guess I don't fucking know," he answers gruffly. "We'll have to cross that bridge when we get to it. But fortunately for us, we'll have her for the entire weekend without interference. And let's not forget, Eros is coming, too. He'll be able to get a read on her and, hopefully, the truth comes to light somehow."

I nod, hearing his logic. "And if it doesn't?"

He shrugs. "Then, I suppose Bird's got one-hundred points to earn."

There's always an air of confidence to his words, but I don't know if that tough-guy façade will even *survive* the weekend. For *any* of us.

"Do either of you believe her?" I glance toward Vince after he asks.

"Which part?"

His brow arches. "About being a virgin."

I shrug. "Who fucking knows. Could've been a tactic to throw us off about that Maddox guy, make her story more believable."

Micah's shaking his head before I even finish speaking. "No. She wasn't lying. Not about that."

Vince and I both eye him, and I note that he sounds completely certain.

"How do you know?"

He meets my gaze. "Honestly? I suspected it the night of the frat meeting, when we had her in my bed," he adds. "I blew the thought off at the time, but... now it makes sense."

I smirk at his explanation. "Not the most in-depth analysis, but it'll do, I guess."

He shrugs and his mouth curves a little, which means his mood's lightened some.

"Then, I suppose we have a plan," Vince says, returning to our original topic. "We'll go about business as usual and observe, listen, and see what happens."

Micah nods in agreement, and just as I do the same, I get a text.

I toss another shirt into my bag, then check the message. And just like that, an okay day officially goes to shit.

I'M HONESTLY NOT SURPRISED THE WOMAN WOULD CHOOSE to take a turn for the worse today of all days. Trust me, I know that sounds like a fucked up thing for a guy to say about his grandmother, but I can't think of a single life event that my family hasn't ruined for me. From birthdays to Christmas, you name it and those assholes have taken a shit on it.

The urgent text from my uncle, Louis, is the reason me and the guys are speeding across town to the hellhole where I grew up, instead of going to grab Bird and get on the road like the rest of our brothers are doing right now.

It's crossed my mind more than once that I should turn my truck around and head in the opposite direction, cut my losses, but I can't seem to make myself do it. Simply because I'd like to avoid yet another aspect of my life filling me with regret. God knows I've already got enough of those. And as it stands, leaving my grandmother on her deathbed to go hang out with the guys might later count as a regret.

The jury's still out on that one, though.

But I have a plan. I'll stop in for a few minutes, avoid my vapid, asshat of a grandfather. The man I'll only ever see as a nightmare in the flesh.

I planned to come alone, but Vince and Micah weren't having it. They know where I come from, what I've been through. Hell, they saw the cuts and bruises I showed up at the group home with. I blamed them all on fights with other kids or injuries from skateboarding and shit, but they never bought those stories. Back then, I covered the scars with lies and long-sleeve shirts, until I got old enough to cover them with ink.

The second I turn my truck into the driveway, it's like a one-thousand pound weight falls on me. I feel angry and anxious, sick to my stomach.

"We're coming in with you," Vince announces. I turn to where he's seated in the passenger seat, and as much as I'd love to tell him they don't have to do that, I'm not sure I can step foot inside this place without them.

When I nod and don't respond, it's enough. They know.

I'm the last to exit the truck, the last one to the sidewalk, the last one on the porch. Micah knocks since he's closest to the door, and I hate what being here does to me. It makes me feel like that same weak-ass kid who used to get tossed around, burned with cigarettes, beaten with extension cords and whatever the hell else my grandfather could find. So, it's no surprise that by the time Louis answers the door, I'm already worked up. It's like he doesn't even notice Micah and Vince as he zeroes in on me, looking me up and down with that same emotionless glare he's always had when it comes to me. Without a word, he pushes the screen door open, then steps aside.

I have that thought again. The one where I'm tempted to run in the opposite direction. It gets stronger when I step into the house. I haven't been here in years, and it looks like nothing's changed. The tile in the entry is still cracked and some of the pieces are missing chunks from the corners.

There's an old dog statue beside the coat tree. My grandfather's had that piece of shit my whole life—a gift from the company he eventually retired from, their token of appreciation when he hit the thirty-year mark as an employee. It's ugly as hell, but has always been his prized possession.

There's dust and cobwebs everywhere. When my grandmother was healthy, she did her best to keep things up, but no one else ever cared quite as much as she did. And now that she's bedridden, it shows.

The scent of cigars and Louis' dogs is overpowering, but reminding myself that this will be over soon keeps me moving forward, following Louis through the kitchen to the small bedroom off the back of the house. My grandfather used to use it as his den, but I'm guessing they converted it when the stairs got to be too much for Grandma.

"Wait here," Louis says, and these are the first words he's spoken since opening the door.

Me, Micah, and Vince are left lingering in the kitchen, standing beside the stove where a pot of chili looks like it's been sitting there a few days. Dishes are piled high in the sink, and as I'm studying the filth these three are living in, a bug scurries up the wall.

"Just fucking great," I say to myself, exhaling to keep my cool.

The door to the bedroom opens again and Louis is just as

monotone as before. "She can't talk much, but she can hear you," he says.

I nod, not seeing the point in turning this into a conversation, but when I step toward the room and the guys trail me, Louis blocks the door with his arm.

"Your friends can wait out here."

He shoots Micah and Vince a look I know isn't sitting well with them. They don't normally take shit from assholes like Louis, but I take their silence as a sign of respect. For me, not Louis. They know this isn't easy. They know I'm already wound tight and ready to punch his ass the first time he steps out of line. So, I appreciate them not making the situation even more volatile than it already is.

I glance at them over my shoulder and it's Vince who meets my gaze. Micah's still got his eyes trained on Louis.

"It's cool. We'll chill here," Vince says, and I don't miss how he places a hand on Micah's shoulder to bring him back down.

So, I guess I'm doing this alone after all.

A vintage lamp on the dresser against the far wall casts dim light in the room, and I walk in holding my breath, feeling a strange mix of emotions at the thought of seeing my grandmother's health decline. Our relationship was complex, layered, but she's still the blood relative I would say I'm closest to. Instead of looking toward the sound of an oxygen tank to my left, I stare at my feet as I cross the carpet, stained from years of wear and tear, and I can only guess no one thought to clean it before stashing her here. In this dark corner of the house to waste away in private.

"You too good to speak to me now?"

The deep, gruff voice catches me off guard. Because up until now, I'd thought it was just me and Grandma in the room, but when I peer up, the bearded, weathered face of my grandfather stares back. Seated against the wall beside the hospital bed, he was easy to miss. Especially seeing as how I *hoped* to miss him.

His words linger in the air, remaining unanswered because I'm not here for him. And regarding his question... yes, I'm too good to speak to him.

240

"Hmph," he grumbles when he realizes I have nothing to say.

I approach my grandma's bedside and in my peripheral vision I see my grandfather's arms cross over his chest as a hoarse laugh leaves him.

"Are you shitting me?" he chuckles. "Look what you've done to yourself. You look like some kind of thug with all those fucking pictures all over your body. Who the fuck do you think will ever take you seriously looking like that?"

I bite my tongue and focus on the reason I'm here, my grandmother. Somehow, I'm able to drown her husband out, cycling through a laundry list of my memories with her. Some good, but mostly bad. I wasn't lying when I said things between us were complicated. She knew everything I was going through and carried on with her day like it was nothing.

Like crying myself to sleep at night was normal.

Like flinching every time someone reached to pass food around the table was normal.

Like hiding in the shed for an entire day when I got a bad grade was normal.

In every instance, she pretended not to know this was all the result of being the focus of my grandfather's wrath.

These thoughts are the reason I pull away when I think to hold her hand. She might mistake compassion for forgiveness, and it isn't that.

Hell, she may *never* have that.

Not from me.

My grandfather huffs and relaxes deeper into his seat, propping his ankle on his knee as he studies me. I'm not making eye contact, but I feel that I have his attention. Always could.

"Holy shit, boy! How do you have time to go to class with all the time you must be spending in the gym?" he asks. "You know what they say about guys like that, don't you? Ones who spend all that time pumping iron and getting ripped? They say they're compensating for something."

He laughs again and I feel my heart racing.

"Is that it, Ash? You compensating for what you're lacking

elsewhere?" This time, he roars, cracking himself up with his own joke while I pretend he's somewhere else.

I'm guessing he takes my lack of a defense as confirmation, but it's actually the opposite. I've got absolutely *nothing* to compensate for.

"Damn, you never could take a joke. I did everything I could to toughen you up, but it never did seem to take," he sighs. "Didn't want to believe it, but your uncle is probably right about you. Some guys are just born pussies."

For the first time in years, I meet my grandfather's gaze. He stares, somehow thinking he can intimidate me like when I was a kid, but he's got me fucked up. In a *big* way.

It isn't until I'm halfway around the bed that he seems to notice he's in danger. But by the time I have his collar in my hand, it's too late. His back slams the wall and I try to stop myself, try to pull back from what I feel happening, but I can't.

There are too many reasons to make this motherfucker hurt and I've never been good at denying myself things I want.

"I've *always* hated your sorry ass," I remind him through gritted teeth, about half a second before launching my fist into his jaw.

"What the *fuck*?" he groans, and the look of surprise in his eyes is fucking everything.

So much that I have to see it again.

I cock back a second time, but only halfway, then slam my knuckles into his nose, enjoying how the bone and cartilage yield to my fist. His sorry ass is lucky I held back. At his age, a full-force hit might've killed him.

I guess I have some self-restraint after all.

"Louis! Louis!! Help! He's insane!"

A laugh leaves me as I drop the old man to the floor, smiling as I motion for him to wipe the trickle of blood oozing from his nose. As I'm backing away, the door flies open and I turn with my fist clenched, half-expecting Louis to be the one rushing in, but it's Vince. He does a quick scan, looking between me and my grandfather as the situation becomes clear.

"We've gotta get out of here," he says, gripping my shoulder as he pulls me toward the door.

But before we make our exit, Micah steps in and does the same scan as Vince. Only, instead of panicking, he smirks, watching my grandfather lunge for the box of tissue on the bedside table, trying in vain to stop the fountain of blood pouring from his nose.

"Fucking finally," Micah says with a laugh.

"And for the record, I was never a pussy. I was a kid," I remind the old man. "I was a kid who stupidly wanted your love. Right up until I realized your sadistic ass wasn't capable of that," I add, backing away before I lose what little self-restraint I still have. "But don't worry, the only thing I want from you now is the opportunity to spit in your fucking casket when you die, you worthless piece of shit."

"Ok, that's enough," Vince says in a hushed tone, pulling me from the room. "Your uncle's in the yard with the dogs and we should probably be gone before he comes back. We don't really need the cops to give us shit."

As much as I'd love to finish what I started, as much as I'd love to give this man even an *ounce* of what I received from him, he had me pegged right. I'm way too good for this shit.

"When she dies, don't call me," I yell out on my way to the front door. "She might be the worst out of all three of you, the worst kind of abuser. The kind who never lifts a hand to hurt you, but also never lifts a finger to help. So, fuck all of you and I hope you all rot in hell."

Micah's finally helping Vince drag me from the house, but not before I can kick over that stupid fucking dog statue. It's a piece of shit. Just like my grandfather's sorry ass.

The guys practically throw me into the backseat of the truck. I'm seeing red, overflowing with rage and frustration. I've dreamed about hauling off and hitting that asshole for so many years, and now it feels like I only got a taste.

"Keys," Vince says when he slams the driver-side door shut. My hands are shaking when I drop them into his palm, suppressing a growl. I don't think I've ever wanted anything as badly as I want to go back inside that house and beat the absolute *shit* out of that bastard.

Micah looks me over from where he sits in the passenger seat, then calmly turns to Vince.

"Hear me out," he says. "Our boy's taken a lot of beatings from that asshole. He might not get another opportunity like this. You and I could *easily* keep Louis in the yard while Ash finishes... working through things."

He arches a brow at Vince, and his suggestion goes ignored by our more level-headed brother. Before Micah can get into his head, Vince speeds out into the street so fast we burn rubber at the end of the driveway.

I lie back on the seat with both fists to my forehead, trying to relax, but it doesn't work. I reached my boiling point today and still don't have anything to show for it. Because my head might be more fucked up *now* than it was before.

Part of me thought the man might actually have grown to feel a bit of remorse in his old age, thought he might've seen the error of his ways as he's reflected over the years, but seeing him again proved me wrong.

He's just as shitty a human being now as he was then.

"Fuck!"

Micah glances back when I can't fight the rage anymore and slam my foot into the back door.

"I should've killed him. I should've *fucking* killed him," I growl, feeling regret sink in.

Looks like I didn't avoid that shit after all.

"Hurting him won't change anything. We know that," Vince reasons. "It won't take back what he did, and it won't make you forget. If there's anything we've learned from the B.S. we've lived through, it's that being blood doesn't mean shit. But we've also learned that our brotherhood is all the family we need."

I close my eyes, trying to let it go. All of it. He's right.

"I just need to get as far away from here as possible, get drunk, and forget this shit ever happened."

The engine revs as Vince presses the gas. "Consider it done."

CHAPTER 36
STEVIE

A s far as awkward car rides go, this ranked right up there with the worst of them. The moment the guys pulled up at my house, I could tell things were off. At first, I blamed it on bad juju lingering between us after what I've now dubbed *The Stable Incident*. But after a while, it became clear that this dark vibe was something different.

And it seemed to mostly be coming from Ash.

Micah's usually the more short-tempered, moody one, but Ash barely spoke the entire four-hour drive here to the lake. And when he did, he mostly gave one-word responses to questions asked by the other two. He stared out the window beside me in the backseat, watching the scenery go by. And then when it got dark, he *still* stared out the window. At nothing. Not sure what happened, but I'm grateful to get out of the truck and as far away from him as possible.

Because if history tells me anything, it's that I don't want to be anywhere near these three when they're in shitty moods.

Micah and Vince exchange a few words and head to the truck bed to grab their things. Ash is already halfway to the cabin with a duffle bag slung over his shoulder. I slam the door shut and round the truck to grab my belongings, but the purple backpack I know was there when we left isn't anymore. However, a quick scan of the guys sets me at ease, seeing that they've scooped it up with theirs.

About an hour before they arrived, Vince shot me a text of what to pack. So, cursing under my breath, I replaced some of what I'd already folded and organized in my bag with what *they* deemed essential—lingerie, short shorts, swimwear. Although, with the wound in the shape of an S with a devil tail on the end marking my hip, I don't think I'll be swimming anywhere. Perhaps they've forgotten having maimed me last weekend.

The thought of it sends a fresh wave of hatred through me as I trudge behind them, making my way onto the porch just as Micah pulls out a key and turns the lock. I wasn't sure what to expect when we got here, and wondered who'd be sharing what houses, but it seems it's just the four of us for the weekend.

Well, until this Eros guy shows up, making it five.

The heavy door creaks and a light brightens the space before I step in behind them. This place is definitely retro, straight out of the eighties. Dark carpet complements the dark wood paneling that covers an accent wall opposite the fireplace. A sectional in the living room is covered in an ugly plaid fabric, and mustard yellow curtains hang at either side of a huge, two-story window overlooking the deck and lake out back. The cabin definitely won't win any awards for how it's decorated, but it's spacious, it's clean, and doesn't have a bad layout.

Vince closes the door and deadbolts it as I move toward the window to take a look outside. An array of identical cabins all encircle the lake, and from here, I can see the yellow glow of lights in the other structures, filled with frat boys and sorority girls sure to take advantage of the privacy and discretion this place affords them.

Already, there's loud conversation and laughter that can be heard even through the glass. The Savages are here and they're ready to let loose. One can only imagine the shenanigans that will take place while we're away.

"This way."

Startled, I glance over my shoulder when Micah speaks. He's expressionless as usual when he turns and heads down a hallway.

The others are gone, and I imagine they're getting settled into their rooms. Which leaves me nervous where *I'll* land for the weekend.

I catch up to Micah's long strides just as he stops at a bedroom and flips the light switch. He sets both my bags on the floor beside the door, and I note that the same drab colors from the main part of the house continue in here. And there's even a plaid bedspread with a similar color scheme to the couches. But again, it's clean and spacious, which is a huge plus.

"This is you," Micah informs me. "Closet. Bathroom," he adds, pointing out the two spaces.

I manage to control the excitement that fills me when I realize I'll have privacy. Which is about the same time I realize they might've given me the master bedroom.

"Get changed," he says. "The girls are all dressing sexy for the bonfire, so you should do the same. Something that shows off your ass."

I arch a brow at his command but don't protest. Mostly, because that would require me to speak to him, which I don't plan to do unless I have to.

"Everyone's meeting up in fifteen minutes. Your instructions are to remain at one of our sides at all times. No wandering off. No funny shit with Enzo or anyone else," he adds, and I hold in the smirk that wants to break free.

To be as big and tough as they are, they really do have one hell of a jealous streak.

He's watching me and a flare of frustration fills his eyes. "Do you understand? Because you aren't saying shit."

I hold his gaze, remembering what they did—tying me up, burning my flesh with their symbol, and my jaw ticks with suppressed rage.

"I'm not saying shit because I don't have shit to say," I reply, which has him glaring with hellfire in his eyes.

"Fifteen minutes," are his parting words, spoken just before he steps out and slams the door behind him.

Infuriated by the level of assholery that just took place, I grab my bag and start digging through it for something to meet King

Dick's demand. Something sexy, yes, but something sexy that won't show or irritate the wound. Easy, right?

After searching for a minute or two, I find a pair of spandex shorts that barely cover my ass cheeks. These should do the trick, so I grab out a black tank to match, then change. I pull the ponytail holder out of my hair and shake it out a bit, letting it fall over my shoulders before swiping on a bit of gloss to freshen up my lips, then I'm done.

I stare at myself, wondering when this nightmare will end, then let out a breath before heading out to see what kind of bullshit the guys have in store for tonight.

Because, trust me, they've *always* got some kind of bullshit in store.

THEY'RE GONE. I WAS INSTRUCTED NEVER TO LEAVE THEIR sight, and now they're nowhere to be found.

Nice.

It's safe to assume they're down at the actual bonfire, but I still glance at each of the smaller groups that have formed along the way—clusters of frat boys seated in lawn chairs, gathering around either coolers or their own small fires while they toss back beer bottles like they're water.

It's during one of my scans that I spot Dahlia. She's already staring when I notice her, and there's hatred in her eyes as usual. We've avoided each other back home. So much that I didn't even know she'd be here tonight, didn't notice she'd left. I'm guessing she's having a similar thought. Then again, she might've expected to see me here because there was no way the *guys* wouldn't be here.

And thanks to Micah, she now believes we're in some kind of a four-way relationship or something. Which, I don't know, I can maybe see why that's believable, but it's not like that. There is no relationship. Only hatred and some kind of sick attraction that makes it hard for us to keep our hands off each other sometimes.

But definitely not a relationship.

I realize she's committed to watching me walk the entire way to the bonfire, so I roll my eyes and let her, but I focus my attention elsewhere. I spot Grace. Well, mostly because she's waving like a wild woman a few yards away. She doesn't come over to speak, though, because she's perched on some guy's knee, eating up his attention as he stares up at her like she's his goddess.

I wave back then smile as I look away. At least there's *one* friendly face here in the crowd. Otherwise, it'd just be me, the guys, and a gaggle of sorority girls with terrible attitudes. I have no clue what this whole *Hunt* thing is, but this turnout is insane. And from the looks of it, everyone's pretty pumped about it.

"Bird."

The now familiar moniker grabs my attention so quickly Micah may as well have called my actual name. I turn and meet his gaze, then he nods, gesturing for me to come to him. Vince and Ash are seated beside him, of course, and I note that all the guys are wearing black t-shirts with the word, '*SAVAGE'* in big, bold letters.

My attention is on Ash as I walk closer. From the looks of things, he's already tossed back a few drinks before I got here. Actually, I was suspicious he'd started drinking before we even got on the road, hence the reason Vince was behind the wheel.

Feeling all eyes on me, including Enzo's, I make my way over, only realizing when I get closer that there's nowhere left to sit. At least, that's what I *thought*. Until Micah reaches for my wrist and pulls me into his lap. I wince a little when pain shoots through my hip, but thankfully, it's fleeting. His thigh is surprisingly sturdy beneath me, and I don't have that feeling I've gotten in the past, when boyfriends would try to hold me like this. Unlike those times, I don't feel the need to balance some of my weight to hide how heavy I am. With Micah's size and build, none of that matters.

He settles one hand on my thigh, and the other brings a cigarette to his lips. I let out a breath, not loving that he's touching me right now. I haven't slept well since the barn. Partly because every time I try, the pain has made it impossible to get comfortable. But even though that's begun to subside the last couple days, I still toss and turn. The trauma of being taken, tied, then burned, cycles on repeat in my thoughts, but the most disturbing part is how they behaved afterward.

As if their obsession with me—or whatever the hell they want to call it—excused their bullshit. Well, I call bullshit. They're damaged, I get it, but we all are. That doesn't mean we get to lash out and inflict pain on others in the name of...

My mind snags on the word that came to mind. Love. There *is* no love between us, so I suppose they do what they do in the name of *lust*.

Whatever the case, it was ugly and I'm not here for that shit.

I feel this heavy sense of being watched, and when I glance to my left, I realize it's Ash. His eyes are a little glazed, but he's got this mean glare set on his face that sends a chill racing down my spine. After a few seconds, he looks away and tips the bottle again, but whatever this darkness is he's carrying, it's changed him. He was never a nice guy by any means, but now he's giving off this menacing aura that doesn't feel like him.

It's... a little scary if I'm being honest.

All the more reason to keep my distance from him tonight.

"This place is great and all, but when do we get to meet Eros? Dude's practically a legend," someone says, stealing my attention. I recognize him as one of this year's pledges.

A smirk curves Vince's lips. "He'll be here sometime tomorrow."

"Is it true what they say about him? That he's saved, like, four of the brothers' lives in the frat?" the same guy asks.

Vince nods. "It's true, but they weren't all brothers. One was a girl who'd been partying with us one night. She had a severe asthma attack and didn't have her inhaler. Eros called 9-1-1, then shut the entire party down to check in with people to see who had a similar prescription. He found someone and got the inhaler to the girl just as she was passing out," he says. "He saved a drunk second-year member who'd fallen into a pool, then there was the time he did the Heimlich on a guy who choked on a fry, and then there was me."

The pledge arches a brow. "No shit?"

"No shit," Vince says with a laugh. "It was a little over a year ago. We threw a party at The Den, but I'd been feeling sick the couple days before. Thought I could push through it, though. Eros was concerned it might be serious, so he kept me with him all night. We mostly hung out by the pool, but wherever I went, he went. Which is why he was with me when I started losing consciousness."

"What happened? What was wrong?" the pledge asks.

"It was my appendix," Vince answers. "Eros carried me to his car and rushed me to the hospital. Got me there just as it burst. If he hadn't been keeping an eye on me, if he'd chosen to party instead of being there for me, I wouldn't be here."

Vince's tone is solemn, but I also note how he seems to genuinely revere Eros. All three of them actually seem to hold the same affection for him. It's similar to the love and respect that would exist between *real* brothers.

I'm still staring at Vince, still thinking about his story when Micah taps my thigh. "Grab me a beer," he whispers.

I don't move right away, frustrated that I'm basically here to wait on them hand and foot. Eventually, I stand from his lap and adjust my shorts where they've ridden up a bit. And when I glance toward the cooler, I lock eyes with Enzo who's seated beside it. We've steered clear of each other since the 'S*pin the Bottle'* situation, but there's no missing how he's focused on me right now. In fact, it's so blatant I'm not the only one who notices.

"Careful, Enzo," Ash warns, his voice deep and menacing.

I lift the lid of the cooler and grab out a drink, pretending to ignore the entire exchange as I walk back to Micah and hand him the bottle. I turn, thinking I'll rest on his knee again since there's no place *else* to sit, but before I get the chance...

"Come on," Ash sighs. "I need to take a leak and you're coming with me."

I frown, wondering what the hell that has to do with me. Does he need a babysitter to keep a lookout for bears or something?

I bite my tongue and don't say these things out loud, knowing these three are known to behave like assholes when I make a scene in front of their brothers. Still, I have no idea what the hell he's thinking.

Ash stands, towering over me with a suspicious glare, then he starts toward the woods. And, well... I guess this means we're going for a walk.

ASH

Noise from the group fades as the distance grows between us and them. Bird's followed without question, tolerating the silence. My guess is that's because she senses I'm not right tonight. My fist aches from the hit earlier, but it's still not enough. I'm stuck somewhere between being grateful the guys pulled me away, and pissed I left things unfinished. God knows that man never left *anything* unfinished when it came to me. He'd beat my ass until he was good and damn ready to stop.

That should have been the case for me. Only, it never would've been enough. Not until he stopped breathing altogether.

"Wait," Bird calls out from behind me. "I can't keep moving at this pace. I'm injured, remember?" she snaps.

The next second, there are no twigs and leaves crunching beneath her feet because she stopped.

I turn and my eyes land on her, observing as she gently massages the skin surrounding the burn, but never touches it directly. My mind glitches and I see that night, see myself holding the hot iron to that perfect plane of skin, and then ruining it forever.

The flash leaves me, and I feel like shit. Even more than I already did. I've tried to drown the feeling out with alcohol, but it isn't working. If I can't drink a problem away, I usually try *fucking* it away, but then I remember that the one girl I'd want on my cock has never taken it before. And there's no way I could be gentle with her in this state. All I have to offer right now is rough, filthy, painful.

Then again, maybe causing pain would do me some good.

Bird's gaze falls to my crotch when I unbutton my jeans, lower my zipper.

"What are you doing?"

Her tone is soft when she asks, almost fearful. It's that glimmer of innocence in her eyes that has me smiling.

"What's it look like? I need to take a piss, so..." My words trail off when I reach into my boxers because... I've got a better idea. "Take it out."

Bird's eyes widen at my command. "What?"

"Did I fucking stutter?" I glance down at my cock and then up to meet Bird's gaze again. She blinks wildly, like she's still not sure she heard me right, but she steps closer anyway. Then, her hand pushes into my boxers, but she stops.

She's trembling, shaking like a leaf as she holds me.

"I don't know what you want me to do," she says just above a whisper, and I feel myself getting annoyed.

"Pull it out and fucking hold it," I snap, prompting her to do as she's told.

With her tits pressed against my arm, she wraps her soft fingers around my dick. She's nervous, so her hands are warm and clammy, but I like the way it feels against my skin. Soft. Moist.

Bracing my hand on the tree in front of me, I relieve myself, not missing how Bird's heart is racing now. It pulsates against my arm where my bicep is wedged into her cleavage, and I can't help but wonder if she's getting off on this.

I finish up and she doesn't seem to know what to do, so I replace her hand with my own to shake my cock, then put it back inside my boxers. Bird's standing there, all aimless and innocent and shit. She looks almost bashful right now. Like seeing me, *touching* me like that, left her not knowing how to feel about it.

And honestly, I've never wanted to defile someone more in my life than I do at this moment.

She gasps when I take her by the throat, then cover her mouth with mine. At first, she tries pulling away, and I feel the tension. She's still pissed at us for what we did in the stable that night, but only because she doesn't understand.

Doesn't understand the hold she has on us.

Doesn't understand the deep-seated need we have to become *her* obsession like she's become *ours*.

I don't let go, squeezing her neck harder as her taste gives me the high I've been searching for in bottle after bottle tonight. I accept that, all this time, she was what I truly craved, and that's when I feel the fight leave her. That's the exact moment her lips finally relent and open for me.

That's it, Bird, let me have you.

My tongue shoves into her mouth and she takes it, *sucks* it as her hands find my chest and gather the front of my tee in her fists. She swallows and I feel it against my palm, imagining my cock in her mouth, imagining myself feeding every inch between her lips, slamming into the back of her throat.

The front of my jeans tightens when my dick swells to the point of there being actual pain. Unable to help myself, I grip her pussy through the thin spandex shorts she wears, feeling the softness of her lips against my fingertips. My pulse races at the mere thought of taking her, being the first to feel her on my cock. Desperately in need of some form of relief, I'm reminded that she's, technically, at our disposal.

I imagine it, her kneeling in front of me like the filthy bitch I plan to turn her into one day, swallowing my cum, inheriting some of my darkness.

My mouth opens to tell her what I want, but the sound of Fletcher's damn voice interrupts.

"We need everyone to join us at the bonfire," he announces over a megaphone, yelling out from somewhere near the cabins. "It's the moment you've all been anxiously awaiting. In approximately ten minutes, The Hunt will officially begin."

"Fuck." I sigh in frustration, thinking of what could've been.

Staring up at me with half-mast eyes, Bird chews her damp, swollen lip. She may have gotten away from me this time, but while we have her here, all to ourselves for an entire weekend, there's nowhere to run.

At this point, having her is no longer a want.

It's a need.

A sh and I join the others, and I'm still not sure what the fuck just happened out there. Everyone's standing around the bonfire, awaiting further instruction, but my attention is on *him*.

My eyes flicker up and he stares down on me. Like a silent acknowledgement of the magnetism still pulling us toward one another. An acknowledgement of the missed opportunity we left behind in the woods.

Micah's hand settles at the small of my back and I swear it feels like I'm in *The Twilight Zone*. These boys give me whiplash, making me the target of their hatred and darkness one moment, then behaving like I'm some prized possession the next.

I swallow hard and face forward, deciding to redirect my focus, because it's impossible to figure them out. But of course, the moment my eyes settle on the flames, they land on Dahlia. Her gaze is locked on mine. Always observing. Always analyzing. Which is why I'm positive she saw me walk up with Ash, and it's also the reason her gaze lowers to my waist as Micah's arm slinks around it. Her eyes snap to mine again, and they're filled with equal parts fury and confusion.

"Alright, people. Listen up," Fletcher says, giving me a new target to zero in on. One that *isn't* Dahlia. He opens the lids of two large, plastic crates before continuing. "For those experiencing The Hunt for the first time... guys, you're the hunters, and ladies, you're the hunted," he explains. "The rules of the jungle are simple: Hunters, if you catch it... you eat it."

No one misses the innuendo, which is why the crowd goes crazy—howling and whistling.

"Now, I'm not telling anyone what to do behind closed doors, but I *will* encourage you to do what feels right tonight. What happens at The Hunt..."

"Stays at The Hunt," the crowd echoes back to Fletcher.

"Exactly, but just a friendly reminder that we're all for fucking and having fun, but fellas... keep it consensual. No doesn't mean yes, and neither does a drunk girl passed out on the couch. So, don't be a dick and ruin this shit for everyone else. Ladies, as the hunted, if someone catches you that you're into, consider yourself paired up for the night. If it's not a match, no harm, no foul. Just have fun."

This... *event*... is starting to take shape. I'd heard mention of The Hunt since meeting the boys, but didn't realize it was an actual hunt. One where a band of horny frat boys chase a bunch of girls through the woods. Now, I'm wondering *why* I didn't put two and two together.

"Alright, so any ladies not captured at the end of the game will be rounded up as will the guys who haven't made a catch. At that time, our singles will have a chance to pair up, giving everyone a chance to make a connection. Understood?"

The crowd cheers in response to the question.

"Good! So, if we can get all our ladies to form a line at *this* crate, and all our guys to form a line at *this* one, we can hand out all the gear and get this show on the road," Fletcher adds, raising a question in my mind.

What kind of fucking gear?

Micah's arm leaves me and he and the others all head where Fletcher designated. Confused as hell, I do the same, standing with the other girls, waiting. I watch from a distance to see what the guys are being given, and first, they're handed matte black lion masks, and what look like leashes.

My attention gets sidetracked when two girls who've just

come from the front of the line pass by, giggling as one helps the other into... *a collar?*

My immediate reaction is *'fuck this'* but then I remember. I'm literally out in the middle of nowhere with no ally. Ok, maybe half an ally in Grace, but still. I'm outnumbered and too far from home to put an end to this shit.

I reach the front and, sure enough, I'm handed a damn collar. One with a steel loop fixed to the front, and a pair of leopard print ears. I step out of line with the pieces, and the guys are watching, standing there in their *'SAVAGE'* tees, lowering black masks over their faces, clenching those leashes as if they know the power they give them.

Shit.

Fuck.

There's no sense in pretending there's a way out of this, so when in Rome...

I fix the collar around my neck, then perch the ears on my head like the rest of the girls. But I'm nowhere near as giddy as they are about it. We're herded to a line of cones, and I follow the other girls there. I glance back, honestly not to look at anyone in particular, but I spot Dahlia. And she's standing very, *very* close to Vince. At first, I try to think nothing of it, but that's hard to do when she begins whispering in his ear.

That smirk on her face when she's done is enough to make my stomach twist in a knot, wondering what the fuck she just said. And to make matters worse, she smiles bigger after realizing I saw her with him.

She meets me at the starting point in her hot pink shorts and halter top, and the bitch has the nerve to speak.

"Good luck, roomie."

"Fuck you," I shoot back, then look straight ahead as she laughs.

"The song chosen for this year's hunt is *'When Doves Cry'*," Fletcher announces. "So, when it stops, you know what that means. The Hunt is over, and everyone should listen for the sound of my voice and check for the strobe light to find your way back home. Now, ladies, on the count of three, I advise you to take off into the woods as fast as you can, because you'll only have a ten second head start before I send the guys in after you. So, ready up," he adds, and then starts his countdown. "Three, two, one... GO!"

My feet move swiftly through the grass as I race toward the tree line. The girls laugh and scream as we spring into the darkness, away from the light of the cabins and bonfire. Dahlia's right beside me, a blur of neon pink in my peripheral. It hits me that I'm still focused on whatever the hell that was between her and Vince.

Did she invite him to catch her?

Does he want *to hook up with her tonight?*

God, listen to me... Dahlia and Vince hooking up is the least of my worries. If he catches her, so what? No, if he catches her, *good.* Hopefully, they *all* catch girls. That'd mean I'm free, off their leash.

Figuratively *and* literally.

My focus should not be on sorting out what Dahlia whispered before we took off. It should be on doing everything in my power to stay ahead of the game. It's as I reach this new resolution that Fletcher speaks through the megaphone again, causing my heart to race ten times faster as he turns the boys loose.

"Savages, at the behest of our founding fathers... go forth and hunt."

F letcher's command echoes in my head and my feet have never moved faster, covering more ground than I imagined possible in such a short amount of time. But even with my speed, one glance over my shoulder at the line of frat boys gaining ground has me certain it's not enough. I'm beginning to see that I don't stand a chance. Not against a brood of well-conditioned athletes.

The guys are easy to spot and they're gaining on me. They're the only ones moving in a pack, and with moonlight filtering through the treetops, I spot Ash's and Micah's tattoo sleeves. Even through the darkness. Vince is in the middle, and immediately· after laying eyes on him, my gaze darts toward Dahlia again. She's still right beside me, and my suspicion grows. Of course, the guys would be on *my* heels, so the pieces are starting to fit together.

She wants to stay visible, wants to stay where Vince can find her.

I face forward again and there's no denying the rush of emotions that flood my head, the heat that fills my veins. I've hated her for months now, but since the guys came into my life, I've found *new* reasons to hate her. Like now, while she's under. the impression I'm *with* them, she's still trying to steal Vince away.

Not... steal him away. Wrong words. He'd have to first be mine to be stolen.

I just mean she's proving that she'd willingly make a move on a guy who was mine if given the opportunity.

I glance toward her again and it's like she's heard my thoughts. A determined smirk has her lips curved in this devious way that makes me want to rip off my sneaker and hurl it at her head.

"Focus," I say under my breath, reminding myself where my thoughts should be centered. On running. On putting space between me and them. Nothing else.

I'm breaking a sweat and I notice the instant that the moisture on my skin causes the bandage on my hip to loosen. The gauze shifts and, within seconds, the tender, pink flesh beneath it starts to burn. At first, it's a gnawing sting, but before long, it's intense and angry. I feel my pace slowing, feel my feet wanting to stop moving altogether.

Sure enough, Dahlia begins to slow down, too, and I envision myself tripping her, seeing her highlighter pink crop top and matching shorts get covered in mud. Now, I'm *positive* this was her plan, using me as bait to catch Vince.

Bitch.

I'm practically limping now, babying the hip, but even *that* is too much to bear.

And that's when I catch the guys in my peripheral vision. They're gaining on us so fast it's laughable, but a sudden burst of adrenaline has me moving again. *Fast.* Dahlia picks up speed until she matches my pace. I'm quick, but it isn't enough.

What gives it away?

The powerful arm that's now hooked around my waist, stopping me dead in my tracks as I'm lifted a few feet into the air.

"Damn, Bird. If I didn't know any better, I'd say you were trying to outrun us," Micah pants into my ear, squeezing me tight against his torso before he lets the soles of my shoes touch the ground again.

A strange mix of emotions floods me, but what's most notably missing is the rage and anger I should feel having been caught.

"What kind of girl lets assholes like you catch her without a fight?" I ask, and I don't mean to sound so lighthearted, so... flirty, but it's too late. Micah reads into it and holds me tighter from behind, his forearm cinching beneath my breasts. I should hate being touched like this by him, but instead I'm hypnotized by the feel of his chest rising and falling against my back as he catches his breath.

I'm winded and frustrated for too many reasons to name, but before I can pitch a fit about being held and slyly groped, I yelp as another arm scoops me up, then tosses me over his shoulder. It's dark and things happen so fast I'm unsure whether it's Vince or Ash at first, but I catch a glimpse of Dahlia's face once I'm able to lift my head from his back. And before I notice the lack of tattoos, the buzzed head, it's her expression that tells me who has me.

The one she thought *she'd* have tonight.

Vince.

He hoisted me up with ease, like I weighed no more than a sack of laundry. The solid muscle that sheathes him like armor across the top of his back and shoulders presses into my stomach and I feel secure as the four of us trudge back toward the bonfire. Not at all like I'm too much for him. Just like when Ash carried me, or with Micah in his bed. These three are more than strong. They're... formidable.

There's that feeling again. The one composed of warmth and satisfaction. The one that spread through my gut the night I pulled up to the house with Micah and all my housemates were there. This time, it's from seeing the queen bitch stand in the middle of the woods, watching as three guys she'd kill to be with seem more interested in *me* than her.

There's just something incredibly special about witnessing Dahlia eat shit.

She fades into the darkness, and I focus on the guys again, their lighthearted conversation as we head back. I lift my head to observe my surroundings. None of the other guys are carrying their catches, so I'm guessing that's just a Vince thing. The other girls are being led by the leashes attached to their collars.

The music's deafening back at the bonfire, loud enough to be heard deep into the woods. One of Vince's large hands spreads across my ass as he slides me off his shoulder and lowers me to the ground. If I'm not crazy, he was careful not to touch my hip. A fact

261

that *would* be sweet if, you know, he wasn't part of the reason I'm currently in pain.

I'd just started scanning the crowd, doing a quick count of how many others made it back from The Hunt, when Ash reaches toward my neck. My breath hitches, but I don't react other than that. I don't even flinch. All because the thought of his hand around my throat doesn't scare me, it *excites* me.

And I'll be damned. He knows.

That smirk on his lips as I lock in on his blue stare tells me so. He's focused, thinking God-knows-what while hooking his leash to my collar. My mind drifts back to the moment in the woods before The Hunt began. This deep-seated attraction between us seems to cancel out all rational thought, including the fact that I should only feel hatred for them right now. But if I'm being honest, there's something else.

Always something else.

The metal component of the leash clicks through the loop at the base of my throat. I peer up at Ash when the soft pads of his fingertips trail my skin, tracing the tendon on the side of my neck.

"Something you want to say, Bird?" he asks. "Looks like you've got something on your mind."

Yes, I want to touch all of you, feel your hands all over me, yours squeezing my throat until I beg for breath.

These thoughts immediately race through my head, but I speak none of them aloud. Instead, I clear my throat and force my eyes elsewhere. Anywhere but into the eyes of the six-foot-something, tatted villain who somehow manages to make me wet even when I hate his ass to death.

He snickers beside me, and I don't give him the satisfaction of knowing that even the sound of it is sexy. Instead, I watch as more strays start to wander back to the bonfire. Most of the girls look happy to be caught, but a few don't. Then there are the ones who clearly got tired of running and gave up, returning to the group unattached. Fletcher mentioned having a plan for them, so I'm sure no one will be sleeping alone tonight if *he* has anything to do with it.

A bright pink spot to my right grabs my attention, and I'm not surprised to find that *Dahlia's* eyes are already locked on me. I've seen her angry, but in this moment she's beyond that—pissed, livid. Eventually, she tears her eyes away and settles beside one of her future sorority sisters, arms folded over her chest, nostrils flared.

I look away, feeling a fresh wave of rage as I think of what she tried tonight. My eyes flit to Vince. Twice I open my mouth, wanting to ask a question, but it isn't until my third attempt that I finally force the words from my mouth.

"What'd she say to you before the race?"

Vince, initially focused on a conversation with Micah, glances down toward me. "What'd *who* say?"

The question, coupled with the look of confusion on his face, is even more satisfying than leaving Dahlia's dumb ass in the woods. When I nod toward her, Vince follows my gaze to Dahlia.

He smirks a little.

"Ah, I see," he says. "But why do you want to know?"

His green stare is fixed on me in such a way that I'm momentarily at a loss for words, letting my eyes wander over his features. All perfect. All adding to the level of unfairness because the guy has zero flaws. Eventually, my attention lands on his lips— pale pink, fleshy... incredibly kissable.

I should know.

I quickly train my eyes on his, sobering up. "I mean, it's not important or anything. I'm just curious, I guess."

He's still wearing that smirk, possibly because he knows how uncomfortable I am right now. Almost enough to regret asking.

Almost.

He doesn't offer up his answer easily, instead making me stew in my awkwardness for a little. Then, eventually, he leans in and speaks clearly into my ear.

"She said that if I caught her tonight, she'd... make it worth my while," he says, clearly being vague with the answer. Possibly to spare my feelings.

He leans away and I can't even look at him. Because I can't take my eyes off *her*. I suspected as much, but hearing him *confirm* what a bitch Dahlia is makes it ten times worse.

Anger flares in the pit of my stomach. I couldn't deny it even if I wanted to, which... I would love to do. Because it shouldn't get to me this much, knowing she came after Vince, but it does. Even with the shit they've put me through, I'm undeniably territorial over these three. That's my twisted truth and I own it.

And I also own the fact that I would *love* the chance to claw her eyes out right now.

As if I spoke those words aloud, a brunette ponytail whips through the air and her cold blue stare is locked on me.

"What the fuck are you looking at?" she yells, her voice carrying over the music. Then, realizing there's drama unfolding, whoever's the DJ for the night decides to kill the music altogether.

The crowd slowly goes quiet, taking note of which direction the infuriated screech just came from.

Dahlia faces me completely, keeping her arms crossed as she comes closer, never blinking. My fists clench at my sides and this moment feels familiar. Only, last time, it ended with flashing red and blue lights, me in cuffs.

That can't happen again.

The judge made that very clear.

"Honestly, why the fuck are you even here?" Dahlia barks out. "You're not pledging. You have no friends here, so what purpose do you even serve? I mean, look at yourself, Stevie," she scoffs. "Maybe if this was a *big game* hunt, it'd make sense that you were invited, but... seriously?"

She looks me over. The disgust in her eyes is tangible as she eyes the way my shorts fit, then my arms where my tank leaves them exposed. I hate her, but more than that... I hate how her empty words trigger me. It's like I'm right back at home, being picked apart by my father, being given a list of reasons I'm not good enough and never will be. The irony is that she's going out of her way to make me aware of how big I am in her eyes, but... I feel so small.

Insignificant.

Invisible.

She turns away from me, facing the crowd now. "In case anyone's missed it, this girl, Stevie Heron, is absolutely pathetic," she announces. "She lives in my basement and, get this, she pays to watch some guy jerk off. I mean, I know no one in their right mind would ever fuck her, but who actually pays for porn in the twenty-first century?"

My face is hot, warm with embarrassment, shame. I'd love nothing more than to shut this bitch up, but having a record leaves me powerless. It's the reason the guys are able to control me, and now it's the reason I'm forced to let Dahlia talk shit about me like I'm not even standing here.

At first, I don't realize I'm breathing wildly, but it becomes apparent when my chest tightens. It's been years since I've had an anxiety attack. The last was when my dad cornered me after performing during a ballet recital when I was seven. He was reminding me to suck in my stomach during our next number. He laughingly told me that it looked like I'd eaten one of the other girls. The only thing he accomplished that night was convincing me not to go back out on stage for the remainder of the performance.

That same wave of shame, that same sense of not belonging... it's eating me alive again.

I take one step back and bump into a wall. At least, that's what Micah's chest feels like, but I can't afford to let anything stop me. With the pure, undiluted fury in my gut, I can't stay here. If I do, there's no telling what might happen, how this might end. So, the best course of action is to let Dahlia think she's won and run for it.

Only, Micah has other plans. I see it in his eyes when I turn to face him, stupidly thinking I can sidestep him.

"What are you doing?" His voice is low and gravelly. So low no one can possibly hear him over Dahlia's rant.

I don't have an answer, and seeing how I'm on the verge of a total meltdown, Vince speaks up.

"I'm gonna shut this shit down," he announces, but the second he takes a step, Micah's hand comes down on his shoulder.

"She doesn't need us or *anyone* to step in," he says, then his eyes leave Vince and land on me as he repeats his question. "What are you doing?"

My eyes slam closed, and I focus on breathing.

Slow and steady.

Slow and steady.

"I'm leaving," I finally answer. "If I stay I'll—"

"If you stay you'll what?" he cuts in, and I swear his eyes darken more than they already were.

"I'll do something I'll regret, something that will land me in trouble again," I admit.

He stares and I feel my heart beating in my throat.

"There's only one problem with that, Bird. You're with us now," he says. I hold my breath when he steps even closer. "So, if *we* don't tolerate disrespect, that means *you* don't tolerate disrespect. Understood?"

I feel my entire body tense when his finger lands in the center of my chest. "Yes, but—"

"But what?"

"I have a record," I admit coarsely, somehow not yelling those words despite my rage. "So, I don't know what the hell you expect from me."

He steps even closer. "Well, the way I see it, you've got two options. You can step back while me and the guys embarrass the fuck out of this bitch and make her crawl back into whatever hole she crawled out of. Or... we could go with option B."

I'm trembling from head to toe. "Which is?"

His lips just barely touch my ear when he answers. "Option B is you let us worry about the aftermath and you handle this shit yourself," he says. "And when I say handle it, I mean I want you to *completely*... fuck... her... up."

I don't know what kind of spell he cast on me with this speech, but I swear I'm feeding off his energy now, feeling like I'm larger than life, untouchable. Or maybe that's simply because I actually believe these three have my back.

A moment later, his fingers are at my throat, pinching the clasp of the leash, setting me free. And from there, the next two minutes are a complete blur. I'm aware of myself charging toward Dahlia. She hears me coming and turns at the last second, stretching her arms out to protect herself, but it's futile. I'm on her ass like a cheap suit. Her back slams the ground after she stumbles, but I have her pinned, and Micah's command stokes the flame inside me until it becomes a full-on blaze.

Fuck. Her. Up.

The first connection between my fist and her face is almost orgasmic. Honestly, it's been a lifetime since I've felt so satisfied, so liberated. The sound of Dahlia's screams for help are like a perfectly orchestrated symphony, literal music to my ears. Several times, she attempts to grab my wrists, attempts to swing back, but she fails until now. The silver ring on her finger grazes my lip when she flails, and the sting only makes me rage more. She doesn't get to talk all that shit about me *and* hit me, too.

Fuck that.

This makes me go harder, *hit* harder. Whenever my knuckles meet the soft flesh of her cheek, her insults go off in my head like rapid fire. In both hers *and* my father's voices, taunting me, shaming me.

I'd never gotten the chance to beat *his* ass, but Dahlia will feel my fucking wrath.

The crowd isn't so silent anymore.

"Holy shit!"

"Daaaamn!"

I have no idea where the voices are coming from, but after Dahlia got to humiliate me in front of them, this is a small measure of vindication. She made a fool of me, now I'm making her bleed.

Seems fair.

There are footsteps to my left, but before I can sort out what's happening, Vince's voice fills the air.

"Savages, control your girls," he calls out—clear, direct, authoritative. "If you can't, they'll be sent packing and your asses will be tossed out, too."

I can only guess a few of Dahlia's sisters were attempting to intervene before Vince spoke up. Honestly, with how raw and unstoppable I feel, I almost wish he'd let them.

My fist rockets toward Dahlia again, but I only make contact one last time before a set of hands slip beneath my arms and lift me to my feet. Feeling like Dahlia hasn't quite had enough yet, I stare down on her, imagining what might've happened had we not been interrupted.

"My tooth!" she yells out. "You chipped it!"

I flip her off with both hands and Ash drags me back. I zero in on Dahlia's pink shirt, at the spatters of blood coloring it. I'm proud seeing her wear her ass kicking like artwork. Before I can be pulled too far away, I crane my neck toward her and spit.

"Bitch."

"Okay, Bird. Enough," Ash chuckles, standing me upright. He keeps both hands on my waist to make sure I don't lunge at Dahlia again. Wise move because I definitely would've if given the chance.

Other than the sweat dampening my hairline and the traces of blood from Dahlia's nose on my knuckles, you'd never know I'd just been in a fight. Swiping my thumb under my nose to check for blood, I try to relax, try convincing myself that what I just did wasn't possibly the biggest mistake of my life.

Movement to the left catches my eye. It's Vince, and he's on his way over to Dahlia. My heart sinks a bit, in disbelief that he might actually try to help her up. Like she didn't just deserve every ounce of that. But then I hear him speak, and his words are a warning. One that brings a smile to my face as he crouches beside her.

"You're free to talk shit. *To* her, *about* her. Any time you want," he says. "Just know there will always be an ass whooping that follows. Every damn time. And I swear, if you or *anyone* breathes a word about this, I'll personally see to it that your plans to be a part of whatever fucking sisterhood you're trying to join are canceled. "

Dahlia stares intently into Vince's eyes.

"I need you to repeat after me," he says. "Say: *This fight was completely my fault.*"

She doesn't speak, so Vince tries again. *"This fight was completely my fault."*

Her enraged glare stays trained on Vince, but our girl Dahlia seems to finally be coming around. "This fight was completely my

268

fault," she echoes, and the sound of it curves Vince's lips with a smile.

"Good," he croons. "So, I've made myself one-hundred-percent clear?"

Dahlia swallows hard, pinching her nose when more blood trickles from her nostrils. She doesn't speak, but does offer a nod.

"Nope, not good enough," Vince bites out. "Use your fucking words. Let me know you comprehend that this fight was your fault. Let me know we're on the same page. You know, so we don't have any mix-ups down the road. I'd hate for the rest of your time here on campus to suddenly turn shitty."

Dahlia stares up at him, hatred in her gaze. "I understand," she hisses, and I'll be damned... those are tears in her eyes.

Pleased with that answer, and probably the sight of Dahlia's tears, Vince smiles, then saunters toward me. And I swear, he's never looked fucking hotter.

Micah steals my attention when he steps into view, blocking my line of sight to Dahlia just as a few from the crowd go to her aid. Fletcher tries to get the night back on track, but me and the guys still have mostly everyone's attention.

Micah grabs me rough, like the brute he is. Without hesitation, he reaches into the back of my hair and tugs until my head tilts back. He scans my face. At first, there's concern in his eyes. I wonder if he expected to find that Dahlia's one hit did more damage, but then a slow smile crosses his face. The slight roughness of his thumb is a new feel, moving heat into my bottom lip when he brushes over it. A streak of blood coats the tip and he doesn't appear to mind.

"And that's how you get shit done," he says with a low growl in his tone. It's the reason there are now goosebumps covering my skin. A pleased grin touches his lips.

And... damn, I'm smiling back at him.

"Head inside and get cleaned up," he orders. "One of us will be up to check on you soon."

I hear the command, but now that I'm a bit more clear-headed, I'm painfully aware of what I've done.

My thoughts spiral, imagining what will happen when Dahlia

269

inevitably gets the police involved. I can't get into any more trouble. I went through hell last time, and it was super clear that I wouldn't get off so easily if I messed up again.

"I shouldn't have done that," I say just above a whisper, staring into Micah's dark eyes as I feel myself coming apart.

He grips my chin, forcing me to focus, staring into me when he speaks.

"I told you I'd handle it and I meant that shit," he asserts, sounding almost offended that I don't have much faith in him. "Now, be a good girl, stop talking so damn much, and do as your told."

He releases me and I turn, trudging toward the cabin. I'm not sure if this rush of adrenaline that has my heart absolutely racing is from the fight or that rabid look in the boys' eyes. Whatever the case, I am undeniably... turned... the fuck... on.

W hat the hell was I thinking, attacking Dahlia like that? I mean, yeah, she deserved it, but what if she calls the police or *someone* calls the police, and I land in hot water again?

Shit.

You fucked up, Stevie.

Big time.

I'm in the middle of pacing at the foot of my bed when I hear the front door open, and then slam shut. Heavy footsteps draw closer and I'm spiraling.

How could I have put my trust in their word? Their promise to protect me? I'm such an idiot.

The knob turns and my feet are still moving when the guys walk in. Well, Vince and Ash, at least. Micah's nowhere in sight. Ash closes the door behind him, and their expressions are a mixture of concern and... *pride?*

"So, how do you feel?" Vince asks, dropping down into the armchair beside the window. He's all casual and shit—arms draped over the armrests, legs set far apart as he relaxes deeper into the seat.

"How do I feel? Stupid," I answer. "You guys have no idea what this could do to me. I could get kicked out of school or... *worse.*"

It's the '*worse*' part that has me worried most. Sure, it'd suck to

271

have to leave B.U., but it'd suck ten times more to be shoved into a jail cell.

"If it makes you feel any better, Micah's making his rounds, doing damage control," Ash says with a sigh as he settles on the edge of the bed. "You don't have to worry about anyone snitching. Not even Dahlia."

He sounds so sure. If only I had that same confidence.

"Relax," Vince says with a chill yawn. "People respect Micah. They won't go against him. And those who don't respect him, well, they *fear* him."

He smirks but I'm not amused.

"And what makes you so sure he's really out there fending for me? For all I know, he's adding fuel to the fire," I scoff. "It's not like you three haven't taken every *other* opportunity to make shit go from bad to worse for me."

I peer up when Vince doesn't immediately answer. His brow is tense with intrigue.

"Maybe, but we've never lied to you."

I'm dumbfounded that he thinks that matters. "Are you fucking kidding me?"

He doesn't blink, just keeps his eyes locked on me while I pace.

"It's true," Ash chimes in. "Yeah, sure, we're assholes, but we've kept every promise we've ever made you. Even the bad ones," he adds, watching me the same as Vince.

A chill races down my spine when he grins a little.

Sick fuck.

"What'd you do, anyway?" he asks. "You're in some kind of legal trouble. That much is clear, but what for?"

This isn't something I talk about. Not because it's difficult to explain, but because it takes me back to a place I fought and clawed to bring myself out of.

"It was right after my..."

My voice trails off before I finish the statement. That's too far to let them in. It may *always* be too far to let them in.

"I went through some family stuff a year ago and wasn't myself for a long time," I share. "I ran into a girl I didn't get along with in high school. She talked shit on the wrong day and I just... snapped. She was pretty bad off by the time someone pulled me off of her. My family lawyered-up and, long story short, I'm... on probation. Which is why I really, *really* shouldn't have lost myself out there."

The guys are quiet and I'm trying to imagine exactly what kind of *'damage control'* Micah might be doing. You know, assuming that's even true.

Vince's words are in my head again. The ones where he reminds me that they've never lied to me. As hard as I try to find a hole in that argument, I can't. Because they've been truthful. As Ash pointed out, they've kept every promise. Dark promises included.

So, I believe them. Believe Micah's out there doing whatever he does to make things like this go away.

"You being on probation is why you agreed to our terms," Ash says, and I nod.

"Yes."

He's thoughtful and I'm locked in his stare. It's filled with something. Not kindness, but maybe... empathy.

"We wouldn't let tonight turn into anything. As far as anyone knows, there *was* no fight. Just some good, clean Savage fun," he adds with a smirk.

Probably because he knows *'good'* and *'clean'* aren't usually words associated with their brotherhood.

"But for what it's worth, Bird... you looked fucking hot out there," he says, every deeply spoken syllable rolling off his tongue like he's reliving the moment in his head.

To which Vince adds, "*Incredibly* fucking hot."

I know these words shouldn't be considered a compliment—them getting off on seeing me beat Dahlia's ass—but they go straight to my head, causing some of the anxiousness to fall away. Then, when Ash stands, my feet are no longer moving. Instead, I'm still, eyes trained on his as he approaches.

"You won out there," he says. "I think that deserves an award."

Air rushes into my lungs when I breathe deep, noting that look he's giving me. It's dark like always, but also not as guarded as usual. Like, he's letting me see more of him. Letting me see that, maybe, there's a soft spot somewhere inside him for me.

I can definitely relate.

His mouth lands on mine and the motion isn't rushed or rough. Nothing like what we shared in the woods earlier. Right now, it's gentle and full of passion and... it steals my breath. The slight sting from my cut lip is jarring when Ash forgets it's there and drags his teeth across it. But when he does it a second time, it's clearly not a mistake. It bleeds again. Only a little, but it's enough to taste the salty metallic flavor on my tongue, which means *he* must taste it, too. And yet, he doesn't back off or seem grossed out.

Instead, he draws my bottom lip into his mouth, like he's savoring it, and then grips my ass with both hands.

Caught up in the whirlwind of him, my hands fall from his chest to his waist, pushing beneath the hem of his shirt until my palms are met with warmth. There's more of the scarred flesh I've discovered on him before, but this time, he doesn't stop me from touching him. *Exploring* him.

The front of his jeans is rough against my shorts, but I'm not as focused on *that* as I am the stiff rod jabbing into me from underneath them.

"I know you feel what you fucking do to me," he breathes, "However... I think tonight should just be about you."

My entire vocabulary is jumbled inside my head like alphabet soup. I hear him, but don't quite register his meaning until he walks me toward the bed, pushing until I fall back with my legs hanging over the edge. Staring up at his devious grin, I put the pieces together. And if I hadn't, I would have by the time his knees lower to the carpet at the foot of the bed, and he tucks his fingers into my shorts to pull them down.

He's careful to avoid my hip, and I realize I trust him not to hurt me when my eyes leave him and land on Vince. He's still seated in the chair, relaxed as he calmly observes his friend removing my panties.

Ash lifts my ankle to his shoulder, and I suck in a breath when he licks a slow trail up my inner thigh.

"Shit..."

274

The word leaves me on a whisper as he finally reaches my slit, lightly teasing my clit with the tip of his tongue.

"Why'd you stop?" I beg when he shifts his attention to my thigh again.

"Because I need you to tell me you want this," he croons, heat from his mouth covering my skin. "Tell me you want me to eat your pussy. Tell me you want to come against my lips."

Weeks ago, I'd have been too proud to admit such a thing, but those feelings have taken a backseat for now.

"I want you to," I say, but Ash tsks in disapproval.

"Those weren't my words, Bird."

I replay his command in my head, but struggle to force his exact phrasing out of my mouth. "I want you to... eat my pussy."

"And?"

"And... make me come against your lips."

I feel his smile against my skin when he places another kiss on my thigh. "Good girl."

He cranes his neck lower until his face disappears between my legs. His tongue, slick with warm saliva, flicks against my clit, sending electric currents scattering through my entire body. He forms a 'V' with two fingers and uses them to hold me open, and the bedspread gathers in my palms. The sound of a zipper lowering has my head lifting from the mattress, expecting the sound to have come from Vince's corner, but it isn't him.

Ash's shoulder moves in rhythm, and although my line of sight is cut off from anything happening beyond the bed, I'm certain he's jerking himself off with his free hand.

I look to Vince again and he's quiet, taking it all in as the front of his pants tents with his erection. Releasing the cover from my fist, I gesture for him to come to me. He smirks and appears to be content just to watch, but he stands from his seat anyway.

The slow, deliberate roll of his shoulders is like an aphrodisiac to me as I watch him saunter over. My hips lift as I grind my pussy against Ash's mouth, craving more friction. I take the feel of him tonguing me deeper to mean that he liked it.

My attention is on Vince again. "Your clothes," I pant. "Take them off."

He barely hesitates, but I notice it, remembering the night I raged on them, telling them all the ways I observed them being broken. Vince was the one I noted to be adverse to being touched. I had an inkling why that might've been, but I honestly never guessed I'd be right. Still, after it came to light that someone from his past *had* violated him, I wished I'd left it alone.

But now that I know, I don't take it lightly that he's giving in to me, removing his clothes, climbing onto the bed beside me.

It means that, despite all the bullshit between us... there's trust.

"I'm... not sure where you want me," he says, and it's clear he's nervous. However, I want him to feel calm, want him to *enjoy* this.

I bring him closer by his hand, staring at his huge cock angled right toward my face.

"Kneel right here," I say, struggling to remain coherent as Ash sucks my swollen clit between his lips.

Vince isn't exactly timid—he's too formidable and sure of himself for that—but it's obvious he doesn't let people get this close. He kneels beside my head, and when I wrap my fingers around his cock, and then wrap my *lips* around it, he hisses a sigh.

"Fuuuuck," he groans.

I stare up at him, watching as his head slowly tilts back, admiring the landscape of him. His body is an absolute work of art. There's no ink like the other two have, but there isn't an ounce of him that wasn't deliberately sculpted into the perfection I see before me tonight.

A bead of precum settles on my tongue as his hand slips into my hair, and I take him in deeper, fighting my body's desire to come so quickly. I'm desperate to draw this out as long as I can—two of my boys entangled with me at the same time.

My mind is so gone I hardly realize the term I've just used for them.

My boys.

But it's what I felt when it came to me. And now I can't pretend it doesn't feel right. Can't pretend it doesn't fit.

In some twisted way, they *are* mine.

And I'm theirs.

276

The bed shifts when Vince rears back on his shins, letting his cock slip free of my mouth with a soft pop. He leans close again, but this time he gives me his lips instead. I don't hate it. There's always something I've loved about kissing him. There's always something incredible that happens between us when we connect in this way.

"I need to tell you something," he breathes against my mouth, and for a moment, I open my eyes to meet his gaze. "I think... we have a secret."

At first, I'm confused, blaming Ash's skilled tongue and the buzz of my impending orgasm for my inability to hear clearly.

"What is it?"

He kisses me again, hot and deep. So much that I think he's going to save whatever this *'secret'* is for later. However, the words, "You've been watching me," are spoken against my lips, but I'm unable to ask for clarity because my mouth is a little busy.

Except, that doesn't mean my mind isn't racing, analyzing his statement.

"I don't—I don't know what you're talking about," I breathe into him, and his response is a cheeky smirk half a second before he pushes his tongue into my mouth again. But without further explanation, he takes my hand, places it against his side, and then moves my fingertips over his skin.

At first, the confusion only spreads, but then I feel it.

A scar.

A thin scar I've stared at week after week. On nights when there's no one else I'd rather be close to. On whatever screen I can get to the quickest, so I don't miss a second of his show.

I can't speak but it's all coming together...

My cam guy being a virgin. Vince's aversion to touch.

Their shared scar and physique.

The camera equipment I spotted in Vince's closet the night I snooped.

It all... makes sense.

"Am I right?" he breathes, moving his mouth to my neck while I find words.

How did I not realize?

277

How did I not catch that they're one in the same?

"I didn't... I had no..."

I get stuck there and a deep chuckle leaves him, vibrating against the damp circle he's just left on the side of my throat.

"Relax. Let's keep it between us," he whispers, and I feel his smile against my lips.

Does this mean the others don't know how he earns cash?

I go from completely turned on to a literal furnace as his admission swirls through my head. Here I was thinking Dahlia airing my secret was one of the most humiliating moments of my life, but now I'm starting to think she did me a favor.

My lips feel chilled when Vince takes his away, but then the thick shaft that pacified me before pushes into my mouth again. He arcs over me like a bridge this time, settling both hands into the mattress on the other side of my head. His body blocks out the dim light from the lamp just before I close my eyes. I tease his tip with my tongue, slurping him in again right after. He's closer to my ear now. Close enough to hear his labored breathing, hear the quiet moans that reverberate in his throat, and it isn't lost on me that I've gotten my wish.

There were many nights I imagined this, pulling him into my world from the screen. Only, I hadn't realized that had already happened. And now, as I smooth my fingertips over the soft skin of his sac, I'm living out my fantasy.

Warm, thick cum bursts from his dick, and I swallow him down. Every ounce of him as he shivers with pleasure just above my head as a thought hits me.

Am I the only one who's ever gotten him off?

I'm distracted when Ash lets out a groan from the floor, half a second before the leg I don't have propped on his shoulder is suddenly doused in wet heat. As he comes, he smooths the head of his cock against my calf, sucking my clit hard and fast until... shit... I'm completely done for.

Words fail me because I refuse to release Vince from my lips until he's limp and empty, but my chest hums with a deep whimper that marks my release. The entire mattress quakes with my body and I realize I've dug my heel into Ash's back. But with his size and mass, I doubt he even feels it.

Vince falls from my mouth, but he doesn't move. He continues to hover over me as my eyes volley between his long, sated dick and the scar, still shocked by what I've discovered.

Ash runs a sticky hand down the inside of my thigh, leaving a trail of his cum on my skin. He's not quite done with me either, placing soft, longing kisses on my clit.

"One of these days," he rasps, "I'm going to mark this pussy, fill it with my cum, claim it as my own once and for all."

My stomach comes alive with butterflies, hearing him speak about me in this way.

"You always have been a greedy son of a bitch," Vince says to Ash with a laugh, giving my tit a gentle squeeze through my bra before rearing back on his shins again.

"Of course, I mean all *three* of us," Ash clarifies, which draws a smile out of me.

"Um, who says I—or my lady bits—want to be claimed by *any* of you?"

After asking the question, clearly being coy, I stare down my body at Ash. He's still smirking, but his brow is arched now.

"If you're not convinced already, you'll definitely be singing a different tune after we fuck you."

I didn't expect him to be so crass, so direct, but I should've. He places a kiss on my knee, then stands, not shy in the least about being nude in front of his friend. That's when I remember they've played hockey together for years, which I'm sure means they've seen one another in the locker room countless times. But for me, a girl who's new to having two boys in the room with their dicks out at once, it's more than a turn on.

I'll certainly lock the image of them both casually walking around the room, dicks swinging as they collect their things, in whatever a girl-version of a spank bank would be.

They don't bother wiping off or even clothing themselves, and I imagine they're off to shower like I will once they're gone. Ash tucks his things under his arm then draws a gasp from me when he hops onto the bed, intending to steal a kiss. And he would have, had I not placed a hand on his chest to stop him.

He glances down at my fingers splayed across his ink, and then meets my gaze with an arched brow, clearly missing why I've kept him at arm's length.

"I just finished... with *Vince*," I add, trusting that he'll be able to fill in the blanks.

And he does, but instead of backing off like I expect, his expression relaxes. I note that there's a faint smile on his lips as he gently removes my hand, then takes what he wants—sucking my tongue and lips like I *didn't* just have Vince between them.

The kiss slows and Ash places one more peck against the corner of my mouth, leaning in close so only I can hear.

"You worry too much," he whispers. "I *prefer* you dirty."

I don't even pretend to understand the complexity of their friendship, but I stop trying when Ash cups me between my legs, smiling as he says one, loaded word in parting.

"Soon."

With that, he climbs off the bed and walks his toned, sexy ass out of my room, closing the door behind him. Vince is on his phone, maybe checking social media or sending a text, but I don't disturb him. When he finishes, I've peeled myself off the comforter and wiped off with one of the spare towels the cabin owner left folded on the dresser.

I'm still not sure what to say to him. Similar to how a person might react to meeting their celebrity crush. Or finally getting close to the hot guy they've only ever had the nerve to admire from afar. But this feels deeper than that.

He takes the guesswork out of how I'm supposed to behave when he steps close, cups my chin. And as if Ash hadn't already left me feeling overwhelmed enough, Vince quiets my thoughts with another kiss. There's nothing rough or empty about it. In fact, my heart leaps inside my chest in this strange way and it startles me because... I've never felt it before.

He releases me, but still grips my chin as he holds my gaze. Something's changed in him. That sense of him holding back is gone and it confirms that tonight was a first for him.

His hand lowers and he takes a few steps toward the door, clothes clutched in his fist.

"Night," he says, and all I can do is lift my fingers with a single wave, accepting that the latter part of this evening has gone in one hell of an unexpected direction.

The door closes and now it's just me. I stare at the space where he stood, and the spell I'm under is only broken when I see the light on my phone blink. An indication that I've missed an alert. And when I check it, I smile, understanding it was *me* Vince had been texting a moment ago.

Vince: Send me your username and I'll send you a code. I won't let you pay to watch something I'd do for you free of charge.

The grin on my face is so big it hurts, texting back with my username as requested, but adding one thing I hope he takes to heart.

Stevie: There are two things I never forget—a face or a promise. So, I hope you know I'm holding you to that.

I set my phone down and head toward the shower, but then double back when he messages again.

Vince: And you already know... I never make promises I don't intend to keep.

CHAPTER 40
STEVIE

"G ood morning."

      Micah looks up from his phone and scans me from where he's posted against the kitchen counter, but doesn't return the greeting. Instead, his eyes slowly inch their way up my figure. From my bare legs where my boy shorts cut off, to my white tank that I stupidly forgot to put a bra underneath.

Yeah, he definitely notices that part. He definitely *enjoys* that part. The smirk on his lips tells me as much.

"Good morning," he finally echoes, taking a sip of water from his glass.

Feeling awkward and a bit overly exposed, I set my sights on the fridge where I'm hoping to find something light to either drink or eat. But before I can get that far, Micah's arm slips around my waist. I gaze down where it locks around me, the faint dusting of blond hair over his tatts.

"Come here," he says.

I take steps in his direction when he pulls me, and I hold my breath as he studies my face, brushing his thumb over the cut on my lip. That look of concern returns from last night and words leave me before I've completely thought them through.

"I'm okay." Right away, I wish I could take them back, because he couldn't possibly be worried about me. Even though all the signs and his actions point toward that, I have to be mistaken.

He must notice when I start to feel embarrassed, because the second my eyes fall away from his, he cups my chin in his hand.

"You did good last night," he says. "I haven't been that fucking proud of someone in a very long time."

The smile that comes next is warm and full of emotion, feeding into my disillusioned thought that he actually cares.

When my internal war makes it difficult to respond, I nod, and then pull myself free from his grasp—both my chin and my waist.

Just before opening the fridge, in my peripheral vision, I see his head lower as he smirks, scrubbing his chin with his hand. My first thought is that maybe he took my response as rejection, but then I remember who I'm dealing with. If anything, he likely thinks I'm playing hard to get this morning.

"How about breakfast," he says, and the next second, the sound of a barstool being scooted out from beneath the countertop fills the room. Which means he clearly wasn't offering to cook for *me*.

"Sure." I'd just closed the refrigerator door, so I open it again to grab the bacon and eggs I spotted.

I have no idea where the pans and utensils are in this foreign-to-me kitchen, so I hunt around for a bit, gathering what I'll need. All the while, Micah quietly watches from his seat. It isn't until the bacon starts sizzling in the pan that he speaks again.

"The guys and I need to make a beer run in a bit. We're leaving once Eros gets in."

I'd totally forgotten they were expecting someone else. Honestly, I'm not looking forward to the new addition. Someone else to wait on hand and foot. Someone else to witness my humiliation.

Fun.

"I'm guessing he'll be tired from the drive up, so he'll probably hang out here with you. That should give you two a chance to get acquainted."

My eyes flit up from the pan when he says that, but he's behind me and can't see my expression. Since when do they trust me alone with another guy? They damn-near broke Enzo in

283

two not too long ago, so what makes this Eros dude any different?

Besides that, I'm not interested in getting acquainted with anyone. Especially another d-bag from their brotherhood. It's only by sheer willpower that I'm learning to tolerate *these* three assholes.

For some reason, that thought makes me smile. They're totally assholes, but... there are perks to putting up with their shit. A flash of how my evening ended last night comes to mind and my pussy clenches at the thought of Ash's face buried between my legs, Vince locked between my lips.

Yep.

Perks.

"Rumor is, I missed a good time last night," Micah says, and my brow tenses at the possibility of him having mind-reading abilities I didn't know about until now.

"A good time?"

He chuckles when I play coy. "You know what the fuck I'm talking about."

I smile, flipping a few strips of bacon. "Is it in your frat bylaws that you guys can't keep secrets from each other?"

"May as well be," he answers. "When it comes to me, Ash, and Vince, we tell each other everything."

I peer up from the pan again, zoning out on the brown-tiled backsplash when a thought comes to mind. After Vince's big reveal last night, I'd argue that Micah's point isn't completely true. There's definitely one secret being kept among their crew.

"But, yeah... don't worry about the Dahlia thing. I took care of it," he says, and I don't miss the seriousness of his tone. "Ash told me what's on the line for you. Told me about your probation, that is."

"Damn, you three really do tell it all, don't you?"

A long stretch of silence passes between us, but the longer it lasts, the more the tension builds. Because I know he has questions, know he's not afraid to ask them.

"What happened?"

And there it is.

At first, I focus on cracking eggs into the glass bowl I fished out from the back of a cabinet, then I give him a one-sentence summary.

"Some chick said the wrong thing on the wrong day, and I lost my temper. End of story."

"No, I mean what happened leading up to that? Ash said something about... family shit?"

The only sound for several seconds is the light clinking of the metal whisk against the sides of the bowl, but then I sigh and give another short answer.

"I lost my sister, and it fucked me up pretty badly."

Silence. That's the response I get from most people, so it doesn't surprise me when this is Micah's as well.

"I get it," he says. "Maybe more than most other people would."

I don't face him. Mostly because, if I did, he'd see the tears pooling in my eyes.

"I lost my sister when I was a kid. I was thirteen," he shares, and my eyes lift to the tile again. "My parents had me young—at age sixteen—then got married right out of high school. I mean, I get it, they thought it was the right thing to do, but they never should've been together."

His voice seems distant, like his thoughts are miles away. Maybe as he recalls all the bad that came from that one seemingly noble act.

"They ended up spending their entire relationship arguing," he adds. "My dad became a firefighter and picked up a lot of odd jobs to afford renovations on the house my grandparents left them. Mom took up real estate, so they weren't around a whole lot. But somehow, in the midst of the busy schedules and all their bullshit, they had my sister when I was six," he says with a distant laugh.

It isn't until he pauses that I realize how rapid my breaths are coming. We don't talk to each other like this, like we're real people. So, I'm a bit taken aback that he's opening up.

"Like I said, they mostly argued. More than they did anything else, including parenting," he adds, his voice sounding far away again, like he's back in those days, reliving it. "There was this one

285

Saturday in particular when things got really bad, and I remember them arguing over the dumbest shit ever. Dad had used Mom's work laptop and accidentally locked her out of it. I swear, they screamed at each other for a good three hours straight before I'd had enough. I walked right out the front door and they never even noticed. That's how bad it was."

"Where'd you go?" I ask. "You were so young."

"I was still close, because there was nowhere *to* go, so I just... walked. For hours," he adds. "Until... I heard the sirens."

I blink as I turn off the stove, somewhat afraid to meet Micah's gaze. I'm not sure I can handle whatever look I'll find there, so I keep myself busy, cleaning the mess.

"I don't know *how* I knew, but... I knew."

I swipe a tear from my cheek, reliving my own tragedy. One that replays in my head every single day of my life. I can't help but wonder if it's like that for Micah, too.

"It was Loren," he shares. "A drunk driver came out of nowhere, hit her, took her from us in the blink of an eye."

My heart's pounding now, and I feel my hands beginning to tremble, too.

"Best guess? She walked right out the front door, just like I did, without either of my parents noticing, and..."

His voice trails off and I force myself to be brave, facing him as I brace my hip against the counter. His expression isn't anything like I expect. Instead of being marked with sadness, I only find anger there.

Dark, deep-rooted, soul-crushing anger.

"Eventually, I shifted my wrath toward the driver who hit her, but before that, I blamed myself, thinking she probably came looking for me when I didn't come right back. And then I blamed myself for not just helping my dad with the laptop to shut my mom up. I've always been good with all kinds of techy shit—computers, software, all of it. I could've had it fixed in five minutes or less, but I didn't bother," he adds. "I was so sick of their bullshit I wanted them to suffer like we suffered, so I let them tear at each other's throats."

He zones out and I know that feeling. The guilt. The constant stream of *'what ifs'*.

"It's not on you."

He peers up when I speak.

"Trust me, you'll have to remind yourself of that every day, but it's true," I say. "Your sister isn't gone because of anything you did or didn't do. She's gone because life can be extremely fucking random sometimes, and shit happens."

He stares, and this is one of the rare moments that he seems human. Like a person with emotions and hopes and dreams like the rest of us. His gaze lowers and I get the sense that he didn't mean to say so much, didn't mean to let me in so far.

"Well... anyway... the point is, I get it. I get why something like what you went through might make you do something you regret."

He ends his statement there, but my gut tells me this isn't the actual ending to the story. Instead, I find myself wondering if maybe this is just as far as he's willing to discuss it. It isn't lost on me that he mentioned his wrath turning toward the driver, but I can't even begin to imagine what that could mean.

Footsteps coming in this direction from down the hallway have Micah and I both shifting gears. He straightens in his seat, and I turn to search for plates.

A tattooed arm reaches around me to the counter when Ash steals a piece of bacon.

"Morning," he says with a grin I spot from the corner of my eye. Right before he grabs a healthy handful of my ass.

Then, a gentle squeeze to my arm focuses me just before Vince warms the side of my neck with a kiss. "Morning."

"Good morning," I say back, but I'm grateful they can't see my face because I'm definitely blushing.

Apparently, I'm not the only one who notices the warmth in those greetings because Micah—being blunt and crass—speaks on it.

"What the fuck did you do to them? These assholes look downright lovesick."

I turn and see his arched brow, which causes my cheeks to heat just a little. "No idea what you're talking about."

"Yeah, I bet," he quips.

I slide him the first plate as he smirks. But before I can fix the others, there's a knock at the door.

"Mind grabbing that for us, Bird? We can feed ourselves," Ash grins.

I yelp when he smacks my ass as I pass by, and of course all three find it funny. Under his breath, possibly when he thinks I'm out of earshot, Micah mentions to the others how he's looking forward to *'breaking me in soon'*.

I ignore the heat that swirls in my core at his words, twisting the locks to greet the infamous Eros. Only, when I pull open the door, the last person on Earth I expect to see... is Tate.

We lock eyes and there are zero words for the look of pure shock in his. I imagine my expression is just as stunned—eyes wide, mouth gaping. I'm not thinking rationally, so my first instinct is to shut him out. So, that's what I do. I slam the door right in his face. Like that will actually solve something.

Did my mother send him out looking for me?

How did he know where to find me?

What the hell will he say when he realizes I've been holed up with three frat boys this weekend?

Shit.

Micah chuffs a short laugh. "What the hell are you doing, Bird? You look fine. I can barely see your nipples through your shirt," he teases.

He walks toward me, thinking I'm freaked out by the guy standing on the other side of the door because I'm not fully dressed. Little does he know, I'm dizzy and feeling like I might actually, honest to God faint because... this is bad.

Very fucking bad.

Laughing and shaking his head, Micah twists the knob, removing the barrier I so desperately needed to remain intact between myself and Tate. And now that it's gone, he stares, and those piercing eyes are asking a million questions.

"What's up? How was the drive?" Micah asks, bringing a very distracted Tate into a bro-hug.

Which means... *what the fuck?*

I'm confused and thinking this must be some kind of twisted nightmare. Because if I'm not mistaken, these two know each other and this is just all some kind of fucked up coincidence.

"The ride was fine. Clear roads the whole way," Tate answers, stealing a glance at me every few seconds. A fact that doesn't slip by Micah.

"Shit, let me introduce you," he says. "Bird, Eros. Eros, Bird."

"Actually—"

"He's the TA for one of my classes," I interrupt, stealing Micah's attention. "Tate, right? Tate Ford?"

Tate's brow twitches again and I find myself praying he doesn't let on that we're connected in any other way than what I just said. I've done my best to keep the guys out of my personal life, and knowing Tate, or Eros, or... *whatever the hell his name is,* has some measure of a connection to me would ruin that.

So, I step up to play the part.

"Stevie," I say, extending my hand to shake Tate's. "You probably don't remember because you see so many faces."

His brow does that thing again, but he's a quick study. "Right. No, I remember. You have one of those faces that's hard to forget."

I nod and shoot him a quick smile that doesn't feel like it quite reaches my eyes. "Nice seeing you outside the classroom."

"Yeah... you, too." He holds my gaze after speaking, even after Micah chimes in.

"Eros and some of the others from the grad chapter still pop in on events every now and then," he explains, closing and locking the door.

There's a sense of finality that hits when he does.

"They've mentioned the name Eros a few times, but... I had no idea it was you," I say, knowing Tate's reading between the lines.

"Yeah, funny. I don't recall them mentioning anything about you either," he replies, his tone clipped.

You could cut the tension in the room with a knife, so I attempt to excuse myself. "Well, I should go change into something more... appropriate," I say, crossing both arms over my chest, remembering the comment about being able to see through my tank.

"Nonsense," Micah quips. "I want you just the way you are. The less you wear, the better."

He smiles and winks, and my eyes immediately flash toward Tate. As expected, he's completely confused by the interaction between me and Micah, especially while I'm not at liberty to explain my way out of it.

Or *lie* my way out of it, rather.

Micah casually tosses his arm over Tate's shoulder, leading him away.

"I'll show you where to put your things. We saved you a room, but Bird got the one with the bathroom this time," he smirks.

I follow them with my gaze, and of course, Tate's eyes land on me several times between the small foyer and the hallway that leads to the bedrooms. For now, he's playing along, but I have a sinking feeling in my gut.

It tells me this isn't over.

Not even close.

CHAPTER 41
STEVIE

T ate and I have been under the same roof for approximately an hour and the world hasn't exploded. Mostly because I've avoided him, aside from breakfast. There were many awkward glances over the table, fake smiles, but now that the guys are gone on their beer run, I've resorted to hiding out on the deck. The last thing I need is him cornering me, making a bad situation ten times worse.

Activity around the lake is already lively. Several people are out on the water—some in boats, some on jet skis, but most just swim. The cabin a few doors over has a speaker on full blast as one of the guys mans a grill. The aroma of fresh seared meat wafts this way, and you'd never guess we're not at the height of summer.

I'm watching a group play Marco Polo down in the water when I'm aware of the glass door sliding open behind me. I sigh and roll my eyes. I came out here for peace, space, but leave it to Tate not to respect that.

"Mind if I join you?"

Offering no eye contact, I sigh again. "I'd say no, but I'm starting to think there's no hiding from you."

He doesn't respond, but does miss the hint, taking the seat beside me. I can feel his wheels turning, wondering why I'm here. But my biggest concern isn't so much what *he* thinks of me. It's what will my *mother* think if he decides to rat me out.

It's this realization of the power he could potentially hold over me that has me committed to being somewhat tolerant of him.

For now, anyway.

"So... Eros, huh? That's a rather interesting nickname," I say, doing my best to sound like I actually care.

"Yeah, uh, it just kind of stuck with me," he explains. "Back in the day, I was kind of... active."

Active.

Which basically translates to *'I was a huge man-whore'*. I distinctly remember Ash's words, stating that Tate earned this name because he *'got more ass than a toilet seat'*.

Also, he said *'back in the day'*, as if he wasn't just living in the frat house pretty recently.

Again with the fucking mind games.

He's quiet and I already know it's the calm before the storm. No way he'd make his way out here and miss the opportunity to pull more of his slick shit, pretending to be Mr. Perfect.

"I think it's time we talk."

And there it is.

"Didn't we just do this in your car not too long ago?" I realize too late that my tone is snappy, but vow to myself to ease up.

"We did," he says, "but I'm officially waving my white flag, declaring this... one-sided feud between us over. I know you don't think I have any right to ask, but... I need you to tell me why you're here. I've tried working it out on my own, but for the life of me, I can't figure out what the hell is going on."

The nerve of this fucking guy. Acting like he's my father or something. Acting like he actually cares.

"Aren't they your friends? Maybe I just enjoy their company like *you* do," I say dryly. "Is it so hard to believe that I'm just hanging out with them? Doing what college kids do?"

"If we were talking about someone else, maybe, but that doesn't sound like you."

"You know *nothing* about me."

"Well, maybe I would if you'd just... shit... let me in."

I have nothing to say to that. He's mentioned this initial spark that existed between us, and I believe he's held on to that. While I can't deny that there may have once been a bit of truth there, the moment has long passed. Whatever flicker there was, it went up in smoke the moment I realized who he is.

What he's done.

"I'm worried about you."

I scoff before he even finishes.

"Fine, you can act like a fucking brat all you want, pretend I'm imagining things, but I'm definitely not imagining that cut on your lip."

When he mentions it, my tongue peeks out, touching the rough line that's sure to leave a faint scar.

"It's nothing."

"Nothing," he echoes. "I've known the guys for a very long time, and I don't think they're capable, but—"

"Oh, my God! They didn't do this!"

When frustration gets the best of me and I finally meet his gaze, there's this look in his eyes that says, *'Good, because I'd fuck them up if they did.'*

I roll my eyes. Can't help it. Just the idea of him playing the role of protector, knowing he's done way worse, is a fucking joke.

"What's your angle here, Tate?"

"If I'm being honest, it looks like you're in trouble. Like you're, I don't know, spiraling. And I'm not sure I shouldn't get in touch with your mother."

A laugh slips, and it's out of pure annoyance. "Are you shitting me? You're seriously threatening to call my mother right now?"

"I won't. Not if you level with me. No more of that surface-level bullshit either. Whatever you haven't said to me up to this point, whatever's *really* behind why you're such a bitch to me, *that's* what I want to hear. I want to know what I did that was so fucking bad that you can't even look me in the eyes."

He finishes and I feel myself panting.

Also, note to self: The Savages are all manipulators.

All of them.

His words swirl in my head for a bit, but when I meet his gaze again, anger rises in my gut.

"You want to know why I'm *such a bitch*? Fine, here it is," I hiss. "You may not have paid the price for your sins, but I sure as hell did."

I haven't even gotten to my point, and I'm already choked up, unable to finish. Tate reaches out like he plans to touch my hand, but then seems to think better of it.

"Finish. Please. I need to know."

First, my eyes are locked on his face, but then they slip down to his arm.

"The brand," I say.

His gaze lowers to the scar. The one identical to the one healing on my hip. He's confused, but I'm not.

"That's what gave you away," I add. "I saw it in the picture. The one from the night you..."

My words fail again.

"The night I what?" he asks, watching from a distance as angry tears spill from my eyes.

"The night you hurt my sister. The night she came home in tears, bruised wrists, torn shirt."

The confusion in his gaze deepens.

Mel begged me not to tell, but I wish like hell I hadn't listened. Maybe Mom would've known what to do. Maybe we could've gotten her some help.

"One month after that, she was gone," I say. "She took herself away from me and everyone else who loved her." Pausing, I wipe the wetness from my face. "She was carrying a lot of shit. That isn't lost on me, but you... *you* broke her."

Tate sinks deeper in his seat, pushing a hand through his hair. "You're saying you think I—"

"No, I don't *think*. I *know* it was you," I snap. "And I know her death doesn't affect you, but that doesn't mean I'm wrong. I watched you that night we talked in your car. When I told you what happened, you were downright callus. You didn't even flinch, and that's when I knew just how fucked up you really are."

"Stevie, you have no idea how sorry I am for what you went through, for your *loss,* but listen to what you're saying. I didn't flinch and now that makes you even *more* convinced I'm guilty? Did you ever consider that I wasn't nervous because I had no idea

294

that was an interrogation? I had no idea I was the one you were suspicious of?"

I completely ignore his questions, asking one of my own. "What do you remember about the first time we met?"

Tate sighs and thinks deeply. "Bits and pieces. Mostly, I remember us getting along really well in the beginning, and then... everything just kind of went to shit. Which I now know is because you saw my brand, knew I was a Savage. But shit, Stevie, do you have any idea how many people are marked with this symbol? Thousands."

He finishes and I reach for his wrist. "Maybe. But how many also have this?"

He follows my gaze to the beaded bracelet he wears. Black beads with Filipino letters engraved in each. After a bit of research, I discovered that the word they spell out is *'Always.'*

He doesn't speak right away, just studies that word like he's seeing it for the first time. I get the sense that it's sentimental, but I couldn't care less right now. In this moment, all I want is for him to own his shit.

"She was seeing someone," I share. "And it was clear that this guy was someone who shouldn't have been in her life. My guess is because she wasn't quite legal yet, and he was older." I glance toward him with those words. "It just... fits. *You* fit."

There's this grave look on Tate's face and I don't miss it when he nods. "It does. But only because you want it to," he adds. "I'd like to see the pic."

I don't immediately reach for my phone, but eventually decide to show him the proof I have, putting him at the wrong place at the wrong time.

I pull up the cropped image I found in my sister's gallery and Tate studies it.

"I remember this," he admits. "And... I remember your sister."

I feel myself perk up, becoming more alert.

"The girl she was with that night is the daughter of one of my mentors—the executive director over a nonprofit that was pretty vital to me after my mom died."

This particular bit of info jars me. Mostly because, before

295

now, I hadn't even considered Mell had been at the party with a friend. But odds are, this is just another of Tate's lies.

"They spotted me and hung around for a bit because Tory knew me from the time I spent with her father—golf outings, family dinners, stuff like that. My gut told me I should've sent them home. God knows girls that young don't belong in places like that."

He pauses and flashes me a knowing look before continuing.

"But after posing for this pic, I lost track of them," he says. "Something urgent came up and I had to bail."

"Like what? What was the emergency?"

He glares a little, possibly annoyed that I've called him on his shit.

"I was kind of on babysitting duty all evening," he says. "Vince's stubborn ass wasn't feeling well and wouldn't go get himself checked out. So, the compromise was that he didn't have to go to the ER if he stuck with me. Turned out that was the right move. About two hours in, his appendix burst. I was able to get him to the hospital in time because I never left his side and noticed when he needed help."

My head lowers and my brow tenses when I think back. Vince had just told this story. By the bonfire last night, actually. Not only that, but I'd seen and felt the scar for myself, and... it lines up perfectly with Tate's recollection.

Not a single discrepancy.

So, it *sounds* true, but... it can't be.

"No offense, but seeing as how the allegations you've made are about as serious as they come, I'm not all that comfortable with you just taking my word for it," Tate says gravely, sounding emotionally wounded by what I've laid at his feet just now. "The name of the girl your sister was with is Tory Horne. I'm sure you can find her social media accounts. I'd appreciate you reaching out to her, maybe setting up a time to actually speak on the phone or in person. She'll be able to fill in the blanks I can't, and hopefully tell you what happened after I took off."

My head is absolutely reeling, spinning out of control when he interrupts my thoughts with a question.

"Does your mom know what you suspected?" he asks solemnly. "I only ask because... it matters to me that she knows I wouldn't do this. I'm guessing you kept it from her, seeing as how she can still look me in my eyes. But if you did, I'd like the chance to clear my own name."

He doesn't sound angry, just... sad. But even with that, I feel his sympathy. There's no gloating, only concern.

The most I'm able to muster is to shake my head, letting him know I hadn't mentioned it. I'm absolutely stunned. Both by the info he's just revealed *and* his conviction. He never faltered.

Still, I must've missed something.

Tears blurring my eyes, I turn to him again. "But... I feel it in my gut that you had something to do with this."

He shakes his head, holding my gaze as I struggle to come to terms with being so wrong for so long.

"I know you want this to be over, know you want closure, Stevie, but... you got it wrong," he says, being gentle with his words. "You needed someone to blame, and I understand why you were grasping at straws. But I didn't do this. Never would. Ever."

My head lowers slowly, and I recall what he shared with me about his mother being a victim of assault, and I feel like absolute shit right now. Accusing him of having caused someone the same hurt he saw her struggle through.

I bury my face in both hands—sad, mortified, frustrated.

"The last thing I have to offer you, in case you're still struggling with believing what I've said, check my socials for the date this all went down. You'll find a time-stamped video where I recorded Vince while he was still in the hospital, high on meds," he shares. "At the time, I was just doing it to make fun of the dumb shit he was rambling about, but now... I hope it helps give you a bit of reassurance."

I feel the shift, feel the exact moment I accept that I was wrong. I'd seen a few possible signs and ran with them because... because I was in pain. I needed a scapegoat and Tate had given me that for the past several months.

For peace of mind, I'll look for the video, but in my gut I already know. He's innocent and I'm... an idiot.

And I'm also back at square one.

"I'm sorry, Stevie. I'm sorry you're in pain. And I'm sorry there isn't anything I can do about it."

His words have me struggling not to fall apart even more than I already was.

He slips my phone from my hand, then I hear his go off with a notification before placing it back in my fingers. "We have each other's numbers now. If there's anything I can do to help, anything you need, call me."

And just like that, I'm losing my shit, turning into a puddle of tears and emotion right there on the deck.

"Thank you," are the only words I'm able to say when I stand and rush into the house without stopping until I'm locked inside my room.

How the hell did I fuck this up so badly?

And... where the hell do I go from here?

D evastated.

Embarrassed.

Angry.

Relieved.

I've spent my entire day getting incredibly well-acquainted with each of these emotions. Every "fact" I held onto as proof that I'd found the one responsible for my sister leaving me fell through today.

In the blink of an eye.

Tate's alibi, finding out Mel had been at the party with a girl I've never met... the entire story I've conjured in my mind has been corrupted. I had it all wrong. Everything. So, instead of my mind creating vividly violent imagery of Tate assaulting my sister, I now see his role in her life that night very differently. It was a brief, innocent encounter that ended with him rushing off to take Vince to the hospital.

While I hid myself away this afternoon, I also reached out to Tory, per Tate's request. Not only did her story line up perfectly with his, she also linked me to more images from that night. Images that placed Mel and her at a park much later. Hours after their time at The Den. In every pic, Mel was smiling bright, having the time of her life.

The complete opposite of the crying mess of a girl who came

home that night, already dying on the inside because of what some asshole did to her. So, I'm left to wonder what happened in the gaps, the dark corners of this story not documented with social media pics and fun hashtags.

I'm back where I started with zero clue who to fucking blame, living with the realization that I'm still stuck.

What I'd give to just... shut it all off. Every emotion, every thought. Everything.

The guys' conversation has been muffled background noise for the past half hour as they relax in the hot tub. I've hung out on the edge, sitting with only my feet submerged. The scent of chlorine and smoke from Micah's cigarette are hardly noticeable at this point, because I'm so deep in thought I may as well be back there. In the past. Reliving it all.

The quiet sloshing of water beside me is the only sound that manages to get my attention. I glance left just as Tate breaks the bubbling surface, and then settles onto the wood slats along the edge. Right beside me. At first, he doesn't speak, just sits with me, staring at both our feet dangling in the water, illuminated by a sinister red light glowing just beneath the steam. It's strange to be so close to him and no longer feel hatred. Instead, there's mostly sadness.

For what I accused him of, how terribly I've treated him, for being so stuck on my own tragedy that I'd willingly point a finger at an innocent man.

"This might be a stupid question, but... you okay?"

I nod slowly. "About as much as I can be."

I don't quite have it in me to look him in the eyes but do see the fabric of his soaked blue swim trunks and his naked torso beside me. His long, tan fingers come into view when he grips the edge of the tub and he's quiet. After what I've done, I can only imagine the terrible things he must be thinking about me. Only, he's too nice and too decent to let it show.

I was such a bitch to him.

"Did you get some rest?" he asks next. "When the guys came back, I told them not to bug you."

"And they listened?" I say with a quiet laugh.

I see his shoulders lift with a shrug. "They do. Usually, anyway. Kind of comes with the territory of being their elder in the frat."

"Hm."

I try to wrap my head around those three taking orders from *anyone,* but apparently Tate is one of the few they revere.

"Not getting in?" he asks.

Among the many reasons I'm not in the mood, the main culprit for why I'm sitting this one out is the wound I'm currently sporting beneath my shorts.

"Not tonight," I answer, pointing at my hip. "I, uh... fell during the hunt and scraped myself up pretty badly."

He nods in my peripheral vision, seeming to have bought the lie.

"Listen, I—"

"I should—"

We both stop and laugh when we try to speak at the same time.

"You first," I offer, because it's the least I can do.

He takes a breath then continues. "I just wanted to put it out there. Not that you're thinking this, but... there's no grudge," he says. "I'm not secretly pissed or thinking bad shit about you. Yeah, things between us were fucked up for a while, but as far as I'm concerned, the air is clear. Like it never happened."

I take in his words. His apology. He didn't have to do that. I wasn't *owed* that, but... it matters. It helps me feel a little less guilty, a little less *mortified,* and I'm grateful.

"I appreciate that. Thank you."

"Don't mention it," he says, and for the first time since he joined me, I finally meet his gaze.

I'd spent so much time hating him, ignoring our initial attraction, that I'd nearly convinced myself I imagined it.

The spark he's spoken of... it's there. Always has been, but I suppressed it for obvious reasons. But now that all the bad shit's been erased, it's like seeing him through a new set of eyes.

"Well, shit! Did I just catch you two eye-fucking?" Micah calls

301

out, causing an audible gasp to pass through my lips when I lower my gaze, staring at the water.

It's never far from mind how their possessiveness quickly turns to wrath. So, my instinct is to avoid it at all costs.

"Why are you always such an asshole?"

Tate's words have a deep chuckle rumbling in Micah's chest. "Genetics, I guess? I mean, my dad's kind of a dick sometimes."

Vince and Ash both laugh, not helping a single thing as they sit back and spectate.

"She's one of my students, for fuck's sake," Tate reasons, but when Micah waves him off, he obviously isn't buying it.

"Hold up a sec. Aren't you the same guy who fucked that professor with the fake tits back in the day? Sure, the tables are turned this time, but still."

Tate doesn't deny Micah's accusation, instead breaking eye contact as he fights a smile of his own.

"This is *me* you're talking to," Micah says. "And relax. If anyone knows how tempting Bird can be, knows how easily it is to forget your intentions, it's us. Let me guess. When she's around, all of a sudden you've got a one-track mind, right? Thinking about all the filthy shit you want to do to her? Zoning out staring at her tits? That magnificent ass?"

He's staring directly at me while he speaks. It's difficult to hold his gaze, but I'm worried he'd think I have something to hide if I look away.

"We were just talking. That's it," I explain. This is my best attempt at denying what Micah sees steeping between me and Tate.

Chemistry.

"Right," Micah says thoughtfully. "Talking and... eye-fucking. I didn't imagine that." His accusation has my heart picking up speed. More so when an exasperated sigh leaves him. "Instead of trying to convince me I'm crazy, why not just... do something about it," he says. "We're all adults here. Nothing wrong with satisfying your curiosity, is there?"

My eyes narrow, wondering what the hell his angle is. I've

seen him freak out over lesser offenses, so what makes this any different?

What makes *Tate* any different?

One corner of Micah's mouth curves up again, and when he nods toward Tate, two words leave his mouth, nearly knocking me off my ass.

"Kiss him."

A laugh from Tate lightens the moment, because I legit almost stroked out from the tension.

"Okay, you've clearly had too much to drink," Tate shoots back, reclining a bit as he rests on the heels of his palms.

"On the contrary. I've only had *one* drink and I'm completely sober. *Mostly* sober," he corrects. "But the point is, I know exactly what I'm saying."

He stops, then turns to me, and there's wickedness in his gaze.

"Bird, you know the rules."

Tate's brow arches. "Rules?"

I volley a look between them, noting the intensity in Tate's eyes, and also the amusement in Micah's. "We caught her during the hunt; therefore, she's ours," Micah explains.

Tate's quiet. So am I while summarizing that rule Micah's just spoken of. A rule that's been in place long *before* The Hunt— '*whatever they say goes*'.

Shit.

A spike of... something jolts through me. I'm not even sure what it is to be able to name it.

Fear?

No, that doesn't feel right. But it hit me with his last statement, when he reminded me that I don't exactly have a choice in the matter. While his next move would typically be to bark out how many points my compliance is worth, he doesn't and I'm grateful. At first, I think he might've skipped that part to avoid embarrassing me, but that couldn't be it.

He's foregone bringing up points to save his *own* ass the embarrassment. More and more, it's becoming abundantly clear just how highly they esteem Tate. Or *Big Brother Eros* as they call him.

Slowly, I'm beginning to realize there's no way around this. So, my gaze flashes toward Tate and he's hard to read. His full lips are slightly parted, and I see how wild his breathing is as his solid chest—thick and tan—rises with each draw of air. With his mouth, he denied Micah's accusation. But with this look, he all but confirms that there's a vibe between us. Something that manifested as flirtation when we first met—despite knowing our parents' marriage would soon make us family.

I lean in, stopping when I realize how awkward this will be, and the loud sigh from Micah means my hesitation has clearly annoyed him.

"Fuck, do I have to give you two instructions? Stevie, straddle him."

Micah impatiently snaps his fingers to rush me, and I blink at Tate. Only, his eyes have left mine. They've lowered to my breasts as he draws a deep surge of air.

I tell myself that I make my next move to avoid provoking Micah, but that's not true. I lift myself from the edge of the hot tub and settle over Tate's lap because I want to. Not just because he's hot as sin, or because I've been fighting this to varying degrees since we met. My reason is that maybe whatever happens next will numb it all.

The pain. The memories. All of it.

I wasn't wrong. Being so close *is* awkward, but I'm curious if I'm the only one who feels this as Tate takes my waist, radiating heat from his palms, gripping me so tight it's like we've done this before.

Or maybe it's just that we've both thought about it.

"Good," Micah rasps. "Now, kiss him."

Behind me, I hear him take a long drag on his cigarette as the tub bubbles and splashes in the background.

"You don't have to do this," Tate says, and it's so low I know I'm the only one who's heard it.

His offer topples the last of the wall I've built between us, hearing him consider my feelings, give me an out if I'm not okay with this.

I shake my head and he seems to understand the unspoken

304

meaning. I'm no longer afraid of him. No longer *angry* with him. And with all the bad burned away, all that remains is the wild attraction.

Steam touches my back where Tate's fingers have wandered beneath my shirt, exposing a small sliver of skin. Micah's command reverberates in my thoughts on repeat and I'm at war within my own head, reminding myself that Tate's not the man I thought he was even just earlier today. It's a constant struggle, but it's true.

The *'good guy act'* he's been putting on all these months was *never* an act. It's just who he is. And as I settle lower onto his lap, I also remind myself that there's no reason not to enjoy this. Not to enjoy *him*.

So, I do it. I push myself, allowing my mouth to connect with his.

"Fucking finally," Micah chuckles.

Things go from warm to hot in a split second as Tate's tongue probes my lips and our curiosity is finally settled. His grip tightens, pushing down my hips until he grips my ass with both hands, squeezing as I grind into him. Hot steel pushes against my crotch as he stiffens, the wetness of his shorts dampening mine as our bodies fit together too perfectly to ignore.

There was always a chance this weekend could take an unexpected turn, but I never imagined *this* being the strange twist of events—grinding on my stepbrother while the others watch.

Three who have given me both hell *and* heaven, depending on the day.

"I've got an idea," Micah speaks up, his voice aimed at my back as Tate's kiss moves to my throat. "Why don't we take this little party inside? We'll grab a few drinks and see where things go? Who knows, maybe our little Bird's feeling adventurous."

A blast of heat moves through me with Micah's suggestion. And while I know I should probably put up a fight, I don't have it in me.

I want this, want *them*, and whatever they have in mind might just be the cure to my pain.

There's a bit of commotion in the water behind me, then a moment later, I understand why. Wet hands come from behind, pushing beneath my shirt and bra as one of the guys grips my tits. The welcomed addition, whoever he is, places slow kisses all over my back while Tate controls my tongue. It's the feel of Ashton's rings against my skin that gives him away, and I enjoy the guys' attention being focused solely on my pleasure.

I feel the heat of Ash's breath when he exhales against the tattoo at the nape of my neck.

"Bird," he whispers. "Let us fuck you tonight."

It's not a question, but a request nonetheless. And right after speaking, the tip of his tongue traces my skin again. It's dizzying, making it difficult to think. Only, I don't really need to.

I've been on the hunt for something to make me numb tonight, something to make me forget all the bad shit, and... I'm starting to think this may be an answer to my prayer.

Ash lifts his head when I push my fingers over his scalp, tearing my lips away from Tate's to speak. And as I glance at Ash from over my shoulder, I lock in on his hooded stare as one word falls from my lips.

The answer he clearly hoped I'd give.

"Yes."

A slow smile curves his lips and then reaches his eyes. He

wastes no time climbing out of the hot tub, then Micah and Vince follow, sloshing water onto the deck as they stand, stretching to their full, impressive height.

Ash offers his hand and I release the grip I have on Tate's neck as I'm lifted from his lap. In the process, I don't miss Tate's attempt to adjust his swim trunks to mask his erection. I can still practically feel the heat and firmness of it between my legs and I'm positive the only reason we were able to contain ourselves for so long was because of my misdirected animosity. Even then, I wasn't blind. I was painfully aware of the attraction, but my hatred was so potent, so *tangible,* that it overshadowed everything else.

Until now.

"Come on," Ash beckons, still holding my hand in his as we cross the deck and enter the cabin through the sliding door. Tate's heavy footsteps trail behind us, and I'm curious what he's thinking, seeing all this unfold. It must feel strange knowing his friends, knowing *me* outside of these circumstances, and now seeing our interaction with one another. I'm also curious if he's wondering things like...

How awkward is all of this going to make standing at the altar during our parents' wedding? Seeing one another weekly in the lecture hall?

Will there ever be a normal family dinner after this? Or will we be passing mashed potatoes across the table, thinking about that time we fucked?

But then a new question pops into my head.

Should either of us actually give a shit about any of that?

My attention shifts to Micah when he pops the fridge open, and I hear the clinking of glass bottles half a second before he pulls out a fresh six-pack.

"I've gotta grab a couple things from my room. Meet you guys in a sec," he says, and then disappears down the hallway.

Ash's gaze lands on me and I'm aware of my racing heart.

"Where will you be comfortable?" he says, and the inquiry has me glancing around the living room, eyeing the sectional.

"Here's good."

307

He nods with a smirk, then wastes no time getting me undressed. He's facing me, slipping my tank over my head, and I feel Vince's hands from behind, lowering my shorts and panties and I step out of both. My nipples warm against Vince's palms when he smooths them up my torso before clasping them over my breasts. My natural inclination is to push my hips back, needing to feel him. He doesn't disappoint. His solid length persists against his swim trunks, and I can hardly believe how turned on I am right now.

"I want you naked," I breathe, and I feed off that devious grin on Ash's face.

"Yes, ma'am," he croons, and with that, he and Vince slip out of their swim trunks.

I sense Tate's hesitancy. We've all gotten used to being with one another in this way, but it's new for him. *I'm* new for him. After a moment of what looks like deep contemplation, he undresses, too, dropping his trunks and then pushing them aside.

I admire all three, taking note of how there isn't a single imperfection. I don't count bruises from hockey or scars from the past. If anything, seeing the shit their bodies have endured only makes them that much hotter and... makes them human.

Next, my eyes lower to their... equipment, and I draw a breath, remembering the answer I'd given Ash. When asked if I'd give in, let them have their way tonight, I made it clear that I'm more than ready, but... based on the sheer size of them, I'm having second thoughts.

Ash steps closer, and my eyes flit to his. At first, I think he plans to kiss me, but instead, he's at my ear. Perhaps because he didn't miss the moment of panic.

"Tate is one of us," he says, "*We* trust him, but if you're not okay with him being here..."

His voice trails off and I realize he misread the look on my face. He maybe assumed I was having second thoughts because of Tate, but even though he reached the wrong conclusion, the fact still remains that he considered my feelings. And that matters.

I take a breath, but don't have to think for long because I know what I want.

Ash's eyes trail me as I reach for Tate's hand, then bring him close. Close enough to push my fingers behind his neck. Close enough to tease his bottom lip with my tongue before drawing it into my mouth.

And with that, Ash has his answer regarding Tate, and so do I.

"Well, shit," Ash says with a husky laugh, "I guess it's a fucking party then."

There are hands and lips all over me. So many that I can't tell who's touching me where. There's a hand on one breast, a mouth on the other, and someone's tongue down my throat. I smooth my palm down one's chest, and squeeze someone's cock in the other. My pussy has become so slick, the wetness seeps onto my inner thighs and we've only just begun.

"Damn, I was gone for less than a minute," Micah says with a laugh.

At the sound of his voice, the kisses slow and, one-by-one, the swarm of warm hands leave my body.

Micah drops down at one end of the couch—the only one of us still clothed—and rolls a joint on the coffee table. He lights the tip, inhales deeply once it's between his lips, then holds his breath as he passes it to Ash, who still has one hand on my hip.

"Shit, I suppose once won't kill me," Ash says to himself, then takes a long drag.

It hits him harder than Micah, and I remember Ash's stance on smoking. He doesn't usually partake, while Micah on the other hand, hardly lets a day pass without blazing up.

Vince takes a hit, then it's in Tate's hands. Being so level-headed, I half expect him to decline the offer, but that isn't the case. His cheeks hollow when he puffs the tip, then his hand stretches toward me as smoke billows from his lips.

I inhale, immediately feeling the smoke fill my lungs. Micah's eyes are on me, maybe wondering if I've ever done this before, so when I don't choke or freak out, he smiles.

"Not your first time?"

I shake my head and hand him the joint. "Nope. I spent most of my weekends high until starting college, but it's been a while."

He nods, watching as I grab the small blanket on the arm of the couch, then cover myself with it before taking a seat.

"I figured it'd help get you out of your head," he says, and the tingle in my limbs means it's already working.

The others take a seat, too, and after finishing the joint, Micah lights and passes a couple more around that we smoke up until they're gone. Eventually, the entire room's filled with a thick haze, and I'm no longer in my head, no longer afraid of the unknown.

Micah's stare has been locked on me for an entire minute straight, and I've attributed it to the fact that he's currently high as fuck. We all are. But when my eyes lower below his waist, I notice he has a hard-on.

Feeling shy under his gaze, I laugh a little. "What?"

One corner of his mouth curves with a smile and he takes another long puff on the joint before responding.

"Do you have any fucking idea how sexy you are?"

The question wasn't what I expected, so I'm positive my face is red.

"Thank you?" I say with a shy laugh, now more aware of being naked beneath the blanket than I was a moment ago.

"Tate, not sure if you know this or not, but tonight's kind of special. It'll be Bird's first time."

Micah's announcement has Tate flashing a concerned look my way from where he's settled on the ottoman. It's the same look he gave earlier, when he spotted the cut on my lip and worried the guys might mean me harm.

"So," Micah continues, "I think we should make it memorable for her, see to it that our girl enjoys herself to the fullest."

That heat I felt in my face a moment ago intensifies. And it's all because of what he just called me.

Their girl.

Tate studies me, maybe noting that I'm not freaking out or afraid, and that seems to ease his concern a bit.

For now, anyway.

"Any chance you're on birth control?" Micah's never one to mince words, and his forthrightness draws a laugh from me.

"I started taking them the summer after graduation. Just in case."

He smiles at that, nodding thoughtfully. "Just in case."

I'm not sure what to expect when he stands, but I'm hypnotized as his shorts fall to the floor. One thing can be said about Micah Locke—his confidence is never lacking. The truth in that observation is clear as he makes his way closer with a cocky stride.

I squirm a little, realizing the slight tremble in my hands. I don't think anyone else notices, but even if they do, there's no need to wonder if I'll back out.

That isn't even a possibility. Not with how badly I want this.

Micha stops in front of me, slowly pumping his dick in his fist. I'm curious what he has in mind when he slowly pulls the blanket off me, then drops it to the ground as his head tilts.

"Turn," he instructs. "Get on all fours."

A breath hitches in my throat, but I obey, kneeling with my palms digging into the cushion. I feel the couch dip when his weight settles onto it, and I brace myself, expecting to feel his dick pushing into me, but instead... a gentle kiss to my hip, and then my lower back.

"Relax," he croons, and I try, holding my breath as his fingers slip into me from behind. "Damn, how are you already this fucking wet?"

The question has a low moan passing from my lips, but it also has my eyes shifting to Tate. I half expect him to be watching in disbelief as I let his friend touch me like this—so freely in front of the others—but I'm wrong. Instead, his cock is stiff, hardening more by the second as he observes.

I face forward when Vince leans in. He'd been seated in the curve of the couch before making his way over for a kiss. And now that I have his lips, I can't help but to reach for his dick. He's far less timid when I touch him this time, and I guess last night established a greater sense of trust between us than I realized. And if I'm not insane, it created a bond that maybe hadn't been there before.

311

His fingers slip beneath my hair and grip my neck. Then, when his breathing deepens, I know he wants more than my hand.

"Lie back," I breathe against his lips, and he follows my command without question, stretching out in front of me.

My mouth envelops his cock, and his head settles against the cushion. The green centers of his eyes disappear as his lids lower, and I love that he's so comfortable with me. The feel of him against my tongue, in tandem with Micah's fingers twisting into my core, already have me in bliss. But then Ash stands from his spot, disappearing behind me.

At first, I'm unsure of his plan, but then I feel lips. *His* lips— warm and soft against my back, and then they're warm and soft... *lower.* At first, he's focused on leaving deep, bruising kisses against my ass cheeks, but then he spreads them. I lose my breath as he introduces me to a completely new feeling, inciting the moan I hum onto Vince's dick.

Suddenly even more turned on by their drive to please me, I suck Vince harder, remembering his taste in my mouth when he came for me last night. I glance up and find him staring down his torso at me, watching as his fingers work into my hair, gently raking them over my scalp.

"You're so fucking beautiful," he pants, but a moment later, he loses the battle to keep his eyes on me when pleasure overwhelms him.

My eyes, on the other hand, are glued to him, recalling the many times I watched him touch himself onscreen, remembering all the times I wanted to touch him in real life. And now, here he is in the flesh.

My wildest fantasy.

I grip his thigh when he tenses, and the feel of him stiffening in my mouth sends a thrill shooting through me. His hips piston toward the ceiling, making the tip of his cock brush in rhythm against the roof of my mouth. Then, as I watch the look on his face become focused and almost pained, I taste him. The salty sweetness of him when he pumps cum into my throat.

"Fuck!" he calls out, and the powerful reaction has me

312

dousing Micah's fingers. He pulls them out and teases my clit before he and Ash back away.

I let Vince fall from my lips and as his spent cock settles against his thigh, he still hasn't caught his breath. He does manage to meet my gaze, though, and I was right. There is a bond there, and I'm beginning to suspect that it runs deep.

"Stand up."

The command comes from Ash this time, and I quickly get to my feet. When he leads me to the ottoman nearby, I don't ask what's next. I just sit, and then lie back when he gently pushes.

At first, I'm in my head, feeling exposed, wishing I could cover myself, but then they swarm me like bees on honey.

Micah and Ash both kneel beside me and my breasts heave with each breath. Micah's hand smooths down my abdomen, slowly cupping my pussy before he slips two fingers inside again. I'm in ecstasy, but that feeling only intensifies when he squeezes my breast, holding it as he eagerly draws my nipple into his mouth. I grip his hair, biting down on my swollen lips when Ash follows Micah's lead. He focuses *his* attention on my other breast, sucking the tender bud at its peak in sync with his brother as I suppress a whimper.

Overwhelmed by all the stimulation, I'm barely aware of large hands pushing up my inner thighs. But when Micah frees his fingers from my core, leaving a trail of dampness on my stomach, I'm alert.

Startled, I lift my head and stare down my body, half-expecting to see Vince's green irises staring back, but my breathing turns wild when I realize it's Tate's stare that's locked on me. The heels of his palms push against my thighs, and I open for him, feeling a million tiny sparks of electricity burst through my body.

But then a thought flickers in my head. It's brief, a fleeting notion that... he shouldn't be touching me this way. Or rather, I shouldn't *let* him. Our familial connection means we'll always have to keep what happens here tonight a secret.

I imagine it... the things my mother would think if she were to walk in right now. If she were to see what I see... my stepbrother opening the lips of my pussy with his fingers, breathing heat over my clit as it throbs in anticipation.

Or his father. Would he be ashamed to see his son kneeling between his stepsister's knees, wetting his lips before going in for his first taste of her?

Probably. But my thoughts in this exact moment are clear. Linear.

Fuck it.

Tate flattens his tongue against my clit and savors me. Slowly. Like an animal relishes its prey.

I can't stop watching him, knowing how wrong this is, knowing this will have to stay our little secret. But also knowing... I don't intend to stop him.

Behind Tate, I spot Vince, watching as the others share me. I wet my lips, wishing he were close enough to kiss, but then my gaze flits toward Micah when my fingers slip from his hair. He stands just as Tate leans away. Confused, I watch them switch places—Tate lowering to where Micah once knelt, and Micah between my knees, settling his mouth against my stomach as he trails slow kisses from my navel to the valley between my breasts. A slow sigh leaves me and Ash's heart beats beneath my palm where one hand remains flat against the firm mass of his chest.

Micah's solid cock grazes my thigh, and at the feel of it, his hips press forward a second time. Only, now, it's intentional. I imagine the motion brings him a small measure of relief, a taste of the friction he craves. But it also spurs my imagination, makes me wonder how he'd feel... *inside me.*

The man I once only saw as a villain.

His mouth trails my neck until his kiss—deep, passionate— finally reaches my lips. His tongue dips into my mouth and I imagine his dick doing the same, dipping into my pussy as it grips him, draws him in deeper. He presses his hips again and my heel digs into the back of his thigh, pulling him closer.

"Fuck... Do you have any idea how badly I want you?" he rasps. "I've imagined how you'd feel since I first laid eyes on you."

Those words, whispered against my lips, cause my back to arch, pushing my breasts to his chest, squirming when my

314

sensitive nipples graze his skin. I'm on fire as he sucks the hollow of my throat, and I recall the fear and hatred I initially felt for them. Over time, it's morphed into something else entirely, something some might say is equally dark and twisted, but I'd argue that they simply don't understand.

This feeling, and these *boys* with all their pain and their scars, have become an addiction.

"Do I have your permission?" Micah's breathy question moves over my skin, causing all other thoughts to fade.

I'm dazed, feeling like I'm floating above my own body. "Permission?"

His mouth is against my ear and the entire world goes silent when he answers, "...To be the first to fuck you."

Every inch of me becomes more aware of him, and when my lips part, I'm unable to speak, aware of this being the point of no return. Aware of how there was once so much bad blood between us I could have literally killed him. Only, that all suddenly feels like a lifetime ago because... fuck.

I want him.

"Yes." As the word rolls off my tongue, I'm aware of Micah aligning his hips perfectly between my legs, aware of the head of his cock already nudging my opening. But a hand cups my chin and turns my head, stealing some of my attention. It's Ash, and my eyes are locked on him as he studies me. There's so much in that look. He once made it known that he only wanted to break me, but when he gives me his tongue, I don't believe that anymore.

Everything's changed.

They've changed, and they've changed *me.*

This connection we all share is far from perfect, far from traditional, but... it's what I need.

I'm not sure when I reached for Tate's hand, but I squeeze it, whining into Ash's mouth as I experience the sweet ache of Micah pushing into me for the first time, patiently stretching me to a perfect fit. Yes, there's pain. That's to be expected. But the pleasure he brings is overwhelming, far outweighing the discomfort.

"That's it, Bird. Let me fucking have you," he breathes,

pulling his hips away before slowly pushing inside again, declaring, "You're ours now."

His words go straight to my head while Ash sucks my lips, my tongue. And in the midst of the lust-fueled frenzy, I actively decide to ignore the red flags. If they want to own me, make me theirs, I won't object.

Not with the potential for there to be more of *this*.

The heat and friction between my legs is positively enlivening, unlike anything else I've ever felt, proving that no toy or device could ever compare. The next sound that leaves my mouth isn't a response to pain. It's a high-pitched moan that Ash swallows down as Micah realizes he doesn't have to be quite so gentle anymore. He slides into me, and then out, pumping his hips faster while the sound of his deep breathing gives me an even better high than the weed. The solid muscles of his thighs brush the soft insides of mine and I'm already hooked, craving this level of closeness before it's even ended.

My fingers warm when I smooth them down Tate's rippled torso until I reach his cock, feeling him grow harder in my hand. It excites me touching him like this, knowing it's about as wrong as you can get, but we can't seem to help ourselves around one another tonight. The thought of pleasuring him while Micah rocks into me, grinding against my clit, has me teetering toward an orgasm already.

Ash's lips leave me, and there's a wild look in his eyes as he turns my attention toward Tate, watching as my hand moves up and down his length. I *think* I understand what Ash wants, but I'm not certain, so I hesitate.

"He needs your mouth, Bird," Ash rasps against my ear, making his request crystal clear when he adds, "Put on a show for me."

My gaze climbs the height of Tate's body until our eyes lock. With his lip clamped between his teeth, enjoying the feel of my hand on him, I don't bother wondering if he'd mind me taking things a step further. So, the next moment, I meet Ash's request and tease the tip of Tate's dick with my tongue before sucking him in. A slow hiss passes between his gritted teeth, and I swear Micah is even harder inside me, watching me damn-near swallow Tate whole.

"You're fucking filthy. You know that?" My eyes drift closed, hearing Ash's deep, melodic voice in my ear as he palms my breast, acting as the devil on my shoulder.

"Do you like the way his cock tastes?" he rasps, brushing his thumb over my nipple. "You open your throat like such a good fucking girl."

I suck harder, twisting my tongue over Tate's tip, feeling Micah push deeper.

"And look at you... You're taking his dick so well, letting him pound that wet pussy like you've done this shit before," Ash says next, and hearing him stirs something inside me.

"I'll bet you're so fucking tight around him right now. Watching you with them has my dick so hard, I swear I might explode as soon as you touch me," he says, and his commentary has me inching closer toward my own peak.

I take Tate in again and he's reached his limit, coming hard with a grunt. I drink him down, swallowing everything he gives me.

"Damn, Bird. You *like* being used as our little fuck doll, don't you?" Ash says, softly tweaking my nipple between his fingers as I writhe against Micah. But I don't even have to think about my answer to his question.

Because it's yes.

A thousand times... yes.

Tate falls limp from my mouth and staggers toward the couch, cursing to himself as he drops down on a cushion not too far from Vince. Both look relaxed and sated as they light up another joint. Tate's taste still lingers on my tongue when Ash turns me to him by my chin, pushing his cock between my lips as my hand braces against Micah's chest. Tension builds in my core and my pussy squeezes around him. Then, a muffled whimper pours out of me, and I come undone, feeling the deepest wave of pleasure I've ever experienced, making me aware of what I've been missing until now.

"Fuck, yes," Micah groans. "Fucking come for me."

317

As I writhe beneath him, he breathes deep, driving his hips harder, faster, until his heat surges into me like a river.

"Shit... You feel so damn good," he pants, pumping his hot cum into my throbbing pussy. I squeeze his chest as my body relaxes beneath him and his rhythm slows. Still catching his breath, he lazily strokes my breast and torso, in no rush to pull out. And I'm in no rush to get rid of him.

"Suck harder, Bird," Ash breathes, and I meet his demand, determined to please *him* as thoroughly as they please *me*. And with one last draw on his dick...

"Oh, fuck... Fuck, yes... Shit..."

He grips the back of my neck and I love seeing him lose himself, love seeing him so turned on that self-control becomes a foreign concept. As soon as he's empty, he backs his hips away, but leans in to press a kiss to my mouth, before lowering to the floor.

Micah lingers, raining soft kisses over my stomach while I come down from the high they've given me. All four are spent and naked, and I...

Well, shit, I might just be the luckiest girl in the world.

W e share another joint, slip into comfortable clothes, then meet back up in the living room where we all drift off watching reruns of old sitcoms. I doze here and there, but never get settled fully. I'm comfortable enough, using Vince's thigh as my pillow while his hand warms my shoulder. And my feet are warm, too, tangled with Ash's beneath the comforter he's shared with me.

But my mind...

It's restless.

Eventually, I force myself out onto the deck to avoid waking the guys. Staring out on the lake as it mirrors the moon and stars above, there's still no clarity, no solace.

Pushing a tear aside, I allow myself to feel it, everything that's somehow decided to hit me all at once.

I sniffle and attempt to wipe my face again when the sliding door opens behind me.

"Everything okay?"

Forcing a smile, I glance over my shoulder and meet Micah's gaze. "All good."

He steps up to the rail beside me, but he's not focused on the water. He's focused on me, likely taking in my puffy, red-rimmed eyes.

"Sorry if I woke you."

"Don't apologize," he says, waving me off, and I still feel him assessing when he pushes my hair off my shoulder. "Do you... always cry when nothing's wrong?"

I smile a little, shrugging when I don't have much else to say.

"Was it us? Were we too rough?"

"No, it's nothing like that," I assure him. "It's just..."

My mind races and I'm not even sure how to articulate my thoughts. All I know is I feel burdened, weighed down by all the secrets. And if seeing how Mel spiraled has taught me anything lately, it's that secrets can sometimes be enough to crush you. So, I'm feeling compelled to let mine out.

In fact, the only one I do intend to keep is Vince's.

"We should talk. *All* of us," I clarify.

Micah's expression is grave at first, but then he nods. "Okay. I'll wake the guys."

I catch his wrist when he turns toward the house. "No, I don't mean right now. It can wait 'til morning."

He arches a brow, shooting me this incredulous look like what I've just suggested is utterly ridiculous. He steps back this way and rests his elbow on the rail, looking me over in my oversized tee and stretch pants. I feel my gaze lowering to the deck when he starts to become too much to stare at, but he lifts my chin with his finger, forcing me to see him.

Forcing me to be seen.

"If *you* can't sleep, *we* can't sleep," he says with a smirk, and then a kiss to my forehead seals the deal before he retraces his steps to the door. "Take whatever time you need out here. We'll be ready when you are."

My gaze lingers on him for several seconds after he's gone back inside, watching through the window as he shakes the guys awake. When I face the water again, I see the warm glow of light coming from the living room in my peripheral vision.

It's been a long time since I've felt so unsettled, so undone, and I attribute the mental torment to how my talk with Tate went down. It shook me to my core, dislodging the small semblance of closure I clung to for so many months. Being physical with the guys was a welcomed distraction, but even *that* has left me feeling

320

unlike myself. Opening up to them was a blessing, yes, but also a curse.

Because now I'm a raw vessel of emotion, letting it all in.

The good.

The bad.

When I enter the house, I have all four guys' full attention. They're pitifully sleepy, but that's not quite my fault. I wanted to wait until a decent hour, but Micah wouldn't hear of it.

I read the room, see they're all receptive and just... let all the things I've held in come pouring out.

"I know you're wondering what was so important that you're awake at three a.m., and... hopefully by the time I'm done, you'll understand."

I drop down onto the ottoman with a sigh, right in the middle of where they're all seated around the sectional.

"There are some things I need to get off my chest and free myself of, so I'm just gonna do this. Fast, like ripping off a Band-Aid," I announce. "First, I don't only know Tate from school."

When I gesture toward him, his brow arches with curiosity.

"In the coming months, our parents are marrying each other, which means, technically, we'll be... kind of related."

"Well, shit," Micah smirks, glancing toward Tate. "Keeping it in the family, I see."

Tate shakes his head then refocuses on me.

"It's not a huge deal, but why keep it a secret?" Vince chimes in.

When I scratch my head, Tate answers. "I started to tell you guys when I first got here, but then I realized Stevie didn't seem comfortable with you knowing yet, so I figured I'd let her tell you in her own time."

"And, actually... my connection to Tate just so happens to be part of the reason I was in your rooms that night," I admit, and my stomach twists as the guys' stares deepen with curiosity.

I'm uncomfortable, but that's why I need to get it all out there, be free.

"My sister was... raped. And after that, she took her life," I finally force out, but decide at the last minute to redact my story some. Instead of naming Tate as my original suspect, I leave him out of it for fear of unintentionally painting him in a bad light.

God knows I've done enough of that already.

"Up until yesterday, I believed a member of your frat had something to do with it," I admit, briefly locking eyes with Tate, hoping he knows I don't intend to point him out. "I thought whoever did it, whoever hurt her, might've been bold enough to confess in writing. In the brotherhood's book of secrets."

This is the first Tate has heard of this at all, and the first the others have heard me fill in the gaps of the story they pieced together the night I trespassed at The Den.

My gaze flits to Micah when he stands from the couch, and when he starts to slowly pace the floor, I can see he's upset.

"I'm sorry for making this all so complicated," I say, feeling like my misguided belief in Tate's guilt caused so much undue drama.

"You should've told us," Micah grumbles.

"I know. If I had, we could've put an end to all this sooner and—"

"Not because of that," he cuts in, staring at the ground as his feet walk a repetitive path in the carpet. "You should've told us because we could've helped, maybe pointed you in the right direction."

I shoot him a look. Does he really believe that? Sure, given the state of our connection *now* this makes sense, but he wouldn't have been this level-headed before. Weeks ago, he would've heard this explanation and thought it as unlikely to be true as the lie I told about helping a friend.

"What made you think it was someone in the frat?" Vince asks. My eyes flit toward him.

"Because... I found a picture in her phone after she passed. It was time stamped with the date of her rape, and I recognized the brand on the guys' arm. There were other distinguishing features, but it doesn't matter because it all turned out to be a dead end. When I talked to Tate yesterday, he helped me see that."

My eyes flash toward him again, and I don't miss the sympathy in his. It's all I've ever found there. Never anger, never

322

resentment, only kindness and a sincere desire to help me solve this for my sister.

"So, it wasn't the guy you thought, but it's *someone* in the brotherhood, right?"

I shake my head when Ash jumps to that conclusion. "Honestly, I doubt it. I recently discovered that my sister went somewhere after she left the party, and I have no idea whose path she crossed between your party and home that night. So, no, I can't say for certain that it was a Savage who did it."

They're all quiet and thoughtful, and once again, I'm impressed. They all seem more concerned about what my sister encountered than my lies, my deceit.

Maybe... they get it.

"There isn't a book."

I peer up and my thoughts halt when Tate speaks up. "What do you mean? Your dad mentioned it and—"

"There *was* a book," he clarifies, "but the brotherhood retired it nearly two decades ago. From what I've heard, it's currently locked in the attic of a senior member, but even then, it's always been more of a novelty, something meant more for visual effect during the old rituals."

If I weren't already seated, I would find someplace to rest because my knees feel weak. I'd gotten so much wrong, so much confused.

"But you got upset when he mentioned it at dinner," I point out, locking eyes with Tate.

"You're not wrong, but that was more so because he was on a rant, telling *all* the brotherhood's secrets, so I just wanted to stop him before he said too much. But it had nothing to do with the book itself," he clarifies.

"We need to know who did this," Micah seethes. "If one of the Savages is responsible, I'll beat his worthless ass myself. We're no saints, but we don't tolerate that kind of bullshit. Ever."

My heart races as his rage peaks, and I honestly believe he'd follow through with every single thing he just promised. But when his steps halt, I stare, wondering what he'll say or do next.

"Shit. Fuck!" He falls silent after those scolding words leave his mouth, the grave expression he wears matching his tone.

He eventually finds it in himself to meet my gaze and when I note the remorse behind that look, I think I'm beginning to understand how this information is hitting him.

"We fucked up. If we'd known the truth, Bird... We... Shit," he says to himself again when words momentarily escape him. "We never... we never would've put you through that shit."

From the corner of my eye, I'm aware of how Tate's posture's just shifted. "What does that mean?" he asks. "What have you put her through?"

"It doesn't matter. It's—"

He lifts his hand and quiets my attempt at explaining, slowly standing to his feet as his eyes remain trained on Micah.

"What the fuck did you guys do?"

All of a sudden, I wish at least *this* portion of the conversation had been had in private, without him listening in.

Micah eventually lifts his gaze to meet Tate's and it's filled with shame, but Vince steps in to elaborate.

"We caught her on camera and thought she was working with Whitlock, so when we couldn't get a confession out of her, we... took matters into our own hands."

Tate's gaze narrows. "What... the fuck... did you do?" he repeats, and he's possibly the only person on this planet I imagine can take that tone with *any* of these three and live to tell the story.

"We put her on the point system," Ash confesses, and I can already see Tate fuming.

"As in, the same point system we use for pledges?" he asks. "You fucking hazed her?"

The shame I initially noted in Micah's eyes intensifies, but he doesn't look away. "We thought it'd get her to tell us the truth, or at least—"

"You—" Tate stops abruptly after cutting in to speak. When he paces toward the window, I'm guessing it's to avoid losing his head. "It ends now," he asserts. "Whatever bullshit game you three were running stops here and if I hear one fucking word that suggests otherwise, I'll report your asses to the dean *myself* and won't think twice about that shit."

Micah's shoulders heave, but he takes it. "It's over."

"It damn-well better be." Tate holds his gaze, and a long moment passes. But once he feels he can trust Micah's word, his eyes land on *me*. I'm not used to having someone protect me, look after me like this, but… it feels nice.

With that, everything that needed to be said has been said.

"What's the next step? For your sister," Ash asks.

I shrug. "Well, thanks to a helpful tip, I'll be meeting up with a friend of hers tomorrow. With any luck, she'll be able to tell me who else they hung with that night, or I'm hoping Mel maybe confided in her about this guy she was seeing."

"We'll take you," Micah offers. "It's the least we can do."

I hear him and certainly appreciate the offer, but I can handle it.

"Feels like one of those things I need to take on by myself," I answer, and when he nods, he seems to get it.

"I know we haven't exactly presented ourselves as guys you can trust with the heavy shit," he says, "but we're gonna prove you wrong. You have my word on that."

I hold his stare, and even though there's sure to be an interesting road ahead of us… I believe him.

"Whatever it takes to show you, whatever it takes to *fix* this, we're committed. One-hundred percent."

A mug of coffee has gone cold between my hands. Nervous doesn't even begin to cover how I'm feeling, knowing how this meeting with Tory can make or break my deep-dive into unearthing the truth about my sister.

The pressure, the thought that this can go in a million different directions, has me feeling a little unstable.

I've glanced down at my phone at least a hundred times in the twenty minutes since settling into this booth. Mostly, I've wanted to call the guys, but that feels weird. I mean, yes, things between us are changing, but we're not at the stage where we pick up the phone just to shoot the shit. Nor are we at the stage where I lean on them for emotional support. Usually, I turn to Maddox for that.

But the problem with *that* is, we haven't spoken in over a week.

There's never been more distance between us, and I think we both feel how it's changing the landscape of our friendship. Maybe forever. After what happened, I was too embarrassed to reach out, despite knowing it's on me. And I'm not even dreading having to face him because of what he *saw*.

It's because of what I *said*.

His feelings for me have been kind of an unspoken factor in our friendship since the beginning. It's the reason I don't talk to him about my relationships. It's the reason he's never really been serious about a girl, aside from that one three-month-long "situation-ship" he landed in senior year of high school. Other than that, he's always been content just hanging out with me, being eternally friend-zoned.

But still, I knew. I knew how he felt, and I threw it in his face simply because he insulted me when hurt caused him to lash out. I should've had the presence of mind to know it'd be hard to move past it, and yet, here we are.

I sigh, staring at the dark phone screen as I finally give in.

"What the fuck do I have to lose?" I mumble to myself, dialing Maddox, holding very little hope that he'll actually answer.

By the fourth ring, I've accepted that he's still pissed and consider hanging up, but then decide to go another way. If he won't *talk* to me, maybe he'll at least listen.

His voicemail begins to record, and I start talking.

"Hey. It's me. I didn't expect you to pick up, but... I thought I'd try anyway. Before I say anything else, I'd like to start with an apology. I fucked up. If I could take back what I said, I would. It was ugly and vicious and not at all how you deserve to be treated."

I pause, wishing he was on the line, giving feedback so I don't feel like this is all for nothing.

"Anyway, I'm at a restaurant right now, preparing to meet someone I'm not sure can even help me, but... you know I'll do anything for Mel. Out of respect for her, I kept a lot of things from you, but I've recently realized that keeping secrets was a huge part of why she spiraled. So, I guess you could say I'm on a mission of sorts. I'm actively unburdening myself of all the shit I've held in, all the shit I've kept from you," I say with a sigh.

"That trip I took to Cypress Pointe... I didn't tell you everything. I left out how I found out that diner I visited even existed. Mel kept a box of mementos. Mostly, it was keepsakes from outings with a guy she was seeing in secret, but there was also a napkin from the diner. I reached out to the girl whose number was written on the back and found out Mel had visited shortly before she died. She went in asking a few strange questions, but it was all kind of disjointed. Not even the people she talked to knew what she wanted. I know you think I'm crazy.

I know I haven't been acting like myself, but I promise I'm okay."

I lean back in the seat, gazing out the window as I gather the courage to say more.

"And I know you don't approve of the guys, mostly because I was hellbent on proving that a Savage was responsible for Mel's attack, but I'm not so sure anymore. I'm *certain* Ash, Micah, and Vince weren't involved, though. Actually, I'm starting to doubt it was anyone from the frat at all. Which means, all this time, I've been looking in the wrong direction, and I'm hoping the girl I'm meeting can fill in the gaps. Maybe she'll give me the answers I need."

I hold the phone a few seconds without words, lowering my gaze to the table.

"But anyway, I suppose that's all I have to say. When you get time, or... if you *want* to... call me."

There's an emptiness in my chest. It seems to grow every day. More so now that he's ignored my call. Sure, I could rationalize that he's busy, but it isn't that. He just doesn't want to talk to me.

A car pulls up in the lot and I straighten in my seat, wondering if it might be Tory. Already, she's fifteen minutes late, so I'm not even sure she'll show at this point.

While I stare at the blue sedan, waiting to see who'll step out, a text comes through.

Maddox: I have a bad feeling about this, and my gut tells me you should stop before you're in too deep. None of this will bring Mel back, Stevie.

I stare at his words, feel the concern in them, but I think he already knows there's only one direction for me to move.

Stevie: I appreciate you caring about me, but I have to do this.

I lower my phone just as a shadow darkens the space beside my table. Well, *three* shadows, actually. I can guess that the tall, wiry blonde in the middle is Tory, but I have no idea who the two guys flanking her might be. When I offer a dim smile, she does the same.

"Stevie, right?" she says.

"That's right."

Her smile broadens now that I've confirmed. "You look just like her," she says. "Mel, I mean."

I nod and glance down at my cold coffee for a second. "Yeah, we got that a lot."

She nods, too, unable to hide the nervous energy she gives off. My gaze shifts to the two guys who came in with her as they settle at a table not too far way.

"Those your bodyguards?" I tease. "Unless this neighborhood's changed drastically in the past six months, I'd say you'd be pretty safe without them."

She grins, but it doesn't quite reach her eyes. "Yeah, sorry about them. They're my brothers. When they heard I was coming here, they insisted I bring them with me."

My brow arches when I don't quite understand why meeting *me* seemed to be interpreted as a threat, but I don't push my luck. I need Tory as comfortable as possible, so whatever it takes.

"I'm glad you agreed to come," I say with a smile. "If you want to order something, it'll be my treat."

"I'm fine. I don't actually have much time, so..."

She trails off, and now that I know we're on a tight schedule, I decide to get right into it.

"I know Mel isn't here to tell you this, but I think she'd appreciate you helping me."

Tory nods. "Anything for her," she says, "And Tate, too. He's a good friend of our family. My dad practically sees him as another son."

Hearing this only confirms how wrong I was about him.

"I'm curious how you and Mel met."

I don't miss how Tory's eyes light up. "My father's youth group," she answers, and I get the feeling she assumes I know what that means.

I force a smile. "I didn't realize she was even involved in anything like that."

"Really?" she asks. "Mel wasn't a member of the church, but she attended most of the weekly meetings. Dad knows most of the local school counselors, so they let him leave leaflets in their offices since the help he offers isn't really about religion. It's about hope," she adds.

"He leaves them with the counselors? Is that how Mel found the group? Was she seeing the school counselor?"

I don't miss how Tory's expression shifts. She tucks her hair behind her shoulder and looks out the window instead of at me.

"It's okay."

She glances at my hand when I place it on the table. I know she doesn't want to spill all my sister's secrets, but I need her to.

Eventually, Tory nods. "From what she shared in the group, she'd been going during lunch for a few months. Every Tuesday and Thursday."

I smile to reassure Tory that she hasn't done anything wrong, but inside... I'm falling apart. The deeper I dig, the more I realize I didn't know my sister at all.

Did Mom know?

Did she know Mel was so broken for so long?

"I know you need to get going soon, so I hope you don't mind me jumping ahead, but... I'm curious about that night you and Mel snuck into the party at The Den."

At the mention of it, Tory recoils.

"We shouldn't have been there," she says. "My parents were livid when they realized I snuck out. Didn't help that I came in a little tipsy," she adds under her breath.

"Hey, I'm not here to judge you." I hold her gaze, making sure she hears and believes me. "You don't have to be ashamed about *anything* talking to me. I just need to know if Mel met up with anyone at the party, or did she maybe meet someone at the park you went to afterward?"

Tory shakes her head. "All we did at the park was drink and smoke a little weed," she admits, and that air of shame is in her tone again. "We knew we shouldn't have been there, shouldn't have been doing those things, but... we just wanted to see what it was like. The whole thing was Mel's idea—the party, the booze, the drugs," Tory explains. "She hadn't been herself for some time and... I think she just needed to clear her head."

"Did she ever tell you what was wrong?" I sound desperate. Because I *am* desperate.

Tory shakes her head again and I can't deny the feeling of disappointment that floods my heart.

"No, she never talked about it. So, I just tried to be a good friend, tried to be there for her."

My gaze lowers to the table and I'm not just disappointed. I'm... devastated. If I'd been a better sister, if I hadn't been so consumed with my own shit, maybe Mel would still be here. She felt so disconnected from our family, so alone that she reached out to everyone *but* me—a counselor, a church group, strangers.

The scope of my failure is absolutely staggering.

"Thank you. For being there for her," I clarify. "It sounds like you were important to her."

"Of course. She was important to me, too."

I nod and reference the mental list in my head of all the questions I need answered.

"Can you tell me what happened after the park? Did you two go anywhere else?"

"No," she answers, shaking her head, but then her eyes shift. "Well, *I* didn't, anyway. I walked home from the park since it wasn't that far. I told Mel she could just stay the night at my house, but she had other plans."

I sit straighter. "Other plans? Like what?"

Tory shrugs. "She was meeting a guy she was hanging out with. Like, a date, I guess."

"Do you know anything about him? A name? Where he lives? Have you seen a picture maybe?"

Another head shake, which means I'm no closer to solving this shit than I was before.

"She was really secretive about him. I kind of wondered if she maybe thought people wouldn't approve? I don't know," she backtracks. "This is all speculation, though, so I'm sorry I can't be more helpful."

"No, you've been *incredibly* helpful. I appreciate you coming," I say with a weak smile, finally able to meet Tory's gaze.

She nods and I can only hope she doesn't think my frustration is on her, because it's not. It's on me.

Everything's on me.

"Well, I should get going, but if you need anything else, you know how to get in touch with me."

My eyes sting with tears, but I force yet another smile, pretending it's all okay.

"Thank you."

Tory stands, lets her brothers know we're finished, and then they're gone. And I'm left to linger in the sadness. This—like so many of my other attempts—was all for nothing.

The waitress returns with the bill, I settle it, then I'm back on the city bus heading toward campus as the sun sets. I'm in a daze the entire ride, feeling like absolute shit. Not even the walk to my neighborhood clears my head, because the devastation runs deep.

Where did she go after the park?

Who was she meeting?

Why didn't she talk to me?

My house comes into view, and I'm filled with a fresh wave of dread. And it's not the *usual* sense of dread I feel when I get home. It's tenfold because of the fight with Dahlia. We haven't crossed paths since our run-in this weekend, and I'm on high alert. It's just a matter of time before I get the notice to vacate, and I have *no* fucking idea where I'll go. But all-in-all, the consensus on the current state of my life is simple.

I've officially become a fuck up.

World-class.

I walk the driveway slowly, hoping I'm able to slip in the back door without having to face any of my roommates. I'm positive Dahlia has already told them her side of things, gotten them to stand in her corner.

Like *that* wasn't inevitable.

With my fingers on the handle, I hesitate to go inside, deciding to give myself a moment to breathe before heading into purgatory. A notification on my phone gives me an excuse to stall.

The screen glows through the darkness as I read.

'We need to talk. There's something you should know. Something I should've told you a long time ago.'

My brow tenses seeing who it's from, and then rereading the message. As *these* words cycle through my thoughts, it's hard not to hear *Mel's* ring inside my head, too—*So many secrets. So little truth.*

I consider calling, but before I'm able to decide or even *react...* everything goes dark. A heavy, cloth bag is pulled over my face and I'm disoriented, clawing at the arm around my neck. My fingers slip over the leather sleeve when I'm so overcome with panic that I'm hysterical, and life begins to flash before my eyes— all the good I've done, all the *wrong.*

Everything.

My airway is cut off when the grip on my throat tightens, making it impossible to scream. And as all sound and light slip away, leaving me surrounded by only nothing but darkness, the only thing I *can* do is hope for peace as I die.

If this is it, if this is how it ends, I'm comforted by the fact that, soon... I'll be with my sister.